AKHUNATON
The Extraterrestrial King

AKHUNATON
The Extraterrestrial King

written and illustrated by

Daniel Blair Stewart

Frog, Ltd.
Berkeley, California

Akhunaton: The Extraterrestrial King

Published by Frog, Ltd.

Frog, Ltd. books are distributed by
North Atlantic Books
P.O. Box 12327
Berkeley, California 94712

Cover and book design by Legacy Media, Inc.
Printed in the United States of America

Library of Congress Cataloging-in-Publication Data
Stewart, Daniel Blair.
    Akhunaton : the extraterrestrial king / Daniel Blair Stewart.
        p.   cm.
    ISBN 1-883319-34-X (paper)
    I.   Title.
    PS3569.T4596A77   1995
    813'.54—dc20   95-356
                                                        CIP

Dedicated to my son, River

1   2   3   4   5   6   7   8   9   /   98   97   96   95

Acknowledgments

Special thanks go to Diane Darling for editing this manuscript and escorting it into its final form when she was editor of *The Green Egg*. Her insights and suggestions shaped the story.

I must also thank Meadow Stewart for her assistance in helping to research this tome, posing for drawings, and putting up with me.

Gary Ferns and Zack Darling tolerated my presence during the months of computer work. Thanks, guys.

Otter Zell, publisher of *The Green Egg*, extended both enthusiastic support and assistance in word processing and computer graphics. Morning Glory Zell shared this encouragement, and both posed challenging questions and extended their own knowledge of the ancient past to me.

Jacques and Janine Vallee gave me valuable information that imparted versimilitude to Part Five. Jacques discussed the UFO enigma in depth with me on several occasions. They both deserve my gratitude for their time and attention.

I thank my principal models Chris Blake, Caragwen Gwendolyn and Meadow Stewart for giving life to these drawings.

My parents, Robert and Elaine Stewart, gave me moral and financial support throughout the grimmest times. Aidan Kelly discussed the ethics of magick with me many years ago, and the essence of these discussions appears in the principles espoused by Akhunaton.

When times got too crazy, Dick Billups, Stuart Potter, John Caraway and Kevin Crosson added their electric guitar sounds to mine so we could all blow off pressure together.

A final word of appreciation must go to my longtime friend and mentor, Fred Adams, artist and visionary philosopher, inspiration to all who know him. His love of ancient mysteries might even surpass mine. His knowledge certainly does.

And now, ladies and gentlemen, I beg for a round of applause for every name mentioned. Thank you.

Genesis, Chapter 6, verse 4:
There were giants in the earth in those days; and also after that, when the sons of God came in unto the daughters of men, and they bare *children* unto them, the same *became* mighty men, which *were* of old, men of reknown.

50. The primordial source of all our religions lies with the ancestors of the Dogon tribe, who got their cosmogony and cosmology directly from the three-eyed invaders who visited long ago. The three-eyed invaders were mute and deaf and telepathic, could not breathe our atmosphere, had the elongated misshapen skull of Ikhnaton, and emanated from a planet in the star-system of Sirius. Although they had no hands, but had, instead, pincer claws such as a crab has, they were great builders. They covertly influence our history toward a fruitful end.

Tractates: Cryptica Scriptura, from *Valis*, by Philip K. Dick

PART I

SOTHIS III

𓅱𓃀𓄿𓊪𓇋𓇳𓅱𓃀𓄿𓊪𓇋𓇳𓅱𓃀𓄿𓊪𓇋𓇳𓅱𓃀𓄿𓊪𓇋𓇳

Chapter One

His name had once been Nagarjaruk. He had wandered the tundra of Siberia during a glacial epoch, an ice age. He had hunted mammoths, fought a cave bear for a home, and eaten the losers of these battles. He had been born on a frozen world where life was niggardly and death was generous.

He had become a shaman. His dreams were prophetic, his mastery of the *amanita* broth unsurpassed. His tribesmen knew he could see the future and he was feared. When his rivals plotted to kill him, he always knew—and murdered the conspirators. He never took a wife.

No prehumans had ever known kindness to outweigh competitiveness, but this fourth wave of evolving humans was even more violent in spirit than its predecessors. Nonetheless, the evolutionary cultivators hoped that these, like *Erectus* and *Neandertal*, would graduate, become translated, and join the galactic community. Then planet Gaia could be converted into a godworld. So, the twelve most powerful human psychics were located telepathically during early stages of human cultivation. Nagarjaruk was one.

Taming this collection of furious males was not easy. They were isolated from each other and individually subjected, through the eye, to a beam of living information, the Gnosis. Culture shock followed immediately.

These twelve Cro-Magnons were the contributors of genes that would be recombined to enhance the race. In dreams of reluctant rapture, Nagarjaruk contributed sperm; in hypnotic trances he contributed brain, skin and muscle cells, bone marrow and blood to the evolution of his race.

Thousands of other prehuman men and women also contributed genes to this process. Recessive genes were eliminated and dominant genes selected for qualities favorable to admission into pangalactic society: cooperativeness, sensitivity, empathy, telepathy. Aboard the starship a humanoid was genetically constructed and conception was accomplished. Since anatomical differences could prevent generation of a viable hybrid from an idealized, synthetic humanoid and a native of Gaia, the brides of the god-kings were carefully chosen. The deciding factor was the width of their pelvic girdles.

After the abduction that cost Nagarjaruk his freedom, the savage shaman was allowed the company of extraterrestrials exclusively. He feared them at first, then grew accustomed to them and trusted that he would not be harmed. When told that

his captors were sending from the stars a king who would rule his planet, he became secretly derisive. He could not envision any of these diminutive humanoids, Procyonians or Capellans, or larval humans like the Zeta II Reticulans, ever commanding respect among tribal humans, who feared size and strength only. So when he met the king he was to serve, he was shocked and terrified. Instead of a dwarf, he faced a giant.

The giant was Thoth. His formidable-looking body was, in fact, quite frail. Thoth could not walk and could barely stand up unassisted. His pelvis was huge, his legs bowed, his abdomen distended. His massive head tottered on a spindly neck. But his immense stature and grotesque proportions inspired awe and fear in the hearts of Thoth's primitive human subjects.

Thoth married a slender, broad-hipped woman of an African tribe who was also a product of genetic engineering She received the full Gnosis through her eye and her brain contained the virtual memory of the Universe. She became Seshat, goddess-human of the Library of the Stars.

Thoth's genetically-engineered brain was over three thousand cubic centimeters in volume. No human woman among the primitives could manage the birth of children with such a father—except Seshat. Though she feared Thoth and his extraterrestrial family, she loved violent, passionate humanity enough to become the bride of this strange king. She knew in her heart that the arrival of the sky people would bring peace to primitive humankind.

Thoth summoned the Siberian to his throne. Nagarjaruk knelt, then threw himself abjectly to the floor. After several moments he looked up cautiously and asked, "What do you wish, O King?"

Thoth smiled compassionately. "Please rise, Loyal One, and face me." Nagarjaruk obeyed. "You have been serving me dutifully for many years, O Priest."

"As you wish, O King."

"You are content with your new land and people?"

"Yes, O King."

"That is good, Nagarjaruk. This is your place, if you wish it to be. That is why I have summoned you. I wish to bestow upon you a new name."

"As you will, O King…"

The priest's new name was *Kahotep*, which meant "the *Ka* is fulfilled." Kahotep was not aware of the irony in it: *Ka* denoted the spirit of the animal brain, the limbic system, as opposed to *Ba*, the soul of the neocortex, the extraterrestrial brain.

Kahotep's early duties as a Priest of Thoth were that of a lab technician. He and his fellow priests washed beakers and flasks, added living chemicals to genetic cultures, used steam to sterilize the glassware that would contain the molecular strands of life. Eventually Kahotep was given more sophisticated tasks. He performed simple experiments and read the holographic data screens of the instruments. In this way he learned that his world was a round planet suspended in space, eternally circling the sun and circled by the moon.

For two thousand years, ageless Thoth ruled the kingdom called Egypt with Seshat, his wife and Kahotep, his priest, when the queen gave birth to a last son, who inherited most of his father's anatomical distortions. The baby had been removed from his mother's womb surgically, for his oversized head could not fit through even Seshat's wide pelvis. Kahotep had seen the miracle of that delivery, awed by the birth. Then he feared the growing boy, the awkward, precocious mutant named Osiris.

From a tribe of Neandertals living in the heart of Australia, a bride was selected for Osiris. Her great pelvic width afforded a generous birth corridor and her cranial capacity was over seventeen hundred cubic centimeters. The name she was given was Isis. Her people called themselves "Children of the Dreamtime." Thus the comely, large-eyed Neandertal woman responded to the Gnosis beamed into

5

her eye with greater acceptance than her Erectus predecessor, Seshat. Isis felt that it was her happy destiny to participate in the cultivation of new humans from this new wave of evolving post-hominids.

Kahotep felt much trepidation at the departure of Thoth and Seshat aboard a lighted disc into the starry sky.

Isis and Osiris reigned for two thousand years, just as had Thoth and Seshat. Kahotep witnessed the unification of Upper and Lower Egypt by Osiris. Instead of commanding an invasion, the god-king had himself journeyed down the Nile into unfriendly territory, protected by a vast army of dancers and musicians, poets and philosophers. The tribal kings were curious, then impressed. After dancing and debating, feasting and celebrating, Osiris had secured their loyalty without conflict or coercion.

When at last the extraterrestrial, Set, arrived to escort the royal couple to the stars, Kahotep felt no trepidation, but calm acceptance. Over four thousand years old, still young in body and mind, he had witnessed one great transition already. Set piloted Isis and Osiris to the star called *Sothis* in Pangalactic, *Seti* or Set in Egyptian.

The sudden departure of their divine royalty provoked uneasiness among the primitive Egyptians, but they were reassured by the appearance of Horus, oldest son of Osiris, upon the throne. Horus was a good king and understood his people far better than had Thoth or even Osiris. He was known for his love of nature, song, poetry and all humanity. Kahotep dutifully served Horus and his queen, Hathor.

Kahotep was the only Priest of Thoth who refused to marry. In truth, he did not respond to women sexually. He was averse to the thin, simian-looking women, anatomically similar to Seshat, who were still prevalent among the early Egyptians. He remained indifferent as robust and voluptuous women began to comprise a growing portion of the population as humanity evolved. He lived among extraterrestrials and god-kings. He worked in the entropy-reversing, euphoria-inducing field emanated by Yod, but Kahotep had an antisexual bias.

This attitude made ascended beings uneasy. Though he was encouraged to indulge in carefree sexual play, he resisted all persuasion to marry. He was intransigent and indifferent, though he was never asked why he refused to even once make love to a female of his species. The beings he served watched him with a slight sadness, for he was dutiful and devoted. In truth, he was grateful for having been saved from the crude, brutal life that was the lot of all humans before the glacial thaw. Nagarjaruk had been born into a tribe with a powerful cult of homosexual violence. Initiation into this secret all-male society, as well as other rites-of-passage for the young men, often included the rape of the initiate by the dominant males of the tribe. At the age of twelve Nagarjaruk had been raped by his own father

He loved each of the god-kings, the *Amentii*, the "visitors from unseen worlds." He loved the goddess-queens, from frail Seshat to lovely Isis and tall, beautiful, brooding Hathor. He had in common with Hathor a heaviness of heart, of spirit, that was more than introspection. Hathor and Kahotep were reserved, hesitant to accept the light of life. The star people observed the queen and the priest and wondered if there was not something inside themselves the two did not accept. Kahotep lived in the bliss of seemingly eternal youth, yet he harbored a fear of death.

Kahotep learned more in his six thousand years than any human had ever known. But he also discovered a terrible secret: the king and queen would soon return to the stars and Egypt would be plunged again into the terrible cycle of birth and death. With only an unproven promise of rebirth to cling to, he sank into a sullenness which he veiled but could not completely disguise.

Horus summoned him and questioned him. When Kahotep admitted he feared death, Horus attempted to explain that only the ego dies. Although Kahotep had lived in bliss among the god-kings for sixty centuries, the the prospect of losing his selfhood threatened him. Horus wisely ended the discussion.

Later that night, Kahotep had an unexpected encounter that burned itself into his memory. He was in the temple laboratory preparing experiments, when he heard voices from another chamber. Hurriedly, he finished the last of his mixtures and slipped down an adjoining hallway.

Two slender humanoids were excitedly discussing something in their strange, fluctuating voices. Kahotep drew near.

"How are the Inner Circle responding to the news of the departure?"

The other voice was somber. "There is great trepidation among the priests."

"Is it because they will face old age?"

"Yes."

There was a long silence, then, "There is a way to circumvent death."

"The Secret?"

"Yes. The Obscene Rite."

"I've heard it is…horrible."

"Yes. It is best kept secret."

"I've never known how it was done."

"You and I have no need of such a process."

"Of course not. But…how is it done?"

"Very simply…" The being hesitated and then simply and uncautiously explained the Rite.

Without a sound, Kahotep slipped out of the temple.

Hathor attained enlightenment. She weighed her heart against the feather of reality and was spared the ordeal of death. Her translation was a festive occasion, but followed by sadness throughout the land.

After the departure of Horus, the Priests of Thoth were retired and replaced by a priesthood led by a mysterious human, Imhotep. The former priests accepted this abrupt change with degrees of resignation. After several years of luxury, lack of responsibility, and leisure, several plunged into despair. Two took their own lives, one passed into insanity, and the unmarried priest disappeared into the desert.

Kahotep responded to the departure of Horus first with stunned disbelief, then with dread as the realization of his own impending death washed over him. Finally, outrage and rebellion arose: he cursed the god-kings for prolonging his life and giving him something sublime to live for, then taking back all of it, even the bliss he had felt in their presence. He was once again in the world they had rescued him from many centuries before. Though not in the shrieking blizzards of the tundra, he was alone in a desert roamed by lions, cobras, adders, and haunted by vultures. Ever-present was death.

Many times at night he raged, shaking his fist against the sky, wondering which of those multitudes of lights was the invaders, with their knowledge-rays and flying discs. Once, as he watched a spaceship cross the starry void above him, he shrieked and leaped in manic fury. In blind hatred he hurled rocks at the stars.

Kahotep had gone insane. For ten long years he did not see another human being. Centuries of bliss gave way to tortured years of dread and loathing. Every night he dreamed of his greatest fear: death. Final, unknowable, ultimate death. Darkness. Extinction.

One morning, he awoke from nightmares unending and cursed a wild and excruciating oath: "They call that ritual obscene, do they? I know the secret of the pineal gland, that resonates with time itself! I have not eaten meat or cooked grains in ten years! I have eaten only the prescribed diet. Let me live! Let me live! The god-kings need not know! They promised to return. Let them find me here, still alive and ready for their arrival!"

His mind was beset by an unconscious paradox: he feared death, yet hated cowardice. So dictated the hunter ethic of Siberia, still alive in him. Cowardice, fear, was weakness. Therefore he, the coward who still despised death, was to be despised. With that maddening contradiction in his mind, he flung his precious ego into the depths of self-loathing. He abandoned all love and morality and trudged south on a pilgrimage to find humanity. He would murder and perform the Obscene Rite, kill innocents and use the eternity-conscious parts of their brains to prolong his own life.

Kahotep knew from the sciences of Thoth and from the Gnosis itself that consciousness is not native to the physical realm of matter that is this Universe of stars and planets. Mind intrudes into the physical realm of electrons and protons and manifests in physical reality as Life. Mind overcomes the tendency of matter to

decay through interaction with energy. Mind, as Life, organizes itself into self-replicating, entropy-reversing forms.

Kahotep was proud. He would indeed perpetuate Mind. His own. Issues of morality, of the preservation of life against the imposition of death, were irrelevant. He regarded ethics as deceptive. He reasoned that the extraterrestrials used logic to keep humanity oppressed and submissive. They had been invaders. They had disrupted nature's balance, and they had promised to invade again.

He journeyed south, by raft along the waters of the Nile and overland through fields and deserts. He skirted villages by night, moving beyond the fringes of light cast by their fires. By day he studied the horizon for the dust-plumes of approaching caravans. He avoided contact with humanity.

On reaching the mountains of the south he made a simple shelter for himself in a shallow cave. Uncounted days passed. The awful necessity of performing the

Obscene Rite obsessed him and he rehearsed it constantly and dreamed it. Often he awoke in darkness screaming.

When he left his mountain cave he journeyed west, toward the Nile. After the third morning he saw the dust clouds of a moving caravan. He spied on the travellers for six days and when he knew which oasis they were approaching, he waited at a vantage point in the hills to stage his ambush.

Guilt and shame overcame him. Several times he stalked away in self-disgust, but then he would see the wrinkles on the backs of his hands, grit his teeth, clench his fists and return to the thorn thicket. He hid and watched the liquid blue mirror in the hollow where the date palms swayed when the air stirred. At sunset a young boy came to water the camels. Kahotep hurled a rock that sent the youth into silent unconsciousness. He pulled the boy out of the water and carried him into the cavern-pitted hills.

Kahotep could sense suspicion that the boy had been kidnapped spread through the encampment below. His only chance to avoid an early death of vengeance lay in his ability to complete the Rite at once and then hide himself and the silent body. He vomited twice as he climbed the rocky slope. So much the better—an empty stomach would best absorb the molecules of Eternity, the precious Serotonin. He reached the cave and prepared. He lit a lamp in the center of a slab of white rock and placed the boy on an adjoining slab. The boy stirred, coughed and sputtered, then blinked. Kahotep lifted his stone hammer and initiated the Obscene Rite.

Choking, he fumbled with his stone blade. He had seen so much blood in many aeons. In Siberia he had killed many men—but he had not murdered in sixty peaceful centuries. The shards of the skull, the grey gelatin of brain oozing through his fingers revolted him.

He suppressed his nausea. Time was precious. He knew the pineal gland was simultaneously discharging and metabolizing Serotonin. Half a minute of near-death would be too long. His stomach, empty of the gastric juices which would digest complex proteins, received the gland and its bitter hormone. The boy's pineal gland was assimilated alive.

Kahotep leaned against the cave wall, eyes closed, sweating, anticipating the dreams that would follow absorption of the source of another human soul. But only the cold shudders of shock and trauma racked him. He had taken too long in his butchery. The Serotonin had been discharged and metabolized during his abominable spell of retching.

He clenched his teeth and fists, eyes glaring wide open, rigid as he sat in the cave. Voices moved in the night. As a search party passed near, Kahotep distinctly heard a voice say, "Who would do such a thing?"

"Evil dog!"

"O Isis, protect us on this night!"

Kahotep quietly growled like an animal.

The search party returned to camp just before sunrise. Undiscovered, Kahotep slept dreamlessly through the day. That night he traversed the desert again, silently, a speck of shadow beneath the eye of the full moon. When he reached the cave that was his home, he rejoiced dementedly. He had not successfully performed the Obscene Rite, but he now knew that he could.

Kahotep lived like an unnatural beast. He selected a remote mountain in the desert west of the Nile, far from the fierce Nubians, for a home. He inhabited caves, preferring darkness to light. He moved furtively, a fleeting shadow.

He lived in no place for more than fifty years, spying on a village, the homes of peasants, a well-traveled caravan route, or perhaps a frequently visited oasis. When rumors arose that a hermit or perhaps a witch lived nearby, he would vanish into the desert again.

He became acutely sensitive. He did not need to hear humans speak to know their thoughts and fears. He would see brief contacts beyond the walls of a village or behind a date palm near a waterhole and know what these exchanges meant: that the people were talking about him. Then he would notice changes: villagers, visitors or strays from the nomad encampments would never walk alone. Groups of women were always escorted by larger groups of men.

For one hundred years Kahotep suffered, either delirious with delusions of grandeur or twisted with the bent rage of self-hate. Bliss, peace, and happiness had left his life forever. He hated his addiction and was reminded of it daily. He longed to eat meat; his Siberian roots called him to the hunt and the glut. But he would never eat honest flesh again, nor cooked grains, cheese, butter, oil, or eggs. He had to rid his stomach of the tendency to produce protein-attacking gastric juices that would break down Serotonin. So he contented himself with raw vegetables, fruits, dates and figs in large quantities, raw nuts for protein, water to drink.

Day after day, he fought his rage by forcing himself to meditate, a practise he had learned under the god-kings. They had also taught him Indian yoga, so in a desperate attempt to preserve the shards of his sanity he forced himself to practise the *asanas* again and again: the Lotus, the Breath of Fire, every one he could remember. Practising what he recalled caused him to remember much more. He found that Kahotep had not been completely shattered by the fall from the Priesthood of Thoth, from glorious service to three god-kings, to the depraved life of a vampire.

Kahotep steadily regained his power. As a priest he had been without motive, except to serve. For six thousand years he had lived on gratitude, knowing that life under the god-kings was infinitely preferable to the frozen hell of Siberia. Now survival was his terrible motive. He had pushed death back a hundred years. He would push it back a thousand! Not just to live, day by day, but possibly forever! He would pospone death infinitely!

No, he corrected himself with a stab of sorrow, *not infinitely. Only indefinitely.* He knew the secrets. He also knew he had acquired the most terrible addiction of all: if he failed to perform the Obscene Rite at intervals no greater than half a century, all of the borrowed time that had prolonged his life would be snatched back.

So he performed the Rite. It was more an act of cannibalism than a ritual. No incense was burned, there were no incantations. Just a swift, ugly act of violence and a frantic dissection, a desperate gulping of the bitter living gland, then an hour of fighting nausea, trying not to vomit the ill-gotten miracle. Finally the hallucinations would come. He would relive the dreams, the living memories of his dead victims. He knew then what tragic lives the peasants led, for Kahotep digested only their bitter memories, assimilated only their hardships and struggles. He acquired contempt for the common people of the land which enforced his desire to live alone.

Against his will he often dreamed of Egypt. He tried not to dwell on his life under the god-kings, the luxury, the

splendor, the magnificence. Instead he glorified his squalor and jealously guarded his latest hovel. Two hundred years of practising yoga and visualization exercises earned him immense power: self-discipline to live for months fasting; staying alert and focused in meditation for weeks; and sometimes leaving his body at will. His memory so eidetic that contemplation of a scene for a few minutes would render it, if he willed, clear in his memory for a lifetime. He lived in and for his mind, devoting himself to the task of increasing his psychic power.

His clairvoyance expanded. He could sense movement far away in the desert.

Often this talent led him to his victims, drawn to the aura of the tragedy of their pathetic lives. He knew the power of a direct look, the hypnotic, telepathic quality of eye contact. He used it on his fifth victim, a young woman. She submitted to him instantly and completely. She slept in the induced fear as he carried her to the tomb of his body. It was after this Rite that Kahotep, moving swiftly north, fleeing the place of the murder, determined to skirt the mountains of the great Valley and navigate the Nile on a cautious return to Egypt.

The despicable human animal was certainly incapable of self-rule. Kahotep sneered. This visit would be easy. He would find only ruins.

From the mountaintops he could see vast bands of green on both sides of the Blue Nile. The White Nile was sometimes visible, sometimes not. He made his way past the place where they joined together, still staying away from human habitation. He was relieved when he was well out of Nubia, for the villages were bigger than he had expected.

There were many caravans and highways. Where he expected squalor, he discovered prosperity. The sparse population of apelike nomads was gone. The humans of the new townships were taller and stood fully erect. They were more…human. The men dressed in tunics or in long, beautifully woven robes. The women wore scarves and veils, their skin smooth and comely.

In truth, Kahotep had seldom ventured out of Memphis during the six millennia he had served the stellar kings. He had been a stranger to much that existed outside of the City of the Pharaoh. Now his preconceptions were soon to be tested.

He camped outside a large city of Upper Egypt, by chance near the site where

Osiris had won the allegiance of the southern tribes. Kahotep remembered how, in the entourage of the immortal king, he had sailed in the royal barge at the head of a flotilla of barges. Osiris had been escorted by an army of poets and musicians, philosophers and artisans, and his weapons had been music, dance, jewels, and irrefutable arguments. In this way the gentle god-king had subdued and peacefully won the friendship of the southern tribes.

Kahotep planned the opposite: he would conquer and subdue.

So completely had he lost touch with Egypt that he shuddered to think how much he had to learn. He listened to the voices of the night, the clairvoyant whispers of distant human thoughts, and tried to perceive their contents. He flew through the astral realm and awakened to struggle to decipher the distant images he brought back. His dreams of Egypt became more intense and they were always filled with fear of the return of the god-kings.

Unable to discern the name of the current Pharaoh by occult means, Kahotep decided to venture into the city and learn what he could firsthand. He walked among the humans in simple clothes. He passed among the street crowds inconspicuously. The mood of the streets was happy and there were bright colors all around. Shops displayed fine wares and Kahotep saw artistry in everything from kitchen utensils to the handiwork of master craftsmen.

He learned much. The Pharaoh's name was Neferkara. It was better to be rich than poor. The marketplace was receptive to barter and jewels could buy much. If beggars were few in those days, men with jewels were few, too. Kahotep had acquired a handful of such treasures when he stripped his victims, and he knew well where more could be had. After his second visit to the city, he was moderately wealthy. Not wishing to be conspicuous, he sold very few of his jewels and only the least precious. Merchants were common in the city and another jewel-trader was incidental.

The local dialect was little different from what he had spoken in Memphis. Kahotep abandoned his cave and kept a room at an inn. He stayed in the white-walled room during the day, meditating. He projected self-assertion, no one cared to talk to him or question his business, nor even looked askance at him in any way. He used his powers to deflect attention wherever he went.

After several years as a gem merchant, he had built himself a substantial personal fortune. He mined kimberlite deposits in northern Nubia. When he befriended the savage Nubians he learned that some still practised human sacrifice. After several years of acquaintance, he was invited to participate.

The ritual was crude and gory. These people were cannibals but Kahotep could not join in the feast since meat was forbidden in his diet. He used the opportunity to stage an event of significance to the Nubians: he set a simple pyrotechnic device to detonate at the pull of a string. At a dramatic moment, after the killing of the old king and queen and before the coronation of the new royal couple, a rocket trailing red and white sparks hissed up through the sky and exploded in a blossom of red fire. The tribefolk were thunderstruck. Kahotep stepped forward and declared that he was a sky-god and that he would never age.

The chief stepped forward and announced to his people, "It is true! He has returned to us many times in many, many years, but he has not aged!"

Kahotep then set the stage for their next cannibal feast. As the wandering stars, the planets, moved into their positions, the visitor from the north prepared. His knowledge was prodigious and the Nubians believed he must be a sky-god. He insisted on honoring the bodies of the old king and queen immediately after their assassinations. Kahotep told the elders that he would eat the source of life that only a god can eat, thus assuring the souls of the divine couple entrance to the Godhead. Then he performed the Rite. Thus as he built his financial empire in Egypt, Kahotep created a religious empire in Nubia.

Pharaohs reigned and died and dynasties passed. Kahotep mastered many tricks of disguise and deception to continue his business with the Egyptians, while appearing time and time again unchanged on his visits to the Nubians. He would start a business or open a store in Egypt using one identity, then buy out an enterprise he had started long before under another name in another city. Egyptians were fanatical record-keepers, but his inventiveness at deception kept his transactions and identities unknown. Also, if any Egyptian were to question Kahotep's ways, he would be mysteriously murdered. Likewise, if any Nubian openly doubted Kahotep's divinity, he was a dead man.

Kahotep was excruciatingly cautious for he knew that if he even cut a finger and bled in Nubia his true nature as a man would be revealed. In Egypt, if someone recognized him in a foreign city and called him by a former name, suspicion might be aroused that could reveal his forgeries and frauds. A prison term would separate him from his essential diet, including the forbidden food he needed every fifty or thirty or twenty years. He would not survive in prison, not even a brief term, and in those ancient dungeons there were no short incarcerations.

Kahotep knew that beneath the veneer of prosperity there was corruption. Abandonment by the god-kings had resulted in tragedy. There was much more death in Egypt in their absence. Kahotep became obsessed by a new goal: he would be king of Egypt and of Nubia.

The people of Egypt during the Old Kingdom succesfully assimilated the genetic characteristics imparted to them by the God-kings. Four generations from Horus, nearly all urban Egyptians had the characteristic god-king skull and women had the enlarged pelvis. Many men inherited the tendency toward hairlessness.

The tradition of sacred incest was a corruption of the original breeding plan of the god-kings. The children of the god-kings and queens were required to be in-

cestuous. The offspring of Isis and Osiris required generations of genetic modifications before they were compatible with the evolving people of the Nile. Their traits were dispersed cautiously among the Egyptians through special matings with peasants who displayed anatomical similarities with the stellar race. Six generations after the departure of Horus, the larger cranium stabilized in size among the Egyptian peasantry. The purpose of the breeding plan that leaned so heavily on incest to assure genetic compatibility was obsolete and long ago forgotten, but the tradition of sacred incest among royal families remained, and much of Egyptian aristocracy was genetically debilitated.

The same process had occurred several times before: in the Tigris and Euphrates River valleys, where civilizations had been built and expanded before the last glacial epoch, as well as before the Penultimate and the Antepenultimate glaciations before that, thus producing three separate waves of human evolutions. The Egyptian people were cultivated in the fourth wave of human evolution.

Had they taken life seriously, the Egyptians would have been more intellectual, but they did not. Their scholars were in love with consciousness for its own sake. Priests discussed ideas for their esthetic merit, not for innate truth and certainly not for logic.

There were those who believed that knowledge was knowable, and those who believed it was not. There were arguments in favor of both assumptions, and neither were taken seriously.

The religions of Old Kingdom Egypt were not segregated : one could worship with the priests of Osiris in the spring, attend the hymn-singing at a temple of Set or Sothis at the rising of the Dog-Star, and go on to meditate with the priests of Thoth, who, with the priestesses of Seshat, tended the libraries and kept old knowledge alive at the universities. Religion was eclectic and nobody cared to devote love or attention to only one deity in a Universe that obviously contained so many. With frequent festivals and Pharaohs who seemed to live just for pageants, religion, like life, was a splendid game.

In the temple of Crocodilopolis, under the high dome painted with a mural of Nuit, the immense reflective pool was alive with bathing crocodiles. The largest were adorned with chains inlaid with precious stones. The priests read poems and sang hymns to the ancient reptiles.

The temple at Elephantine contained a vast courtyard in which a herd of sacred elephants roamed. The Temple of Bast was home to a million prowling cats to whom priestesses gave offerings and sang hymns hourly. Egyptians believed in the Mind within every animal, plant, even minerals.

They were not inquisitive. They established no sciences of their own and trusted their priests to keep alive the old sciences, the mathematics, chemistry, and physics imparted to them by the god-Kings. If the priests could do that accurately…

Against this backdrop of jovially conflicting beliefs, the long-lived sorceror Kahotep moved, playing on the innocence of Egypt's humans. None suspected that a six thousand four hundred year old Priest of Thoth was alive in the city of Kalabsha, or walked the streets of Elephantine, or dwelled within the fortress of Thebes.

Kahotep loved Thebes. After a brief return to Nubia, where he made a reappearance as a sun-god, he resumed residence there. He liked being a sun god and he still entertained a desire to be Pharaoh—or, far better, to control the Pharaoh. To dictate directly to the king would be ideal.

Because he was literate as so few citizens were, Kahotep sat in on many council sessions, lending his service as a scribe. He was sometimes appointed to public office and often passed laws from which he realized no immediate benefit. After serving for years and then retiring, he might return as a merchant or a monarch, or play the role of a mere camel dealer. In each new lifetime he would take advantage of the legal systems he had previously created.

Old Kingdom Egypt flourished in a time of plenty. The fertile banks of the Nile flooded every 56 years with the rising of the Dog-Star, which was the Terminal of Worlds circling the black hole closest to the Ra system. This fact, which only Kahotep knew for certain, was wondered at by the Priests of Thoth in Memphis and debated in hushed voices in the privacy of their temples.

However, no one took such matters seriously. The lush valleys that stretched inland on both sides of the mighty river gave life to millions of people. Every person tended a garden. There was abundance. The many tributaries of the Nile provided fish and game. Festival days were celebrated throughout the year, and the Pharaohs enjoyed celebration and were generous. This meant many feasts for everyone. Poverty existed only in the biggest cities, as did crime, usually theft. Rape was unheard of and murder was almost unknown, but not quite.

𓅓

For over a century Kahotep's attempts to teleport himself through timespace were the main focus of his meditations. He concentrated his visualizations on the projection of psychoholograms, the first step toward altering the vibrational rate of the electromagnetic resonance field of his body. His goal was to harmonize with the timespace continuum of the place he visualized until enfoldment occurred. He knew from his training as a Priest of Thoth that enfoldment was the point at which the mental image, the psychohologram, becomes more real in experience than the world beyond the thinker's closed eyelids.

The technique was to visualize a remembered image of a scene visited firsthand until the remembered image overtakes the fading sensory impressions of the external world and the ego of the thinker "dies." Then the projected image overwhelms the senses, the psychohologram is unfolded and a limited act of teleportation, or timespace dislocation, occurs.. Kahotep believed he had reached that point several times, but because of his tired, suppressed rage, it never happened. Kahotep remained imprisoned in his linear timespace continuum.

He never mastered wave-shifting.

To prevent a wave-shifter from dancing out of one reality into another, all that is needed is a viewer. Line-of-sight contact with another sentient being anchors the wave-shifter to the location of the second percipient.

Kahotep feared he was being locked into place by antagonistic wave-shifters who opposed his usurpage of souls to prolong his life. So, before attempting meditations in his secret cavern hideaways, he would shout threats and curses to all listening ears to drive away "the Little People." Instead, he evicted bats, desert mice, and terrified insects, and he feared that they were wave-shifting spies from the far past or future of his race.

In truth, he had never learned ego-death.

He had forgotten the heart's relationship to Ma'at. At the end of the journey, at the instant of body death, the soul was said to meet Osiris, the Judge of Souls. Osiris

18

stood before a balance scale, one tray of which was empty. The other tray held the feather which was Ma'at. If the heart of the dead human's soul weighed as little or less than Ma'at, the Feather of Truth, then the soul would be admitted to Heaven. but most souls, it was said, outweighed the feather, and Baba, the Soul-Eater, a crocodilian monster, would consume them instead.

Kahotep knew his similarity to Baba, the Soul-Eater. This made him resent his addiction even more.

Wave-shifters did, in fact, spy on him. His usurpation of power, his unholy activities among evolving humanity did not go unnoticed elsewhen. Kahotep never came upon any evidence that wave-shifters had secreted themselves in his cave-hovels, or the houses he owned in Thebes, or Onn, or the townships in the desert of Egypt. They were skilled at their mental craft, and it was their purpose to observe evolving humanity without intervention and sometimes to influence, subtly, that evolution. They knew that Kahotep was beyond influence or persuasion. He was amok with motive power of his own.

Centuries of Egyptian history passed. A gradual change in temperament came over the Egyptian people. It showed in their myths of the Other World, where the gods and goddesses lived and out of which the early people had come, long ago.

By the middle of Old Kingdom the departure of Osiris was no longer depicted as a smooth ride into the stars after a pleasantly received invitation from Seth, the god. Set/Seti/Seth/Sothis was no longer known simply as the bright Dog-Star in the constellation of Canis Major. Seth was an evil deity now, the assassin of beloved Osiris. Seth menaced Egypt herself and after several generations of retelling, the people of Egypt feared the Dog-Star itself.

Although worship of Isis and Osiris persisted with vast popularity among the common people, the aristocracy of Egypt embraced more exotic religions. Some Pharaohs worshipped Thoth, oldest of the gods-on-earth, in whose name the repositories of knowledge were tended. Thoth was the source of wisdom, god of the oldest priesthood. Worship of Thoth implied mercy mixed with intelligence. To worship Thoth assured the respect of the peasants, or so the Pharaohs hoped.

The Nubians had long been raiding the towns and cities of Upper Egypt. Once isolated, scattered tribes, content with in-fighting and ritual cannibalism, over the years they had become unified. They unanimously owed allegiance to their sun-god, known only as the Nameless One.

Egypt responded by building a great army. The general who led the army claimed to be a Priest of Thoth. Kahotep became vizier to the Pharaoh Besh at the beginning of the Third Dynasty. The vizier-general built the Wall of the Hundred Gates around the city of Thebes. Again he resided in Thebes, far from Memphis and the Pharaoh Besh. No one knew that this was the storyteller who, generations before, had retold the myth of the departure of Osiris as a battle with Seth, as a war story.

A sun-god cult sprang up in the east, in the rising city-states of Mesopotamia. The deity worshipped was called the Unknown One. He was male and demanded tribute of human sacrifices. Since few Egyptians knew the language of the invaders, the resemblance of this new eastern sun-god and the solar deity of the Nubians went unnoticed.

Raids out of the east surprised the Egyptians, but Egypt already had a vast army from which to dispatch legions to dispense with these hordes. The nameless war-god in Hatti incited the eastern tribes to invade Egypt. For two centuries the attacks had been sporadic and ineffective: now, the invaders came in conquest.

Struggling against the ravages of inbreeding, King Unas attempted to be a good king. Like all Pharaohs, he was as good as his entourage of advisors. Not even his manservants knew Unas was murdered in his old age by a subtle poison, administered by the world's most skilled assassin. King Unas was succeeded by King Teti I, a war king,

Teti I drove the eastern nomads from Egypt, then from their own turf. He pushed them back to the banks of the two rivers from which they had come. The generals were superbly informed and the Pharaoh seemed to know the terrain his troops would cross well in advance of their departures. He attributed this foreknowledge to his dreams.

Teti I was Egypt's best military commander. He conquered and held vast territories for Egypt. It was even said that the sun-gods of Nubia and Mesopotamia deserted their homelands and people while King Teti I ruled Egypt. The name Teti meant Seti, Set, or Seth, names for Sothis, the Dog-Star.

Teti had a son by one of his many wives, a queen of indescribable beauty. The boy grew to be the great war-king, Usurkara Ati. He continued Egypt's conquests abroad and suppressed captive peoples. Egypt dominated Africa and Asia Minor and was the greatest military power in the world. The Sixth Dynasty after the departure of Horus saw multitudes imprisoned and slaughtered inside the cities and townships of Egypt. Some gods, notably Seth, demanded human lives as tributes.

King Ati fathered a reincarnation of Teti I, Meripa Pepi, who bore an uncanny resemblance to King Teti. The memories of people old enough to have seen both kings attested to this. King Pepi I was as ruthless as his predecessors. He was an effective military strategist and tactician. He was also an advocate of human sacrifice. Slavery crept into Egyptian society. Only a percentage of the multitude of war prisoners could be sacrificed to the gods—the rest were tamed and employed at hard labor.

Pepi I had been a great patron of the arts. He held many pageants in honor of himself, but during his reign a subtle change took place. As his son Merenra Mehtiemsaf I grew, Pepi held fewer and fewer cultural events. Royal support for art and festivity ended with the boy's coronation pageant.

Mehtiemsaf added a new crime to the list of atrocities of his line: he burned the history books. Scrolls, papyri, all ancient records were burned. Though fanatical mobs had destroyed much in the past, this time it was sanctioned by a king. Lists of documents to be banned were drawn up by the Pharaoh himself. He also employed many anonymous scribes who recorded Pharaoh Mehtiemsaf's version of what the burned texts had contained.

Kahotep controlled Egypt from the death of King Unas on. Each war-Pharaoh was an initiate into his Inner Circle, which included implantation of a limbic-system demon into the brain and addiction to the Obscene Rite.

Succeeding Pharaoh Mehtiemsaf was his "son," another direct reincarnation of King Teti, another Teti/Pepi lookalike. His name was Neferkara Pepi II, and the people of Egypt knew him as a secretive king, celebrating few pageants and commanding many victorious battles. He was a great antiquarian who passionately gathered all art pieces of great age, especially artifacts from the temples of Thoth and Seshat: everything that dated back to the age before the departure of Horus.

King Pepi II reigned for over forty years and quietly turned his throne over to his "son," Merenra Mehtiemsaf II. He was another secretive Pharaoh, almost unseen. He held no pageants. He demanded vast tributes in human sacrifices, and confiscated and burned all sacred texts and scrolls of great antiquity. He requisitioned art objects from the temples. These treasures were never seen again.

Mehtiemsaf II was succeeded by Pharaoh Neterkara, who persecuted scholars, poets, intellectuals, librarians, and visionaries to a degree no other Pharaoh had. Prisons were filled with genius. Those suspected of possessing psychic powers, such as the ability to communicate with animals or foretell the future with their dreams, were sacrificed to gods associated with Seth, the Dog-star.

Under the reign of Kahotep's last initiate, Pharaoh Menkara, the remaining Egyptian thinkers and visionaries were arrested, placed aboard a barge and sent into exile, to drift out of the Nile River and into the currents of the Mediterranean Sea. With this, the empire that was Egypt finally fell. As the last intellectuals and poets floated away, rumor spread among the tormented people about the truth behind the Sixth Dynasty Pharaohs. The population arose in revolt. Someone in the military was the source of this disclosure: the king's own guard had witnessed something too terrible to describe.

All that was known was that, in the evening after a festival, a disturbance had caught the attention of the king's guard. Several of the king's courtiers had fled from their posts. The king was nowhere to be found.

Later that night, a courtier approached the General of Egypt with grim news. The two were alone in the commanding officer's chambers.

The king's personal advisor was in shock. He could not speak. When he tried, he doubled up in pain and vomited uncontrollably. Then, he gathered his strength, stood and faced the general.

"It is the king…" He shuddered convulsively.

"What is this? Is the king in danger?"

The young man shook his head, then said in a voice strained and tense with horror:

"I come to you with a strange and terrible secret. I have witnessed something inhuman…"

He told the general what he had seen. His words shocked with revulsion the sensibilities of that warrior who had seen vast slaughter on many battlefields.

It was decided that great evil had come to inhabit the royal palace.

A coup was staged but the king vanished in time to avoid assassination.

Without a king, the masses succumbed to blind panic. In the chaos, the content of the unrecorded rumor was forgotten.

A dark age ensued that lasted for centuries.

Repeated invasions of Nubians and Hittites commanded by an unnamed solar god devastated Egypt. Culture ceased and occupation and servility began. The unseen presence of Kahotep moved like a shadow behind the destruction.

The Seventh Dynasty began when.Egypt was reunified and liberated by King Neferka. Though palace intrigues and assassinations were frequent among the ruling houses of Egypt, the many invasions from outside tribes and empires subsided. The people of the Nile were choosing to reunite and cast off oppression.

By the beginning of the Eighth Dynasty, peasants had been granted basic rights and men had the privilege of voting for their local nomarchs and judges. They could petition to challenge court decisions or even repeal unjust laws. By the Eleventh Dynasty, the Pharaoh was a figurehead, symbolic protector of his nation. He did not inflict purges and persecution upon his people, but remained a passive overseer and commander of the armies abroad.

At the end of the Eleventh Dynasty a viper lay coiled in Egypt. A rumor circulated through the city of Thebes about the return of a forgotten god, a deity known only as "the Nameless One." In the center of Thebes was the Temple of Amen, an Earth-god. He was god of the umbilical cord and called "the Hidden One" by his priests.

As the sun arose on the first day of spring on the last day of the Eleventh Dynasty, a Priest of Amen announced that Amen, "the Hidden One" was about to make himself manifest.

"First," the anonymous priest insisted, crying out to the sleepy, but waking populace, "Amen must settle some discrepancies in the myths about who he was and his place in the Universe. It is hereby revealed that Amen is not an Earth-god. Amen is a sky-god, a solar god—the only sun god! All others are secondary or false deities."

As the crowd became a hostile mob, the Priest of Amen only laughed. His arrogance intimidated his shocked audience, who restricted their antagonism to shouts of: "Heretic!" and "Blasphemer!"

Undaunted, the priest continued his diatribe:

"Amen is not god of the umbilical cord. His consort is not Muit, goddess of the placenta. No. Amen is married to Amenit, goddess of cobras, to be identified with Upper Egypt where the deadly serpents are found in great numbers in the jungle delta of the Nile. Muit is forever to be identified as goddess of vultures, to represent Lower Egypt, symbolized by the vulture. These things are so because Amen decreed them to be!"

Although many who had assembled now jeered insults and threats to the heretical priest, no soldiers came to arrest him. Startled merchants, opening their shops, looked about for a guard to silence the orator.

"Amen is—Osiris!" the priest cried. "Amen is Osiris! For it is Amen who weighs the souls that enter Heaven at death. Osiris, the son-of-Amen, is not he-who-weighs-the-heart. The Feather of Ma'at is in the eyes of Amen. He is a war god. To please Amen-Osiris you must kill the enemies of Amen! It is the hearts of the enemies of Amen that shall be weighed against Ma'at, and the Feather of Truth has grown weighty!"

With those words the Priest of Amen drew a scimitar from beneath his leopard robes. He shrieked a war-cry. The Egyptian Guard stepped out of hiding, slashed their way out of baskets and leaped out of doorways. Their swords and daggers gave the new Amen his first hearts to weigh.

Thebes was subdued while the sun was still new in the sky. The Egyptian Guard was no longer a familiar constabulary, but an invader from within. Simultaneous uprisings in local townships throughout Upper Egypt overtook news of the coup itself, and every messenger who escaped the burnings was slain on the highways.

By noon the War-Priests of Amen had conquered all of Upper Egypt and were amassing their victorious and virtually unscathed army for a surprise attack on Lower Egypt and the conquest of the capital city, Memphis. An army of war-priests marched on their neighbors to the north, unwinding like the great cobra they represented in their new mythology. The army was the new god Amen and also the new goddess Amenit, who was Upper Egypt and who strikes and kills. Thus killing, the cobra left much human carrion for Muit, goddess of vultures over Nekbet.

The Priests of Amen in the northern nomes had been similarly unified by common designs. Although their numbers were too few to constitute an army, they hid themselves in the countryside to ambush emissaries from the rural townships which had been attacked enroute. Every citizen who did not possess an icon of Amen was murdered. Those spared were given a chance to fight side-by-side with the soldier-priests. By the second morning of the revolution, an army of six million war-priests was purging Egypt of men whose loyalty to Amen could not be proven. Women and children were arbitrarily slaughtered or imprisoned.

23

That dread day, Pharaoh Sankhara Mentuhotep IV awoke to word that no fewer than a million invaders surrounded Memphis. Even as he assembled his personal guards, another terrified emissary informed him that Memphis had been invaded. To the Pharoah's sickened dismay, a third messenger told him that the High Priestess of the goddess Apit had been slain in her temple.

With the death of Pharaoh Mentuhotep IV, the Priests of Amen established themselves as the sole ruling force in Egypt. The Twelfth Dynasty of Egypt began with the reign of a High Priest of Amen, spokesman for "the Hidden One." His name as king was Sehetepra Amenemhat I.

Amenemhat I ruled with an iron fist.

Amen demanded many human sacrifices and the Pharaoh's duty was to send home the souls of the victims. Amenemhat became known as "the smasher of foreheads."

The method prescribed by Amen was for the Pharaoh to grasp the victim's forelock with his left hand while holding a small stone hammer in his right. After the shattering of the skull, the body was tossed to the side of the altar, out of sight of the crowd and of most of the priests.

There the shattered skulls were eagerly awaited by "the Hidden One" and his twelve High Priests, all Amen's Inner Circle.

Many generations lived and died under the threat of the Pharaoh's hammer. All Egyptians shared a reminder of this threat: the unshaven forelock, which the Pharaoh's hand might grip at any time.

Kings reigned and were succeeded by kings. All served "the Hidden One."

As the dynasties passed, Egypt regained prominence as a military power. Other civilizations rose, equal in stature, in the east where the Tigris and Euphrates Rivers flowed: Hatti, Chaldea, Sumeria, and Mitanni. Among the tribes of Hatti, a war cult grew. Tribes on the outskirts of Mitanni were uniting under a king named Hyksos, who claimed to be immortal.

Throughout the Twelfth and Thirteenth Dynasties of Egypt corruption riddled the royal houses. Sacred incest between kings and queens resulted in genetic degeneration of the Pharaohs under Amen.

When forces gathered in Hatti that threatened invasion from the east, the Pharaohs of the Fourteenth Dynasy seemed to take no notice. Even as Amen still demanded tributes in every city, it was apparent to many that "the Hidden One" had withdrawn his support from the Pharaoh. The power of the king, and of Egypt, suffered greatly and the Fifteenth Dynasty of Egypt collapsed under the chariots of invading nomads.

These tribes were named after their god, the king-who-lives-forever. They conquered Egypt swiftly and not even the name of the Pharaoh, whose death marked victory for the invaders, was recorded or remembered.

The conqueror King Hyksos was eternally young, some said immortal. He extracted much labor and tribute from the Egyptians he ruled. A tyrant fond of human sacrifice, King Hyksos was never seen by anyone outside of his circle of personal attendants. When he vanished, after three hundred years of relentless oppression, the Hyksos tribesmen were left without a leader. Anxious rumors spread among the eastern warriors: the gods no longer favored Mitanni. The Hyksos had been abandoned by their long-lived king.

The Egyptians overthrew their oppressors. The coup was brief, with much bloodshed—and the iron chains of the Hyksos were cast off. Amen had returned to Egypt—the Egyptians rejoiced. Organizer of armies, god of military might, "the Hidden One" was back! Egypt would be strong again!

The Pharaoh Aahmes reigned briefly and was assassinated. The very old priesthood of Thoth had attempted to overthrow Amenist rule, but the plot was uncovered and the conspirators murdered.

The next Pharaoh who assumed the throne was Amenhotep I. His name meant "Amen is Satisfied."

Chapter Two

Two spaceships materialized out of the event horizon of the black hole. Near-infinite mass of lightspeed forced their deceleration. Time had ceased for the occupants of the starships when they entered the Omniverse, thus emergence from the Omniverse was instantaneous. They exited in the Sothis system, on the spiral rim of the galaxy. Tme resumed and mass decreased as the starships and their occupants folded out of two-dimensional limbo into three-dimensional completeness. They were back in the Universe.

The spaceships skimmed the photon ring of the black hole in hyperbolic arcs. Their magnetic scoops combed the shell of captured light and energy reservoirs were filled, retrorockets fired. The ships, the *Atet* and the *Sektet*, were discoidal. The hyperbolic loops they flew stabilized into graceful orbits before they shot through a gap between the terraformed rings that encircled the gravity vortex.

The rings had been built billions of years before by the earliest generation of timespace explorers. The initial black hole expeditions were followed by the first terraforming projects, whose purpose was to remodel the bands of orbiting asteroidal debris into immense ringworlds encircling the black hole itself. The limitless gravity of the black hole held an oxygen-nitrogen atmosphere in trough-shaped rings a thousand miles wide, their sides bordered by walls hundreds of miles high, like water cradled in an aqueduct. Two stars orbiting the black hole gave the forested ringworlds day and night.

The ships decelerated over the world rings, soared over mountains, canyons, rivers and fields to the village of humanoids where the intelligent energy body of Yod resided. Existing as vast electromagnetic minds, Yod and other Elohim were capable of reversing entropy in their proximity. They had been born the instant the Universe exploded into existence.

Three humanoids piloted each of the discoidal spaceships. In the *Atet* were Geb, a male from Capella V, and his wife and copilot Nuit, from Procyon IX. They escorted Set, a male humanoid native to and named after the world they were now approaching: Sothis. Set had been studying humanoid evolution in the center of the galaxy when he had been called upon to remedy an emergency on Gaia, formerly the second but now the third planet orbiting the star Ra.

Set's wife Nephthys was aboard the *Sektet*, which was piloted by Isis and Osiris. These genetically engineered proto-Earthlings had served as god-king and goddess-queen to the people of Gaia. Due to their genetic kinship to the Egyptians, Isis and Osiris remained in telepathic-empathic contact with them. Isis, a Neandertal woman, had declared the emergency: something terrible was happening on Gaia. Osiris must return, after soliciting help from the Galactic Community. All agreed that Shu, the scholarly dramatist who had inhabited the body of Horus thousands of years earlier, must be contacted. Although Shu chose not to live in the body of Horus after his departure from Gaia, he retained rudimentary telepathic contact with his evolving human progeny. They assumed that he and his wife Tefnut also knew of the emergency.

Isis knew no other body than the one she had been born into but Osiris had left his native body in hypersleep thousands of years before so that he could retain advanced telepathic contact with the Gaians of Egypt. Shu, however, had been married to Tefnut at the time of the experiment and subsequently left the body of Horus in hypersleep and returned to his native humanoid form. Because all human/ extraterrestrial offspring were the result of genetic engineering, he was not truly sexually married to his human goddess-queen, Hathor. The conception of their children was arranged *in vitro*, the developing cells injected into the uterus of the sleeping Hathor, who was dreaming in rapture of being in the arms of her husband, the god-king.

The *Atet* and the *Sektet* followed the negentropic emanations of Yod to the village where Shu and Tefnut lived. The two spaceships hovered over the village and Geb agreed to descend. Osiris was uncomfortable in one-Gravity due to his immense pelvis, an evolution-enhancing trait, which made walking or standing awkward on surface gravity conditions.

Geb, Nuit, and Set descended toward the mountainous landscape of the ring-world. They could see the canyon, then the river, then the circle of buildings far below the energy body of Yod. The trees and flowers were native to Gaia except for vegetables cultivated in the gardens of the non-Gaian residents. As the rotating disc neared the ground, a sparrow flew to the branch of an oak tree to observe. When a tall delicate humanoid emerged with smaller humanoids beside him, the bird warbled: "Who are you? What is your business here?"

Geb sang back in an avian dialect: "We have come for our friend, Shu."

"Shu is my friend, too."

"Then tell him he is needed."

The bird hesitated, then flew off.

Shu was only a short flight away, cleaning the ashes from his combustion stove and preparing to mix ash and loam into his compost system. He saw the bird looking down from a bough of a fir tree and knew the sparrow had come to warn him. He had sensed the approach of the two spaceships and had all along been receiving nightmare signals from the people of Gaia in his dreamtime. He sang to the bird:

"Have my friends arrived?"

27

"Are they your friends? Are they your friends?"

"They are indeed! I must depart with them."

"You-must-stay-here! You-must-stay-here!" the bird twittered.

"No, I am sorry. Tefnut and I must depart. Yod must depart. We will be back." Shu continued in his thoughts, *long after you have died, little friend*.

The bird flew away, frightened by a rustling in the berry bushes. Tall, stately Geb emerged with Nuit, followed by the social scientist, Set. They greeted Shu with raised hands.

"I am ready," Shu said, finishing his task. "I have arranged for my neighbors to watch after my home on this world while I return to Gaia."

"Where is Tefnut?" Geb asked.

"I am here," said the diminutive Reticulan woman. They turned to see her emerge from the log house, her white skin shining in the light from the two suns.

"You know that something terrible is happening on Gaia," Geb said to her.

She nodded.

"Do either of you know the nature of this emergency?"

"The Gaians are evolving in a direction similar to the warlike tribes of the moons of Ra IV, the exploded gas giant which now orbits Ra as a band of asteroids," said Shu. "Evolutionary forces are running counter to the development of empathic consciousness on Gaia. This fourth wave of humans are becoming too hostile to survive on their mother-world."

"That is the essence," Geb nodded, "and there is more. Yod has summoned Vau and He to take his place on Sothis III. We will escort Yod by starship to Gaia. Isis and Osiris agree: intervention in human evolution is necessary to prevent ultimate disaster, the death of Gaia, the last life-bearing planet in the Ra system."

"Intervention has been forbidden by the Elohim," Tefnut said.

"Yod suspends the ban. Limited intervention will be arranged."

Tefnut shook her head. "Three mother-worlds in the Ra system have already died. One was scorched by the explosion of the gas giant. The moons whose races duelled and lost were also mother-worlds. Intervention was not attempted then; why now?"

Geb replied: "Probability curves showed many variables, even the detonation of the gas giant, were triggered by the war. We cannot risk such variables again. Gaian humans are evolving into a more aggressive, hostile species than even the human-oids of the moons of Ra IV. Indications are that very soon, in six to eight thousand Gaian years, war will end life on Gaia. Technological war will result in spoilage of the oceans which supply starships with heavy water throughout this region of the galaxy.

"We therefore have two reasons for considering intervention: idealistically, we would enjoy cultivating humanitarian beings out of the evolving humans. Pragmatically, we must preserve the oceans as a source of heavy water.

"Limited intervention can be accomplished," Geb continued. "The course of evolution can be altered without force. Historical cultivation through information dispersal can divert the evolutionary forces at work, but extreme caution and subtlety must be used.

"We will escort you to the starship that has just received the energy body of Yod. Then Yod will inform you directly."

"We must depart," agreed Shu. He and Tefnut followed the three humanoids to the field where the *Atet* hovered. The spaceship stabilized its spin at Geb's mental command. An aperture dilated and a ladder extended. The crew and passengers climbed aboard. The aperture closed, the disc resumed spin and shot into the sky.

Above the atmosphere the *Atet*, joined by the *Sektet*, entered the belly of a vast interstellar starship. The *Aton* was piloted by a humanoid known as "Father Tem," a title of respect bestowed upon starship pilots of male gender. Although too big to survive black hole translation, the starship *Aton* could comfortably support millions of humanoid occupants for voyages of many years. The immense, multi-leveled disc was the same starship that brought the cultivators of evolution to Gaia four million years past, when hominids on three planets in the Ra system were observed evolving toward humanness. Starship *Aton* was returning to the Ra system. Instead of carrying multitudes of busy humanoids, the huge starship was home to nine corporeal occupants and one god.

Shu emerged from the Atet holding Tefnut's hand, escorted by Geb. The tiny Father Tem greeted them. As they walked down a gleaming metal corridor the small entourage conversed in Pangalactic, a language more sung than spoken.

Shu began: "Has it been decided, Father Tem, that intervention is completely necessary?"

"There is no answer yet."

Tefnut inquired, "Were multiuniverse models used in formulating the probability curves?"

"Yes," Tem replied. "All conceivable markoff chains led to catastrophes. At best Gaians will bring extinction to themselves and no fewer than twenty million other species."

"My race," Isis sang, "remained benevolent. What little quarreling we did never resulted in warfare."

"That is true," Tem agreed, "but your race acquired a somberness and intense introspection that kept many of your people, especially your young males, from becoming translated. That is why your ancestors have laid their bones in lands far from Egypt."

"That is true," Isis concurred sadly.

Tem reached to embrace her. He caressed her naked back, her muscular shoulders. She was very beautiful. Her black hair was braided in knotted strings and beaded with thousands of jewels.

They resumed their walk down the long corridor. Soon Tem stated with few words and much emotion that Yod was safely aboard and had stated unequivocally that intervention was necessary to save the life of planet Gaia. In lieu of forceful overthrow of existing kingdoms, they would stage a return of the sky-kings to be recorded for posterity in art and stone. This would impart to future generations of Gaian humans information about the relationship between their planet and other worlds in the body of Ptah, the Universe.

Osiris knew. He had remained in his misshappen body for six thousand years in order to maintain telepathic empathy with the race he had literally helped to father. What he knew about the people that had sprung from his loins and the womb of his queen, Isis, caused him much psychic agony.

"Their males murder each other in hordes. The dominant males perpetuate their violent tendencies by raping surviving women and girls. In this way," the god-king

Osiris continued, "after several generations genes imparting such traits as sensitivity and compassion are removed from the pool. Only dominance-oriented humans are born, and only males with uncontrollable aggressive urges survive."

They arrived at Tem's navigation dome. Their discussion resumed around a table in the center of a simulated starry sky.

Tefnut said, "I have dreamed that someone is controlling this process, using warfare to eliminate males unfit for warfare. It is not self-perpetuating, but a cycle being exploited by a human entity or elite society." Tefnut fell silent as she locked eyes with Tem, then studied the eyes of everyone else at the table. Yes, they had all dreamed the same: a parasite was alive on Gaia and borrowing life while breeding a new, murderous race of humans.

"The Obscene Rite!..." Tefnut gasped. Tem reached across the table and held her hand. The empathy field of Yod intensified. Tefnut whispered, "That has never happened before. After we have cultivated a race and suspended contact to watch the race mature, the inner circle who were closest to the god-kings might borrow secrets from the sciences to perpetuate their own longevity. Such methods are always self-destructive. As the populations evolve they overthrow the elites who inflict tyranny upon them. Longevity is the greatest gamble there is! The Obscene Rite has never succeeded for more than a few generations and never before failed to bring violent death to its purveyors."

Shu felt something deep inside him sink into sadness. He knew his wife was right.

Turning to Shu, Tem spoke, "Yod summons you. You have been selected to return to Gaia to intervene. You spent two thousand years in the body of Horus, last of the star-fathers. You will have a living memory of Egypt imparted to your mind directly, if you agree."

"Agreed."

"Then we depart," Tem announced, and led Shu to the chamber wherein the energy body of Yod resided.

The living presence of Yod held Shu aloft.

Yod had been watching Egypt through the eyes of the vampire-priest, Kahotep. Now Shu knew firsthand the severity of the situation in Egypt. Suspended in air, his right eye ached from the transmission of Kahotep's entire memory into his brain. Yod gave Shu a brief empathic blessing and lowered him onto a ledge in the wall of the chamber. The diminutive humanoid hurried out of the vast magnetic bottle that housed the living energy-god and vanished into a corridor as the door slid closed behind him.

Tem and Tefnut escorted Shu to the star pilot's chamber. They joined hands with other passengers at Tem's circular table. Shu closed his eyes. They breathed together, deeply and meditatively. Their mindmeet was perfect. The spirit of Thoth, the Heart and Tongue of Ptah, manifested in their circle. By means of empathy, then telepathy, Shu shared the information, the living logos, imparted to him by Yod.

When the circle was complete the nine participants reawakened to the remembered truth about what was happening on the beloved mother planet, Gaia, Earth. As their shocked silence dissipated, the immortals prepared to discuss intervention in Egyptian society, the task of deflecting human history from the impending disasters that Kahotep had generated for the future.

Ethical constraints had been imposed by Yod himself on their act of limited intervention: a ban on interfering directly with the activities of Kahotep, and restraint from inflicting harm on any form of life, including the vampire priest. It was understood among the humans aboard Starship *Aton* that intervention was to include only the dissemination of information throughout Egyptian society. A demonstration of the divine origins of humanity was to be encoded in art and history for the benefit of future generations. Assuming that there would be survivors after Kahotep's cruel age.

Starship *Aton* departed the Sothis system. Vast and discoidal, its engines pushed through the infinite night.

Unlike the smaller hyperspace vehicles capable of the nearly instantaneous acceleration necessary for black hole translation, *Aton* was a true starship, designed for interstellar flights of several years' duration. Filled to capacity, over a million humanoids could co-exist, dining on native foods hydroponically or hydroplanktonically grown, and enjoy comfort on her decks without crowding. The velocity of the giant starship approximated their commmon native gravities.

As the first year of the journey commenced, the constant one-G force of acceleration marked the approach to lightspeed. Inside the starship, time did not seem to slow down; the relative mass of the occupants did not seem to increase; the lengths and depths of objects did not seem to foreshorten. The effects of relativity were measurable only by observers outside of *Aton's* place in the timespace continuum. Within the starship reality was perceived as normal in a rapidly moving Universe.

Meditations and discussions followed each of Shu's further communication with Yod. The humanoids and the Elohim were drawing up a plan whereby large numbers of evolving humans could be awakened to the outer Universe. Generations of Earthlings would peacefully be made aware of their place in a community infinitely larger than the collection of quarreling tribes on their native world.

"After his failure to maintain control over Old Kingdom Egypt," Isis offered, "I doubt that Kahotep will again attempt to rule directly. He has his Inner Circle of twelve High Priests for that, and they remain under his absolute psychic control. He will remain like a shadow behind them, unnoticed unless we ourselves unmask him."

"That would be risky," Shu said. "Culture shock, fear and blind panic would result from such a radical intervention. We need to set in motion a wave of information that runs counter to Kahotep's propaganda and religious dogma. In this way we will preserve the knowledge of human celestial origins for more enlightened generations to perceive and interpret correctly."

"How can we do this?" Isis asked.

"One way would be to stage a return of the god-king system and a re-creation of a seed-race which can hybridize with the natives successfully. Then this experiment must be rendered in sculpted stone and pigment. It must be clearly recorded what our intentions are. We must establish a record of a complete ethical divergence from the morality of the time. This last point, connected to our origins off the planet, is the greatest indication we can provide of our peaceful intentions."

"This will mean taking control of Egypt out of the hands of Kahotep's puppets," Tem stated cautiously. " How can this be accomplished without force?"

"We must stage a vast demonstration of a power older and greater than that of one corrupt priesthood," Shu said. "The rest will fall into place of its own accord."

"Will we not be risking the chaos and panic of culture shock?" Isis objected.

"We will be risking that, yes. But a measure of culture shock will permanently record this act of intervention in human history."

"Then what?" Isis remained skeptical.

"We will continuously feed the native people information that conflicts with Kahotep's propaganda. After an incubation period of four thousand years or so, we will recolonize Gaia. When her inhabitants are finally made ready to accept their place in a cosmic society, she will be reconverted to a godworld."

"This is a bold plan, Shu," said Tem.

"It is indeed risky and it might fail," Shu admitted. "The alternatives are to intervene forcibly and murder Kahotep and his Inner Circle, or to refrain from intervention and watch this human race meet planetary disaster. Both are unacceptable. Our only real option is limited intervention without force, imparting its significance to future generations who will have discovered the process of experimental science and followed it to a vision of the Universe that is not so solipsistic."

"Solipsistic," Tem said, "as described by the egotism of Kahotep and voiced by his followers."

"They can lie to the people of the world forever," said Shu, "but they will not be believed forever."

Kahotep had used many names during his covert reigns of Egypt, Nubia, and Mitanni. None of his followers knew him as Kahotep, "the animal soul is fulfilled." His followers in Egypt called him Amen, "the Hidden One." The Inner Circle of direct initiates, themselves addicted to the Obscene Rite and ridden with telepathically implanted demons, referred to the vampire-priest by his secret name. Kahotep insisted on being called "The Beast."

PART II

EGYPT

Chapter Three

To the peasants, what the Priests of Amen said could not be true because it was so unbeautiful. Without Osiris in their hearts to greet them after death, the Egyptian laborers looked with eyes darkened with envy toward their Pharaohs. Worship of Amen prevailed, a reign of fear. The people felt two fears, and these guaranteed their servility. One was fear of capture, imprisonment, torture, and death at the hands of the Priests of Amen. The other was fear that Amen's cosmology might be valid after all. Lacking the spiritual food of beauty daily contemplated, they hungered for a new religion, one more soul-fulfilling, more like their original faiths. A vision was needed that would alleviate the fear of death that Amenism brought.

The pharohs of the New Kingdom proceeded across the generations of the Eighteenth Dynasty, feigning a strife between the priests of Amen and Thoth. These conflicts were carefully contrived and staged by the Hidden One, The Beast. Nothing was unplanned. The first Pharaoh to rule after the Hyksos was overturned was Amenhotep I. His son and successor was Thothmose I, a devotee and Priest of Thoth, alleged to be a member of Thoth's Inner Circle. Thothmose II was not truly his son. After three years marked by the theatrics and event-staging which were the devices of The Beast, he died and another "son" took his place.

Rumors of this king's depravity and loathsome practises were silenced quickly by his queen, the hard-jawed, masculine Queen Hatshepsut. She was a cruel woman, if indeed she was a woman, and she sent many spies throughout Egypt. To whisper a word against her was suicide. Daily the streets of Egypt saw arrests and executions under Queen Hatshepsut and King Thothmose III, until the gutters of Thebes ran with blood.

Hatshepsut became commander of the Egyptian army. Under her, Egypt prospered as a military power. She directed the invasion of Punt, conquered after two years by her architect-general, Senemnut. The resulting settlements were anchored by mighty fortresses. She ruled Egypt and called herself king, not queen. Hatshepsut established uneasy truces with Mitanni and thrice invaded, colonizing the eastern empires. Egypt warred with Byblos and Sumer. Settlements for her armies reached far beyond her borders. New boundaries were drawn, far from the Nile. The cobra of Amenism would strike and Muit, Mother of Vultures, would oversee the assimilation of the victims.

Thothmose had a son, named Amenhotep II. Although the king was a member of the cult of sexual adoration of the phallus, he did not molest his son, but loved and worshipped him with words of praise and acts of discreet affection. It had been arranged that with the birth of the son of Thothmose III the "rivalry" between Amenism and the religion of Thoth would be resolved. In fact the Inner Circle of the Priests of Thoth were the same as the Priests of Amen, since the Hidden One claimed to have been a Priest of Thoth long ago. This was known to very few: that Amen had once been human, but became a god.

Queen Hatshepsut died, poisoned by Thothmose III. After an elaborate funeral pageant she was buried closer to the Valley of Kings than any Egyptian queen had ever been. Her tomb was hewn into a rock cliff overlooking the valley. But her body had been secretly disinterred and the corpse of one of her handmaidens put in her sarcophagus in her place.

Amenhotep II reigned for a generation and fathered a mighty son, Thothmose IV.

Thothmose IV was so obsessed with his role as king that he believed himself to be immortal. He received regular assurances that he would live forever from a secret voice that called to him from the dark chambers in the temple of Karnak. He was told that his claim to immortality would be realized through his son, Amenhotep III. He and his son truly believed themselves to be the same being, their love for each other so strong that they shared one mind incarnate in two bodies.

"It is like dangling two feet in a pool," Thothmose IV explained to his son. "Two feet that connect to one body, but which enter separately the water of human time."

It was during the reign of Thothmose IV that a new religion suddenly arose in Egypt. To the orthodox ancient priesthoods it was unwanted, but to the peasants who toiled to feed the armies, it was gladly welcome. The Song of the Oppressed Peasant was sung quietly in the fields and rumors of the arrival of a new deity were uttered behind the backs of the guards who patrolled with whips.

This deity was not inaccessible as was Amen, the Hidden One. Seen occasionally blazing colors in the night sky, it skimmed the horizon by day. Sometimes it approached quite close to the ground and to look directly into the god's rays imparted visions directly into human eyes: visions of Heaven and who and what the gods really were.

The starship *Aton* had returned to the Ra system. The night sky was ablaze with visitors once again.

Chapter Four

S tarship *Aton* decelerated into a stable orbit around the largest gas giant in the Ra system. It maneuvered into the vicinity of the moon Ganymede. In the city under the frozen, crystalline world many beings from past and future worlds lived. The presence of vast water ice deposits made it a refueling stop as well as an outpost where scientists could conduct experiments and study the evolution of life in the atmosphere of the gaseous planet Earth dwellers would someday call Jupiter. The laboratory that produced the bodies of Thoth, Osiris, and Horus was located in the subsurface city.

Aton fell into a toposynchronized orbit above the outpost. Pilot Tem remained aboard when the other occupants departed in the *Atet* for the world below. They landed on a small platform at the bottom of a crater and descended below the surface. The airlock chamber was pressurized and the crew disembarked to join a small group who awaited them at the spaceport. They proceeded to the genetic laboratory, conversing and thoughtsharing as they walked.

Hem was a genetic engineer whose specialty was Gaian vertebrates. With Tefnut and Shu he created holographic designs of the anatomy of the new god-king. This one would also possess the giant pelvis that Thoth, Osiris, and Horus had imparted to their progeny.

"The new king won't be able to walk well with these hips," Hem remarked.

"He won't need to walk much at all," Shu insisted.

"If he lives in danger and cannot walk…" Hem gestured with an insectish shrug. He sensed that Shu and his companions were desperate. The gamble was theirs; the outcome would be…dubious. In any case, life in the artificial body, the genetically engineered breeding device, could be abandoned at will. Hem studied the images on the screen.

"It is all for theatrics," said Shu happily, undeterred. "I want the face and body to be the subject of many, many portraits."

"According to my meditations and dreams, the future rulers of Egypt will have them destroyed."

"Many, yes. But a few will survive. Kahotep himself will probably see that the best will be preserved."

"How do you know that?"

"I will make certain that he records much about me. When I leave, he will spend much time writing about my visit."

"You will have to live in that body until it dies of its own decay or is killed."

"That is true."

"You could be caught and tortured."

"I can also share my suffering with my captors, whether they wish to receive the pain they inflict or not."

"He must have taught his Inner Circle some things. He knows many tricks. Suppose your tormentors have no volition of their own, or are desensitized to pain by drugs. Or are better magicians than you expect. They may be able to create powerful empathy blocks."

"This visit will be fraught with danger, of course. If worse came to worse I could project a psychohologram and enfold it. I could use reality displacement for an emergency return to the starship."

"If you got a chance! Were you captured, someone will surely keep a constant eye on you. Their ruler will surely know you are a wave-shifter."

"We have many plans!" Shu said joyously. "But we have only one goal. We shall succeed."

🜨

Aton approached planet Gaia from the night side. She plunged into the rich atmosphere, dove into the ocean and descended into the abyssal depths. The deuterium tanks were filled. The vast reactors blazed with colliding atoms of heavy water. Sliding through the sea, *Aton* moved swiftly toward Africa.

Bursting again into the night sky, the rotating starship soared over the coastline of the tropical land. Herds of wildebeests and zebras stampeded, terrified by *Aton's* lights. Ethiopians cast frightened glances skyward and uttered fearful words to ward off the dragon who no doubt would eat not a few of the king's cattle. The Nubians were more terrified as their newly-returned sun god had warned them of evil things born by night winds. Sometimes monsters stole their children or young women not yet betrothed.

Lights glared in myriad patterns on the bottom of the vast disc. Cloaked in a mirage of folded light, Shu and Tem astonished the primitive humans by displaying brilliant, multicolored rotating rings that illuminated the earth below. When Isis asked, "Why is this?" Tem merely replied, "To attract attention."

🜨

In the days of Thothmose IV, a man named Hapu, a stonecutter, was exiled from the tiny desert town of Kech on suspicion of being a witch. He roamed Egypt with his tiny, fragile wife until he came to an oasis where they created for themselves a permanent encampment. His wife, a girl of twelve, was pregnant and her belly was beginning to show. The old, brown-skinned man assisted her attentively through the months of her pregnancy. Her labor was disastrous. She died in Hapu's arms and the baby slid into his lap. It squirmed and cried, wrapped in purple placenta and a twisted blue umbilicus. Hapu took the baby into his arms as his wife slipped into the Tuat. The afterbirth was ejected, then a lake of blood.

The baby lived.

The tiny boy survived on goat's milk. As he grew he suffered bad dreams, even as an infant. At first Hapu thought the baby had chronic colic. When he realized the boy suffered nightmares, Hapu again feared persecution for witchcraft.

When he went to the marketplace and trade his dates and garden vegetables for sacks of millet and barley, he inquired of the merchants of any news, especially politics. One day he was astonished to learn that a new Pharaoh had ascended to the throne. His name was Amenhotep II.

Hapu exclaimed jubilantly, "That is a coincidence! I, too, am loyal to Amen." He pulled the baby from a cloth sling on his back. "My boy is named Amenhotep. I am Hapu. He is Amenhotep, Son of Hapu."

The merchant laughed. "He is a fine looking boy. Where is his mother?"

Hapu lowered his eyes. Slowly, he folded a corner of white cloth over the quiet baby's face. "My wife, she was young. She should not have suffered childbirth."

The merchant patted Hapu's shoulder. "Well, maybe he will grow to be a great warrior. Maybe he will please Amen with the hearts of a thousand dead unbelievers."

Hapu looked up, defiant and proud. "He will! He will serve Amen on the throne of the Next World, and lay the souls of multitudes at the feet of the Judge."

The merchant folded his arms, fists to his shoulders, over his chest in a private man's salute to the Hidden One. The merchant said, "Amen."

Hapu repeated the two syllables, bowing his head. Then he looked into the merchant's eyes. There was an instant of contact and of suspended belief. They were both pretending. They knew it, though they would never admit it, especially in a crowded marketplace.

Hurriedly, they negotiated a transaction. Hapu purchased some dried figs and sacks of oats and millet. He furtively left the marketplace and returned to the oasis in the hills by way of a dusty, narrow road. He held to his chest his quiet, mysterious baby whose name now was Amenhotep, Son of Hapu.

Hapu the stonecutter learned what the bad dreams meant, even when the child was very young. At the age of three Amenhotep, Son of Hapu, awoke with screams in the long hours of the night. Then the boy fell into convulsions, muttering unintelligible sounds until he uttered the word "serpent." As his father listened, fearful and overawed, the boy repeated this several times, then fell asleep. When his father shook him, the child did not awaken.

In the morning Hapu found that his ass had died. The beast lay next to the tree to which it was tethered, its tongue protruding and black, and a foreleg swollen. Then Amenhotep, Son of Hapu, crawled out of the tent on his hands and knees, groping as if blind. Hapu rushed to him: the child was in one of his trances. The boy crept to a crevice between boulders, shrieked and scurried away like a frightened animal. Hapu did not comfort the wailing boy, but peered into the crevice. In the bottom lay a coiled cobra.

Hapu realized then that his boy was a seer, perhaps a prophet. Such was Hapu's misfortune to have been accused of witchcraft! He resolved to move from his encampment and take the harvest of his garden to a different marketplace.

Such was the life that Hapu's fears imposed on him: he feared that the Priests of Amen, who had forbidden witchcraft for as long as anyone could remember, would hear rumors of his strange, autistic child and kidnap the boy and murder him. Hapu's constant lonely nomadism, his tenacious clinging to the boy, finally drew attention.

At the bazaar near Thebes a man espied the boy, Amenhotep, Son of Hapu, just five years old: his distant gaze, his constant chatter and his father, who barely spoke at all. The boy, inclined toward strange behavior, had not been at the bazaar for an hour before he slipped away from his father who was dickering with a shoe merchant. Amenhotep ran into the crowd and was quickly seized by a fat-bellied man wielding a long, curved knife.

The boy immediately fell into a trance. In his trance he saw stars, multitudes of stars. Then, as if moving among them, he saw great colored lights. One of these, with which he felt a kinship, was a blue ball with sharp-edged brown and green areas. It was white at the top and bottom. and patterns of white swirls moved slowly across all of it. He somehow knew the surface of the ball was blue with water…

He awoke from the trance into great pain. His eyes were strapped shut by a blindfold that was much too tight and his hands and feet were bound. He smelled straw and felt around him the rough sides of a basket bouncing in the back of a cart.

After a time the cart stopped and he heard voices. He strained to hear a man ask another man if he was the one.

"Yes, he is the one."

"Can he foretell the future?"

"Yes. His father, the witch, is said to have summoned an incubus. The boy's real father is a demon. We know this. It is true."

The sound of tinkling metal told the boy that coins had been dropped into a purse. He, Amenhotep, Son of Hapu, had been sold, exactly as in his dream the night before…

The man who bought the prophetic boy often kidnapped or purchased such children. He knew the signs. He had imposed a ban on witchcraft several hundred years before—and eleven hundred years before that, and three hundred years before that. Three times he had come to power in Egypt alone. He knew human nature and watched for errant behavior. Such as when a stonecutter of some talent is accused of witchcraft, then cannot keep a job, is forced to move again and again, against his will, and keeps a child alive at great expense...

This child had the Sight. In his great occipital lobe, wrapped around his pineal gland, nestled in the curve of his hypothalamus, was that ineffable Other Eye, the eye that sees an energy other than light. In this child, that eye saw more strongly than his natural two.

When finally the boy was brought to The Beast, he was naked. He had eaten reluctantly, after a long fast and was in no pain other than the animal hostility that captivity evokes. The Beast looked the boy over. His mouth was open slightly, but the look in his eyes offered no hint of desire, only interest. Cold, intellectual interest. Nothing more.

The Beast looked at the guard who had brought the boy in. Then he stared long into the boy's eyes. After the child burst into tears, The Beast looked again at the silent guard and said:

"Very good. He is surely the one. Now go and put his eyes out so that his Other Sight can prevail. He shall be my seer."

Sunless days and moonless months passed, folding year into year. Amenhotep, Son of Hapu grew accustomed to his blindness. Often he mixed lies with his prophecies, but when discovered it evoked the wrath of his tormentor and he suffered much. Frequently he uttered words while asleep or dreaming, or in one of his many trances. These were overheard by The Beast directly, for the ventilation duct near the throne conducted all of the blind seer's utterances to his ear.

Amenhotep, Son of Hapu grew to be a young man. The Beast was proud of his prize. He commissioned a sculptor to carve a stone bust of the brooding psychic, rendered with the eyes normal, unscarred, with eyelids meditatively closed.

It was after the fifth year of the reign of Thothmose IV that the blind seer began experiencing nightmares of a different kind than any he had ever dreamed before. These new dreams filled him with strange fire and jubilation. He mocked his captor. His nightly mutterings yielded no clue as to the content of his dreams. The only meaningful phrase Kahotep could decipher from the seer's mumbled gibberish was: "They are here! They are here!"

The youth knew intuitively that The Beast understood what those words meant. He deeply desired to remember the content of his dreams, but they faded immediately upon awakening, every time.

Amenhotep's waking clairvoyance was acute, due to his blindness. One morning, during Kahotep's interrogation, he sensed abruptly that his captor was withholding important news, something crucial to the meaning of his dreams. The Beast questioned him more intently. Amenhotep, Son of Hapu, accused his tormentor of knowing the truth. Kahotep denied that he knew anything of the meaning of his captive seer's dreams.

When The Beast at last departed, Amenhotep, Son of Hapu, "followed" him, by means of his clairvoyance, out of the chamber and into the hall. He sensed Kahotep in his room. The blind boy lay down with his ear to the ventilation duct in the wall by his bed of rough blankets. The Beast did not suspect that the youth might be listening, for he had not blocked the opening although his hushed conversation was obviously confidential.

Amenhotep, Son of Hapu could not hear the conversation well, but he knew that The Beast was talking to at least three other men and that the discussion became argumentative in parts. The only words he could understand were: "return", "prepare", and the name of the god, "Aton." The name of that forgotten god of the Old Kingdom was repeated several times throughout the exchange.

Then The Beast paused to muse over his plans—and sensed a dangerous intrusion. He knew telepathically before he even reached the wall that the blind seer was listening on the other side of the ventilation duct. The Beast threw down a stone slab that blocked the opening and bellowed in rage.

Beyond the stone wall, Amenhotep, Son of Hapu sat upright on his coarse blankets and wondered if the god Aton had returned, and why this infuriated his captor so greatly.

🪲

The appearance of the spaceship inspired a religious movement among the peasants.

In the fifth year of the brief reign of Thothmose IV, the genetic decay inflicted by royal incest plagued the king's health. He was anemic and epileptic. He showed autistic tendencies, especially violent fits of uncontrollable rage.

Kahotep was delighted that the queen had taken a lover and thus Amenhotep III was not so directly related to the Pharaoh. The Beast would have to preserve this new bloodline. Amenism was intellectually bankrupt and metaphysically menacing, merely a mythological extension of Kahotep's imagination. The sudden appearance of a new tribal religion gave him new ideas.

Aton was an Old Kingdom deity. The name meant the material solar disc, which Amen had usurped as an aspect when The Beast overthrew Memphis from his temple in Thebes, thus ending the Eleventh Dynasty. This was the Eighteenth Dynasty. Why was an insignificant Old Kingdom deity making a comeback in the south of Egypt and Nubia? Kahotep contemplated this from his inner sanctum beneath Karnak.

He knew for certain, from the descriptions of the aerial god, that the real *Aton*, the starship that had landed many times during the ages of Thoth, Osiris, and Horus, had returned for some unknown reason. Kahotep's immediate response was fear, then defiance. He dreaded the return of the ones who had created Egypt and given him access to the knowledge which enabled him to prolong his life for these many centuries, however violently.

He knew that spaceships had been sighted many times over the years, to the north and east of Egypt, flying in and out of the ocean, soaring over the Nile, sailing high in the atmosphere, tracing the skies with ionized trails, the sunlight glinting off curved metal discs. Sometimes Kahotep would don disguises and stroll the streets of Thebes. He would move among the crowds, eavesdropping on his unsuspecting subjects. His disguises were so perfect that he could spy on his own cabinet of courtiers, priests, and military officers. If any questioned the will of Amen, they died or mysteriously vanished.

When word of multiple sightings reached Kahotep, he waited until he was certain that the sky people had not returned in full force. Assured that the promised return of the god-kings had not taken place, The Beast slipped unnoticed into the crowds of Thebes. At sunrise he sold a few rubies that his spies would retrieve for him and by noon assumed another role that nobody questioned. He sought to appraise the degree of contact, if any, and learn what rumors still persisted.

The chatter of the buyers and sellers yielded much information. Women carrying babies excitedly shared the stories their husbands brought back from the outlying townships: a spectacular light in the sky had caused animal stampedes. Some rural people said that the muticolored rays of the metal disc of the sun imparted visions to them. And there were disappearances: children were gone, and more than a few young women. Some men claimed that angels made love to them. Angels of the Amentii.

Kahotep was dressed in the widow's black robes of mourning. He was leaning over some fruit baskets, pretending to sample some figs, when words caught his attention that made him stiffen. "The new god has made many Bedouin girls pregnant. Aton must be a god of fertility as well!"

He had heard all he needed or wanted to hear. The two women speaking noticed that widow stooping over a basket was listening to them. They avoided eye contact, in consonance with Egyptian customs of modesty. The widow hurriedly made a purchase and vanished into the crowd.

When night came, Kahotep ducked down a decaying hallway and under a wooden slab. He emerged inside an ancient wall, hollow with a concealed corridor. It led to the subterranean inner sanctum beneath Karnak.

When he arrived, he could hear the manic laughter and hysterical screaming of Amenhotep, Son of Hapu. The boy was delirious. The Beast felt a surge of rage.

"So—you know! You know, do you? You know!" the blind seer shrieked from beyond the stone wall. Kahotep stared at the ventilation slot near the floor. "You know that the Aton disc has returned."

"I know that much, yes," The Beast finally reponded.

"You know about the sky gods! They are back, they are back!"

"I know that a desert deity is suddenly popular," Kahotep cried, struggling to control his fury. "But Aton is a very important aspect of me. I am Amen, and Aton is only one small part..."

"Aton is not a part of you! Aton is something bigger. Aton usurps Amen!" Amenhotep, Son of Hapu, lapsed again into hysterical laughter.

The Beast sat sullenly in his throne of meditation. He clutched the armrests of brass and gold. The captive seer would not have dared hurl such an insult to The Beast before the return of Aton. He was rapidly becoming uncontrollable.

Suddenly, the laughter stopped. Amenhotep, Son of Hapu cried out:

"Beware, O Beast! For the day will come when a king shall rule Egypt with two queens. And that king shall divide your kingdom in half!"

Chapter Five

Starship *Aton* assumed a geosynchronous orbit over the Libyan desert. During the day, Shu, Tefnut, and Tem in the *Atet* , and Set, Geb, and Nuit in the *Sektet* embarked to survey the townships visited so grandly by the *Aton*. Their greater intent was to monitor the people who had been selected for contact and to continue contact with the human community.

The two shuttlediscs were enfolded in mirage screens. Their occupants meditated in deep telepathic states and listened to the minds of the Egyptians who had witnessed the arrival of the vast starship. All of Upper Egypt was alive with rumors and exciting stories repeated urgently from village to village.

Priests and Priestesses of Thoth were sought out. Hermits in the outlying mountains were contacted. Priestesses of Bast and Isis beheld cosmic memories. Visionary knowledge was imparted to minds which the starship had scanned and found receptive to selected elements of Yod's memory. To gaze with corporeal eyes into the light that is the body of Yod is to receive the living memory of electromagnetism. Many of the lights that blazed from the rim of *Aton* were portholes, not points of illumination nor gravimagnetic stabilizers.

Some of the witnesses would be visited again by daylight. A merchant in a caravan caught a glimpse of a silver disc skimming a few degrees above the horizon. He called to his wife and pointed to it. When he turned away, the disc vanished behind the spacefold of a mirage screen. The woman never saw the disc. She was not meant to.

A woman exiled in the desert as a witch received a second visitation from a skydisc. It was smaller than the immense lighted rings she had seen by night. Upon glimpsing the landing craft, a thought formed in her mind, as if imparted from another: "You are greatly loved." The woman fell to her knees, called out her blessings, and rejoiced.

Throughout Upper Egypt, old temples, now only windhewn ruins, were yet secretly frequented by the hermit priests of Aton. These were visited by the *Atet* and the *Sektet*. Peasants in the southern nomes knew of the hermit priests and the self-exiled families of the devout. To the servants of Amen, they feigned ignorance.

Outside a village, Tem, Shu, and Tefnut perceived the excited mood of the villagers. Visions were recounted by the Priests and Priestesses of Selket, goddess of occult lore, witchcraft and alchemy.

Moving farther south, the *Atet* flew, fully visible, in a line that passed over several ancient temples, including two temples of Aton. Witch-priests and priestesses gathered on hilltops to watch the flying disc. Some were fearful, but most were not.

The *Sektet* remained invisible to humans and beasts, pausing over the great cities, sometimes descending. The three occupants telepathically overheard the talk below. Many of the citiy-dwellers had lived their lives steeped in Amenist dogma. Some found the visitation disturbing and terrifying. The mood of the cities ranged from dark anticipation to joyous celebration by those who knew the sighting was an omen of something very good to come.

After a day of surveying the cities and townships, the two spaceships met in the desert on the outskirts of Nubia, in a region unexplored even by the nomads. There a temporary camp was established to serve as a field !aboratory for the genetic survey of the local population. Long after nightfall, the Atet and the Sektet flew out separately seeking people who lived near the ruins of the ancient temples. Invisible even to the senses of animals, the hypnotic power of the occupants in meditation contacted the minds of humans who would be most receptive to the sky-people in the disc. Discretion was essental as many human minds would be cast into madness if greeted by powers they could not understand.

A girl of twelve was sleeping under the stars. She was awakened and compelled silently to rise. She walked into the desert. A shining light lured her into the hills. She dreamed a vivid dream of a beautiful man with glowing white skin and flowing golden hair that fell past his shoulders. He made love to her passionately in a realm of colored light while their bodies floated together in space.

This girl contributed many fully-formed ova, a few brain cells and tissue and blood samples. Her vision of love would be a cherished recollection for the rest of her life. The elders of her tribe would regard the visitation as divine favor upon her.

Another young woman from a nomad encampment declared that she had been seduced by a god. The skin of the deity was white and shiny, and he wore the collar of a Pharaoh. His hair was golden. This woman contributed many more fertile ova.

A shepherd, youngest of three brothers, was seduced in his dreamtime by a cat-faced woman. He found the experience overwhelming and he dreamed of this goddess from that time on and found human women disappointing after having made love to a goddess.

Many humans received visitations the first night of the survey. Contact was cloaked in dreams. Blood samples, ovum cells, sperm deposits, were taken from sleeping donors whose minds were wild with rapturous encounters with incubi and succubi.

By morning the genetic materials sampled represented twenty human bodies. Chromosomes were surveyed, catalogued, and broken down into individual genes. Contact resumed the next day, with visions of cosmic order imparted to the Priests and Priestesses of Aton in rural temples.

For five days and nights the immortals of the starship *Aton* conducted their genetic survey of the people of Upper Egypt and the outskirts of Nubia. Hundreds of samples were taken. In the daytime, rural communities buzzed with rumors of angelic visitors, lights in the sky, and men and women receiving the sexual favors of divine beings. Witchcraft was sometimes mentioned, but no longer unfavorably. The incubus and succubus were not considered threatening by the tribal people of the desert.

⚜ ⚜ ⚜

His father had been a Priest of Aton. The Priests of Aton were encouraged to marry and teach their secret knowledge to their wives, who were excellent priestesses. Mothers represented the Goddess Herself. Monastic life had purified his father's son, so he, too, sought a wife. Remembering the example of his father, he left the mountains and joined a caravan. He met a young woman and journeyed with her for several months, then returned with her to his home among the rocks. He led her into his religion as well. He summoned his god one night with an act of magick, then he left the temple. In the morning his wife was pregnant. Nine months later, she bore a son. The boy was named Yuia.

Yuia was initiated at an early age into the mysteries of the sect of Aton. To him, Aton was *more* than the tangible, physical essence of the sun. Aton was the material, some said "metal" or "silver" disc that is *like* the sun, but is not the sun. It is the disc the gods ride in.

Yuia was twelve when he met Thuya. She was slightly older than he, fifteen years, if her illiterate parents were correct. Both children had blonde hair, which was unusual for southern Egyptians. They teasingly became lovers and were married by their parents with the rising of the Dog Star.

Yuia and Thuya were intelligent, charismatic children. Their families were proud of them. Because Thuya had a talent for arithmetic, and her honor and sincerity were known throughout her village, she was chosen to take inventory for the local tax office.

People paid their taxes in the form of material donations. Peasants contributed a share of the grain which they grew in the fields alloted to them by the Pharaoh. Craftsmen and artisans paid by giving the best of whatever they made. Thus musical instruments, jewelry, earthenware pottery, furniture, and works of art all had to be appraised, often at great expense. After serving as an auditor, Thuya was hired as a clerk and accountant. She became a civil servant of the royal tax office, and eventually became confidante and scribe to the local nomarch.

After the first genetic survey of the people of Upper Egypt, the *Aton* returned to Jupiter. It arrived over the outpost on Ganymede and the two shuttlediscs transported the living specimens to the laboratory under the ice. There scientists hurried to disassemble the chromosomes, then the genes, into individual units. All human traits were charted.

Two hypothetical bodies were conceived and rendered holographically. One was a human woman, indistinguishable from any other member of her species except that her hips were designed to accommodate the birth of a baby with a huge head. Her pelvis had an extraordinarily wide birth corridor.

The other body took much longer to design: a male of the genetically enhanced seed race. The head would be immense, containing a brain several times as large as a normal human brain. In addition, to insure that all of this male's descendants would survive childbirth, the torso and abdomen were arranged around a giant female pelvis. Only the sexual organs distinguished it as male.

Even as theorists constructed a DNA molecule encoded with the design of the synthetic male body, the nucleus that would produce the female was being implanted into a living ovum cell. When viable, the fertilized ovum was placed in a time stasis and Starship *Aton* returned to Gaia.

❧

During the third year of her marriage, Thuya was visited by an angel of the Amentii. As priest and priestess, they had summoned the god according to an ancient ritual. Now both sat silently, waiting in the candlelight.

They sensed the approach of the spacecraft moments before they felt the powerful vibrations that pulsed through the stone upon which they sat. Yuia and Thuya grinned breathlessly, in joyous anticipation. Out of the circular opening in the temple dome, a single moving star brightened as it crossed toward the center of the sky and stopped. It continued to intensify, as if descending.

Yuia and Thuya threw their naked bodies on the altar, reaching out their arms to the source of the brilliant rays. On the hillsides, thorn bushes writhed as if tortured by winds, though the night air was still. The radiant beams seemed opaque, but no dust flew. The ground shook as if quaking to a terrible roar, but the silence itself was deafening. The disc neared the earth.

A thousand feet above the Temple of Aton, the huge starship dispatched a shuttledisc. The *Atet* sailed down until it hovered twenty feet above the aperture in the center of the dome. Yuia stood with arms outstretched to greet it. A beam of living light flashed into his right eye, and he received a complete vision of the Gnosis: the memory of the Universe penetrated his optic nerve and illuminated his brain.

Thuya was teleported aboard the hovering shuttledisc. She was received by two small, silver-skinned beings. She knew she had been aboard this strange boat before and was confident that she was safe in the loving hands of Lord God Ptah. She materialized in bubbly shrouds of sparkling colors, and her body tingled as it coalesced in the center of a shaft of light. She closed her eyes against the glare.

When she opened them she was lying on her back on a padded table in a vast room. The walls and ceiling were made out of living jewels. She knew she was in the Amentt, on the edge of Heaven. Still the light hurt her eyes, and she closed them again.

She felt a presence approach her from the side. The entity stopped and stood beside her. She had felt him before, she did not need to open her eyes. He was familiar, unseen, and somehow she knew that he was a man, a beautiful yellow haired human man, enveloped in light which emanated from a silver disc. . Thuya felt the rapture of his presence overhelm her. He made love to her again and again and she yielded joyously to his embrace. Thus she learned many times that there was no difference between a man and a god.

Ecstasy became sleep. One dream dissolved into another. Dreams dissolved into oblivion and Thuya was seduced by the Void.

When she awoke briefly the next morning she was lying on the altar in the sunlight. Her head ached and she quickly returned to blank sleep. Yuia was nearby, singing hymns and waving incense urns as he walked in circles around the altar.

Thuya experienced one last dream. Her astral lover returned to promise that their union would result in the birth of a child—a very special child.

Yuia celebrated the news in the Temple of Aton. He sang songs, chanted and meditated while his wife slept in the bridal chamber. At night, he lit many candles and continued singing hymns of joy. Still his wife slept soundly.

Chapter Six

The queen of Thothmose IV had been impregnated by a wave-shifter summoned by a Priestess of Selket in a secret fertility rite. The baby born to the queen, the next King of Egypt, was three when he learned of the visitations by the solar god Aton. Already the prince was being heralded by the priesthoods of both Amen and Thoth as a great emissary of the gods, a child-priest who would at last unify the two rival sects.

The boy's name was Amenhotep III.

At five years old he was intellectually trying to reconcile Amenism and Atonism. He ignored the exhortations of his father and uncles to study the papyrus scrolls of the religion of Thoth. He was more interested in this new peasant religion, the worship of the Material Disc.

The reign of Thothmose IV ended less than a dozen years after it began. A child of nine, Amenhotep III became Pharaoh. He was surrounded by advisors and executives who presented him repeatedly in pageants and kept him out of politics. This was most agreeable to the moderately intelligent, well-intentioned young man.

All his life he had heard stories of a beautiful and precocious peasant girl, born, as he had been, by the seed of a god-man after her father, a priest named Yuia, had invoked the god Aton. Her mother, a priestess named Thuya, had received the sacred seed. Their daughter was already a priestess.

Her name was Tiy.

Even as a baby, Tiy seemed endowed with knowledge and understandings far beyond her years. She spoke her first words at four months, learned to walk by nine months and was learning to read and write by her first year.

While her mother worked by day keeping records for the government and overseeing the local tax office, her father conducted the affairs of temple-priest. Thuya taught her daughter astronomy, mathematics and religion, including the secret history of Aton.

Her parent's sudden rise to prominence had not escaped the attention of The Beast, who scrutinized the life of the precocious peasant girl from afar. Kahotep had been contemplating a new plan ever since the apparent departure of the star-people and the resurgence of Atonism among the desert people.

He wished to avoid another brief, ill-fated debacle like the reign of Thothmose IV, who had been demented largely due to inbreeding. Though Kahotep did not suspect that Amenhotep III had been fathered by a wave-shifter, he knew that the queen had had a human lover and credited the genetic fitness of the boy to a man who was not the king. According to tradition, the boy-king was to marry his sister, but this king had none.

The Beast watched Tiy from afar, through his emissaries, family acquaintances. Tiy was intelligent, charming, charismatic, gifted in music and mathematics. She was fully literate. She was also very beautiful.

Stories circulated about her. She had been visited more than once at night by Aton, so said her neighbors. Her parents were good and loving people, beloved throughout their village. Tiy had a reputation as a healer: her empathic abilities were so great that the sick and the crippled came to receive her touch, which alleviated their pain. Her blessings rid them of afflictions.

When she was ten she was given a job as a scribe in the court of her local nomarch. She performed her duties with such competence that she was given greater and greater responsibilities. Complicated tasks did not intimidate nor confuse her. Her problem solving abilities were quick and clever, especially regarding the appraisal of art objects, for which she and her mother were often consulted. Tiy also settled disputes between the taxed and the tax collecters. She judged all questions on principle. All who knew of the child prodigy named Tiy respected her.

Tiy had a younger brother named Ai. He was a quiet and alert, catlike boy, he was studying to become a Priest of Aton. Also highly intelligent, he devoted his full attention to studies to becoming a temple priest like his father.

That Amenhotep III had been chosen to personify the union between the priesthoods of Thoth and Amen was a great irony. Though Kahotep carefully scripted all the debates, discussions and proclamations made by the new Pharaoh, the new alliance between the rival religious factions did not distract the common folk from their new religion of the Disc. The sect of Aton did not prescribe any dogma, describe Heaven nor dictate any system of beliefs.

Amenhotep III was somewhat serious and overly dignified, and far from being an intellectual. Intense philosophical debates or lively discussions lured him haplessly into rounds of intense questioning. When he defended his own positions he revealed himself to be so naive that The Beast frequently ordered the words of the king censored. The false proclamations and discussions attributed to the king flattered him, and he frequently revised his memories to conform to the image that his priests contrived of him.

When word of the king's fascination for Atonism reached the people, rumors quickly spread predicting that Amen and Aton were soon going to merge as one priesthood. In truth, Kahotep was counseling his priests to negotiate just such a bloodless, voluntary collaboration. This prospective union sent messengers from Amen's temples to the temple of the Priest and Priestess of Aton, Yuia and Thuya.

They discussed religion and politics into the evening and learned that the couple had a son and daughter who were studying the priestcraft of this new religion.

The emissaries of Amen later returned with the news that the king himself offered a private audience to the gifted children, especially Tiy, who was older and already an initiated priestess. Tiy consented eagerly and her parents agreed to let her go. She departed for Thebes the next day, charged with the task of representing her religion to the Amenist king.

A royal caravan escorted her to the Nile, where she boarded a royal barge. The sunset and moonlight drifted with her on the slow, black water. On the morning of the third day the elegant barge was tethered to a mooring of wooden planks and towering stone columns. Between the pillars approached a contingent of soldiers carrying a throne. In the throne sat a regal figure, lavishly adorned with jewels and clothed in filmy white cloth.

Tiy was escorted off the barge. The royal throne was placed before her and she knelt. She carefully kept her head lowered but glanced up discreetly. The king was handsome and seemed genuinely friendly. He smiled. She arose at his command that was more like a polite request, and then their eye contact was mutual and prolonged.

The king ordered a throne brought forward for Tiy and they were carried side by side down the avenue between the two rows of pillars toward the royal palace in Thebes. They parted on the palace steps and Tiy was led away to spend her first evening among handmaidens in the future queen's suites.

The next day Tiy was summoned by the king's vizier to the first discussion, to be conducted in extreme privacy. Secret metaphysical matters were to be discussed, important ideas equivalent to magical formulae.

A bush finch settled on a papyrus blossom in a reflective pool near the king and Priestess Tiy. The bird listened intently as they discussed cosmology and cosmogony.

"This Aton...it has imparted prophecies, no doubt?" The young king was searching for words. "Has Aton disclosed, ah, wisdom about the future?"

"The Metal Disc has visited many priests and priestesses and imparted knowledge of the Universe. We view Aton as a messenger of Ptah and not the body of Ptah Himself."

"Do you believe in Ptah as distinct from Amen-Ptah?"

"We do not know if the spirit of war, which is Amen, is the greater part of Ptah, who is God."

"So, if Ptah is God, who is Amen?"

"He could be god of war."

"God of war only?"

"War is only an aspect of the Universe, of Ptah. It is not the only aspect of Ptah that there is."

"What other aspects are as important as war? If Egypt is overrun with enemies again, like the Hyksos or the Nubians, what would happen to Ptah? How many desert savages could worship or even comprehend Ptah?"

She stroked his arm and smiled. Her broad lips parted for a moment. She whispered: "Amen is not god of lovemaking, is he?"

Ashamed, Amenhotep III looked away. His few male companions were already boasting of their erotic adventures and though he had passed puberty, shyness prevented him from obtaining experience with the opposite sex. The king was a virgin.

"Have I offended you?" Tiy touched his shoulders.

He turned toward her, feigning indifference. "Oh, why should your question bother me?"

Tiy withdrew her arms, but not her gaze.

"I have delved into many matters," Amenhotep III said, "and have joined the theologies of Thoth and Amen, which some scholars said could never be done. So, Amen is not god of love, but that is not an important aspect of Ptah."

"If it were not an important aspect of Ptah, then what future would Egypt have without the love that couples share? Without love that makes babies, one generation would age and die. Egypt would have no children to take care of their parents. A generation without love would be the last generation born."

"I understand." The king sat silently in deep thought for a long time. "These children born, fathered by the god-in-the-Disc…"

"Shu: Shu-in-the-Disc."

"Yes, the god Shu-in-the-Disc-of-Aton. You claim to be such a child. My own mother confessed to me more than once that she had no mortal lover, not even my father the king, when I was conceived. What of this? If a deity, perhaps one of the Amentii, can impregnate a woman with divine seed, then will not there always be generations born?"

"Of course! Aton is a god of love. Shu-in-the-Disc is my father, summoned by my mortal father. My mother became my mother on that night."

"But then, I also am a child of Amen! Amen impregnated my mother. She told me this when I was a child. I was conceived during her fertility rites. She was examined and judged to be a virgin by the court physician, and so my own true father is divine!"

"Is it not true that Amen has no fertility rituals? That he abolished them long ago?"

Amenhotep III sighed. "It is so. The rites of my mother were secret. Not even my father knew she attended them."

"I see. What religion did your mother practise?"

"Worship of Selket."

"Then she was a witch."

"Please… keep that as a secret. Do not tell anyone. Please."

"I will not. Do not worry."

He relaxed. "My father hated witchcraft, especially that of the women who worshipped in the mysteries of Selket. The Priestesses of Isis have their secrets, too, but their music and songs gladden the heart! Amen would never abolish the sacred music and dance of Isis. But Selket, her priestesses, aroused the fear of my father, who felt threatened by sorcery. He awoke many times hearing voices in the night …"

"So I have heard."

"It was natural for him to hate witchcraft."

"I understand."

"But this is a novel proposition, that making love is as important as making war. I will consider it."

Tiy gave him her warmest smile and they parted.

The bush finch fluttered off the papyrus and into the sky. It flew over the palace, over the city streets, over the marketplace to a slot between stones set in the wall of the Temple of Karnak. This bird had made this flight many times. He dove into shadow in the shaft and flew straight down, then swept up and shot through a horizontal corridor, around several corners and straight down again toward a dim light. Alighting, the finch advanced into the deep central chamber where lived The Beast.

Kahotep turned slowly and looked at the bird. He whistled the trill of notes that comprised the bird's name, then asked in Egyptian:

"You have observed them, the king and the priestess, during their meeting?"

The bird warbled his answer.

"And what did they talk about?"

The bush finch sang his interpretation of the conversation, decribing it from a viewpoint not unacquainted with human ways. Kahotep had taught his little spy as much as the bird could absorb about human customs, behavior, and tribal codes. He could understand the Egyptian language, though he could not speak it. However, speculations about God and the deities did not touch the bird-mind, and philosophy was lost on the tiny avian.

The bird sang that the king and his guest shared a secret. Yes, the bird trilled, a secret about the king's father. He sang the words his master had taught him to use in the context of secret births.

The Beast knew what to ask. Yes, the bird had heard the name Selket spoken, and witchcraft. Yes, the queen was a secret worshipper of Selket.

The Beast fed the bird a sweet, freshly baked breadcrust, which the tiny spy pecked at furiously while The Beast contemplated this news. His worst fears were confirmed: the king was star-begotten. As the young priestess was, as well…

"You may go now," he said to the bird, who picked up the remaining scrap, flew to the dark shaft and was gone.

Kahotep brooded darkly. He did not like the fact that the young king had no queen, but Kahotep was confident that the future was still in his grasp, for in no case could Amenhotep III marry a commoner.

Chapter Seven

The next day the young king met with Priestess Tiy over breakfast. He had perfumed his shaven head and worn his most ornate corselet: appearing before her *sans* crown was a sign of informality.

Tiy wore her long black hair in knotted and beaded strands. Amenhotep commented that Atonists "defied the law" by refusing to shave their heads and wear only a forelock. Tiy reminded him that victims of human sacrifice had to be so shaved, and that only tradition exhorted people to "prepare for sacrifice so prematurely."

Her words impressed him. He summoned a courtier, who confirmed Tiy's opinion that Atonists defied tradition only and not the written law.

Then Amenhotep complimented Tiy, telling her how beautiful her hair was. "It would be a shame to cut it," he whispered.

She laughed and her eyes sparkled. Amenhotep touched her. Together they ate, chatted romantically, speaking only of intimate things and no philosophical discourse. They contributed no new theology. The meeting was a success: the king wished to see her that evening, and the next day and the day after that. He arranged for tours of magnificent Thebes, to occupy her time while he was tending to matters of state.

At the end of one week, Amenhotep III announced his heartfelt intention: to marry Priestess Tiy and rule Egypt with her as his queen. He made it clear that she would be no mere concubine.

Tiy was stunned. Never had a daughter of peasants served at the right hand of the king. She accepted his proposal of marriage at a banquet given in her honor. There, though grim faces watched the king, others smiled. Some were taken aback when the king openly displayed affection for the priestess, for praise for his chosen queen was not unanimous. To the king's displeasure, he felt compelled to defend his decision, lamenting the fact that no suitable sisters occupied the royal houses anymore.

☥

Laden with gifts, treasures carried by soldiers, Tiy returned to her township to tell her friends and family the news. She prepared to move to Thebes and take her place beside the king. She spent a month finalizing her business at home. Her parents were promoted to Officers of the Civil Service by order of the Pharaoh Amenhotep III, which made them direct courtiers of their nomarch.

The month did not pass smoothly for Amenhotep. When his advisors criticized his choice of a bride, he would hear nothing of it. In a fit of anger after an argument with General Horemheb he smashed the heads of a dozen prisoners of war, all of them Nubians, spontaneously, without ritual preparation nor public display.

When Tiy finally appeared before him again, the controversy that had raged in her absence had been suppressed. Lavish gifts were bestowed upon Egypt's future queen, and gifts were sent to her parents. A generous dowry was paid by the happy king.

The marriage was performed between sunrise and sunset by the Priests of Amen. That no arrangement had been deemed possible under which Aton could be represented in the services caused Tiy some grief. The king promised that from then on her religion would be represented equally with Amenism.

Sunset brought the ritual to an end and the royal feast began. The royal couple, both wearing the Uraeus of the Double Plumes, dined on meats roasted with jungle fruits, fish, many exotic kinds of fowl, grain cakes, pastries dripping with honey, and delicacies

from the far east, from the kings of Mitanni. Their wedding night ended in raptures of nuptial bliss. For Tiy the consummation of the marriage was more than a holy pleasure, it was the realization of the fondest dream any girl in Egypt could have: to wed the Pharaoh, the young god-king of her people.

Although there was displeasure at the peasant queen among the royalty, the love that the populace held for Tiy was evidenced by her unanimous popularity among the peasants. The aristocracy was forced to vanquish their pride and support this queen who was much closer to the people of Egypt than they were.

Kahotep was furious that Amenhotep III had ignored the advice of his courtiers

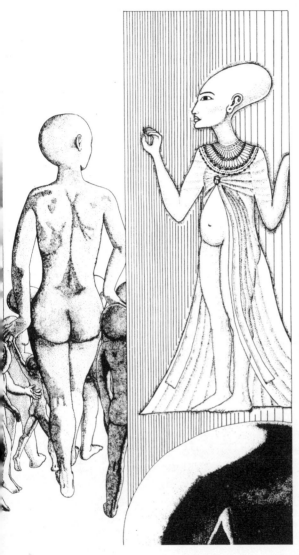

(many of whom were employed by Kahotep and under his hypnotic control) to take Tiy as a concubine only, not as queen. But Amenhotep III wisely saw in Tiy decisiveness, intelligence and charisma. Deep inside he knew he lacked such qualities himself, and to find them in a woman brought him great joy. His love was undeniable. Kahotep, from his vault beneath Karnak, was terrified at his apparent loss of control over the throne.

Stories of Tiy's wisdom and fairness in diplomatic matters circulated widely. Decisions she made on important issues benefitted all of Egypt. Amenhotep III boasted that his wife was his closest advisor and best friend. Tiy was given new names among her people: "the Solver of Problems" and "the Wise One." Her judgements satisfied everyone.

After her first five years as Queen of Egypt, Tiy returned home to visit her family while Amenhotep III took advantage of the opportunity to hunt lions in the thorn forests to the south.

Upon her arrival, even before she arrived at the home of her family, she was informed that her countryfolk had seen signs in the sky again, indicating that Aton had returned. She was greeted by her mother in the courtyard of their new palace. Immense love was shared in their embraces as breezes stirred the fronds of palm trees overhead and the scent of lilies sugared the air.

After dinner, Thuya took Tiy by carriage across the desert to the ruins of the ancient Temple of Aton. They tied the horses to a crumbling obelisk, then descended the steep corridor to the repositories of inner mysteries. They strode through a hallway illuminated by torchlight passing on both sides chambers which contained religious artifacts from archaic ages, forgotten for centuries. Sculpted colossi of grotesque, forgotten star-kings loomed overhead. Their elongated heads were enhanced and not hidden by the crowns they wore. The false plaited beards of the Pharaohs did not disguise that these kings had been of another race entirely.

Thuya led her daughter into a room which, though smaller than the rest, was yet immense. Messages in hieroglyphics were painted on frescoes showing discs, many with the wings of the Horus-hawk, others decorated with solar rays.

Tiy paused to examine one painting that aroused in her a deep anxiety and suspicion of hidden meanings. In it, woman was being led by two smaller figures toward a disc that radiated shafts of light. Under the disc stood a figure, taller than the rest, with arms outstretched. This slender personage wore a mighty crown.

"Even now the Disc approaches," Thuya whispered.

Tiy's eyes widened.

"It has been seen by the Nubians. They are afraid of it. The townships to the south and east and west have all seen Aton by day and by night. By night with rays of light and by day a disc with invisible wings, the Disc approaches. Aton approaches even now."

"'Will I see it? Will it reveal the living visions to me, the way it did to you and father? Is this what my religion leads to?"

"Yes, Tiy, and more. You have been chosen for two honors, not just one."

"I am Queen of Egypt! What greater honor is there?"

"A god rides in Aton, a sky-god. He has chosen you to be his goddess-queen. Aton has watched over you, Tiy. It is no accident that you have become Queen of Egypt.

"Early in my marriage to Yuia I consented to bear a child of Aton. You are that child. Now a god-king has chosen you to bear a son for him, a son who will rule Egypt after the Pharaoh has peacefully ceased to exist."

"Why? What do you mean? What will happen to him?"

"No harm will come to your husband. That we do know. We know also that you will have one son. That son will be special. He will be divinely, not humanly, begotten."

Tiy nodded silently, struggling to accept. Her mother's message was clearly illuminated by the murals and sculpture. The figures beneath the winged discs suddenly became real to her. She would be received by one of these, just as her mother had been.

Tiy studied the murals again, this time in awe. The sequence of the pictures, the meaning of the wide-hipped men with elongated heads became apparent. She whispered:

"They are not of our race."

"No, they are not."

"They must be from another race—perhaps from another world."

"They are."

"Then it is true: the wandering stars, the planets, they are brighter than the other stars because they are closer, are they not? And they, too, are worlds, just like this world?"

"Yes, and the other stars are suns, just like our own."

"This is why you taught me astronomy! So that I could learn cosmology!"

"Yes, but the new cosmology must remain secret. Do not reveal this knowledge even to your husband, the king."

"What? To keep such a wonderful revelation secret...!"

"Hush!" Thuya whispered. After a space she murmured, "Yes, all people should know. But the Priests of Amen have banned this cosmology as a heresy. It is a crime to even speak of Worlds-in-Heaven or of the old kings as sky-gods. But look!" She extended her arms. "It was a noble experiment! Look at us ! We are almost like they are."

In a hushed voice, Tiy ventured: "When will the god-king arrive?"

Thuya leaned forward, "If all goes well, tonight."

An immense circle had been dug into the desert. Under a shallow layer of wind-polished volcanic pebbles lay a deeper layer of silt. The black stones had been removed, leaving a perfect ring. In the center was a shallow pit in which an obelisk had been erected. The tip of the obelisk was a perfect, terminated quartz crystal.

Yuia cast a magic circle by walking in a clockwise direction upon the ring drawn in white silt. North, then east, south, west, while Thuya chanted in the center of the circle beside the obelisk, they invoked the cardinal points of the horizon as Yuia passed them, until he was standing again on the northern edge of the circle.

When the circle was complete their daughter, Queen Tiy, stepped from the eastern quarter, through the psychic boundary her father had drawn, and walked toward the obelisk. She sang a prayer facing the stone, then sat cross-legged beside it, facing east. East was the direction of rebirth, and Tiy was facing a rebirth, through her body as mother-goddess, of Horus, god-king. Another Horus, a son of the Divine Race, whose bodies linked humanity to the Amentii.

While Yuia and Thuya intoned chants in a prehistoric language, one star flickered into being. It gleamed and brightened in the center of the sky, descending. It cast down a brilliant blue-white beam of light. The ray struck the obelisk and gleamed prismatically from the crystal tip.

Yuia and Thuya lowered their voices and rolled the chant into a long: "Ahhhhhuuuuuuummmmmmmm…"

The peripheral lights fractured into discrete rays and rotating bands but from the center the intense electric-white beam continued to shine directly upon the obelisk and upon Queen Tiy. The disc covered the entire sky.

Yuia put his hand on his daughter's arm and said, "You will be gone for a short time. We will greet you again at the temple. Close your eyes. Do not look directly into the light. You will ride the light itself into the Aton Disc."

Tiy stood beside the obelisk, steadying herself against the stone, her eyes closed. Yiua and Thuya stepped away from their daughter, the queen.

The disc hovered, rotating. The central light intensified until its glare obscured Queen Tiy completely. When the ray faded to darkness she was gone.

The disc ascended.

Clouds of blue-white glare dissipated and Queen Tiy stood in a multicolored shaft of light that made her skin tingle. These rays also swiftly dimmed.

She felt elation, excitement. Her eyes adjusted to the soft light inside the starship. A very beautiful African woman with long, beaded black hair greeted her, smiling. Beside her stood two smaller beings, very odd-looking, not human. Tiy gasped and stepped back. To her relief, one of the strange humanoids smiled. Their facial expressions and eyes made them seem almost...human.

The dark-skinned woman spoke: "I am Isis."

Tiy felt a thrill of excitement to be standing in the presence of the Goddess. She followed her into a corridor. The walls looked alive and the ceiling was nothing but light. Isis paused and an aperture dilated in the wall. Light spilled out. The human goddess gestured for Tiy to enter, saying,

"These are the mysteries of your people. Here you will see the secret beginnings of your race. A star man awaits you on the other side."

Tiy walked past holograms of the families of Egypt's first three kings: Thoth, his vast head supported by an ornately jeweled crown, sat in his throne beside slender, broad-hipped Seshat, who was obviously of some very old human race. They were surrounded by fantastic children whose elongated, high-domed heads resembled those of the hairless, white-skinned humanoids who had accompanied them down the corridors of the Disc of Aton. The queen wondered what wondrous age those strange children must have lived in.

Tiy gasped when she saw the likeness of Isis standing beside the image of Osiris, also a huge-skulled humanoid of a nonhuman race. Their children possessed their father's strange cranium, but to a lesser degree than the children of Thoth and Seshat. Horus and Hathor had four sons, who in turn had fathered many sons and daughters. All showed the characteristic wide pelvic bones and huge skulls, but with great variation among them. Most of the grandchildren of Horus and Hathor appeared to be normal humans.

Then Tiy saw a rendering of herself standing beside a strange and beautiful man. He was much taller than she. His head was elongated, his face goatlike, his skull immense and extended far back, balanced upon a slender neck. His hips were wide and his thighs were huge. His belly protruded grotesquely down from his pinched chest. He was of the race of Thoth, Osiris, and Horus.

"Will this be my husband?" Tiy asked breathlessly.

"This will be your son," answered Isis.

She examined the lifelike images of nine children, seven of whom were girls, six with fantastic heads. "Will these be my children?"

"They will be your grandchildren."

They came to another aperture which slid open noiselessly. They walked together through beams of light. In the center of the room was a coshioned table of shining silver.

A tall, slender being, nearly as tall as Isis, approached. He extended a hand in a friendly gesture. "I am Tem," he said.

Tiy bowed respectfully. She looked up and saw that he held a crystal jar filled with green liquid.

"Permit me to anoint you," Tem said.

Tiy bowed again. Tem touched her forehead with oil. Her body tingled all over. She was breathless. Many small arms and strong hands supported her and led her to the padded silver table. Tiy closed her eyes, blinded by the glare.

When she opened her eyes, she saw a towering human figure standing over her, silhouetted by the curtain of rays. He leaned over and embraced her. They kissed, her senses dissolving into tingling rapture, her consciousness dissolving into bliss.

She made love to the god-man again and again, until time itself ceased to pass.

Tiy returned to Thebes with many mysteries. She had a knowledge of the nature of the Universe, which she felt a nearly overwhelming urge to share with her people. She dared not, for Thuya had told her in the ruins of the ancient temple, "If you dare speak of our world as a a ball that travels a course around the sun, then death will punctuate your final sentence!" She understood: the cosmological beliefs of the Amenists were rigid, and death was meted out to heretics.

Tiy wanted to tell her husband of the favor that her god Aton had bestowed upon her. She dared not, for it was of the gravest importance that the king think the baby was his own son, divinely conceived of course, but his own child nonetheless. She dared not tell her husband the greatest source of her heartbreak: the plans that had been laid for the boy. Her husband was a highly volatile element in a very unstable drama. Tiy regarded him as a cause for concern, herself as a focal point in a dangerous plan, playing a role of such vast importance that the eyes of the very stars watched anxiously.

Amenhotep greeted her at the royal landing on the banks of the Nile. He gave her kisses and long embraces. She slid her arms under his corselet and put her head on his shoulder, her eyes closed.

He escorted her to the palace and there bestowed many gifts upon her. She accepted the jewelry and ointments and perfumes graciously, then shared gifts of her own with him: canes and staves, carved by the people of her native province, vases of earthenware and bowls of blue fiance purchased from merchants along the way.

After a dinner feast of millet and baked waterfowl, the king and his queen made love. He had been celibate for the duration of his wife's journey. She sweetened his heart with her love, and she put out of her mind the ecstacy she had experienced aboard the Aton Disc...

Amenhotep III was a kind and childlike husband, remarkably innocent, due to the sheltered life he had lived as king. But he had so completely taken for granted himself as Pharaoh that he had no real feeling for his people. In his elevated world, to vent his rage by delivering the death blows to human sacrifices was an unquestionable law of nature, not merely a royal privilege.

Tiy now saw her people as struggling toward a psychic and evolutionary leap that she herself could barely fathom. For the first time in her life she felt that some secret, taboo thing had happened to her people and that a great deadly force held Egypt in its grip. She understood that this insight had been instilled in her in the Aton Disc, along with the need for her to practise secrecy in a world controlled by Amen, the Hidden One.

The queen continued to question what of her people's beliefs were superstition, such as the idea that the world was perched atop a pedestal on the back of a huge desert tortoise wandering a labyrinth under the belly of a vast cow who was also a woman painted half blue and half black with glowing white specks, which were the stars. Since this was false, what else was merely imaginative guesswork hurled in the face of vast ignorance?

Tiy witnessed Amenhotep III launch into a rage after an argument with his military commander, General Horemheb. She did not understand what the argument was about, but she saw her husband storm from the palace toward the Temple of Amen. Hours later she learned that he had put to death over a hundred slaves.

Tiy was appalled and grief-stricken, though Amenhotep reminded her that it was natural for the Pharaoh to be a "Great Smasher of Foreheads." She knew that arguing would be fatal—not for her, but for many others—so she kept silent.

The king was kind and sympathetic toward his queen, who suffered severe nausea and abdominal cramps during her pregnancy. Her body was reacting to the alien baby growing inside of her. Amenhotep comforted her: he would stroke her hair and speak softly. She loved him for his gentle side, for he never directed his rage against Tiy. Amenhotep loved his queen, peasant girl that she was. He was intrigued by the stories she told him about her brother and herself, her family and friends, all of whom lived in a society he had never known.

He secretly feared the peasants. Perhaps every Pharaoh had, at least as far back as the Old Kingdom. There were so *many* peasants. The king stood atop a pyramid not of stone. It was a human pyramid of toiling laborers. Tiy was his only connection with them. He was not at all envious of the adoration that the common folk

heaped upon her. He was confident that through her he was popular among the common people of his land. Continued popularity was his only assurance that he would not be dethroned the way Pepi II had been, or lose favor with the common folk like Sesostris III just before the Hyksos invaded. Tiy was more than a peasant queen; she represented his security.

As the months of her pregnancy passed, Tiy was seen less and less at festivals and pageants. She was tended by a flock of handmaidens and her husband spent as much time as he could beside her, though his duties as king occupied most of his day.

When her last month of pregnancy arrived, Tiy fought a tendency toward depression and doubt. Several times she nearly broke down under the strain for she knew that her husband would be outraged by the news that would accompany the birth of the baby.

Tiy's water broke at midnight and labor immediately followed. The blood in her waters portended an intense labor.

Amenhotep summoned the Priests of Amen, but when Yuia and Thuya unexpectedly showed up in the harem, Tiy gratefuly fell into her mother's arms. The priests arrived to find everything under control, though there was no explanation of how the queen's parents managed to slip past them and enter the palace.

Amenhotep was escorted to the inner temple of the palace. All fathers, even kings, were forbidden from viewing the event of birth. Before the altar to Amen, surrounded by candles, the king sat, meditating, chanting prayers, and singing hymns to deities, all of whose names were prefixed with the name of Amen.

Tiy and her parents vanished. Tiy's personal priest of Aton reassured the Pharaoh's guard that everything was proceeding normally. This was no untruth, for Tiy had gone with her own father and mother willingly, so all was well in the eyes of Aton.

Hours passed. The night melted before the dawn. Tiy's bedchamber was searched by her personal guardians for intruders. After the room was declared to be completely empty, the door was sealed and guards were stationed throughout the hallway.

Somewhere above Thebes, the Queen of Egypt was giving birth to a boy. Her father and mother assisted, but the midwife was a jovial wave-shifter, a huge-headed woman with a lovely face. Attending the birth were diminutive Amentii of several stellar races. The infant born had a similarly elongated head.

Many worlds witnessed that birth. Visions of it swept past the moons of the giant planets of the Ra system, illuminating the colonies on Io, Ganymede, and Titan. Holographic images of the sacred birth were sent to the inhabitants of the ringworlds encircling Sothis III. Holograms of the event could be viewed by visitors to the Ra system for all of Eternity.

A new god-king had been born.

The guards loyal to the queen were startled to hear sounds from the queen's bedchamber. They pried open the door slab and pushed aside the curtains to see the living queen and her priestess-mother and priest-father beside her. She was reclining in bed, but was not asleep.

Yuia held up one hand, indicating silence. "All is well."

"How did you enter?"

"That was arranged by Aton."

"But how?"

"Hush!" Yuia snapped.

When Amenhotep learned that his son had been spirited away immediately after birth, he rushed from his temple to Tiy's bedchamber and looked pleadingly at his sleeping wife. He tried to awaken her, but Yuia and General Horemheb restrained him.

"Why this concealment? Why can I not see my son? Take me to him! Take me to him!"

"The baby was born…deformed," Yuia said sternly. "It is best that you do not see the boy yet."

"Deformed? My son—a freak, a monster?"

"By human standards, yes. He would appear to most people to be disfigured, perhaps grotesque."

The king hung his head and wailed loudly. He was led from the bedchamber as his eyes ran with tears.

Tiy had been sedated. She slept, oblivious to the cries of the king's grief. When she later awoke, Amenhotep was still weeping. He had insisted on returning and now knelt beside her. She caressed him. He looked up at her and moaned "They *took* him!"

She nodded. "I know."

"Was he…?" Amenhotep could not voice his question.

"It is his head. We thought it best—all of us, myself included—we agreed that you and the boy should be separated."

"What?" He stared at her, not comprehending.

"It is best, my dear husband. The deformity is extreme. It is best for you and for all of Egypt as well."

The king was silent for a long time. Finally, he said, "The baby is a boy?"

"Yes, a boy."

"The baby is alive?"

"Yes, alive."

"Have you named the boy yet?"

"No, he has no name."

"Then, if he lives, let him be known as Amenhotep the Fourth, in honor of me, his father."

"Let it be done," Tiy said. "If the boy lives, let him be named Amenhotep IV, in honor of…his father."

"Where is he now?" the king asked.

"In the care of Aton."

"When will I see him?"

"I don't know, my love. Maybe soon. Maybe never."

Amenhotep III was stunned into a long silence. Tiy caressed him. She whispered "You yourself saw little of your own father…"

He shook his head. "He still saw me. He liked to dress me in my jewels and tell me he loved me."

"You saw little of him. Once or twice a year he visited you, no more."

"That is true." The king sat upright, regaining his composure.

Tiy saw, with amazement, that his sorrow was beginning to pass already. He had adjusted. He was so childlike and strangely uncaring.

He kissed her. They embraced and he felt the new shape of her body, her belly still flabby and fat, but no longer stiffly swollen with another human body within.

Yuia and Thuya departed abruptly for their home. In the days and weeks that followed, Amenhotep asked occasionally about his son and Tiy reassured him that all was well. The king ruled upon his throne, deaf to the rumors that something supernatural had happened to his firstborn son.

Chapter Eight

The years Queen Tiy spent with Amenhotep III were idyllic and nearly unmarred. The king loved his royal wife and she bore him a family of daughters, whom he adored. He gave them many gifts and built Tiy a temple to Aton as well as several temples to Amen and Aton. He also caused to be built, in the Sudanese city of Saddenga, a temple where Tiy was worshipped as a goddess. In the western district of Thebes, Amenhotep III built his queen a lake. It was immense: more than 3,700 cubits long and over 700 cubits wide, excavated by legions of slaves in a single fortnight.

The architects employed by the Pharaoh were twin brothers named Her and Suti. Because twins had customarily been slain at birth in Egypt, only intervention by the Priests of Amen , for unknown reasons, had saved these talented builders. They designed many of the king's temples.

During the years that Tiy bore him daughters Ast, Henttaneb and Satamen, Amenhotep fought one battle, a tribal rebellion in Nubia. 312 Nubians were killed and 740 were imprisoned for prolonged labor or sacrifice to Amen. Many murals were commissioned of Her and Suti, depicting the war-king Amenhotep III in Nubia slaying multitudes of Amen's enemies.

The empire had never been bigger. Amenhotep III ruled Egypt south along the Nile well past the Second Cataract as well as all of Phoenicia and Syria. These had been conquered by Thothmose I and held in the time of Amenhotep III's father. Amenhotep III ruled these lands and more: the Egyptian Sudan was his, down to Napata, well inside the former borders of Nubia. Friendship with kings abroad had been established by his father, Thothmose IV and continued to provide him with powerful allies.

Babylonian kings regularly exchanged gifts with him, from sculptures carved in marble, bronze or limestone to jewels and even their own daughters, when they reached marriageable age. Thus King Amenhotep III acquired many concubines. His own mother had been a royal concubine, presented by her father, Tushratta, King of Mitanni. Thothmose IV married Mutemuua, the witch whose communion with a wave-shifter had produced Amenhotep III.

In the tenth year of his reign, after the completion of lake Tcharukha, the Pharaoh took as a concubine Gilukhipa, a princess presented to him as a gift by the Mitannian prince Shutarna of Neherna. Shortly after, Tushratta presented his grandson Amenhotep III with his daughter, Tatumkhipa. Amenhotep gratefully accepted these young girls as wives, and placed them in his harem, and betrothed Ast, who was nine, Hentaneb, eight, and Satamen, age six, to marry into prominent Mitannian families in a few short years. Amenhotep was glad to strengthen Egypt politically without having to go to war.

Tiy accepted the acquisition of concubines with matronly patience. She considered herself mother of Egypt and, yes, mother to this spoiled, naive, sometimes arrogant, angry, and often deluded king. She saw through his vanity. She overlooked his violent tantrums and knew that to the king she represented something dark, secret, and frightening. Something occult. A mystery…

The Pharaoh and his queen sailed together on the great lake he had built for her. The torchlights on the embankments and on other slow barges flickered in the black, still water. They called their royal barge *Atontehen:* "Sparkling Rays of Aton." They drank wine and talked about religion, about the lovely family they had raised, always avoiding the subject of the hidden, deformed boy.

"I think it is true that my mother was a witch," he said one evening, gazing at the firelit shore.

"Why do you say that?" Tiy asked, knowing they were safe from the ears of the Amenists.

"I think it is…eastern. Those Mitannians have always secretly been magicians, all of them. The kings especially. And…I think Amen came to her in spirit form. My father…is then not my father."

"How can you know?"

"I have thought about it long and hard. He never had a true queen. He loved my mother most of all in his harem, but she could not be queen. She was not Egyptian. Still, he always seemed very astonished to have fathered me."

"Astonished?"

"I see things now in a way I did not see when I was a boy. My father always seemed amazed that Mutemuua bore him a child."

"He must have loved her. Although she was not accepted as a royal queen, he gave her a royal name at their wedding. The people themselves saw it as her coronation."

"Yes, she was "Hereditary Princess, Great Lady, President of the South and North, Great Royal Mother." So, she *was* a Mother of Egypt even if the Priests of Amen could not accept her as such."

"Then why do you doubt that he was your father?"

"Because I have come to accept many things. I have come to accept that goddesses make love to mortal men and gods can impregnate mortal women. I have come to accept the supernatural as natural."

"I see."

"Let us drink a toast!" He lifted his wine cup. "I declare that henceforth this day shall be a holiday in honor of you, my queen."

"Not of me, my love. Of Aton."

"Very well, then, to Aton. On this, the season of Akhet, on the third month, on the sixteenth day, I declare this to be Aton's Day. It is very close to the time when the veil between this world and the Tuat is thin, as the priestesses of Selket say. It is now that the most magic happens in the world."

"This is true." Tiy lifted her cup.

They drank the toast and tossed the last drops of red wine in their cups to the waters of the Nile as an offering to Aton.

Though the king mysteriously disappeared one year later, the day remained sacred to the common people of Egypt thenceforth.

Amenhotep III had been declared Pharaoh of Egypt at the age of nine. He had ruled for five years when he married Tiy; she was fifteen, he was fourteen. He was nineteen when his son, Amenhotep IV was born. Birth defects were common among the royal houses, afflicted by deformities caused by inbreeding, the result of Egyptian sacred incest. Amenhotep III had long recovered from his grief at the loss of his first son. It was common for a king to never see a child born too deformed. Kings were encouraged to forget such things.

Amenhotep III was not himself defective. He was brave and enjoyed chariot racing. He enjoyed fishing along the Nile and the hunt. His favorite sport was hunting lions. He would ride his chariot through the deserts to the south, beyond Sinjar, to the edge of the savannahs, and there he would run down the great maned males. He always aimed his spear truly at the base of the lion's neck. The grasslands were as hot as the desert on a summer day, and he preferred hunting lions in the thorn forests during the fall. To get to the thorn forests took a journey of several weeks, and ended in a seven-day chariot ride through acacia-swept plains. He would camp at the outskirts of the thorn forests beside the river Khabur and beat drums to drive lions out and into the ambush that awaited them.

On this fall day he was looking back on his years as Pharaoh with pride as he drove white stallions over the yellow grass, the heavy red sun at his shoulder. He remembered much, and none of it echoed even a brief suggestion of the sorrow he had felt, once, long ago, for his missing son.

He was remembering the battle, the chariot ride into the village, this very chariot, with arrows streaking through the dust-churned air around him, spears tossed and scimitars ringing like bells against swords and shields.

It was much unlike this ride. The acacias leaned in the direction of the strong prevailing wind. The air was clear. The only sounds were the hooves of horses all around, from his little army fighting a war against one lion. The king knew he was in no danger.

Without warning, the horses were released from their traces. They shot ahead while the chariots rolled to a stop. The Pharaoh of Egypt was struck speechless as light began to pour down from the sky, blinding him. A vast starship descended and hovered, radiating brilliant light upon Amenhotep III and his hunting party.

Then the king was lying on his side in a field where many men were toiling under the hot sun. He could not remember anything, not even his own name. Something exploded just above his shoulder and a violent sting jolted him to his knees. A soldier of Amen drew back the whip again. The naked man stumbled to his feet, still uncomprehending. The masses toiled, the guard whipped the confused, stumbling former king.

After the sunset and the end of the day's labor, the amnesiac king and workers sat around their campfires and joined their voices in song. The song they sang was one of pain they had felt every night for centuries, since the overthrow of Memphis by Thebes and the refutation of the rights of the peasants by the priesthood of the god Amen.

> "Work, my brother, rest is nigh—
>   "Pharaoh lives for ever!
> "Beast and bird and earth and sky,
> "Things that creep and things that fly—
> "All must labor, all must die;
>   "But Pharaoh lives for ever!"
>
> "Work, my brother, while 'tis day—
>   "Pharaoh lives for ever!
> "Rivers waste and wane away,
>   "Marble crumbles down like clay,
> "Nations dwindle to decay;
>   "But Pharaoh lives for ever!"
>
> "Work—it is thy mortal doom—
>   "Pharaoh lives for ever!
> "Shadows passing through the gloom,
>   "Age to age gives place and room,
> "Kings go down into the tomb;
>   "But Pharaoh lives for ever!"

Chapter Nine

The Queen took the news of her husband's disappearance with a stern countenance. Some of her handmaidens wondered if she had expected it.

Tiy ruled for five years. Her brother Ai, a fully initiated Priest of Aton, was her closest advisor, virtually her co-ruler. A just and merciful leader, she was beloved of the people of Egypt. During her reign no wars were fought and only one minor tribal uprising along the Nubian border had to be suppressed. This queen was not like Hatshepsut, who sent several slaves a day to the World of the Dead. Instead, Tiy shut down the sacrificial altars, allowing even the Priests of Amen only a few victims for sacrifice to their god.

General Horemheb was her military advisor, having become leader of Egypt's military under Amenhotep III. He used no force but instead used persuasion by musicians, poets and philosophers to expand Egypt's empire into Nubia. It was the same method by which, in ancient times, Osiris had joined Upper Egypt with Lower Egypt. Horemheb backed up his talented elite with ranks of spear-throwers and archers, but the effect was the same. Horemheb had become general of the court of the Pharaoh because he had learned and applied a lesson of history to the politics of his time.

Behind the palace walls the woman who was Queen and Great Mother of Egypt was making peaceful decisions and merciful judgements in political matters. The beauty of her judgements gave rise to her names among the peasants of Egypt: "The Solver of Problems" and "The Wise One." There had never been, nor would there ever be, such a loved and cherished Egyptian queen.

Tiy proclaimed many festival days and honored each seasonal celebration with greater and greater feasts. The Nile Valley was prospering: the trees offered their fruits on heavily laden limbs and the fields poured forth their grains. Abundance was everywhere. Worship of Tiy as a goddess spread through Egypt. The great queen who never seemed to age was the object of much mysticism.

𓂀

From the instant of the artificial conception of his new Horus-body, Shu lived in two bodies. His native body floated in a tank of hyperoxygenated water. Sometimes he awoke in his native body and other times he woke in the cellular cluster that multiplied inside the womb of Queen Tiy. This transfer of his personality had been made electrically before the implantation of the fertilized ovum cell.

The process of implantation had been one of horrible pressures, considerable pain and power surges, accompanied by a feeling of closeness with another human being: a soft, gentle mother who surrounded the growing embryonic body. The sleepy, floating times that followed were familiar to Shu from his gestation in the distant past as the genetically engineered star-king, Horus. The long dreamy process was experienced by a mature, intelligent mind rather than by a sleepy tadpole of human life in a uterus.

When Tiy walked, Shu felt the rhythms of her steps and knew that she was walking. When Tiy slept, Shu could feel the position of her abdomen, the sounds of her body, her breathing and heartbeat, and knew when she was asleep. When his embryonic gills turned into tiny foetal ears he could hear her voice when she spoke. She discussed political matters often. Sometimes she sang hymns to Aton or Isis or chatted with those friends whose company she enjoyed most.

When the time came for the sacred birth, the laboring Mother Tiy, her parents and her unborn child were teleported aboard the *Aton*. Fully awake in the body of the child, Shu again experienced the momentous contractions and pressures of corporeal birth. The pain was excruciating, the thrust of delivery ecstatic. As the tight birth aperture slid away from the baby's slippery body, Shu coughed the mucus from his mouth and nostrils and inhaled his new body's first breath of air.

The midwife who was also his wet nurse and the infant remained aboard the starship after Tiy and her parents were teleported back to the palace. Then *Aton* left orbit around Earth and returned to the city on Ganymede.

After the adventure of birth Shu lived only in the huge-brained Horus-body. Years passed, mere units of time to Shu, who was already over a million years old. He spent much time learning to function with those slender, elongated limbs, to stand upright first in light gravity and then in heavier and heavier fields until the one-G environment of Gaia was duplicated. Then he struggled to walk, hampered by his exaggerated torso. Under full gravitational pressure his limbs frequently collapsed and his wide pelvis refused to function.

"Very good," he told Tefnut and Tem after the first few attempts to stand and walk. "The pelvis is adequate: I am crippled."

Tefnut did not understand and her emotions emanated concern.

"Do not worry," said Shu in the strange body. "Thoth and Osiris were crippled, too. Horus could walk little better than this."

"But Horus was not living in danger, as you will be."

"Bless you, Tefnut. Your love for me manifests in such tender concern. I will be in far less danger than you imagine."

Tefnut was silent.

Shu continued working with his pathetic arms and legs. His swollen, distended abdomen was the result of his abnormal pelvis and his strange intestines: the descendants of this god-king would be meat-eaters, carnivorous humans, in order that the new race might survive a cataclysm. It was known that five hundred years after his reign as Amenhotep IV, the last big piece of asteroidal debris left by the exploded gas giant would plunge into the north Atlantean Ocean, vaporizing immense volumes of water and creating a volcanic scar, an island of conical lava. The ensuing ice age would devastate Europe and the north of Africa. New Kingdom Egypt would barely survive. The descendants of this extraterrestrial Pharaoh would have to live in a world bereft of vegetation, with nothing but the flesh of animals for sustenance.

Shu measured time not by years but by accomplishments. He forced the body to walk and learned to draw and paint with his new hands. He had Yod beam the Gnosis into his giant brain and created a memory of the Universe in its neurons. He inhabited the body as if it were his own. It matured and when it stopped growing it was quite large, taller in fact than Osiris. Shu functioned perfectly in the body. He looked forward to his return to Gaia. He grew eager to journey back to Egypt.

Stoneware alembics boiled over leaping flames as the Beast worked in his laboratory, experimenting with drugs. He was attempting to enhance his stolen memory of extraterrestrial science, which he applied to look like magic to the peasantry and to his priests. He recorded the results of his laboratory and psychic experiments in a book which he hid in a stone vault in the floor of his secret chamber. A series of papyrus scrolls written in hieratic script, it was Kahotep's most closely guarded secret.

The appearance of *Aton* did not impress him the same way it affected the common folk of Egypt. To The Beast it was not a god, but a visiting spaceship, a return of the star people who had cultivated the first humans out of primitive hominids. It was also a direct threat to The Beast. He was certain they knew of his existence, his method of prolonging his life, and his role as god in the worship of Amen, the religion of war.

The Beast had long ago experimentally determined certain patterns of heredity. He knew that some traits, including an animal's temperament, could be selected for. It worked in rats and dogs and it was working well in his breeding schemes to create permanently hostile dominant male humans. The inbred drive of males to kill other males, combined with the powerful desire to rape the women of conquered tribes, was designed by The Beast to overcome and negate the very traits imparted by the interstellar races to produce humans out of hominids.

Now the extraterrestrials were observing the effects of his genetic program. The starship people, the Amentii, had returned. They were openly displaying their starships to the people of Egypt. The Beast had no choice but to claim credit for the miracle of the sightings. The Priests of Amen declared that Amen was showing his material aspect. The peasants listened, but their simple minds understood that Aton was the most important aspect of Amen. Aton, the material disc, was manifesting to be worshipped. Thus, worship of Aton could include worship of Amen, god of war. But Amen remained hidden and Aton was revealing himself. So Aton could include Amen the way a pond or a lake or an ocean could contain a pebble.

The Beast considered that it was good that Amenhotep III had chosen to marry and make his queen the priestess of Aton, Tiy. Chosen before his birth to reunite the rival priesthoods of Thoth and Amen, Amenhotep III had also served to unite Amenism with the newly-emerging Atonism. The Beast had been spared the momentous task of scripting the unification of two religions, one of which he could not control. Amenhotep III had done it for him. But to what end?·

The Beast placed a dish of bread and seeds in the cage. Whiskers twitched from a shadow. In the next room, glass bottles glistened in the light of candles. The Beast had kept alive the ancient art of glass blowing and he hoarded several hundred alembics and bottles. His war-drenched economies had overburdened him with the expense, and his laboratories had deteriorated. Still, this laboratory was complete and he could function as chemist and biologist quite efficiently.

Returning from his hive of wire rat cages, The Beast sat on his throne in meditation. From the next room emanated a wave of fear which exploded into madness. A few moments of silence passed. Then the agonized voice of Amenhotep, Son of Hapu wailed:

"He is *coming!* He is *coming!*"

The Beast sat in silence, listening, remembering. The blind seer was more trouble to keep alive than he was worth.

"He is approaching!"

The blind seer always screamed these words, that someone, a man, was getting closer. For three, maybe four years, ever since the disappearance of Amenhotep III, this had been the pattern behind the seer's drastic fits of insanity.

When the Aton Disc had first returned, his words had been, "Beware the king who will rule with two queens!"

But many years had gone by since the Aton Disc had been seen over the cities. It reappeared only occasionally in the remote regions, the papyrus swamps or the deserts beyond the cliff-walled Nile Valley. The Beast interpreted this pattern as threatening. It had been too easy. Tiy had been whisked to the throne of Queen of Egypt because of her beauty, her precocious and charismatic intelligence, and partly due to events and circumstances that The Beast had not himself controlled. He feared an armed uprising of the peasantry and knew that Tiy alone stood between the assimilation of his religion of war by a stellar religion of peace. So Kahotep tolerated her. The fact that her only son had vanished after his birth gave The Beast no comfort, for The Beast no longer ruled Egypt, though he skillfully balanced the armies he yet controlled to maintain peace for Egypt. He did not want a war to break out while Tiy was in power for all orders and battle plans would come directly from the royal court, not from the Priests of Amen. So, for the duration of Atonist rule, The Beast could retain power only by prolonging peace along Egypt's borders.

He sent many spies to search for Tiy's missing son, Amenhotep IV, though he knew it was in vain. He knew that starships had a way of teleporting matter intact, including human beings. He knew starships could render themselves invisible. The Beast reasoned that the son of the king was not on the surface of the planet.

In his six thousand years of contact with the star people he had only once been aboard a spaceship and they had robbed his memory of the experience. He had tried many times to project his consciousness into the interior of a starship but could not. His imagination could not depict it and his out-of-body flights, the work of his deepest meditations, never revealed to him even a glimpse of such an image.

He had often plotted Tiy's assassination, but every time his plan fell to ruin because he knew that murdering her would result in the downfall of Egypt, the down-

79

fall of Amenism, and the time was fast aproaching when The Beast could no longer command the armies of Mitanni, of Babylon, of Nubia, nor of Egypt.

Now, for an uncomfortably long time, the starship Aton was gone from planet Earth and with it, the rightful heir to the throne of Pharaoh. He needed to know what those aboard the *Aton* knew of him, and what they would decide to do about him.

The Beast alternately listened to and tried to block out the manic ravings of the blind seer in the room next door. If only the chopped phrases would convey an entire message, like what their possible strategy against him was, or a premonition of an attack, confirmation of an invasion, a second coming…

Nothing. More noise. The seer was a lunatic, quite worthless. The Beast would evict him soon. Or kill him.

"He's coming! He's soon going to be here! He's *on his way,* do you hear, on his way, do you hear? He's on his way, his way, his way *home!*"

The Beast rose. He walked across the floor to the slab of stone, inset in the wall over the shaft through which the voice rose. There he froze. He heard something he had not heard from Amenhotep, Son of Hapu in years, twenty years at least. Not since the time of the sightings of Aton, north in a line over the Nile River.

Amenhotep, Son of Hapu, cried:

"Beware the king who rules with two queens!"

And then he broke into fits of tortured laughter.

PART III

THEBES

Chapter Ten

N o living thing witnessed the arrival. The tall, strange-looking man walked into the perceptual field of a cobra sunning itself on a rock. The snake reared back and hissed. The man with the long face and immense bald head glanced fleetingly to the side and half-smiled, not pausing in his weird, skipping gait that never touched the ground.

His appearance was awesome. The shape of his body was as unearthly as the shape of his skull. His shoulders were straight, his arms like a normal man's, but his abdomen protruded grotesquely and his hips and thighs bulged to the point of being huge.

His pelvis and skull had been designed to complement each other morphologically, but the purpose of the pelvis was twofold—to assist his female descendants in difficult childbirths, and to indicate in art to future generations the special origin of the human race.

The man was living Horus, returned.

No Egyptian would know the significance of the man's anatomy, except for the sullen, fearful and contemptuous Priest of Thoth who huddled in a secret chamber beneath the Temple of Karnak in the city of Thebes. The city, surrounded by its hundred-gated wall, was only a few miles away.

The man moved swiftly, his feet always a few inches above the ground. Under the deep dome of the morning sky, thin lines of light sparkled down like puppet strings, connecting his strange body to some unseen point in the sky.

When the sun had risen higher these rays became invisible. The man was striding between ploughed fields and peasant farmers were beginning to take notice of him. A slavemaster who caught sight of him screamed and ran away.

The new Horus glanced down at a dust-covered scarab beetle rolling a dung-ball through the dirt. To the tall, strangely beautiful man, the dung ball represented the planet that would one day be named after its soil: Earth. To him the beetle was like the Greek hero Atlas.

Another mile down the dirt road he came upon a man kneeling in fervent prayer. The man was dressed in a loincloth. He looked old, but was not. His skin was lined from harsh weather. He hastily ended his prayer, then looked up to see who approached.

"Do not let me disturb you," said the tall man with the huge skull. His voice was deep, yet calm and resonant.

"I was praying for my wife," the man said. "I prayed to both Amen and Aton. Her soul will face the Judge of Souls, whom I believe to be Osiris, but if it is Amen-Osiris, then I fear that Baba, the Soul Eater, might devour her. You...you are the answer to my prayers! Ah, but I thought the Amentii were small people! You, tall man, you—I can tell you are of the Amentii!"

The overpowering figure bellowed a booming laugh, then smiled down at the peasant. The small man jerked himself quickly to his feet after bowing three times dutifully.

The deep voice said: "Yes, the Amentii are often of small races, but many are your size and some are bigger. May I ask you, fellow human, do you doubt that your wife was happy and good in her lifetime?"

"Oh, she was a sweet and wonderful woman!" the peasant exclaimed.

"Then have no fear. Baba, the Soul Eater, shall find himself hungry again today." The huge man laughed.

The peasant bowed from the waist, then looked up eagerly again. "You have come to impart knowledge to me," he said, voice trembling. "Tell me, I must know: who is supreme, Amen or Aton? I am much drawn to the celebration of music and dance that Aton requires as tribute, but I am still mortal and...if Amen is truly Amen-Ptah, the One True God, then I am unworthy to meet him in the afterlife."

"You are not unworthy."

"I tremble in fear at the thought of killing someone, even if the enemies of Amen are not truly human beings, being unbelievers. But...I am an unbeliever, or at least, such puzzles fill me with doubts about both Amen and Aton."

"Have you ever seen Amen?"

"He calls himself 'The Hidden One'. He is everywhere, yet never seen."

"If Amen hides, then Amen is a coward. How can the One True and Only God be a coward?"

"You have come to bring me knowledge. My prayers have been answered. So—Aton is the One True God."

"Ptah is God. Ptah is the Universe, from soil to stars, and Ptah is the Original and Greatest Mind, in whose realm all things happen. There is no other God, no higher mind, than Ptah."

"Then...what is Aton?"

"Aton is that part of Ptah you can hear and touch and see, which comes from the stars, just like Ra comes out of the east to shine upon the land. Aton is the physical, material disc filled with living fire just like the blood of the sun itself."

"I will try to believe," the man said, raising his head and puffing out his chest. "I would like to see Aton."

"You will."

His eyes gleamed. "I have spoken to people who have witnessed the coming of Aton. In my grandmother's generation it is said that the Aton Disc even descended upon Thebes itself. The Disc of the Sun was seen blinding bright in the night sky."

"So do you believe," the towering man said.

"I have not seen Aton, but I see you with my living eyes." He bowed again, with awe and much reverence. "Thou art truly a mystical being," he said, addressing the mysterious being in the formal phrasing of his native tongue. "Tell me, if it doth not offend thee, but who art thou?"

"Your question does not offend me at all! Every living thing has a right to all the knowledge it wants. I am your king, and you are—Parennefer. Is that not your name?"

The man's eyes widened. His hands trembled. He bowed again, kneeling, with his hands folded over his head.

The giant man laughed again. "Do not be overzealous in your humility, fellow human. You and I are equals, even though I am your king and of the race you call the Amentii."

"Then you *are* the Amentii. That is why you look…so strange to my eyes. That is why you can read my thoughts and know my name."

"The Amentii are of many races, fellow human. One of those races is your own."

"Bless thee, O King!"

"Bless thee, wise human," the huge man sang, and then walked on the royal road to Thebes.

Tiy had shaved her head again. For the second time in her life, Egypt's queen had shaved her head.

The first time had been during the trip she had taken back to her homeland, a few years after her marriage to Amenhotep III. The journey of the conception of her first child, the one who had vanished the day of his birth. Now in her palace she shaved her head again, including her forelock, which was always spared the razor under Amenist tradition.

The Priests of Amen had departed the palace when a disturbance in the streets of Thebes drew their attention. A terrifying figure was walking swiftly through the avenues. As the figure approached, citizens fled in terror. It was the form of a bizarre, misshapen man. He was very tall, with unnaturally huge hips, a bloated, drooping belly, and an elongated, dome-shaped skull three times the size of a normal human head.

The man was naked. Amen, the One True God, had commanded all people to cover their loins. Genitals of both sexes had to be hidden by a scarab. This terrifying figure was naked. The people, shocked and horrified, knew by this that it was a demon.

The terrible man was walking straight to the Temple of Karnak.

A small contingent of War Priests of Amen surrounded the fast-walking figure and aimed their speartips at him. They remained at safe distance, however, for the figure so terrified them that they thought their war god himself might have to manifest and dispatch this demon. It was widely known that Amen lived in the Temple of Karnak. This demon, now climbing the wide steps of the temple, would find the One True God awaiting him!

As the towering figure reached the top step, the Queen of Egypt emerged from behind a pillar, also shockingly naked. The warrior priests drew back, spears lowered, as their queen walked forward with open arms and embraced the mysterious being.

The eyes of Thebes were upon them as they held each other for many long and loving moments. A vast crowd had assembled on the streets, pushing up to the steps of the temple. Multitudes poured out from their hiding places and pushed in massive tides. Curiosity was overcoming fear.

Queen Tiy and the strange man parted, still gazing lovingly into each other's eyes. Turning to face the crowd, Tiy lifted her arms and announced:

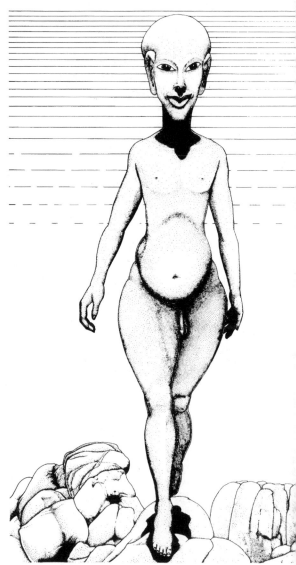

"Hear me, fellow Egyptians! I am your Queen and High Priestess of the god Aton. On this day I have been reunited with my only son who is your king, born of the race of the Amentii and a true son of Horus. He is Amenhotep the Fourth."

As her words fell upon the ears of the masses, murmurs rippled from mouth to ear, and from face to face uncertainty traveled, glance to glance. At length the realization that before them stood their Queen of Egypt with her new King gave rise to hails and cheers.

The strange-looking man bowed once, apparently painfully, then stood erect and looked out over the people of his nation.

After ordering the war-priests to disperse, Tiy and her towering son walked the passages between the pillars, strolling leisurely through the vast, dark temple. At first their conversation was sparse and consisted only of a few words of love sprinkled through breathless pauses and happy gazes, from eye to eye. They held hands as they slowly wandered the halls of Karnak.

"You have spent seventeen years in the Heavens," Tiy said at last, as her elation settled into bliss. "Tell me about the realm of the Amentii."

"The Amentii are many races. Many live in the Amentt, the world which surrounds us but which we cannot see. The world of space and matter emanates from the Amentt. The Amentii who who manifest in this world also live in space and matter, but separated from this realm by vast spans of time."

Tiy mused over this for several minutes, "The Amentt... the Amentii are many races? The Other World and the Heavens are home to different races of Little People?" Like all Egyptians, ideas fascinated her for their complexity and beauty, not for logical order nor demonstrable truth. She was excited. "The Amentii live in the Amentt—*and* in the Heavens?"

"The Amentt pervades all of Heaven and Earth. The Amentii live in worlds like this one. Some travel through time and space through the Amentt, the Other World that is invisible yet everywhere. Some move through the Heavens in boats of the sky that sail with the wings of Horus. This is how I have come."

As they talked, there stirred in the deep recesses of the labyrinth a trembling fear in the empathic field. In the buried room where the maze ended, the one who called himself Amen sat upright in his throne: a shiver chilled his spine and sparked his brain with alarm. He sweated and peered into the shadows of his dim chamber. Someone or something walking the corridors of the temple was disturbing Kahotep's clairvoyant field. When he sensed the presence of Queen Tiy, Kahotep was furious. He was trapped.

He summoned three from his Inner Circle of Twelve Chosen Guardians. Both of the High Priests and the High Priestess had been implanted with demons fashioned from The Beast's holographic imagination. Mere eye contact with the Hidden One meant risking such an implantation. The Twelve Guardians of the Hidden One unwillingly shared their minds with their master. When Teti, Pepi and Hatshepsut, Kahotep's three flesh-and-blood puppets, arrived through the chamber gate, Kahotep ordered them to their hiding places. He felt confident of these vantage points: when his disciples returned, he would see in their eyes whatever they had seen.

The three mute sentries took their posts. Hatshepsut peered down from a slot through a cornerstone. She could view four separate hallways. Pepi climbed to a tower overlooking the temple grounds, with a view that included the main entrance. This tower was the ceremonial obelisk at the start of the Avenue of the Sphinxes, built by Amenhotep III.

Seti, third of the Guardians, occupied a central vantage point over the zenith of the Central Dome, overlooking all the innermost corridors. These were perfectly dark, a labyrinth of sorts as these halls could not be navigated in darkness. Anyone wandering by torchlight would be revealed.

The new Horus stopped in the main hallway, feeling the presence of a spy nearby in some secret place. He held his human mother's hand and gazed into her eyes. "Egypt has bestowed some great names of respect upon you," he said in a soft, bottomless voice. "I have heard you have been called "The Wise Woman" and "Resolver of Problems." I am grateful that my beloved Egypt has been in such loving and gentle hands."

Tiy's wide lips drew back into a vast grin. Tears filled her kohl-edged eyes and she embraced her son.

They moved behind a pillar and sojourned away from where the ancient king sensed the woman spy was stationed. As he and Tiy neared the courtyard, Shu-in-the-body-of-Horus glanced at the obelisk and knew immediately that it was hollow. Even Amenhotep III had not known this. The new and ancient king also knew that another spy peered down from a horizontal slot at the top. As he strolled with Tiy, who did not suspect, he kept well back from the edge of the stone slab above their heads. Anyone in any of the vantage points he had sensed so far would only have glimpsed their feet or their shadows.

"You have been blessed with times of peace, Mother Tiy," the new king remarked. Tiy nodded. "Egypt has been blessed."

"All lands have been blessed, Mother Tiy."

She gazed up at him and nodded. "Nubia is discontented. But Horemheb has overseen diplomacy there. We have made many concessions to their freedom. We wish to coexist, not conquer."

"That is good to hear, Lady Tiy! I rejoice at the sound of those words. It is wonderful! We must always have peace with our neighbors."

They turned a corner and walked down the main corridor that led to the central shrine. Not even Queen Tiy had been allowed by the priests to enter there. They were met by a small band of defiant men, but the towering creature who called himself the new King of Egypt bellowed at them, "Be gone!" and they scattered.

Tiy volunteered to fetch a lamp, but her son declined. "I am accustomed to the darkness," he assured her.

They moved quietly down the corridors to the central shrine which was under a vast dome, unlit and drowned in absolute shadow. In the silence and a blind darkness only Amenhotep IV could see the terrifying fresco, the huge idol painted on a limestone slab rising above the altar.

The Horus-king sensed his mother's unease and led her out through the black tunnel. At the end of a sunlit corridor they found an exit and left the temple, having eluded completely the eyes of the spies of The Beast.

Walking up the steps to the palace, a bird perched on a flowering thorn tree glared with its beady eye at the queen and new king. It took flight abruptly.

Go, little messenger, thought the extraterrestrial king. *Tell your unholy master about me.*

The bird flew over the temple dome and down a shaft that led vertically into the depths. Through tiny tunnels and ventilation shafts the bird arrived at The Beast's chambers as he dismissed his unlucky servants. "Nothing," cursed Kahotep. "Nothing. No one saw it, whatever it is."

From beyond the stone wall came the voice of the blind seer:

"He is *back!* He is *back,* he is *back!*"

"Go, you! Mock me no more!"

The Beast leapt from his throne to furiously cover with the stone slab the shaft that communicated with the madman's chamber. The mocking, babbling prophet was alone in his cell.

The bird waited for silence to return to the room, then it sang a greeting in its native tongue.

The Beast turned abruptly, then slowly smiled. "Come, come, my little friend," The Beast whistled in a language he had taught the bird. "You have news for me. I can tell."

"Monster, man friend! A monster walks with the queen!"

"A monster?" Kahotep scowled. "What did it look like?"

"I cannot make picture," chirped the bird.

The man whistled a series of notes: "Please describe."

"Not-a-man," the bird sang.

"Please describe," The Beast warbled.

"No words."

The Beast scattered a handful of seeds for the bird. It hopped forward and pecked a few, then looked up. Both the tiny bird and the man heard a muffled laugh. It was the voice of the delirious Amenhotep, Son of Hapu, ringing through the wall.

Immediately upon entering to the palace the new king was greeted by the Inner Circle of Aton's priesthood: Ai, brother of the queen and High Priest, Yuia, High Priest and father of the queen, royal astronomer and calender keeper, and Thuya. mother of the queen, High Priestess of Aton and of Isis, royal scribe, philosopher and recipient of the Gnosis, imparted from the Aton Disc.

They were truly glad to see their true god-king in a living Horus body. Amid the glad chatter and shared smiles loomed the immediate matter of finding Horus-king a queen. His coronation should take place immediately to secure to him the throne of Egypt.

The meeting of the twelve prospective brides and the new king was arranged for that same afternoon. There were many priestesses of Aton to consider. The list of royal favorites was read.

Long before the secret time of the arrival of the new king had been whispered from ear to ear among Aton's Inner Circle, a tentative selection had been made: a beautiful young woman of eighteen years and high intelligence. She was adept at arithmetic, dabbled in astronomy, excelled at music and dance and she was the living image of Hathor. Her name meant "The Beautiful One Has Come": Nefertiti. She was loving and sensitive and her likeness to Hathor represented Horus and Hathor together again in Egypt.

This priestesses were informed in their rooms that the queen's firstborn child, her missing son, had returned. The star child was grown to manhood, one of the Amentii. Although the announcement had been made to all of the young priestesses, there was among them an understanding that the message was for Nefertiti. Instead of rushing to their polished silver mirrors to reline their eyes with stibium paint or don jeweled wigs, the young women encircled the loveliest priestess among them. They poured their adoration upon Nefertiti whom they all deeply knew would be Egypt's queen. Then the priestesses set about adorning themselves with their jewels, scarves, applying makeup, and preparing for the biggest moment of their lives.

Meanwhile, the royal tailors were trying to fit together a costume for their king, who was yet naked. The tailors and seamstresses were not taken aback by Amenhotep IV's unusual anatomy—they had been told that his body would be very different from theirs—but they were uncertain of their ability to fit him with clothes.

A belt was made to cover his loins, in keeping with the laws of modesty imposed by the god Amen.

The extraterrestrial king scoffed at this custom. "There should be no shame of the sex organs of the body," he chided High Priest Ai. "I know this," replied the slender, catlike man. "The Priests of Amen pour shame over everything."

The members of the royal household laughed, for Ai was testing the king's sense of humor. A huge grin pulled back the remarkably broad lips and the king's darl eyes sparkled.

"You seem not to take Amen's customs so gravely," observed Amenhotep IV.

Ai stood upright as if at attention. "Oh, but people who live under the Material Disc find it hard to take much of anything gravely."

Again, the small entourage burst into laughter. The king from the stars grinned immensely.

"If I would be lighthearted when I meet Osiris and the scale that shall weigh my heart," Ai said, "then I will practise lightness while I am here in this realm."

"That is supremely wise," smiled the king.

Ai bowed very slightly, then smiled.

Soon Amenhotep IV stood up from his stool and was fitted with a kilt of cotton woven so finely that it looked like a white film over his hips and thighs. A royal collar had been fitted with extra beads to widen it and it encircled the king's neck nicely. His eyes were lined with black stibium and his chin fitted with a plaited beard, glued on with resin. Sandals made for a very large man fitted his feet adequately and, although his walk was somewhat awkward, he strutted around the chamber in a humorous self-caricature that made the priests and courtiers shriek with laughter. The immense man responded with sillier poses and gestures, until his hip gave way and his huge body tumbled. Ai rushed to his side and, with another priest and a tailor, prevented the king from falling. They helped him back on his stool, whereupon the king laughed. Amenhotep IV was ready to receive the priestesses, among whom was his prospective bride.

He could barely fit in the throne of the former king. The armrests dug into his thighs, it was too small, too low to the ground, like a child's chair. Still, he squeezed into it, relaxed and allowed a smile to brighten his countenance. As strange as his face was, his smiles were glorious.

The young women were admitted into the reception chamber. Although they had been told that their king was not of their race, that he was physically different from them, they did not know what to expect. Being of the Amentii, they thought he would be small. He was not. He was over seven feet tall. His head was both dome shaped and elongated—and huge. The oddness of his hips and thighs made him look feminine, yet, they had been assured, he was truly a man.

Their initial response to the sight of their king was shocked surprise and horror, which they quickly suppressed. The king smiled knowingly as the twelve young women tried to regain their composure. Several shook uncontrollably. One of these was Nefertiti.

The High Priestess called their attention to the ceremony. They quickly overcame their surprise and performed what they had practised. They lined up before him and invoked Isis, shaking their sistrums and reciting poetry. One by one they read verses or sang hymns to the goddess, and then bade Isis farewell and broke the circle. The king was impressed. The Sisters of Aton danced before the king individually and took turns playing flute, lyre, oud, and drums as accompaniment. The Twelve Sisters of Aton ended by dancing together for Amenhotep IV while the High Priestess played a doumbek and High Priest Ai plucked intricate melodies on an oud. At the end the young women were lighthearted.

"Magnificent," said the strange looking man in his baritone voice, "You are all very beautiful."

"Speaking for our circle," said the High Priestess, "we are most gratified, O King. Bless thee. In the name of Aton, bless thee."

"With much thanks and deep gratitude, I receive your blessings, O Priestess."

Then the king gazed deeply upon the twelve Sisters of Aton. They lowered their eyes before the strange man cramped in the throne. Their smiles faded as the realization that one was about to be chosen to be Queen of Egypt dawned. Silence fell quickly over the room.

"There is one among you who looks at me," the king-to-be said slowly. "And the rest of you look at her."

It was true: one of the Sisters had taken a few small steps back, unable to look away from Amenhotep IV. The other priestesses glanced furtively at Nefertiti, to see her perhaps for the last time as a mere priestess.

Nefertiti stood tall and slowly a smile overcame her features, claiming first her mouth, then animating her eyes. She took one tiny step forward.

"Thou art a picture of perfect beauty," the king said to her. "You must be the one called Nefertiti, Please come forward."

The young woman with the black braided wig and modest crown of the Aton Disc walked gracefuly to a spot just before the throne and bowed. Then she stood and faced the strange king and smiled with absolute composure. In a melodious voice she said, "I hope my efforts please my king."

"I was most pleased and am certain Isis herself was greatly pleased." Amenhotep IV grinned, his huge mouth and wide lips drawing back over his great, elongated jaw.

Nefertiti gasped and fled, but was intercepted by her sisters at the door to the chamber. They huddled on the floor with her, heads together, stroking her shoulders and arms while she briefly wept. Then, after a time, she stood up.

"I frighten you," said Amenhotep IV bleakly.

Nefertiti nodded, her lower lip trembling.

"Is there not one of you who is unafraid of me?"

The sisters averted their eyes completely from the sight of the star-begotten man.

"It was explained to you that I am not of your race, but of the original race that came here from Sothis, even before the pyramids stood. Is that not true?"

"Yes, O King," the High Priestess said, "they were told. I informed them myself that there would be unusual physical differences."

"I understand. And still they were unprepared for the sight of me. I anticipated some surprise…even aversion."

"Forgive us, O King!" the high priestess exclaimed.

"Forgiven, of course. This was not unexpected."

The high priestess bowed several times and then backed away.

"Nefertiti," said Amenhotep IV, "you have the spirit of Hathor inside of you. Call upon that spirit whenever you need assistance, guidance, or protection from the danger or doubt. Self-doubt is your weakness. Remember Hathor and know that she is as much the spirit of beauty in a poem as in a blossom, of song and dance as well as dawn. The beauty of the love in your heart is as lovely as the grace in your face and body.

"Go now, Nefertiti, and know that as queen you shall live in the comfort of this palace and you shall be loved by all."

Nefertiti thrilled to the sound of the word "Queen." She lowered her eyes, then looked deeply into the immense, elongated eyes of the extraterrestrial man. Hastily, she bowed. The king raised his hand and blessed her, then she was gone.

☥ ☥ ☥

The king had chosen.

Nefertiti had displayed the most versatile musicianship. She performed with every instrument in the ensemble. She had been the most graceful dancer. As she overcame the shock of seeing the king for the first time, her tension was released as she performed. Her poetry was lyrical and sensitive. This, too, impressed the king. He praised her for her talent. Word of his choice spread rapidly throughout the kingdom.

Returning to the Sister's Harem, Nefertiti was received with adulation. She was also comforted by the priestesses and handmaidens, who anticipated the ordeal of such a marriage. All of the priestesses had been terrified by the appearance of the king. The high priestesses entered and told Nefertiti that she had been granted the choice of refusing to sit as queen beside the king. This was a gift from Amenhotep IV himself, with no mention of a royal reprimand.

"He will see you privately in an hour, Nefertiti."

Nefertiti found the king less grotesque in appearance than her initial impression. In fact, she marvelled at the perfect slenderness of his face and the immensity of his elongated eyes. He was reclining on a mountainous pile of cushions instead of sitting cramped in the throne. He looked more relaxed and even natural. He had removed his crown, but not his plaited beard. She gasped in awe at the size of his skull.

"Bless you, young blossom of the Nile," said the mysterious king, pleased to see that she was not as fearful of him as she had been.

"Forgive me, O King, please forgive me. You were not…what I had expected…"

"I am not anything you *could have* expected, Nefertiti," smiled the king.

"That is so," whispered Nefertiti. She moved closer to him, warmed by his understanding. The huge eyes of the king had begun to look infinitely compassionate in their depth, and his huge smile was no longer grotesque to her, though she was far from accustomed to his appearance. She knew empathically that he was not malevolent. She saw him as a weird giant, but she trusted him.

"You do not have to claim the throne, Nefertiti," said Amenhotep IV. "I can offer you the throne and my promise to be kind, gentle, and loving. You will be asked to do no more than any other Egyptian queen. You will dance at the festivals, sit beside me in pageants and greet visitors. We will do these things often, should you decide to join me. We will make ourselves accessible to many."

"My dear king," Nefertiti murmured as she sat gently upon the couch beside him, "I have much to offer ...the throne..."

"Of course you do, Beautiful One!" Amenhotep IV gazed down upon her with tender eyes. "Thou art far more than merely a lovely vessel of flesh. Thou hast been blessed with a deep and sensitive soul. I can see this in your eyes. State what is in your heart, Nefertiti."

Tears filled her eyes and her ears rang with the praise from the man from the other side of the sky.

"I have received an honor I fear I do not deserve. I stand in awe of you, for you are like no man or woman I have ever seen. Egypt has truly been blessed by Aton. I now see...that there is great beauty to your strange body. I feel little and insufficient beside you..."

He took her hand in his own and pressed it to his lips in a delicate kiss. He said quietly:

"You are the living image of Hathor reborn. I have seen your face two thousand years ago, when I walked this Earth as Horus, son of Osiris. For two thousand years I lived in bliss with Hathor, and for two thousand years she shared bliss with me. She was loved by Egypt just as you shall be, if you decide to be my consort. If you do not, I shall step to the throne without a bride but accompanied by Queen Tiy, who shall be my counsellor in any case."

"I understand," said Nefertiti, contemplating the significance of Tiy as the companion of her son at the coronation.

"It is your decision. You are under no obligation to me or to anyone, except your true self. Look into your heart now. Stroll by the fountain, wander the gardens, take as long as you like, Nefertiti, to think about it..."

"I have considered this deeply," she said, gathering firmness in her voice. "I will accompany you, Horus-reborn. I will be your queen."

"If you later reconsider..."

"I will not reconsider. I remember what you told me. At the pageant, when I saw you the first time..."

"Did you remember the spirit of Hathor?"

"Yes, and I remembered what you said about Lady Hathor as the spirit of beauty, and how beauty is not confined to any one form of beauty."

"Does this give your heart strength?'"

"Yes," she said breathlessly. "Yes it is what my heart needed to hear. Thank you, my King."

When the word reached the temples of Amen scattered throughout Thebes, the priests assembled in their council chambers to discuss their concern: that the Queen of Egypt had been tricked into letting an unholy monster claim the throne of Pharaoh.

Two challenges were agreed upon. In the catacombs of the Temple of Karnak a relic had been preserved. Taken from a remote, long-crumbled tomb, it was a huge triple conical crown, displaying the disc of Ra and the double Ma'at, the feathers of truth, fitted with a double Uraeus. These were the symbols of the cobra and the vulture, representing Upper and Lower Egypt in the battlefield mythos of the religion of Amen.

The priests felt that any demon claiming to be a successor to Horus should be challenged to wear this crown, attributed directly to Horus who lived many centuries ago. On the chance that the demon's infernal head might fit the crown, a second challenge would have to be made, but the priests were slow to decide what it should be.

Setuhotep the Wise, the High Priest of Karnak, offered to handle the challenge. He would face the claimant to the throne, the crown hidden in a huge box to be carried by four temple guards. They would enter when signalled, and the first of the two challenges to the Atonist king would be laid at his unsuspecting feet.

If a second or even a third challenge had to be made, Setuhotep the Wise had his own ideas of what it should be. He could enumerate no set plan, but he had some ideas. The weary and anxious priests agreed to leave matters to him.

The High Priest of Amen and his contingent arrived at the palace shortly after Nefertiti's departure. The guards bearing the giant box went to a side entrance while Setuhotep the Wise strode to the main entrance and requested to be taken to the man claiming to be the only son of Queen Tiy. He was immediately taken before the living replicant, who stood by the pillars of a small reception area beside the main palace rooms.

Setuhotep the Wise halted in his tracks and proceeded forward with cautious slowness as the giant turned to face him. The priest froze when the being looked him in the eye and grinned.

"You wish to see me?" Amenhotep IV asked.

The High Priest of Amen avoided looking into those laughing eyes again. He shuffled his feeta uncertainly, muttering to himself, "No, no, I cannot be deceived. This is not one of the Amentii. This is a demon! I cannot be deceived...!"

Then, gathering his courage, he rushed toward the extraterrestrial man and cried: "Demon, in the name of Amen, be gone with you!"

Amenhotep IV's eyes overflowed with mirth. He threw back his head and bellowed deep laughter.

Setuhotep the Wise choked back a scream. His throat gurgled and his eyes bulged. His knees shook violently.

"Tell your god I wish to meet with him," Amenhotep IV gleefully demanded..

"N-n-no one sees Amen," the priest finally choked out.

"You summoned Amen to banish me. You still see me. Where is Amen?"

The High Priest of Amen backed up against a pillar and forced himself to stand erect. The creature before him was only mocking his god, not attacking him physically, so he feigned courage. "We will see if you are a true son of Horus. We will see! For—here is the very crown that Horus once wore!" He shouted a command.

Footsteps echoed between the columns. The guards hurried in carrying the heavy wooden box containing the crown. When they saw the monster, they halted, deposited the crate near the door and backed fearfully away, tumbling over each other in their haste.

"Are those the guards of the War Priests of Amen?" sneered the big creature.

"Here! In this b-box is…is a crown once worn b-by Horus h-himself! If you are a true son of Horus, then this crown will f-f-f-fit you…!"

As he struggled to open the box, the high priest began to have doubts about the Crown of Horus as a definitive test to put to this demon. His head looked so big— and so long!

Amenhotep IV helped the trembling priest open the big box. The frightened man recoiled from his presence. The son of Queen Tiy smiled and recognition flashed in his eyes as he lifted the crown.

"Ah, my old crown!" smiled Amenhotep IV, his voice rolling with satisfaction. He lifted it to his immense head and fitted it on. Perfectly.

"No, no, I cannot be seeing this!" the High Priest of Amen moaned, crawling away on his hands and knees. "N-n-n-no! No, no! This cannot be!"

"What other thing must I do to convince you? I am a true son of Horus. In point of fact I *was* Horus in another body, two thousand years ago."

"No! I do not believe you!"

"Then, behold! I summon the Amentii!" Amenhotep IV raised his arms. In his hands were the crook and the flail. He was in telepathic contact with the captain of the starship *Aton* and these gestures were a prearranged a signal for a "real" manifestation. Two holograms of a pair of particularly large-brained humanoids from a planet in the Procyon system were projected in pillars of light on both sides of the man who had come to claim the throne.

Setuhotep the Wise could not tell a hologram from a living thing and scrambled wildly away on his knees. He snatched an amulet from beneath his tunic: the Utchat, the Eye of Horus, most powerful of all protective symbols. The terrified priest screamed the first few words of an exorcism prayer. But when Amenhotep IV realized that the symbol of his former incarnation, fashioned out of ceramic and glass, was being used as a magickal weapon against Horus himself, he bellowed with laughter

Leaning forward, he caught the piece as it fell from the hysterical priest's hand. "Let me see this trinket, this Eye of Horus." He examined it, held it up to the light. "The workmanship is not bad," he hummed.

The holograms of the Procyonians continued to stare at the horrified priest until he panicked utterly and fled.

"Please deliver two smaller crowns like this!" the king called after the fleeting figure. "Hathor had many made. Please find those other two that are not too large in size!"

The king's baritone voice echoed louder than the running footsteps. He knew that Setuhotep the Wise had certainly heard him.

As the Priests of Amen were reconvened to hear the terrifying tale told by Setuhotep, the coronation of the new king was beginning. The citizens of Thebes were assembling on the garden hillsides of the royal grounds adjacent to the temple of Aton. The word of the arrival of the new king had spread among the peoples of Egypt as if whispered by the wings of many falcons.

While being attired in his dressing room, Amenhotep IV summoned Ai. The priest was being adorned in costume for the part of Horus. Amenhotep asked him for the script to the ritual. A page returned with the king's scroll. Amenhotep IV read it critically.

"This is the version that the Priests of Amen have left us. I have a few changes to make." Drawing a writing brush and an ink stick from a box beside his elbow, he ground the ink stick in a stone water tray the royal scribe placed before him. He frowned while he read.

Shortly he announced, "I will remove the part of Seth entirely. Seth is not the enemy of Osiris. Osiris resides much of the time on Sothis. So Seth must have a different reason for delivering a riddle to Osiris. I will submit a version consistent with the reality of the Aton disc, which all of Egypt will see again. It will be one in which the riddle is not accompanied by a pantomime of conflict. I will omit this mock battle of staves before the riddle is stated. I will substitute Thoth for Seth. That shall be the greatest amendment. There are other minor changes to be considered."

"Is this permitted?" a priest of Amen asked cautiously. He had listened in mute astonishment to this violation of tradition.

Amenhotep IV looked at the priest, then to Ai, then to Queen Tiy. "It is permitted if it is permitted by the Queen of Egypt."

Queen Tiy was grinning expecantly. "Of course I permit it."

The changes were made.

The high, stepped outdoor theatre in the vast courtyard of the Temple of Aton was filled by legions of worshippers of the Material Disc. They sat on the ground in rows between the eight aisles radiating from the stage toward the cardinal directions: north, south, east, west and the cross-quarters. The innermost row formed a circle around the pyramidal, flat-topped stage. Between that row and the stage itself was a circular white wall, a model of the hundred-gated wall that surrounded Thebes itself.

In the center of the stage was a circular table upon which was a heart-shaped box made of rubies. It contained a ceramic scarab, a balance scale and a ceramic feather. Around the ruby box, in a circle, was a crystal ball in the north , a tray of incense burned over a candle jar on the eastern side, a bowl of salt, a wafer of oats crushed with ground barley, and a crystal vase filled with spring water beside a silver goblet in the west.

Beyond the table, before an obelisk jutting into the sky, stood three thrones. Two Priests of Aton walked through the eastern and western aisles up the steps of the stage and seated themselves on the smaller thrones beside the royal throne. On the west sat Horus; to the east sat Thoth.

The new king also arrived out of the east. The horizon of the rising sun was symbolic of rebirth to the Egyptians, and every coronation was a time of national rebirth. However, the crowd stirred with awe and muttered misgivings. Many of the common people who had been frightened earlier that morning by the strange human being who had then, too, appeared from the east, again saw that same terrifying apparition in the form of their king. The rumor of the new king had been accompanied by word that he was somehow different from ordinary human beings. But the huge, strange man before them stretched to the limit the meaning of the word "divine." To many, the strange man looked evil.

The king ascended the eastern stairs. He stood before the table, facing Horus and Thoth in their thrones. Both stood to greet the king. They faced him, holding the crook and the flail crossed over their chests.

Thoth challenged the new king with a riddle to test his authenticity as Horus. "What is the meaning of the Sphinx!"

Amenhotep IV smiled. "The Sphinx is the essence of the tribe of men. For men have the nature of the beast in their bodies, the essence of love and the beauty of Hathor in their faces, and they all aspire on the wings of spirit, which they are still learning to master."

Thoth and Horus exchanged glances. Then they nodded. Thoth proclaimed the riddle correctly answered and they handed a crook and a flail to the new king, who accepted them and crossed them over his chest. The remaining crook, held by Thoth, and flail, held by Horus, were placed on the table.

The succession of Horus to Osiris was begun by Horus, bowing to the king, the Horus reborn. He blessed the king with the fragrance of incense and said, "May you cherish the essence of intelligence." He offered the king a goblet of spring water. "May you be blessed with the essence of love." He tossed a pinch of salt over the left shoulder of the king. "May the Earth nurture you." He offered the king the wafer. "May you draw from these grains the fire that is the essence of life." Horus and the new king bowed to each oather, then bowed facing the crowd.

The immense size of the king's head was a matter of amazement to everyone by now, and those nearest the stage were most uneasy. They were calmed when the new king spoke a few words about the crook and flail, about guidance and wisdom and restraint from any form of violence. The strange new king spoke clearly and eloquently.

He was crowned symbolically twice, once for Upper Egypt with a red crown presented by Thoth and again with a white crown presented by Horus. Both crowns were ridiculously small for his head. Thoth and Horus stepped back. The eastern and western thrones were elevated. A small procession approached from the east bearing Queen Nefertiti and a similar procession out of the west bore Queen Tiy. Four men carried a box up the southern aisle and all met at the base of the stage.

The crowd was beginning to see humor in the coronation, in which the man-sized crowns were perched like tiny birds on the king's huge head. With the sudden appearance of Tiy and the beautiful Nefertiti, the crowd was awestruck. The two queens mounted the steps, as did the men carrying the huge box. All met upon the platform and the box was opened.

"Behold!" said the new Pharaoh, "The triple-crown of Horus!"

The crown was lifted from the box and placed on the head of the extraterrestrial king.

Beside him to the west sat Tiy, and to the east, Nefertiti. They wore crowns identical to his but only a third as big. Their crowns also fit perfectly.

Pharaoh Amenhotep IV stood again and was led by Horus down the stairs to the circular white wall. Climbing steps over the northern arch, the king faced the obelisk and walked around the wall three times clockwise, then sang a hymn of promise to protect Egypt forever, even after death.

With Horus about to become the new Osiris and Amenhotep IV about to become the new Horus, the priest in the Horus mask lifted the ruby-inlaid lid of the heart-shaped box and raised the scales to eye level. As he placed the ceramic feather on one tray, Amenhotep IV placed the scarab onto the other, and the two trays remained level.

Then Thoth opened a scroll and addressed the new king, asking him to recite his sacred tutelary. The Five Great Names of the King consisted of his Horus name, his Neby (Two Ladies of Upper and Lower Egypt name), his Golden Horus name, and his prenoumen and noumen. Four of these names were magickal in content, and would only be heard in public once. Only his noumen would be used as his name.

Turning to address the crowd, holding the crook and flail crossed over his chest, Amenhotep IV announced: "The king of the south and of the north, Nefer-kheperu-Ra-ua-en-Ra, giver of life, son of Ra, loving him, Amenhotep, God, governor of Thebes, great in the duration of his life and the great royal wife of Nefertiti, living and young."

With that, the coronation was complete and the king held out the crook and flail at arms' length and announced:

"Let the Heb-Sed Feast begin!"

The king's entourage noticed that the king ate only meats, not grains nor vegetables. His diet was different, he explained, because his descendants would live in a world without any plant life and in which dead meat would not only be plentiful, but it would not rot for years. When asked to explain, he merely stated that no one present was ready to understand, but that eventually many people would.

As the festivities went on into the night, it became obvious that Nefertiti was experiencing some growing discomfort. Her lovely face was hardened, eyes downcast, mouth unsmiling. After the feast and during the music and dance, Amenhotep IV asked her to slip away with him for a brief walk. They strolled by a great rectangular pond, far from the crowd of celebrants.

Amenhotep IV knew what was bothering his new queen: she was brooding over her aversion to his physical strangeness. She was struggling against the dread she felt at the obligation to please her strange husband sexually. As a priestess, she had chosen to retain her virginity as a commitment to a king she might have been asked to marry, and now that she had ascended the throne of queen, she felt revulsion at the prospect of consummating her marriage.

The man in the bizarre, genetically engineered body determined to set aside all of her doubts. He took her arm in his and gazed at her, smiling.

"Do not fear me, Nefertiti. You are lovely in face and body, and far lovelier still in your heart. You are very sensitive, so much so that you are vulnerable. I want your marriage to me to be one of love. Know that I will not hurt you, especially in our marriage bed."

Upon hearing his words, Nefertiti burst into tears. The king put his arms around her and embraced her sympathetically. Slowly she wove her own arms around him, and hugged his birdlike chest and swollen belly.

She spent the night dreaming in her bed. Beside her sat the strange being, her husband, the King of Egypt. He stayed beside her all night, seated with his legs folded under him, his hands were cupped in his lap, his head erect. His eyes were half closed in meditation.

By morning it was apparent that the strange king did not sleep in the way of ordinary humans. When Nefertiti awoke, she saw the yellow sunlight falling upon him, sitting in the same position as when she had fallen asleep the night before.

Chapter Eleven

The day after the coronation of Amenhotep IV, all of Egypt echoed with the news of the arrival of the king from the stars. The words were not entirely favorable: the Priests of Amen described the new king as a monster, possibly a demon. Furthermore, the High Priest of the Temple of Karnak had resigned from his post the very day of the coronation. It was rumored that Setuhotep the Wise had gone mad.

Although the new king overheard these rumblings, it was apparent that the dark mood was not shared by all Egyptians. The peasants were relieved to know one fact: that Queen Tiy had not stepped down from her throne. The news that queens Tiy and Nefertiti would rule Egypt as equals to Amenhotep IV himself gave the citizens the reassurance they needed that the one they venerated as the "Wise Woman," the "Solver of Problems," the "Mother of Egypt," was still to be their queen, and her power would be shared and not usurped by the strange king she called her son.

Amenhotep IV was eager to tour his new land. After a breakfast of baked river perch, his tour of Thebes began. The king, his two queens, and his uncle Ai, High Priest of Aton, rode chariots down the Avenue of the Sphinxes between the Temple of Karnak and the Temple of Luxor.

On the steps of the Temple of Luxor they were met by a Priest of Amen named Xepuru-Ra. He was a young man, overzealous and well-versed in the dogma of his war god. He announced his intention of conducting the tour. Amenhotep IV consented. The young priest did not seem to fear the tall, odd-looking king. But he also did not seem very intelligent, neither imaginative nor logical. He was enthusiastic, but even then about nothing in particular.

Xepuru-Ra expounded the history of his temple. Inside he immediately and proudly led the entourage to a mural painted in honor of the builder of the temple.

"This depicts your father, Amenhotep III, in glorious battle against the Nubians. It was in his fifth year as king. He rode in his chariot with the Egyptian army, and even led the victories fought by his friends in Babylonia and Mitanni, and even the armies of the Assyrians. So great was his reputation as a general that the kings of friendly empires called upon him. This battle scene depicted shows the Nubians slaughtered in a battle fought entirely by Amenhotep III. Here it shows him slaying his enemies firsthand—"

"Say no more. This is repulsive to me."

There was a shocked silence. The young priest of Amen was stunned. He stared.

His jaw fell slack and he gasped audibly.

Ai began to smirk, covered his mouth, chortled, then burst into laughter. Nefertiti looked bewildered, then embarrassed. Tiy smiled in amusement. Ai continued to laugh hysterically, then regained his composure.

The King spoke. "So, Pharaohs still fight wars? Egypt has not grown wise, Egypt has grown terrible. When Thoth and Osiris came to this world, we saw primitive people fighting *everywhere*. We hoped this would change. Were we fools? Can human beings *not* be cultivated from savages?" The awesome king strode past the stunned priest. "What do these scenes depict? The taking of captives?"

Defiantly, the temple spokesman said: "More than *three hundred rebels* were killed, and more than *seven hundred captives* were taken. Seven hundred slaves! And the more noble of the captives were sacrificed to Amen...!"

"*Slaves?* Human beings sacrificed to Amen?"

"The slaves lighten the labor of the peasants! Women slaves make good pets. And Amen demands sacrifice. Remember, these are not human beings. They are Nubians. Black-skinned. The more noble, the more intelligent, become food for the Hidden One."

"Human sacrifice. To Amen. How obscene."

"No! These things have *always been!* You mentioned Thoth: we still offer Thoth sacrifice of intelligent dark-skinned manlike Nubians. Remember, the Enemies of Amen are not really human, they do not have souls..."

"Even blades of grass have souls."

"No! They are judged by Amen-Osiris in the Tuat, after death..."

"All things are judged equally after death. Then all things are reborn. Death purifies. Only when a world is sick does death lead to more death."

"No! No! You speak lies! You are an enemy—an enemy of Amen!" Xepuru-Ra thrust forward a double Utchat and covered his own eyes. There was silence until Ai started laughing again.

Xepuru-Ra peeked through his fingers at the "demon" still standing before him.

Amenhotep IV asked: "If Amen is the One True God, how could he have made so many enemies?"

"The world does not yet believe! When all worship Amen, then Amen will have no more enemies and the world will be pure. We are making the world pure!"

"Then will war cease?"

"Yes!"

"Then will human sacrifice cease?"

"Yes!"

"Then will slavery be abolished?"

"Yes. I mean, I think so...No, no, you tricked me! You ask too many questions! Amen says that only clever deceivers ask too many questions. Amen says it is better not to ask any questions at all, unless you do not understand orders or the will of your superiors…"

"Say no more. Are people being held nearby, awaiting human sacrifice?"

"Of course!" Xepuru-Ra beamed. "Amen lives in Karnak, so those chosen to give their lives for Amen are kept in the temple grounds."

The king looked at Queen Tiy. "Has human sacrifice been conducted during your years as queen?"

Tiy was ashamed. Her smile vanished in a gasp, and she stammered, "I…I tried to forbid it. I even composed a formal proclamation against it, but the scribes would not record it because they feared breaking tradition, and the Priests of Amen openly defied me."

"The Priests of Amen defied the Queen of Egypt?"

"I beg you!" Xepuru-Ra stepped forward, albeit cautiously. "I recall no such proclamation, with pardons, O Queen."

"You were not informed of them because no one would carry my words on this ugly matter. Not beyond the walls of my own palace."

"Enough!" said Amenhotep IV. "Take me to Karnak and where slaves await this so-called 'honor.' "

A messenger was sent to the palace to summon the royal scribe. The king, two queens and priest Ai walked back along the Avenue of the Sphinxes to Karnak. Xepuru-Ra had been ordered to accompany them, despite his growing resentment.

Within the Temple of Karnak twelve men were held in a dark cell awaiting sacrifice. Others were confined in a corral of plaster and brick walls set in a trench several cubits deep Many other slaves in groups of a hundred or more were confined in similar enclosures within all the other temples of Amen throughout Egypt.

The king and his entourage, plus one offended priest, arrived at the outer chambers for the sacrificial victims just as Apy, the royal scribe, appeared between the clay and brick hovels.

"So these are the condemned," spoke the King in his rumbling deep voice which was shaded in tones of utter sadness. The king's huge head bent to peer down through the loose slats of the ceiling boards at the starving, terrified mortals. They scampered back into the shadows, turning into pairs of eyes peeping over folded knees. Whimpers and moans of fear and misery stirred the dung-stenched air.

Then, the weird king faced Xepuru-Ra and asked: "Where are the others?"

"There are six more inside the temple."

"Apy, please record everything that is about to transpire."

The royal scribe nodded, dipped his brush in ink and poised it above a papyrus scroll.

"Do not fear me," said Amenhotep IV, speaking into the darkness in which the doomed were huddled. "I am your new king." Then, to Xepuru-Ra: "What have these men done to deserve such punishment?"

There were murmurings from inside the pit.

"They have done nothing," stammered Xepuru-Ra, his voice holding back notes of anger and fear. "It is an *honor* that they have been chosen for sacrifice to Amen!"

"Honor? What honor? I know of no honor that separates people allowed to live from others marked for death."

The priest was furious. "It is *tradition*! It has nothing to do with deeds done. It is *tradition*! But when criminals are condemned to death, the High Priests of Amen call in the ones among them who know the secret sciences of Amen. The heads of all the captives are measured and those favored by Amen are—"

"Measured? Their heads are *measured* for sacrifice? Is that how Amen's victims are chosen?"

"I do not know! It is a secret science—"

"Secret sciences and temple mysteries! Secrets, secrets are everywhere! This is foul! I will meet with the High Priests of Amen."

"They will not meet with you."

"Why not?"

"They say you are a demon which, no doubt, you are."

"They serve a demon, since they serve death to their god Amen."

"That is blasphemy!" Xepuru-Ra leaped back, arms held out, trembling. "You defame the One True God!"

To Apy the scribe, Amenhotep IV said: "Record this: on this, the second day of Epep and the first day of my reign as King of Egypt, I, Amenhotep IV, declare that all human sacrifices to Amen or Thoth or any other gods shall hereby be abolished forever and care will be taken to swiftly return all who have been interred to their homes and families. Furthermore, all shall be returned well fed, bathed and suitably clothed, and with the blessings of Aton upon them. This is by order of the King of Egypt, Amenhotep IV. So be it."

Silence stood in the chamber until Apy looked up from the hieratic figures that danced across the papyrus scroll. "It is written."

"Good. We shall continue." To Xepuru-Ra, he commanded: "Do not run away from me. Stand still—by order of the king! We have much to converse about, my poor friend. Tell me about these 'criminals.' This one, stepping from this hell-pit, what was his crime?"

"*I* know not. Ask *him*."

"Yes, I will. Please, fearful one, approach me and know I am not of your race. Who art thou and what was thy crime?"

"I am a peasant. I work the fields of the sacred granaries and my family was starving, for they also toiled. I was accused of stealing grain."

"I understand. Did you steal it?"

In psychic agony, terrified of lying to the strange man, the peasant finally answered: "…Yes."

"Set him free. If any in Egypt are starving, let them be fed from the sacred granaries."

The shocked silence that followed ended when Xepuru-Ra uttered, "The sacred grains...*fed to the vulgar folk?* No!"

"Do the gods ever claim these offerings of grain?"

"We store the grain for them for when they will come!"

"Have they ever come?"

The priest of Amen was silent.

"Answer me."

"I do not know. I have never inquired into that matter."

"I have." Ai stepped forward.

"Oh? And what happens to the sacred grains?"

"They are stored for seven years, then removed to make room for more grain."

"I see. Where is the old grain removed to?"

"Far from the towns, where it is scattered over the land. By day the birds feed on it and by night the rats dine."

"But not the poor people of Egypt."

"Oh, no! The Priests of Amen say the grain is too good for that! It is fit only for the gods. So, of course, the rats get it."

"What a horrible mockery of religion! What a gross application of the principle of paying tribute to the soil! No! This condition must cease! Apy, have you recorded all of this thus far?"

Apy nodded, grinning.

"Very good. I continue my pronouncement: on this, the above date, I, Amenhotep IV, Pharaoh over all of Egypt, consign all grains previously reserved as offerings to any and all gods to be diverted to the poor and hungry among the peasantry. Furthermore, all scribes and recordkeepers previously employed to take inventories on grains shall be assigned to the task of dispersing all grains. Finally, all priests whose tasks included gathering sacred grains shall serve a duty of seeking out the poor and hungry and delivering grains to the cooking houses where it shall be ground into flour and baked as breads, or soaked in water and cooked and served in that way. I, the king, shall delegate the necessary duties to chosen representatives and shall recruit overseers to coordinate these feasts. By order of the Pharaoh, Amenhotep IV, so be it."

Apy recorded the pronouncement, then looked up.

"Who shall you choose?" Xepuru-Ra snapped defiantly. "Who can you trust to this?"

The king looked compassionately at the bent, crippled figures moving awkwardly out of the mud brick prison. "I shall find people willing to move food to the hungry among them," he said.

"This is obscene! Everything you do and say is obscene!"

"Do you truly think so? Is not this pit of misery obscene to you?"

"It is common! It is *normal* for the chosen to suffer in their final moments! It even makes their departure to the Tuat all the more swift. Their suffering is *humane*."

"There is no humane suffering. Ask them. You are too well fed to know of what evil you speak, Xepuru-Ra, High Priest of Amen."

"Thou art surely a demon," he gasped.

"If I am a demon, then exorcise me from this realm!"

Chanting an incantation, Xepuru-Ra flashed an Utchat, then a double Utchat in front of the towering figure. When they failed to have any effect, he swiftly replaced them in his bag and drew out an ankh. He held it in the Pharaoh's face and screamed a long list of commands and threats, always ending with the words: "In the name of Amen—be gone!"

Soon his voice faltered, his knees shook and buckled, and when every spell he knew was exhausted, the devastated temple priest fell to the ground. Everything he had been taught to believe to be true crumbled in his mind. He trembled and fainted, still clutching the ankh.

"I, Amenhotep IV, hereby proclaim that theft of the food that has been reserved for temple offerings to be no longer a crime. I proclaim that the displacement of any peasant from his land to be a crime punishable by a fine equal to the value of the acquired land, and that such fines shall be paid to those who have been displaced. Further, all death penalties shall be suspended and never again shall death ever befall a citizen of Egypt for the commission of any crime whatsoever. By order of the Pharaoh, Amenhotep IV. So be it."

The last of the suffering skeletal figures had hobbled through the gate and all were standing at the edge of a dry field, looking bewildered and dazed.

"Bring water," the king ordered his messenger. "Immediately."

The boy ran between the hovels toward Karnak.

When the temple servants arrived with water gourds, they nearly refused to serve the former prisoners. The king towered and commanded them personally, and repeated his dictates. He assigned Ai to oversee the feeding and bathing of the hungry citizens of Egypt. Then the king and the two queens walked back toward the palace.

Tiy and Nefertiti noticed that the king himself was suffering, though neither suspected how painful it was for this strange creature to walk under the gravity of Earth.

By noon the heretical proclamations of the new king had been announced from the temples of Aton throughout all of Thebes. By evening, most of Lower Egypt knew that all sacrificial victims had been freed and food offerings to the gods were being distributed to the poor and hungry.

As he recovered from his bone-crushing walk from Luxor and his chariot ride to Karnak and back, Amenhotep IV continued to employ the royal scribe at the task of recording conversations.

"Mother Tiy, you mentioned that court officials were reluctant—in fact you said *unwilling*—to cooperate with you in abolishing the sacrifice of men to the gods. Why do was this so?"

Tiy shook her head angrily. "I think it was because Amen is so feared, both as a war god and as a hungry god. Sometimes I fear it was because I am a queen instead of a king, my son."

Amenhotep IV nodded. "I think both are valid reasons, Mother Tiy."

"What can we do to change the way things are?"

"We can change our lives to fit what we ought to be, then offer ourselves as examples of how best to live."

Tiy nodded thoughtfully.

Amenhotep IV looked at Nefertiti "Have you anything to say, my Queen?"

Nefertiti looked away abruptly. She was silent.

He returned to Tiy. "Let it be known that I, Amenhotep IV, shall weigh the opinions of any woman present in my court as equal to the advice of my male court officials."

Apy scribed.

"That is informal. It is not a proclamation. I only want it recorded for sake of posterity."

There was another quiet interval, then Tiy inquired of her stellar son about her vanished husband, Amenhotep III.

"You really loved him, did you not?"

"Yes," she said, "although I perceived much ignorance in him. He could have learned much, and yet he loved playing the game of being king, acting out the role of king, so much that he heard no voice but his own."

"I understand that."

"Tell me, where is he? In the Tuat, the Realm of the Dead?"

"He is not in the Realm of the Dead. He is in the Amentt—the Hidden World."

"So you told me yesterday. That is one of the first things I asked you."

"Yes, Great Mother!" He laughed gently. "How we were diverted from our first conversation by the business of the coronation! There will be five more days of the Heb-Sed Feast. Now we will be feeding the mouths of those who need a feast most."

Tiy sighed and nodded. Nefertiti blinked back a tear.

"Please do not fear for your former husband! He now lives in another Egypt, and although he is not king there, he has become a rather prosperous peasant. He shall grow old and die with a little wealth, if not some happiness. He does not remember having been king, so he has no sadness of loss."

"It is well. He tolerated much that I privately felt was evil."

The king gathered his mother's hands in his. "Speak boldly to me whenever you see or feel the presence of evil and I will banish it. If need be, I will even summon the Aton disc to intervene. You are right. There is great evil in Egypt. You will rejoice, for there is at last great good at hand."

⚱ ⚱ ⚱

That evening the first group of what would become multitudes of pilgrims arrived to see the King from the Heavens. The cluster of eager peasants consisted of two men, both residents of Thebes, who had been released from sacrificial bondage, plus the remnants of their impoverished families. All had participated in the feast and wore new clothing for the first time in their lives. The three children had never before eaten well. The two families, seven people in all, still shocked by the unexpected reunion.

They were stopped at the palace doors by guards who nearly refused to admit them. Ai overheard and came to investigate, then took it upon himself to jovially invite the trembling, grateful peasants inside.

"Yes," a man whispered to his wife, "He's the one I told you about, the man who's always laughing!"

They were led to a simple unfurnished room of great size. By a far window sat a large figure on a high stool, gazing out at the yellowing sun. They rushed toward the man in their eagerness, but fell short of him and groveled, prostrate, with their arms outstretched.

"Bless thee, bless thee, O King!" they sobbed, their voices quavering with religious passion. "Thou art a *good* king, thou art *good!* Bless thee, bless thee!"

"May much good be upon thee," said the king. He smiled at each one, looking into their eyes, relaxing them with his empathic gaze.

"We rejoice!" one of the men exclaimed shakily.

"I am glad," laughed the king.

The women and children regarded him from behind lowered lids. The crown on his vast cranium fascinated them. They had expected the plaited beard on his chin, which oddly seemed to fit his elongated face. His smile conveyed benevolence.

"Tell me your names."

"Hep," said one.

"Aref," said the other. He put his arm around the young woman beside him, obviously very proud to be married to her. "This is my wife, Nifu."

"Bless you, bless you all. Have you joined the Heb-Sed Feast?"

"Why, yes!" Hep was first to stand.

"May we?" Hep's wife lowered her eyes. "Would it be…proper?"

"Have you ever been excluded from a festival before?"

"Yes…" the woman started to say, but her husband silenced her with a prod of his elbow.

"Please tell me," said Amenhotep IV.

"We beg for scraps left after the feast. Often…we are excluded."

"Tributes," said Hep. "Tributes are expected from us. At each festival."

"I understand. Go now. That is another injustice that will change. Go. And bless thee."

They showered him with their blessings once more, then Ai led them down the corridors to the palace's festival grounds.

Things are far worse than I expected, thought the extraterrestrial king as he laboriously stood and walked to the door.

☥

The bird had been no help. The demons in the eyes of his Inner Circle had been unable to glimpse any image of the new king. He must be extremely clairvoyant, the Beast deduced, for he has walked the grounds of Karnak and turned every corner and remained behind walls and pillars that kept him out of view of their hiding places. The twelve spies were useless, seated at the stone table, staring sightlessly into the darkness. Kahotep ordered them to return to the invisible slots in their hideaways to further attempt to catch sight of the king.

In the hours of the day, one by one, the Beast would summon them to his inner chambers and gaze into their vacant eyes, attempting to visualize the hologram of the brain. But even when the demons he had placed in their minds sparked back and forth across the optic nerves of his possessed priesthood like electrical discharges, they revealed no significant information to Kahotep, their creator. They returned to their hypnotized hosts like baby dragons to curl up and doze or romp about in the cave of the skull that each demon called its home.

Reports had already reached Kahotep about the king's heretical proclaimations. He had abolished human sacrifice, outlawed the death penalty and in fact all of the practises that gave Kahotep and his Twelve Chosen their vampiristic longevity. Without access to the living pineal glands of human brains, the ancient priest and his circle would face gradual age and death. The plan of the Hidden One would collapse. Whoever or whatever this monstrous-looking king was, he knew about Kahotep, the Obscene Rite—everything. And he was about to destroy it all.

The words of Amenhotep, Son of Hapu, rang in Kahotep's ears. Tiy had not stepped down from her throne. The new king was ruling Egypt on an equal basis with his wife and mother.

"Beware the king who rules with two queens!"

☥ 𓃭 𓄿

The night after the second day of the coronation feast, the king and his royal wife retired. She slept in her bed as she had the night before. The king sat beside her crosslegged, his eyes rolled back in deep meditation.

He had left his body and was in psychic communion with Yod, the vast energy vortex aboard the *Aton*. The eight humanoid occupants also participated in the telepathic communion.

Things are much worse than I anticipated, Shu-who-was-the-king *thought. Kahotep is a masterful psychologist. He uses religious propaganda skillfully. Osiris is no longer the god most favored by literate Egyptians. Even the peasants believe Osiris to be merely a god of grain, and not the Judge of Souls in the afterlife. Amen, Kahotep's false god, has usurped even the role of Osiris, and meets the soul as Amen-Osiris, whose criterion for a 'good soul' is one who lays the hearts of others on the scale of Ma'at, and not his own heart, light as a feather.*

The method of selecting humans for sacrifice to Amen, who is, in reality, Kahotep and his Inner Circle of Twelve Chosen initiates, shows a carefully considered methodology: he measures the size and shape of each shaven head. He pays close attention to the dimensions of the occipital lobe and studies the frontal lobe as well. This suggests he is trying to breed a less intelligent strain of humans whose males will be aggressive and violent. Kahotep seeks to reverse the genetic tendencies we have released into this species of hominids and which made him and his kin human. Kahotep will rid the Egyptian gene pool of large-brained individuals for his own obscene gluttony.

Given a few more generations, he could not succeed. Given a few centuries, he could cultivate enough uncontrollably violent males to police large populations and enforce his genetic plans. Given another two to four thousand years, Kahotep could redirect human evolution

Of course, this must not happen. My plan is to lure him out into the open by doing what he fears the most. I will gather the artists and scribes of Egypt and have them meticulously record, in writing, sculpture, and murals, the creation of an artificial race for hybridization with an evolving human race. This will compel Kahotep to preserve this experiment for me as a beacon for future generations who will discover it during the times when ignorance subsides and scientific knowledge replaces superstition. I will create a little time-capsule of artistic and scientific treasures—and I will assign the task of custodianship to the man who hates and fears me the most: Kahotep. He will be the guardian of this cultural and scientific treasure.

Chapter Twelve

By the morning after her second night with her alien husband, Nefertiti was assured that he was not an incubus, the lusty spirit she had feared he would be. His predisposition was entirely the opposite of erotic. He emanated love, so much so that passion seemed removed from his spectrum of feelings.

She had overcome her aversion to his strange anatomy and was even growing accustomed to the hugeness of his head and elongation of his face. She was beginning to develop a good rapport with Queen Tiy and Ai and participated more freely in their discussions.

All agreed that the events of the day before had been good. The proclamations that the king had made seemed just and fair. Queen Tiy had been born among the peasants of Egypt. No matter how many years Tiy had been queen and Ai had been her royal priest, neither could forget how their parents had toiled in the fields in the days when they were children. Even as Priest and Priestess of Aton their sympathies never lay entirely with the nobles and court officials.

By noon many pilgrims had come to see the king. Amenhotep IV held court on a palace balcony for the increasing number of visitors. Caravans of peasants from neighboring cities and towns had begun to arrive. Many were curious. Some had seen the Aton disc two generations before, on nights when it had illuminated villages and cities with light as bright as day. Others had seen smaller Material Discs over the desert and now they wanted to see their king from the Other World.

All were excited, though many felt trepidation. Unprecedented were the edicts issued thus far by this new king. The nobles and aristocrats feared that Egypt would be threatened, not from the outside by some external enemy, but from within by a heretical king.

By evening nobles, temple priests of all Egyptian religions and former court officials of Amenhotep III were arriving to bring gifts to the strange king. They brought their own eagerness and anxiety as well, but most were relieved when they greeted the man in the throne. Their hearts were generally lightened by viewing the living miracle, though the more a man dreaded the loss of power over other human beings bestowed by his social status, the more disturbed or even fearful he became in the presence of the new king, reflected in their shock and horror upon viewing his awesome face and unnatural body.

The king encouraged nobles and peasants to dine together but noted that the royalty often rejected that idea. He also noticed that, although the peasants seemed to have mixed feelings about his physical strangeness or the radical content of his proclaimations, the aristocrats were almost unanimous in their hostility toward him.

The only thing people could talk about anywhere in Egypt was the return of Amenhotep IV from the Heavens, brought back by the Aton Disc itself. During the third, fourth, and last days of the Heb-Sed Feast, the king witnessed throngs of pilgrims from all over Lower Egypt pushing their way through Thebes to view his face and body. Their numbers swelled until, on the last night of the coronation feast, the masses gathered before the palace steps. The king walked to the edge of his balcony and addressed his people. In a deep voice that all could hear, he announced:

"I, Amenhotep IV, arrived to fulfill my rightful claim to the throne five days ago, on the first day of Epep, the third month of summer. I returned after seventeen years in the Heavens, inside the Aton Disc, which is the Material, Physical, Metal Disc that is like the sun in appearance. Before my birth as your king from the womb of Queen Tiy, my Royal Mother, I was a man of one of those races which together you call the Amentii. I lived near Seti, the Star of Anubis, sacred to all Egyptians. I lived near a vast dark body that cannot be seen by human eyes, near two stars that together appear as one in this world's night sky. My native body is asleep inside the Aton Disc. My original name is Shu. The strange body I now inhabit enables me to father many children. For this reason that I must explain something very important. Amenhotep III was not my father. Queen Tiy is indeed my true mother, for I created this body for myself out of her flesh and blood. The truth is that *I am my own father*. I know that other Pharaohs before me have said this, but I stand before you different from you in face and figure, which no other Pharaoh could claim. I stand taller than the tallest of you. My hips and thighs are those of a woman, and my belly contains internal organs that are similar to but not the same as your own. Look upon this body and remember it. I have come from another world, another horizon apart from this world's horizon, to tell you great truths and to rid the land of pain and death.

"I have returned to Egypt after two thousand years. I last walked these fertile green valleys as Horus, and there was peace throughout the land. There was plenty. Food was so abundant that a great surplus was shipped to primitive lands to the south and east. Vegetables were offered to the gods and goddesses of the land. Offerings were returned to the soil directly. There was peace and plenty. We whom you call the Amentii, the Hidden Beings, saw that all was good. People could speak and most could read and write. Some expressed great genius at numbers. We rejoiced. Then, we departed.

"I was summoned back to this world after two thousand years because we learned that it had fallen into spiritual and political ruin. I had prepared myself to see much suffering in the land I once loved for its peacefulness and fecundity. Now I see sacrificial murder of living people to gods like Thoth, who never demanded such tribute when he was your First Pharaoh, and to Amen, whose name means 'the Hidden One.'

"Amen *is* a Hidden One, but not in the sense that the Amentii are hidden. The Amentii live in many worlds that you cannot see, and are thus hidden from your senses by dimensions such as vast distances or long ages of time. It is said we live in the Amentt, which is the Hidden World. Know this, Egyptians: there are many hidden worlds, not just one. And know this, too: *no* true gods or goddesses ever demand that humans die as offerings served to them. Service to the gods can only come through life. Why else would we live? If death is an act of faith, then is birth an act of sin? No. I tell you, no truth comes to minds wrapped up in contradictions.

"Amen is the Hidden One, for Amen has demanded human death as his tribute and Amen knows this is evil. That is why the Hidden One hides. He is a coward. He knows that he is not a genuine god at all, but an ancient priest who has become a criminal, a parasite upon the people of Egypt. Amen does not reside in the Amentt. Amen resides in a stone chamber deep beneath the Temple of Karnak.

"You see me, creator of my own body, standing before you. The Priests of Amen have used their spells on me, as if I were a demon to be commanded about by superior magick. One by one, their exorcisms failed, and I was not banished from this Earthly realm. I still stand among you, unscathed by the charms and rituals of the priests of Amen.

"But where is Amen? The Hidden One, who demands so much Egyptian blood, is not as bold as I. Amen hides; I walk among you. Amen claims to be god, but I am Egypt's rightful king, the first true god-king to walk Egypt since my Horus incarnation. Still, Amen hides.

"If Amen is the One True God, let him show himself! If the Hidden One truly is creator of this Universe, let the almighty manifest! How long will we wait for the Hidden One to show himself? Minutes, perhaps? Days? Years?

"The Heb-Sed Feast is over, but let the feast of plenty for all of Egypt begin in its place!"

A long silence drifted over the crowd, and then multitudes raised their hands and glad voices and called out generous blessings to the king.

"So, your husband crushed a slave rebellion in Nubia. He vanished in the thorn forests of Kash while hunting lions." Amenhotep IV was speaking to Queen Tiy. "Both matters disturb me. I wish to abolish slavery and I think that I will abolish the hunting of lions as well. Surely, your husband did not eat the lions he killed."

"Many noblemen hunt animals they do not wish to eat,'" said Tiy. "They return with pelts as proof of their bravery."

"A man who hunts lions from a chariot is not brave."

"My husband was not brave. Only king."

115

"I will abolish all hunting for vanity. Vanity compounding vanity! The conceit and hubris of humanity is terrible, but it is worst among the royalty. Summon Apy. I wish to make an official proclamation."

By noon of the king's sixth day as ruler of Egypt the hunting of animals for any purpose other than sustenance was abolished. Provisions were made for the liberation of slaves and the negotiation of payment for services previously rendered by slaves. Each new piece of legislation increased the happiness of humans and wild beasts. Each new pronouncement increased the strength and joys of multitudes formerly oppressed by tyranny, including the women of Egypt. The king had observed their lack of political status and sought to end that inequality under the law.

"I see no reason to observe traditions that harm women or Negro people. I see no reason to observe traditions that inflict harm on *anyone*, human or animal. I see many traditions as evil. Many I have already abolished."

"But my king," said Nefertiti, "Too much change can weaken our nation."

"If Egypt has weaknesses so great that she succumbs to change, then Egypt may have to pass away so that stronger nations of men and women can exist."

These words shocked the two queens. Even Ai gasped.

The king shrugged. "If change can destroy Egypt, then Egypt is weak. A hammer cannot alter the flow of water. Water embodies the spirit of constant change."

Ai nodded thoughtfully. Tiy and Nefertiti pondered this in silence.

By the end of his first weeek as king, Amenhotep IV had abolished human sacrifice, the death penalty, the hunting of animals for entertainment, slavery, laws that restricted the Negro citizenry, laws that limited the rights of women and the law that required the sexual organs be hidden from view behind the image of a scarab beetle.

Each new pronouncement seemed more radical than the last. Ancient traditions were being struck down by the hammer of the new king. The only thing that reassured the bewildered Egyptians was the fact that Queen Tiy was still Mother of Egypt and she in her wisdom endorsed the proclamations, one after another.

The seekers who visited the palace in Thebes had increased from small groups of pilgrim families to vast throngs. Many were peasants or liberated slaves. Many had never before in their lives felt the comfort of a full belly. To them such a king could not be evil simply because he was of a race from another world.

It was during his second week as king that Amenhotep IV announced to Queen Nefertiti that she was to join him in the bridal chamber of the Temple of Aton that night. Nefertiti felt her sudden optimism depart. She gravely accepted that she would be the literal wife of this Man from the Heavens. Once more aversion to his strange body filled her.

He sensed the chill that came over her and told her simply that she needed not fear. "You will enter my world in order to make love with me. It cannot be done in this world. Once you are in my world, every care or worry you have ever had will pass away. Even the pleasures of this world will seem dim compared to the raptures awaiting you there."

Nefertiti turned to face Tiy, who smiled knowingly.

That night the king and queen entered the temple together and walked together through torchlit corridors to the bridal chamber. Inside, they faced the altar on which many priests and priestesses of Aton had experienced the sexual love of the Amentii, beings from the Hidden World who, strangely, were also human kin.

He offered her the sacrament of bread and dark wine. In the wine were a mild sedative and a hypnotic drug which took effect immediately and subtly.

He led her to the altar. She was lighthearted, happy, not at all entranced. They reclined together on the warm stone. He gazed into her eyes. She looked up at the gleaming diamonds set in the night and a single star appeared, outshining all the others. It slowly grew until Nefertiti could see that it was actually descending. Soon it filled the sky, then it filled the bridal chamber and her eyes with prismatic rays.

She felt herself lifted gently off the stone slab, floated on clouds of light. She did not know if she was standing or reclining until she saw a blurry, silhouetted figure approaching slowly through the multicolored glare.

It was the king. He was smaller now. His head was normal, his hips were less thick, his belly less pendulous. She tried to see his skull but the back of his head vanished in the glare. He embraced and kissed her and she closed her eyes, feeling his love.

The starship *Aton* received the shuttlecraft and within minutes Nefertiti was lying on a cushioned table beneath a scanning eye, her body bathed in brilliant hypnotic lights.

The cellular scan revealed that Nefertiti was in excellent health and that her strength and high intelligence were products of her genes and not of just a favorable environment. She had no obvious genetic defects and the chromosomal survey showed no susceptibility to cancer.

"We will try a normal controlled conception *in vitro*," said the King of Egypt to the crew of star travelers. "This will establish whether or not my genes are compatible with hers."

A crystalline box was brought by Pilot Tem, who placed it on the cushion between Nefertiti's legs. From an aperture in it slithered a thin transparent tube, animated and alive. It streaked out of the box and slipped into the sleeping woman's vagina, into her uterus, and into the fallopian tube that was enlarging to accommodate the passage of an ovum cell. The very tip of the tube, narrowed to fit the fallopian tube, now narrowed still further. It became a microscopic hollow needle of living glass, and it pierced the ovary of the queen. It sought out the ovarian follicle nearest to expelling a mature egg. It plucked the genetic sphere, then the slender strand withdrew swiftly from the body of Queen Nefertiti.

Amenhotep IV reclined beside Nefertiti on a similar cushioned table, and he, too, fell into a trance. His penis became erect. Tefnut placed a condom over it and attached the nipple in the tip of the condom to a similar clear tube emanating from an identical crystalline box between the king's feet. Then Tefnut left the laboratory and went to the adjoining room, which contained the glass chamber in which the body of her husband, Shu, floated in clear liquid.

She climbed up rungs on the wall to the top of the tank and lowered herself into the warm fluid. She submerged her head and forced herself to inhale the hyperoxygenated liquid. It filled her lungs warmly, and when the last bubbles of air from her nostrils floated away, her urge to choke and expunge the liquid subsided. Tefnut breathed the same fluid that gave her husband's body life.

As Amenhotep IV closed his eyes, Shu opened his. He felt good again in his native body, and saw, swimming toward him, his beloved wife. They embraced and Shu and Tefnut shared ecstacy in the weightlessness of the watery medium. As their bodies merged, the body of Amenhotep IV responded sympathetically. The nipple in the condom was filled with semen, which passed through the living glass tube into the crystalline box.

Tefnut remained with Shu in the tank for many long moments, then her eyes closed. Geb and Nuit pulled her to the surface and placed a cup over her nose and mouth. When the oxygenated fluid was suctioned from her lungs they lifted her out and descended the rungs beside the tank.

Amenhotep IV sat upright, his eyes fully open.

A genetic scan quickly cataloged the millions of sperm cells in each drop of semen. The single sperm which showed the greatest genetic promise was placed in a microscopic tube which led to an infinitesimally small glass sphere in which had been deposited the selected ovum. Conception was observed under magnification and when the fertilized cell began to divide and divide again, it was placed in the queen's uterus by the same animated tube that had borrowed the ripe egg just hours before.

When the discoidal craft returned to the sky, it left behind two sleeping figures on the warm stone bridal altar. Their arms and legs were intertwined and they stayed perfectly motionless until the warm glow of dawn awakened them. Then they embraced and returned to sleep. Nefertiti, nestled in the arms of the strange king, smiled.

When Nefertiti awoke, she found that the king was sitting beside her, caressing her. She slid her body against his. He drew her into his arms. She curled up to his chest and he embraced her. The memories of the night of rapture filled her. She knew it had not been a dream. She no longer feared sexual union with his strange body. In fact, she longed again to share a night of ecstasy with him in his world filled with light.

Upon returning to the palace, she was greeted by Queen Tiy. For the first time since their meeting, Nefertiti understood what was behind Tiy's knowing, complacent smile. Nefertiti appreciated the look of wisdom and otherworldly experience in Tiy's vast eyes. She spent the day in quiet contemplation of the new life stirring within her womb.

Chapter Thirteen

Ai met Nefertiti in the hallway.

"Where is the king?"

"Have you not heard?"

Outside thousands gathered at the balcony. The peasants had been joined by throngs from the higher classes. Nobles, robed scholars and multitudes of guards and soldiers, all were voicing the shocked utterances of thousands more who were viewing the spectacle of the king's attack from the streets.

"What is he doing?" Nefertiti demanded tearfully, trying to peer out past the balcony. Ai restrained her.

"All is right, my queen," Ai said. "He read another proclamation this morning. In it he said that he was not the son of Amenhotep III, that the third Amenhotep was not the father of his body. He reminded them of his strange appearance, saying that he had created his own body in the Aton Disc. He said he was creator of his own body, that he was his own father, and that the Pharaoh before him had committed abominations. He also said that no Pharaohs had been descendants of Horus since Khufu, and that all the Pharaohs under Amen have been imposters."

"Oh no!" Nefertiti stepped back into the shadow of a pillar. "He made similar statements immediately after his coronation but I do not think anyone was offended. Many kings have said those very things about themselves, true or not."

"Of course kings say those things about themselves!" Ai laughed, but his chuckle was mirthless. "Apparently our new king wants to draw attention to this fact. He has demonstrated his adamance."

"No." Nefertiti moaned with dread.

"He is walking from monument to monument, erasing the name of Amenhotep III wherever he finds it. Erasing that name with a hammer and chisel."

"Oh, Lord Ptah!"

"Yes, O Queen."

"Where is Tiy?"

"She is in the sentry tower watching the streets from above."

"No. No! She cannot let him do this! He will kill his own father in the Tuat, *his own father!* Even if Amenhotep III is not his true father, then Amenhotep the man will die in Heaven…"

"The king has also made a pronouncement about that. He says that Egypt is steeped in superstition. He says that what happens after death is a mystery. He says that life should be lived for its own sake and that the Tuat is a sealed secret. *A sealed secret*—to be kept from our eyes on this side of the grave—forever!"

"No! No, that cannot be…!" Nefertiti felt suddenly weak and groped desperately for a chair. Ai assisted her to a huge pillow by the wall. Two handmaidens rushed to her side, fanning her and offering her water.

Nefertiti recovered briefly, just as voices thundered from the outer hall. She feared that the mob had begun to riot and had broken into the palace. She started to rise, but was held back by her handmaidens.

The baritone timbre of the sacreligious king could be heard above the other voices. He bellowed commands as if reciting *en rote*. His voice was loud and expressionless, deliberately flattened to a monotone.

Most of the angry voices became silent. One voice heard loudly shouting insults was that of the priest, Xepuru-Ra. The words of Xepuru-Ra became distinct:

"I will have you know you murdered your own father! You murdered your own father! He has died twice now, died a second death in Heaven itself because of you!"

Another voice cried out:

"Yes! Yes, thanks to you, you—you killed your own father's *ka!* You killed his *ka*, and if his ghost dies, then his immortal soul must perish!"

Amenhotep IV would not countenence it. "Superstition! Superstitious nonsense. Amenhotep III is dead. He was a primitive barbarian. The fact that he was king drenched him in hubris. And because of his delusions of grandeur, he committed many atrocities."

Xepuru-Ra cried out: "No more than any Pharaoh! No more than Thothmose III, by your own atavistic standards. How about his queen? How about Hatshepsut? Oh, you would have *hated* her!"

"I hate no one. I demonstrate to Egyptians that I am a god-king, physically different from all other Egyptians, and that I do not share these superstitions!"

"You cannot change the minds of all Egyptians!" cried the rapid speaker.

"I do not seek to. I seek only to communicate those simple facts to the minds of Egyptians and people all over the world who are as yet unborn."

"*What?*" many voices gasped in unison.

The fast voice demanded: "Of what significance will this be? To Egyptians, to people yet unborn?"

Xepuru-Ra was excited. "For people who are not yet alive you shatter the name of a single king from his own temple? His own colossi?"

"Yes," said the deep, satisfied rumble. "To make a point to people who will not be born for several thousand years at least."

In the silence that measured the shock of abject disbelief, the king's uneven footsteps echoed down the colonnade. The two priests of Amen shuffled off in the opposite direction. The fast-speaking voice whispered:

"Let us record this!"

"Yes, we must...!"

"On this day Aton's king has gone mad!"

"Yes, that explains it," Xepuru-Ra intoned slowly. "I think it is his head. It is too big. I think he must have gone mad because of his big head!"

Nefertiti was in tears. Tiy arrived in her co-regent's chamber, smiling elatedly. She tried to comfort the younger queen, but her sympathy was not well received. Tiy could not help grinning excitedly. Nefertiti turned away.

"He means no harm," Tiy stated gently.

"How can you say that? He defiled his own father's name!"

"My husband was not his true father. You know this. You, too, have met your god-king in the Amentt. You know what he means when he says that he is his own father."

"He is mocking our faith."

"He knows what he is doing," Ai said, entering and sitting near them.

"How can you *say* that?" Nefertiti snapped.

"Because I know what he is doing," Ai replied simply.

The silence that followed thundered in the young queen's ears.

"I can tell that you have not received visionary knowledge," Tiy said sadly. "It is unfortunate that you have not."

"There is much more to his appearance among us than merely ruling one nation under the sun for a handful of years," Ai said. "There is so much more to his return than just that."

Tiy added excitedly, "There is much danger in bringing a man down from the stars. Egypt is in great danger, even greater danger. Amenhotep IV is prepared to die just to record this visit of the Aton Disc for the future of all time."

"Then he is a fool." Nefertiti sobbed in pain. "He heightens the danger! I felt good about him when he abolished killing and human sacrifices and slavery! But now he has gone too far!"

Ai shrugged. "He has to tell the people who will live in the future about his total lack of faith in our ancient religion, and this will be emphasized in connection with his strange body. That is all."

"You are all mad!" Nefertiti gasped.

"Oh, no," said Ai, laughing again. "It is just that we have received knowledge that you have not. That is all."

"You have been very close to it," Tiy whispered to the distraught queen. "Remember the night you spent in the Other World with him? That is all. When you need strength, when you face danger, remember that night in the Other World and have faith in the illuminated Material Disc. That is all."

"We have visionary knowledge," Ai said. "my sister and I and our parents, Yuia and Thuya. We have received visions from the rays of the Aton Disc."

"In the name of Ptah Almighty!" Nefertiti trembled all over. She inhaled and held a long, slow breath. She gazed at the floor and shook her head as she slowly realized that she was an integral part of a political conspiracy of a dangerous and unknown nature.

Ai sat beside her and spoke slowly. "My sister and I were not born of earthly parents. My sister was fathered by an incubus in an abandoned temple because the new god would need a mother in this world." He gestured with his hands around his head. "It is the size and shape of that skull, you know. If his mother had had too small a pelvis, he would have gotten stuck on the way out of her belly." He pointed at Tiy's wide hips and curved thighs. "That is why she greeted him naked. My sister's pelvis is almost identical to her son's."

"And you wish future generations to know that he behaves like a madman?"

"Is that all you care about?" Ai rose in fury. "Only what other people think and say here and now in Egypt?"

"He is offending multitudes of Egyptians and you are telling me he is doing this to convey some obscure riddle to people in some future time. That is absurd! Is that how the god-kings manipulate us? Is that the message they bring?"

"Yes," said Ai.

"This cannot be. Perhaps...perhaps..."

"Do not think it, Nefertiti," Tiy said sternly.

"He is...unnatural, that is all."

"But he is *not* a demon."

"He is a real human being, like me or you," said Ai.

"How can you say that?"

"Nefertiti," Tiy said gently, "a great deal of the difference between us and the Amentii is in what we know, not what world we were born on."

"No. No. This is absurd! I cannot believe any of it."

"Why not, O Queen?" Ai asked sadly.

"Because," Nefertiti sobbed again, "I cannot *understand* any of it! It frightens me!"

⁂

For five days Amenhotep IV assailed the statuary and monuments of Amenhotep III. Although he did not defile the works of art themselves, he erased his predecessor's name in hieroglyphs wherever he found it. When at last he returned to his palace in Thebes, he was hounded by jeering, cursing multitudes restrained by angry, bewildered but obedient guards.

The king retired to a bath in a vast pool of hot water, then to meditation in his personal chamber. His campaign had been continuous, without rest. Nefertiti had slept fitfully in his absence, but under the rising moon which peered through the

123

tiled archway like the ghost of a star, the young queen slept soundly for the first in several nights.

Outside the palace, even at that late hour, Egypt was still echoing uneasily with frightened rumors, accusations, utterances of disapproval that ran deep through the society of Egyptians. In the beer halls where the peasants drank the barley ale, voices were grim. In the backrooms of the pleasure dens and in the private houses of nobility, voices turned tense with discontent, hushed with fear.

The strange king had gone too far.

"Why, why, why, why, why, why?" Nefertiti was furious.

"Because I wished to demonstrate a point for all time," the king said nonchalantly. "I did the statuary no harm. I only erased a specific man's name whenever I found it."

"Not in his temples, did you?"

"Yes, I removed his name from the temples he built. I erased it everywhere."

"No! You did not!"

"Yes, I did, and the man did not die a second death in the Tuat, either."

"How do you know?"

"Because I have been there! When I left my Horus body for my native body, I, too, made the journey through the Realm of the Dead."

"Only days ago you said death was a mystery. Now you say you have been there. You contradict yourself!"

"Nefertiti, I said death was permanently concealed from humans on this side of the grave. *I* have been on *both* sides, when my mind was being transferred from one body to another."

"I see. So we are inferior, we Egyptian people."

"You are not inferior. Your race need not evolve any further in body to attain the wisdom and knowledge of the society of the stars. Some will be prepared for this knowledge now, this very day. Then another three or four thousand years may pass before great numbers can be prepared all together for translation into the stars. Or maybe no one will ever be prepared for translation, ever again. It depends on how bad will be this world's self-chosen fate."

"If Egypt is in such danger, then do not invoke more harm by angering the gods who sent you!"

"I cannot anger the gods who sent me, Nefertiti, because they are all personal friends of mine. I seek only to anger and terrify one god who is not even a god but an impostor, a tyrant to this world and a coward who lives in Karnak."

"You talk in riddles," Nefertiti scolded. "Why are you so evasive?"

"You are unprepared to receive visionary knowledge," said the king. "You would be wise to prepare yourself. You must meditate every day, especially in the morning. Play your musical instruments and dance. And study astronomy. Yes. Study astronomy."

"What will this do? Meditate, play music, and study the stars while my husband, Egypt's king, defaces monuments and temples? This is how I prepare myself to receive visionary knowledge?"

"Yes!" The huge king laughed. "That is a very good way to start. These are excellent things to do while I deface temples and statues."

By the end of his first month as king, Amenhotep IV had turned the focus of his rage (if, indeed, it *was* rage) from the name of the king who had preceeded him to the name of the god of many temples throughout the city. He returned to the palace every few nights, traveling from temple to temple by day. Always surrounded by armed guards who escorted him and loyally protected him during his acts of vandalism, throughout his attack he erased only the word "Amen." Never before had this been done. Beginning with the Temple of Karnak, the king's first visit lasted seventeen hours. He briefly turned his attention to the Temple of Luxor, striking out the name of the Hidden One wherever he found it, then returned to Karnak.

Word reached the palace that the king had gone berserk. He had overturned tables, shattered icons, chiseled out the very name of Amen everywhere he found it, from wall murals to statuary. Many statues of Amen he destroyed. The war priests stood by helplessly, unable to intervene.

He penetrated the central shrine in Karnak by torchlight. His hammer and cold chisel swung in his arms as he strode down the narrow, high corridors. At last he saw in torchlight the secret icon, Amen's own self-depiction. There, in the bloody colors of the war-god's own fresco on a vertical limestone slab, looming over the vast domed room, was the terrifying mural.

Amen revealed himself and his symbology in all of his demented, depraved glory. The primary symbol was the god's fully erect penis, seen from the side in consonance with the rigid tradition of Egyptian figure drawing. Above the waist the torso rotated full front, but one arm was hidden, holding the scourge that Amen used to whip his own back, a symbol of discipline. To Amenhotep IV it was a symbol of perversion.

The right arm of the figure was held in an Egyptian military salute. The face of the Hidden God glared across his temple shrine. His teeth were bared in defiance and he was looking back over his shoulder, alert for his enemies.

Let me be one of his enemies, Amenhotep IV thought. Then he chiseled out the name of Amen from the towering mural.

"It is all utter nonsense," boomed the baritone that was like thunder. "The *ka* must live so the *ba* can live and the *ba* must live so the *ka* must be treated as if it was alive—this is all so much superstition! A corruption of a magick so sublime that it cannot even be adequately explained by the vulgar Egyptian language anymore. Discussion or practice of this ancient theory is secret knowledge, forbidden by Amen. So who says that I am intolerant? You cannot murder the *ba*, the immortal soul, by erasing names! And you cannot kill the *ka*, the ghost, by erasing names! I do these things to defy tradition, to mock superstition."

Nefertiti was exasperated beyond all measure. "For centuries we have observed the same rites, the same traditions, and now you upset all! Always for the same reason. 'You cannot kill the *ba* by killing the *ka*' and so on! You mock Egyptians! You make us to be savages because of our beliefs, like primitive Nubians, or worse!"

"Egyptians of another age will understand."

Ai and Tiy arrived in the sunny courtyard. The worried cries of Egyptians were far away, beyond the palace walls.

"Is everything pleasant between you two?" Tiy was concerned, having overheard some of the argument. She went to Nefertiti's side, but the younger queen withdrew.

"You endorse everything he does," she said.

Tiy turned to Amenhotep IV and said, "Please, my son, refrain from continuing this onslaught against the Temples of Amen. Or at least soften your attack. I believe all of Egypt observes your point by now."

"You do not understand, my mother. I wish to lure the Hidden One into the open."

"Then you believe Amen is a god?"

"Not a god, but a living thing like you or me. Amen is real. Amen resides in Karnak, in a cavity beneath the floor. He does not reside in the Amentt, which is the Hidden World, the Other World from which I have come."

"I think all of Egypt knows your claim to the throne from the Amentt and that you say Amen does not live there."

"Yes, O Mother, but I wish to prod The Beast from his lair. I want to end Amen's rule over Egypt by exposing exactly what their war god is. Then they will turn away from that creature and he will at last age and die."

Nefertiti was staring at the king, aghast. Finally she ventured, "So, you believe that although Amen is a false god, Amen is also alive? Somehow not human, but also not a god?"

"Exactly. And who and what he is would be repulsive to his own followers, if they knew whom they serve."

Nefertiti cast her eyes downward. She blinked, then closed her eyes, then opened them slowly and stared.

"Tell me about this Egyptian infatuation with death," demanded Amenhotep IV.

Ai nodded contemplatively, then said, "So much of our religions have much to do with preparing in this life for what will happen or where we will go in the next life, if indeed there is any. It becomes obvious to me that there is a secret fear of death somewhere in our spirits."

"Is this so? How about your spirit, Ai?"

The priest shrugged. "I have looked within myself and can truly say that some of the time I am accustomed to the thought of death and sometimes death makes me uneasy."

"Why?"

"Because I know that everything I have every heard about death is only words and I fear that my mind might cease to exist after I die."

"I understand. Your thoughts are well received."

"Most Egyptians do not examine their own feelings so deeply," Tiy said. "They are uneasy about death because they fear Baba, the Soul Eater, who will try to wrestle them away from Osiris. The Amenists fear Amen-Osiris himself, so death is a worry for Egyptians because the *ba* is so vulnerable when it departs from the body."

"I understand. And yet it was not this way in the Old Kingdom, when it was assumed that everything alive would return. Somewhere else, in quantity and in another form but without the direct memories of its previous existence. Many people remembered previous existences, as every living body stores vast hereditary knowledge. But now in Egypt doubt and death go hand in hand."

"And what of you, Pharaoh?" Nefertiti cried out. "Since the beginning of time, kings have taken great pains to deliver themselves intact, their bodies fully restored, to keep from entering the Tuat like ordinary men do."

"This elaborate funerary rite is the first sign that Egyptians fear death. I find it important beyond measure that the kings of Egypt were first to express this fear through their funeral customs."

Tiy spoke. "Is the year-long embalming ritual not a survival of that which was was observed before King Zoser and Imhotep inherited the throne from Horus?"

"Yes, but it is a gross misinterpretation of two facts. One is that all Egyptians watched Osiris, then two thousand years later Horus, ascend into the sky on a beam of light. This was such a momentous act that it was engraved in the myths and traditions of all Egyptian religions throughout the land.

"The second fact exerts a corrupting influence on Egypt still: a promise was made by Horus to Zoser, and repeated by Zoser to his successors, each one, that the god-kings would return one day and all death would be abolished. The old kings would return to Heaven-on-Earth someday.

"Remembering the ascent of the true god-kings into the night sky on a ray of light, plus the promises made by the successors of Horus, has caused the fear of annihilation of the soul by death. Which has been expressed most prominently in the funerary rites of the kings."

"You, I suppose, have no such fear," Nefertiti said.

"I am just as vulnerable to death as you are and, no, I do not have such a fear."

"Well, I am glad for you! Suppose you die? What do you want to be done with your body?"

The king pondered, then laughed. "My bones would make a very unusual display for a temple of Aton, but my flesh and blood? The fields can claim that."

Ai laughed but Nefertiti was shocked. She pursed her lips and then stated: "I find hardest to grasp that you seem to mean everything you say."

"That I do," said Amenhotep IV. "My bones—yes, they should be preserved for posterity. That is partly why I created this body thus. But I am not better than anyone else just because I am king. So my corpse should be offered to the soil, as is natural in the cycle of birth, death and fertility."

"So—do you wish to ban the funerary traditions for your own body when you die?"

The king thought about that for a moment, then said, "Summon Apy. I have a new pronouncement to make."

A court messenger returned with the royal scribe, and minutes later a new proclamation had been written.

The year-long, magnificently elaborate funerary rites of mummification were to be abolished, along with ceremonial sacrifices, the death penalty, trophy hunting, slavery and laws limiting the rights of women, Negroes, and destitute peasants. The new order was read aloud by the king from the balcony to the many people who lingered there to observe his strange head and figure. Copies of the pronouncement were posted outside all temples of Aton throughout Thebes. Messengers spread the word throughout all of Egypt.

As for himself, the king would arrange for a simple cremation to be followed by a restoration of his skeleton to be displayed as a curiosity and a reminder of the strange skulls and pelvic bones of the god-kings who lived so long ago…

Chapter Fourteen

Amenhotep IV awoke to the news that an enclave of sacrificial victims had been discovered in Medamud just across the Nile and to the north of Karnak. The prisoners had been liberated, but they had been kept in dungeons for so long that it was impossible to locate their families. The king sent for the men, seven hundred in all.

The King deduced from their number that The Beast had been gorging his brain with chemicals distilled from the glands of multitudes of victims, thus enhancing the life-prolonging effect of the Obscene Rite. *This must cease immediately,* the great king decided, and awaited their arrival at his palace, midway between Luxor and Karnak, on the east bank of the Nile.

The trudging horde of men assembled in a line along the royal avenue leading to the palace. Many did not believe the news that had been told to them. They feared that the new Pharaoh would trick them, that he was about to select his first round of sacrificial victims. With the shackles at last gone from their arms and legs, they yet responded submissively to the guards who escorted them. Their thirst slaked and their bellies full but with dread in their hearts, they went to meet the King-who-was-not-a-human being. Many dropped to their knees and groveled in fear when they saw him.

He stooped beside one trembling figure and asked: "What was your crime?"

"Treason," said the man.

"Were you guilty?"

"No. I was accused of selling swords to the Nubians, but in truth I sold slaves to the King of Egypt."

Abruptly, the king stood and walked toward a man who was praying fervently. "What are you praying for?" asked the king.

"Deliverance from suffering!" The fearful man choked out, then added, "O King!"

"Are you suffering?"

"I am suffering from uncertainty, O King."

"What is your name?"

"Hui."

"Look into my eyes, Hui. Do not be afraid. I have returned in peace from the stars. Yield to the feeling in your heart." The man relaxed, breathed deeply, slowly, calmly. "Now, tell me why you were imprisoned for sacrifice to Amen."

"My dreams were prophetic! I told my family, and someone accused me of witchcraft."

The king placed a hand on the man's clean-shaven scalp. He was measuring the size and shape of his skull. Then he stood and announced, "Hui, I wish to make you one of my courtiers."

The man was stunned. He gasped, dropping to the ground, then scampered forward, kissing the feet of the extraterrestrial king.

The king shook his head and with his own hand raised the trembling man to his feet. "Do not do that. Stand, gather your dignity, be happy. If you feel humble, feel humble. If you feel proud, feel proud. But stand in my presence."

Ai, the Laughing Priest, laughed again.

Hui stood, then impulsively threw himself forward and hugged the king. The king's beaded collar rattled. He laughed. The thin, trembling man clung to him, then stood back weeping.

The strange king walked to another man, who watched with eyes wide with astonishment.

"What is your name?"

"Mahu."

"Are you amazed by what you see, Mahu?"

"Yes."

"How do you feel?"

"M-my heart is light as a feather, O King."

Amenhotep IV laughed. "Bless you." He placed his hand on the man's head. It was large and well-formed, with high parietal lobes. "I choose you to be another of my personal courtiers."

"Bless you, O King!"

"Who among you has been treated unjustly?"

Every man responded with outcries. The king faced them one at a time, closely observing each skull's volume and conformation.

"What is your name?"

"Penthu."

"What is yours?"

"Rames."

"And yours?"

"Aahmes."

"What is your name?"

"Nefer-khepuru-her-sekheper."

"Please come with me, Penthu, Rames, Aahmes, and Nefer-khepuru-her-sekheper. You are all to become my personal courtiers."

The great king walked past the row of excited, anxious men. No one knew by what method he was choosing, but sometimes he would grip a head, measure it with his fingers and almost always choose that person to follow him. The next of his first dozen courtiers were Merira I, Merira II, Api, Tutu, Mai, and Ani.

After a long search, the remainder of men liberated by the king were led to the grassy hills beside the Temple of Aton. They were told to group according to their native homes and cities in preparation for a return to their homelands.

The newly-selected courtiers were taken to the palace and questioned about their families. Survivors would be contacted and brought to the palace. All of the men had been peasants when they were arrested and consigned to sacrifice to Amen. To their astonishment, they were now safely out of range of the death-hammer and preparing to become the personal attendants of the strange, otherworldly king who had saved them.

Gratitude filled the palace. Gratitude pushed back the murmurings of discontent that refused to subside throughout Egypt.

"Has Ai found me a suitable vizier?" Amenhotep IV asked Queen Tiy.

"He is returning from Edfu with a man of great promise. An architect-astronomer with an unusual mathematical talent."

"What is his name?"

"Nakht."

"Are there other prospects?"

"Yes, there is Ramose, of the temple of Aton west of Sakkara."

"Have him summoned, too. I need a personal vizier with a good knowledge of mathematics and chemistry. I also need a general vizier to supervise architectural and engineering projects throughout Egypt."

Thus Nakht became personal vizier to Amenhotep IV, and Ramose, who was a superior sculptor and architect, became chief vizier.

The king summoned the twins who had served Amenhotep III as architects, sculptors, and engineers. He commissioned from them a statue of himself. It was to be larger than a bust but less monumental than a colossus. Her and Suti went to work immediately, completing much in their first day of sketching studies and molding prototypes out of river clay.

For three days the king sat for them, and they eagerly chiseled out a visage from a great block of limestone. As the stone head neared completion, the king expressed doubt that it was right, but the sculptors, eager to please, refused to permit the Pharaoh to take a look. On the fourth day Amenhotep IV insisted on peeking around the edge of the block. What he saw seemed to infuriate him.

"You mock me!"

Her fell to his knees and cried out frantically, "No, no, no, good King, we do not mock you! See how beautiful we have made your nose and your jaw! Look at how round we have made your head!"

"You have made me look like a normal man!"

Suti threw himself forward pleading, "We do not wish to offend you!"

"I must be portrayed exactly as I am!"

"What!?" Her was shocked. Every king commanded his sculptors to flatter him—Amenhotep III certainly had. But not his successor, this huge and weird-looking man. Her repeated over and over, "N-n-no! No...no...N-n-n-nnooo!"

"The world must not see this statue." The king picked up a large hammer. "No one must see this statue."

Suti fell to the floor, scurrying crablike sideways to the stairs. When he reached the bottom step, he stood with his back pressed against the wall and watched horrified as the king lifted the hammer and swung it. The nondescript face shattered and fell in fragments to the marble floor. Satisfied, he turned to the twin sculptors.

"Do you think you can sculpt my face exactly as you see it?"

Her shook his head and scowled incoherently with fear and rage.

Suti stood up slowly and said, "I think I understand...You want us to *emphasize* the differences between you and ordinary men. Is that correct?"

Amenhotep IV nodded in satisfaction. "That is correct."

"You want us to preserve your differences for your posterity."

"That is so."

Suti was excited by the prospect of such a rare, unusual challenge. "Then I must try!"

His brother, more architect than artist, had crept to the doorway and was ready to bolt. "I see nothing decorative about. . .your face, O King." His eyes were ablaze with contempt. "Pardon me, but I cannot understand why you would want to. . .to flaunt your own ugliness."

"You do not believe I am of the star race?"

"No, I do not," Her said. "I think you are a freak!"

"Her, no!" Suti cried out to his brother.

"Let him speak. He has the right to express himself, especially in the presence of the king!"

"That is all," Her said, and fled from the room.

Suti remained. Amenhotep IV offered to teach him a new system of symmetry and form which would be applied to the sculpting of ordinary faces, like Nefertiti's, as well as the king's elongated, grotesque head.

"I am somewhat of a sculptor myself," the king stated.

"I await your instruction on this new method of design with eagerness. My only regret is that my brother could not appreciate this challenge."

"That is a pity. I will choose a small company of artists and artisans and train them personally. I wish to break away from current traditions and styles. We will create a free and realistic rendering of people and nature, a complete departure from the rigid stylization that flattens human figures and crowds the murals all around me. That is my wish. It begins with you, Suti. You are my first student."

Amenhotep IV had a visitor. Nakht awakened him from a deep meditation and announced that a very excited little man was at the gate of the palace. The visitor said it was most important to see the king. He had a personal curiosity to satisfy, which could only be done if he could see, firsthand, if Amenhotep IV was "the one."

Intuitively sparked, the king consented to see the "little man." The guards had said he was a peasant, which never failed to evoke a positive response from the Pharaoh.

The man looked familiar. Amenhotep IV recalled that this was the first person he had met upon entering the fields surrounding urban Thebes.

"Parannefer!"

"O King, you remember my name!"

"Of course, Parannefer. I remember our meeting quite clearly."

The man nearly danced with delight. "Then you *are* the one! You were not just an unnatural spirit posing as a new king, as such wicked entities are known to do. You are the real king, and I did see you! Praise Almighty Ptah!"

Amenhotep IV laughed. "I was not any trickster spirit or demon. My arrival was unannounced and unexpected, particles of chance being what they are."

The peasant's eyes widened. "You *are* a star-being!"

"You are Parannefer, a good soul, pure of heart. What leads you to seek me out now?"

"At first I was afraid to seek the Pharaoh on my own, to confirm my doubts or vanquish them, and then I came upon this man and he told me how accessible you are, so I decided…" He shrugged, then smiled. "Here I am!"

The king laughed. "So you are. I told you I was your king, and now you see me here. Is this not a great moment?"

Parannefer laughed. "Yes, yes it is! Let me tell you something important to me. After I saw you and spent the day in the fields, I went to sleep after dinner, under the stars and I had a dream! In the dream I saw my wife's face! Yes, she glowed with light against the stars! She was telling me things, things that I wanted to know about death. She told me about the laying down of hearts before Osiris, that Osiris is a blazing white light, and *all we have to offer him on the scale of Ma'at is the sum of our good memories, light as a feather!* That is *all!* That is what she told me!"

The king laughed again in his deep voice, soothingly. "Parannefer, you have ventured to the edge of Eternity in that dream and you have received much truth. Take what your wife's *ba* has told you to heart."

"It was her *ba* that spoke to me?"

"Yes, but much of what has been said about the *ba* is nonsense."

"If that is so, then what is the *ba*?"

"Every man and woman has more than one brain. Each of these is like the mind of an animal. A man has a mind like a dragon in his spine; thus, the fire of the spine can be raised by the *asanas* practised from ancient times. The head has a mind of a beast, like the body of the sphinx, which is a reflection of its meaning as a riddle of combined forms. Third is the brain that emanates the mind of the spiritual essence, the mind of the angels. It is this mind, emanating from this great human brain, that all men and women have in common with all of the Amentii."

The peasant's eyes bulged. The king had said that he, a mere peasant, by virtue of his large human brain was equal in consciousness to any of the Amentii!

"Parannefer, what did your family think of this dream?"

"I have no family, O King."

"I understand. What about your friends?"

"I have a few friends. We seldom talk. Lately, they go to the beer-halls. But I find that...not a pleasure."

"I perceive that you are a good man, Parannefer. I therefore make you the most intimate of my courtiers. You shall be called 'Best Friend of the King and Innermost Confidant.' Does that suit you?"

Parannefer's eyes widened and he grinned and nodded his head uncontrollably.

"Good. Gather your belongings and bring them here. A room shall be prepared for you."

The man laughed and glanced down at himself. He was naked except for a loin-cloth. "I have brought all of my belongings."

The king and the peasant both smiled with mutual satisfaction. The king ordered a room prepared for his new Best Friend.

Artisans from Upper and Lower Egypt were called forth to show their works to the new king. He was looking for talent that had heretofore been unappreciated.

One woodcarver struck the king as being unusually gifted with an eye for realistic detail. He was a small, thin man with an elfish grin. His name was Bek. Another wood carver, who had experimented with stone when he could afford it, was Cato. He was a serious and intense young man, and also caught the King's eye.

A liberated Nubian slave arrived one afternoon with an entourage of dark-skinned Nubians who were very surprised to find themselves treated as equal to Egyptian citizens under the new king. They sought to keep watch below the king's balcony in hopes that they might catch a glimpse of him. He summoned them at once in his private quarters where they talked jovially of their new conditions. One, called Panehsi the Negro, remained after the discussion. He, too, became one of the king's personal courtiers, frequently asked to give advice on racial politics, especially with regard to Nubia.

When fifteen personal attendants, courtiers, and royal artisans had been assembled to tend to the needs of the king, and when his art students seemed to be freely assimilating his ideas, a calmness settled upon all of Egypt that soothed the doubts aroused by his attacks on the temples of Amen.

Then the king arose from meditation early one morning, summoned all the generals of the Egyptian army to his throne and ordered General Horemheb himself to seize every piece of gold, every jeweled ornament, every metal statue, all icons and effigies—virtually all of the wealth contained in the Temple of Karnak. He ordered him to take these treasures and lay them on the grounds outside his balcony.

He thus confiscated the riches of the Temple of Karnak itself.

Chapter Fifteen

Nefertiti complained of abdominal cramps. Ordinarily, a mother more than a month pregnant would be suffering discomfort occasionally, but Amenhotep IV was very concerned. He had been informed by the occupants of the *Aton* that something was wrong with the fetus.

It was three times the size a human fetus should be at a similar stage of development. Furthermore, the mass was amorphous. It contained no details of organs or skeletal structure. Something of a skull should have been present, but this fetus had no identifiable head.

Preparations were made to abort it. Contact between Amenhotep IV and the *Aton* was made telepathically while the king sat in meditation. The termination had to be effected with a minimum of shock and trauma to Queen Nefertiti. How this could be best accomplished, no one yet knew.

The following day the king continued to sort the confiscated treasures. Jeweled relics poured out of the temple. Soldiers, harassed by the priests for having obeyed the orders of their king, brought ever greater treasures, from sackfuls of jewels to immense gilded statues.

The king seemed indifferent to much that was being brought before him. Most he considered mere baubles. Some works that excelled in their artistry he set aside, but most of the pieces were separated into rows or piles according to what they were made of: gold, silver, or *tcham*, a sacred metal composed of copper thinly plated with gold. Other piles were made of pieces encrusted with diamonds, emeralds, sapphires, and rubies.

Only the king seemed to know what he intended to do with these treasures. He refused to discuss the subject of the massive confiscation with Nefertiti, who presented her objections to Tiy. The elder queen listened intently and promised to get an opinion out of the king one way or other.

"Persuade him to talk to me," Nefertiti pleaded.

Tiy assured her that she would try. "He is being unnaturally obstinate, and he knows it," Tiy admitted. "This is not like him. He insists on meditating—even right now!"

It was true. Amenhotep IV was in telepathic contact with the beings in starship *Aton*. Preparations were being made to teleport Nefertiti aboard.

As the queen retired to her bedchamber, the starship waited miles above and directly over the palace. No Egyptian saw the starcraft hover far above the atmosphere. The sunlight glinting off it made it look like just a star in the darkening dome of Nuit's vast belly.

Nefertiti was sedated by the yellow Egyptian wine and by a telepathic suggestion imparted through her final eye contact with Amenhotep IV before he departed from the dining hall to his chamber to meditate. He had as usual refused to discuss politics with her. Still angry, she nonetheless yielded quickly to sleep.

She materialized aboard the starship under a blaze of lights. When she awakened briefly, the hand of her ultrahuman husband gripped hers and reassured her, and she again fell unconscious.

Tem lowered a biomagnetic eye from the canopy of lights above the cushioned table.

"Scan her entire body twice and then focus on her abdomen."

Tem scanned Nefertiti from her ankles to her forehead and then retraced to her ankles. He lifted the instrument, then lowered it toward her abdomen and positioned it six inches from her navel.

A hologram appeared between two lenses on the table. The image of the queen's huge pelvis and leg bones glowed white, as did her spine. The edge of the hologram glowed blue, following the contours of her skin. Her internal organs, uterus, vagina, and ovaries all glowed transparently with their own inner blue shades.

The mass in the uterus was coiled, bubbly, erupting with appendages.

"It must be removed," said Tem.

"Yes, it must," agreed Amenhotep IV.

"What could have caused that?" wondered Nuit.

"We will not know until it is removed, dissected and given a genetic scan."

"How shall we remove it?" Tem asked.

"Give Nefertiti a dream of rapture, of great metaphysical relief of no specific cause. We will induce premature labor with hormones. As soon as the fetus is aborted, she must be teleported back to her bedchamber. I shall accompany her, then return here."

The injection was prepared. Hypersleep was induced and a dream of rapture imparted by empathic suggestion. The injection caused rapid labor which resulted in nearly instant expulsion of the fetal mass because the queen's body itself rejected it. Nuit and Isis received the unnatural blob of protoplasm in a crystalline dish. Then Nefertiti and Amenhotep IV dissolved in multicolored beams of light.

They materialized in the bedchamber. Nefertiti moaned and writhed as if in pain but did not awaken. She still slept when the king dissolved into beams and columns of light. Nefertiti became quiet and perfectly still as the rays faded and he was gone.

The king materialized aboard the *Aton* and studied the results of the first genetic scan.

"It is interesting that this was the result of a natural conception *in vitro*,'" remarked Tem at last.

"Yes," said Amenhotep IV sadly. " It would appear that there is no compatibility between my sperm and Nefertiti's ova. My artificial sperm were unable to communicate their genetic message to her natural ovum cell. The oncogenes reproduced wildly and produced this incoherent mass of protoplasm."

"It is very similar genetically to a malignant tumor," sighed Tem.

"So it is. Yet, it is *structurally* different. These curved needles of calcium are rudiments of bones, and in a way it has the precursor of a gastrointestinal tract."

"So it has. Yet, the oncogenes have gone wild and disrupted the structural possibilities." Tem's voice was unbearably sad.

Amenhotep IV patted his hand and said cheerfully, "We do not need to dissect it. It is not complex enough to warrant that. I will return to Egypt with it. It will be part of my time capsule."

"What!? You wish to preserve this for posterity as a first experiment?" Tem was amused.

"That is exactly my intention! Record the data; return me with the foetus in a crystal jar."

So it was: back in his palace, the king transferred the terrible nonliving thing to a new repository, an earthenware jar filled with salt water. When the crystal jar gleamed into rainbow rays and teleported back to the *Aton*, the king fell into the repose of meditation in his bedchamber once again.

The hours of the night ebbed away from the edge of dawn.

Chapter Sixteen

Upon awakening and feeling the absence of life in her womb, Nefertiti was melancholy. Amenhotep IV was gone. He had risen early, allegedly to oversee the last of the confiscations. Nefertiti was glad. Comforted by her handmaidens and Mother Tiy, she gloomily hoped she would never see her unnatural husband again.

The final treasures had been delivered, the last few pieces loosely catalogued and placed on the appropriate piles. The king ordered the gold and copper separated from the rest of the treasures—especially the copper.

By evening, when he joined his two queens, his young bride's attitude had softened. He knew her anger toward him was justified. He had known Nefertiti would be deeply saddened by the loss of her first baby, a star-child in whom she had placed all of her hopes. At least her dreams had been ecstatic. She had been again to the Other World, if only to suffer a great loss. But a new mood of acceptance had blossomed in Nefertiti, and she was even glad to see the Pharaoh. He sat beside her at the royal dining table. Although their conversation was sparse, it was loving, and the young queen became affectionate toward the him, who had just finished confiscating all of the treasures of Karnak.

Later in their private rooms she spoke to him of the disappearance of her unborn child.

"I was indescribably sad at first," she said weakly, still reluctant to speak of the loss, especially to him. "But I remember saying goodbye to the little soul in the Other World, and Mother Tiy comforted me, and I remember how painful it was when I awoke in the morning and something felt wrong. I started feeling better toward the end of the day. Thank you for being with me, my husband. I still fear you a bit, but you have never hurt me. I have no reason to fear you, although your ways are strange."

The king laughed. "I know that my actions are both strange and appalling to you, but have no fear. There is a purpose for everything I do."

"I have been hearing of your plunder of Karnak, and I wished for so long to talk with you! But now—forgive me! I cannot talk about anything right now."

He embraced her and she clutched his high chest. Her eyes were closed; she scarcely breathed. They remained together for a long time, until she fell asleep on the low mound of her bed on the floor.

He meditated beside her for several hours, then arose and slipped from the sleeping queen and down the palace hallways unnoticed to a chamber in the interior of the palalce. It was like many rooms: lacking windows, with a high roof and with only one doorway and two small vents. The intended purpose of such rooms was to store dry grain in case of famine or drought. But now it was a laboratory.

There Ai was teaching Parannefer some simple laboratory techniques. They were embalming the cadaver of the result of their first genetic experiment, using a greatly modified version of an ancient royal funerary rite.

"Why are we doing this?" Parannefer asked Ai several times as they prepared solutions of solvents and distilled oils. "I thought the king outlawed all royal funerary protocol."

"He outlawed the year-long funerary rite. But he wants this specimen preserved as an embalmed king. Everything the Pharaoh is doing here in Egypt has great relevance to a real future."

"Is that so? Shall there be Pharaohs ruling until the god-kings return again from the skies to live among us in that future time?"

"There shall be a long age without any Pharaohs of Egypt, and even a brief time without any kings at all!"

"What?" Parannefer was shocked. He blinked in disbelief, but when he saw how serious the priest was, he shrugged and accepted the notion. He was glad that he would never live to see that terrible, anarchic day.

"Do not worry," Ai reassured the Best Friend of the King. "You are gaining valuable experience you will need if you wish to work with him."

"I am glad," Parannefer said, carefully washing a glass beaker.

When Amenhotep IV arrived, Parannefer repeated his question about embalming the grotesque cadaver.

"That this poor deformed thing was embalmed as a king will be a message," said Amenhotep IV. "It will tell people something of the nature of the firstborn of the king who arrived in the Aton disc."

"What will it tell them?"

"It will tell them of the difficulties god-kings face in order to father children by the daughters of Humanity."

"I see…" Parannefer sank deep in thought.

The king placed a huge hand on Parannefer's shoulder. "Do not ponder these things too much, Dear Friend."

"I will not. I accept that I have a vast opportunity to serve you, O King."

"Thank you. Now may you cleanse your soul in dreams and awaken refreshed in the morning."

"Bless you, O King," said Parannefer.

"Bless you, O King," said Ai.

The Priest of Aton and the Best Friend of the King departed.

The creature who called himself The Beast clutched his throne and glared defiantly into the darkness. Kahotep could feel the presence of the king in the temple above him. For hours The Beast sat frozen with terror and paralyzing hate. The riches of his greatest temple had been plundered by a man from the stars who had sworn to prod the Hidden One out of hiding!

He sat alone and in silence for he had long ago sealed the aparture between his chamber and the chamber of Amenhotep, Son of Hapu. For months, all that the blind seer had cried out was:

"Beware the king who rules with two queens! *He is back!*"

He felt the presence of the extraterrestrial king move out of the halls of Karnak shortly before dawn. The Beast slept briefly, then summoned his Twelve Chosen. He instructed them to eat and take shifts sleeping. The Depraved One then slept again. When he awoke with disturbing dreams it was early afternoon. He had slept far too long.

His priesthood had assembled in their bare temple. Xepuru-Ra was praying in the hidden room below the central shrine, waiting for an oracle. Two wheat and barley biscuits and two cups of beer had been placed in the miniature Temple of Amen set in the wall behind the altar. No prophecy had been imparted yet, but the priest knew the ritual and had received visions from Amen before. He would repeat the rite and wait again, though six repetitions of the Subjugation Rite had not brought acceptance of the offering to the Hidden One. Amen was choosing not to manifest.

The faith of the remaining High Priest in Karnak was shaken, while The Beast, against his own wishes, slept. There was no sign, not even the materialization of a slip of paper! Xepuru-Ra was disheartened, though it was still early in the day. *Amen frequently prefers manifesting at night*, Xepuru-Ra reminded himself, *even in times of great crisis*. But the unholy confiscations had been complete for more than a night and a day! It was futile to wait for night again.

The priest was repeating his prayers *en rote*, fast and loudly now, and did not hear the sliding of a human body across the vast single slab of stone that comprised the ceiling of the central chamber. The stone above his head was painted with complex, multicolored hieroglyphs. Some of the black lines surrounding the name of Amen-Thoth were actually slots in the stone. Directly above, through such a slot peered the long-lived Priest of Thoth who called himself the Hidden One.

The desperate Xepuru-Ra prayed repetitively and vociferously. He again finished the traditional litany, then blinked and looked up. A piece of papyrus parchment fluttered down from just a few feet above his head. There! A wondrous materialization! Xepuru-Ra marveled over the pen-drawn hieroglyphs. Each one was perfect. The inscription read:

"O Dog of Little Faith! How irony has bestowed undeserved honor upon impiety. Repeat your prayer of worthiness and acceptance one hour after sunset. Your Protector, Amen."

This was one of many such messages that The Beast had created long in advance. He had chosen his temple priests for their gullibility—this paid off limitlessly. Seeing the perfect, ink-dry hieroglyphs appear silently during a prayer impressed them every time as a miraculous message from a hidden god.

When the sun had set and the said hour was at hand, the eager temple priest placed a tray bearing two biscuits and two cups of beer on the tiled floor of the altar of the Little Temple, where the spirit of Amen was said to dwell. On the other side of the wall was a secret room. Inside was a man in a black robe. From the slots in the decorated ceiling of the miniature temple he could see within without being seen. Looking straight down from above he could see the tray of food and beer in the tiny Temple of Amen.

Xepuru-Ra backed away, kneeling in prayer. He faced the door through which he had entered. Behind him was the altar, the tiny temple and the tray of food. He recited his prayers audibly, as he had been taught many years ago. The tiled floor of the miniature temple rotated silently. The tray of food disappeared.

The man in black removed one of the biscuits and one of the cups of beer. He drew from his robe a tiny ceramic vial filled with rose-colored fluid. Opening it, he held up the crystal stopper, which tapered into a glass tube. He lowered it over the remaining biscuit and deposited one drop from the tip onto the brown crust. Then he swirled the tube in the remaining cup of beer.

The Beast noiselessly rotated the floor back into place in the wall of the temple. From an unseen slot he watched the kneeling priest, back turned, eyes closed, finish his prayer and examine the food on the tray. Exactly half had been accepted. Suppressing his eagerness, the priest reached for the cake and cup. Xepuru-Ra ate the sacrament.

Soon the indole-based chemical passed through Xepuru-Ra's fasting-purified stomach via the alcohol in the beer. He knew he was being possessed by the spirit of Amen! He would be transformed for the next twelve hours. His pineal gland being stimulated induced a dreamlike state of waking consciousness. Xepuru-Ra had ingested a powereful dose of ergotamine, a natural form of lysergic acid, a powerful Serotonin-like drug.

When Amen saw in the pallid face and swaying eyes that the full effects of the drug were in force, he delivered his oracle.

First, a long, rising moan. The voice of the Hidden One echoed throughout the temple. In the ears of Xepuru-Ra, it rang on waves of adrenalin chills. It climaxed with a sudden shouted command:

"Come to attention!"

"Y-y-y-yyeesss!" Xepuru-Ra staggered and whirled in the center of the room, blinking blindly and gasping.

"Hear the voice of your master!"

The priest fell to his knees, then toppled on his side and convulsed briefly. He tried to draw himself to his knees again to listen through the rippling, glowing colors in his mind.

"Hear me and respond, Xepuru-Ra! I am Amen, your god and One True King."

"I h-hear, O Amen!"

"You have been chosen to rid the world of this evil one."

"I have tried, O Amen, I have tried! Y-y-yes, I h-have t-t-t-t-tried!'"

"I know your efforts. Your magick should be more substantial. At morning you will find a magickal knife on the altar of this temple. Be careful, for the blade has had vast magick imparted to it! It will kill instantly any man or animal it touches! Carelessness will be fatal!

"Access to the palace will be opened for you, though the guards will not be sedated. Kill them if you must. Silently kill the monster king. Then kill yourself. I will meet you in the Tuat. I guarantee your soul admission into Heaven!"

The Beast repeated these instructions loudly in the bellowing echo chamber of his secret room. His threatening commands seemed to resound from all directions simultaneously. The simple instructions were repeated hour after hour as the crude lysergic acid burned the serotonin receptors in Xepuru-Ra's brain with electrochemical fireworks:

"Kill the demon king then kill yourself and we will meet in the Tuat."

Convulsions blended smoothly into sleep, and as Xepuru-Ra slumbered he urinated in his robes.

When he awoke, he defecated into his robes, then took them off and cleaned himself with an unstained corner. He crawled naked across the floor to the miniature temple set in the altar wall. His ears rang and he had lost his balance, yet he prayed he wrongly remembered the instructions from his god.

His memory had preserved the dark message: there, on the tiled floor of the temple miniature was a long, elegantly curved scimitar. The silver handle bore a cobra and a vulture, the two animals most sacred to Amen.

Amenhotep IV had ordered his guards to hide. They vanished, secreting themselves throughout the rooms of the palace, each instructed to report the presence of an intruder directly to the king.

Finding the promised easy entry, Xepuru-Ra, armed with his poisoned scimitar, slipped down deserted corridors aimlessly. Unfamiliar with the palace, he peered into several dark rooms, until, to his own great surprise he emerged to confront the terrifying king.

Ai, Parannefer, and Queen Tiy approached from the rear. Behind them followed a contingent of guards brandishing spears.

The priest of Amen froze, transfixed. The huge, unnatural king looked deeply into Xepuru-Ra's eyes as he walked towards him. The terrified priest broke his trance and ducked into an adjacent room. It had no furnishings. Only a window parted the wall for a view of the courtyard well below and a pool where the sacred crocodiles basked.

The priest pressed his back to the wall beside the doorway, waiting for someone—anyone—to step inside. He waited with fear-filled senses for the chance to cut the flesh of the king.

He feared most that he might be taken alive after some brief struggle. Then he would have to face the king. He fervently hoped that instead he would be killed instantly.

The deep voice bellowed from beynd the doorway. "This is your king!"

"Aiiiiieeeyyaaaa!" The assassin wailed, spun through the doorway, then froze, his knife curving over his head.

His eyes met and merged with the eyes of the king. He slashed only empty air with his poisoned sickle. He dared not scathe the king. He screamed, *"Thou shalt not judge me!"*

"Feel no guilt in my presence."

Pain broke through the fear that gripped the priest of Amen. The plunge was spasmodic and reflexive, his knife inside his own belly.

"Take him out of here just as he is," said Amenhotep IV to his guards. "Be careful with that knife. You will find deadly poison on the blade."

"Where should we take him?" one guard asked.

"To Karnak. The priests in the temple will know what to do with him."

An account of the suicide reached the ears of The Beast by his secret emissaries. Now he was alone. One high priest had gone mad. The second had killed himself. Karnak was not without temple priests, but now had no ordained high priest. Worse, all of the temple accoutrements had been taken: tools of magick and age-old science, ornamented wands, cups, swords, crystal pyramids, jeweled scepters—all gone, filed away, presumably, in the treasure trove of the new king.

Also gone were hundreds of sacrificial victims, men imprisoned young so that they would be available for sacrifice when Amen's physiology again demanded rejuvenation by the Obscene Rite. The length of his cycle and volume of Serotonin required to sustain him had increased since its inception. Thirty years had passed since his last ingestion of living Serotonin. Kahotep calculated that he had twenty years to live.

His fortune was ill. He had no representative inside the palace now, not even Suti.

The last Amenist King had vanished in a thorn forest hunting lions. A queen of another religion then had ruled in his place, a very popular queen. And now all of Egypt was being shocked and mortified by a king with a grotesque body, who shouted heretical pronouncements and banned Egypt's most sacred customs! Obviously these events had been controlled!

Kahotep felt wave after wave of regret that he had not murdered Tiy long ago. That would have raised chaos and anarchy, and probably a peasant uprising. But Kahotep now faced the closure of his greatest temple in his capital city!

The Beast had no way to stop this new king. He did not even have a high priest! No other priests in Karnak had been trained in the ritual of preparation and acceptance of the Oracle of Amen. None other at all, in fact, except the High Priest of Luxor. Every Priest of Amen, including the High Priest of Luxor, feared the new king. When he came to their temples with his small troupe of guards, the defilements, the temple confiscations had been done with theatrical flourish witnessed by the guards alone, for without exception, the temple priests fled in panic at his approach.

The day after the assassination attempt, the Priesthood of Amen suffered another blow: Amenhotep IV ordered the riches in the Temple of Luxor confiscated. The Egyptian army would spread its treasures before the king's palace.

Deep in his catacombs, The Beast raved uncontrollably. Above Kahotep's chambers the ground trembled with the footfalls of soldiers marching in unison. After a few hours, heavier footsteps shook the streets: the soldiers returned bearing treasures of statuary, jewels, and gold.

Three days passed, during which the Temple of Luxor was emptied of its contents. The treasures were sorted efficiently in rows and piles according to the system used for the closure of Karnak. As inventory was taken, the artifacts were hauled to the Royal Tax Houses.

When the temple was completely empty, the king made another pronouncement: since Amen had not at any time shown himself, had not manifested in any form, therefore he, Amenhotep IV, Son-of-Aton, was going to display his star-begotten body in frequent pageants and festivals. Only a coward hides, said the strange new king, and Amen must either be a coward, and therefore a god of limited power, or Amen might not even be a real god at all.

So be it, were the final words posted on the archway over an abandoned temple.

The Beast sat hour after hour in his throne without even a mortal servant. Kahotep did not know that Nefertiti had conceived a first child and lost it. He did not know of anything that happened within the palace walls, except what he learned through the small animals, the birds and rodents, who did not make the best witnesses.

Kahotep was alone and he knew it. He would still be given offerings of food by the faithful at his local temples, all of which were interconnected by secret tunnels. He could steal food offerings to royal ancestors at the mastabas of the houses of Thebes. He would be unsuspectingly cared for by his temple priests. And then he would live twenty more years only to die of age and cancer.

No. He would not have it! He would gather his resources and meet this new threat without revealing himself or else escape from Egypt and seek refuge somewhere that would welcome a blood-craving war god.

Chapter Seventeen

In the weeks that followed, Nefertiti the queen seemed to heal very well in both body and spirit. She accepted that she would yet be mother to a new race, in the same way that Tiy was mother to Amenhotep IV. There would be risk, but no extreme danger. She knew she would be again taken into the Amentt to receive the seed of the god-king in his astral home.

The distribution of the sacred grains to the hungry poor had been a brilliant and necessary reform. Its success brought the king vast favor among the peasantry. The appointees in charge of the food distribution had been so effective that, despite his extremely unpopular acts of confiscation of the treasures of Karnak and Luxor, the great majority of the people, the peasants who comprised most of the citizenry, supported their king enthusiastically.

Feeling thus secure in her heart, and with the understanding that her husband's attacks on the temples of Amen had ceased for a time, Nefertiti was led once again to the bridal chamber in the Temple of Aton. This time she was escorted by both the king and Mother Tiy to the altar under the ceiling of the temple dome. She reclined on the cushioned stone slab, gazing thoughtfully through the circular port at the starry night sky, until a wonderful warmth spread throughout her body and enticed her eyelids to close. Her husband's large and strong hand held her right hand and Mother Tiy's small fingers interlaced with her left. The king's mother's hand was also held in his own; thus a circle was formed.

One star in the center of the sky grew brighter than the others. The room was bathed in light, at first prismatic, then white. A gleaming, cloudy white light. . . .

Nefertiti reached toward a figure running slowly toward her. It was the human, the beautiful human figure of her husband's real body in this world of white light! They made love and dissolved into orgiastic lightwaves of colorful pleasure. She reached a mystical orgasm as soon as he entered her body. He deposited his gift in her. She floated in nerve-numbed bliss, her eyes shut against the glare, content with the knowledge that her husband was near.

Tiy had been aboard the starship *Aton* the night before. Then she had contributed two ovum cells, painlessly plucked from her fertile ovaries without benefit of the masking memories of induced raptures and hypnotically-imparted dreams.

The Mother Queen was forty years of age and still youthful. Her body had not aged significantly in more than twenty years. She, alone, could contribute genes that would be completely compatible with the king's artificial sperm. Also, she was quite capable of giving birth again, should that ever be necessary. The wise Mother of Egypt knew much: that the world was round, not flat atop a pedestal balanced on the back of a turtle. That the Aton Disc was a starship of immense size from one of the stars in the night sky. She knew that there were many, many worlds in the sky, some like her own.

She observed as the nuclei of both ova were removed and all oncogenes systematically combed from the chromosomes. After a limited purge of recessive genes and restructuring of dominant genes, the nuclei were returned to the ova. The gods of the *Aton* thus hoped to achieve a high probability of compatibility with sperm cells of the king's genetically-engineered body.

As the tube slithered out from between Nefertiti's labia, they witnessed a successful implantation of two fertilized ova from the body of Tiy. As the nuclei split, the cells doubled, quadrupled, the ova adhered to the wall of Nefertiti's womb. The queen was now pregnant again.

The young queen slept much the next day. The second night of her sacred pregnancy, she remembered being drawn again into a realm of light, and in that cloudy brilliant world she met two little spirits, a boy and a girl...

The fetuses bore no defective traits. Even so, Nefertiti would be brought aboard in a week or so and scanned again. This pregnancy must not end in another disaster. The two tiny ones were going through a healthy chromosomal dance, developing normally, anchored to the wall of the nurturing uterus. One was developing into a female; the other was developing into a male.

The queen would be the mother of twins.

A week passed. Nefertiti chatted with her mother-in-law and husband about their new religion, the news from around the kingdom of Egypt, and the arrival of the babies. Nefertiti insisted her dreams had revealed to her that she would give birth to twins.

"How can you be so sure?" Tiy would tease her.

"The night after I made love with...him...in the Amentt, I returned to the Amentt to receive two spirits, a little boy and a little girl. I remember this! It was too vivid to be an ordinary dream..."

"I will not argue," Tiy would say at that point, and give Amenhotep IV a secret look. The king would smile.

As the days passed their conversations centered more and more on the births. When a week had passed, the starship *Aton* again assumed a geosynchronized orbit above the palace. Aboard the spaceship, Nefertiti again dreamed in rapture, and a very sexually fulfilling dream occupied her consciousness while the electromagnetic eye and other instruments scanned her body. The scan revealed that her womb contained two very healthy normal embryos. They were developing rapidly. Neither would give their strong, young mother any foreseeable problems during her pregnancy.

The next morning she remembered the realm of light and erotic rapture. When she awoke to see her husband, the king, sitting beside her, she reached for him immediately and hugged him to her breast.

The two little lives in her belly felt good and warm.

When the queen was three months pregnant and the twins she carried healthy and strong, Amenhotep IV announced that he was about to build a new temple of Aton. It was to be erected exactly between the temples of Karnak and Luxor, right in the center of the Avenue of the Sphinxes. A few of the sphinxes would have to be hauled away for what would be a very deep foundation for a rather small building.

After a week of digging, twenty feet underground a horizontal wall of stone was uncovered. The king ordered the work crews to break through it. The limestone was very hard and in fact the most effective work against it was accomplished at night and in secrecy. Morning after morning the wall was found broken and fragments were removed by the laborers.

The slab was clearly a ceiling. When it was finally opened, the king looked into the tunnel that ran between Luxor and Karnak. A rumble thundered out of the blackness, climaxed in a deafening roar and a powerful gust of wind that burst from the stone hall.

"Listen!" the king ordered.

A second roar erupted from the tunnel out of the south, from Luxor. It thundered, then fell silent.

"The tunnels have been sealed," said Amenhotep IV. He knew that two immense stone slabs had been dropped, permanently, triggered automatically or by a mechanism operated by The Beast himself.

Since the first tunnel to be blocked was the corridor that led to Karnak, the king surmised that The Beast had sealed himself in his chambers beneath that temple. The sealing of the tunnel in of Luxor may have been automatic, triggered by the tremor caused by the fall of the first slab.

That is good, thought Amenhotep IV as he left the excavation. *The Depraved One is trapped in his tomb beneath the Temple of Karnak. He will either flee, in which case he will be apprehended, or he will die there.*

The Temple of Aton between Luxor and Karnak was completed at the time that Nefertiti was due to give birth. The pregnancy had been carefully monitored. The two babies were healthy and strong inside her. The son had inherited his father's enlarged female pelvis and the daughter had inherited the king's huge elongated head.

During her pregnancy, and following the seizure of the temple treasures of Luxor, the king let up his assault against Amenism to be with his queen. He spent days with his art students, painstakingly teaching them how to perfect the contours of the human face and body, in contrast to the rigid traditions spanning the centuries. Bek most of all was responding favorably to the new rules of proportion and anatomy. Cato was showing signs of developing talent. Suti had successfully broken ties with the stylized past of his half-lifetime of creative work. Tutmose, a younger man, joined them after displaying his works of great genius carved in stone before the critical gaze of the Pharaoh.

In his brief tours of the local temple of Aton, Amenhotep IV met and befriended Auta, a priest who, although not an artist himself, showed such enthusiasm for both paintings and sculptures that the king invited him to the palace to become "Overseer and Vivifier of All Art Objects." After working closely with the artists, Auta started taking a hands-on interest, first doodling with ink brushes on paper, then molding heads and faces out of clay. Soon he, too, was learning the proportions and the symmetry of the human body and producing admirable renderings. The king posed frequently with his two queens.

When the first few labor pains led to the breaking of the queen's waters, Nefertiti was escorted to her chamber. Her husband was beside her and Queen Tiy was at her feet. Instead of teleporting the queen aboard the *Aton*, a midwife would be teleported down to oversee the births.

A light gleamed behind the laboring queen and subsided. Around Nefertiti walked a small human woman who wore silver robes. Her head was huge and high-domed. Their initial eye contact seemed to jolt the royal mother outside of her body.

Her consciousness hovered over her bed, near the ceiling of the room. She could see her body bathed in multicolored rays of light. She felt each contraction as if her mind were connected to her body by a long cord. Distant sensations, the pain was real but impersonal. She met each contraction with a push, push against the two little beings in her belly.

One slid out, blue and bloody. The other followed with the next contraction. Both were wreathed in their umbilical cords. Another pain filled the distant body, and out came the afterbirth.

Then Nefertiti felt drawn up and up, faster and faster, toward a blazing pillar of light. It was alive and regarded her with curiosity and love. She greeted the light with her most cheished memories. It saw through her eyes. Nefertiti went past the gleaming light into a dark and comfortable realm in which she felt her spirit could bathe forever in the healing water of sleep.

When she dreamily awoke, two perfect mouths were suckling at her breasts. She felt two tiny bodies on her belly. Comfortable, she sensed people around her. Filled with happiness she went back to sleep.

The little boy was named Smenkhara. His twin sister was Meritaton. They were both odd children, as Nefertiti had anticipated they might be.

The boy looked normal, with an egg-shaped head and bowed legs. His disposition was recalcitrant and he rarely slept but moaned almost incessantly as if from internal discomforts. He nursed often and greedily, then he would cry as if from colic. He seemed to be an unhappy baby, almost from the moment of his birth.

Second to leave the womb, Meritaton was much happier by disposition. She had inherited her father's elongated head to the extreme and difficulties had threatened as her head moved through Nefertiti's birth corridor. But Meritaton's skull was considerably longer than it was wide, and her mother's body had accommodated it. Meritaton was born with her eyes wide open and fully alert.

As the days passed, both babies looked out at the world with eager, intelligent gazes. There was little question as to their health or strength, although Smenkhara had difficulty moving his little legs in their pelvic sockets. Though he suffered from gastritis from his mother's milk, he bonded to her and to Tiy and responded to Ai's smiling face. But the huge, looming face of the king, his father, terrified the boy. This filled the king with great sadness.

After the twins were born, the queen fell into a melancholy state that persisted despite the best efforts of her family and her strange husband to cheer her up. She seemed to develop a subtle aversion to the babies and soon gave up breast feeding them and employed a wet nurse. Nefertiti was much happier.

Their daughter was not afraid of her father at all. She bonded with him in that mystical union that unites almost all parents with their blood children. Nefertiti thought that the affection Meritaton and the king displayed for each other was justly to compensate for the his failure to inspire the love of his son.

Amenhotep IV tried very hard to win Smenkhara's heart. He cradled the baby in his arms until the child's screaming became too painful for the king's grieving ears to stand. He observed the boy in his sleep, the only time the king could gaze upon his beloved son without evoking terror in him.

Nefertiti did not welcome her husband with an open heart during the days and weeks that followed the birth of the two odd children. Whenever he approached her, her manner became distant, her conversation disjointed and shallow. She grew indifferent and submissive. His attempts to be with her became less and less frequent.

Near the end of his first year as king, Amenhotep IV incurred the hostility of Nefertiti when without warning he ordered the army to march to Lower Egypt and seize the entire contents of every temple of Amen in the land. For weeks treasures flowed to the palace grounds and were sorted, inventoried, then carried to the taxation warehouses. The warehouses of the treasury were filled to overflowing. Immense piles of jeweled and golden artifacts were stacked against the white plaster walls. The king still ordered raid after raid until the confiscations were complete throughout Lower Egypt.

Without a pause, the army was ordered to march south to raid the temples of Amen in Upper Egypt, until all riches had been carried off and guards posted to prohibit the worship of the Hidden One. Months followed, during which caravans of treasures came in from all directions . Gold, silver, copper and jewels were piled high on the palace grounds or stacked against the walls of the tax offices.

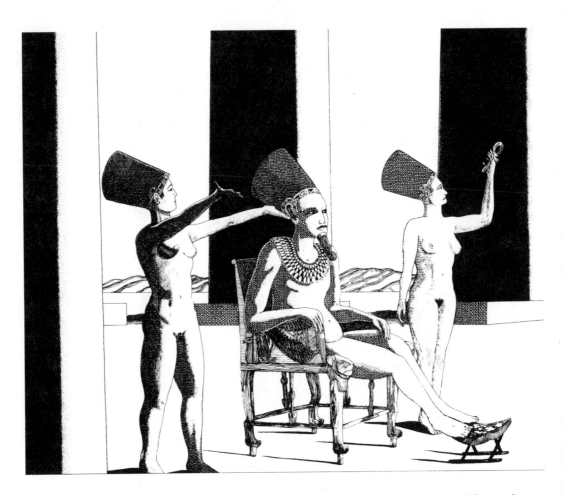

Then, throughout the land of Egypt, the religion of Amen, worship of the Hidden One, was banned by order of the king. The temples of Amen were closed.

This provoked outrage from Nefertiti, who compared the king's latest attack on the religion of the war god with the oppressive nature of Amenism itself.

"Nonsense." Amenhotep IV dismissed her words with a wave of his hand. "I murdered no one. I declared no war. No weapons were used."

"Weapons were brandished!"

"It was a dangerous task, taking the teeth out of Egypt's war-dragon!"

They would argue deep into the night, but to no avail. The strange king read aloud one proclamation after another against the religion of the Hidden One, and ordered the new series to be copied by hundreds of scribes and distributed throughout the land.

"I have trapped the Hidden One in his own temple catacombs. I have cut into his secret tunnel with the foundation of my own temple. The sacrifice of human victims to feed his unnatural geriatric addiction has been stopped. He will face death in less than two dozen years."

"True, O King," said Ai, "if Amen does not retaliate against you. You have attacked the Hidden One unmercifully. All of Egypt knows you hate Amen. But they also know that, like Amen's own priests, you treat the Hidden One as if he were a real man, or a living creature of some kind, if not human. Thusly do you reinforce faith in Amen throughout Egypt. You sow the seeds of your own unpopularity in doing this."

"My uncle, I have lifted fear of imprisonment and death from the hearts of Egyptians. I have ended persecution of the poor and of the darker races, and have distributed foods once reserved for the gods to the mouths of the hungry and homeless.

"Furthermore, the harvest at the end of my first year as king has been so bountiful that the peasants credit Aton with having blessed Egypt. Even now, with food being given to the peasants in vast shipments, there is surplus. Abundance unprecedented in our history is attributed to Aton. These words are being repeated all over Egypt.

"The temples of Aton are filled with believers. The temples of Amen are abandoned. The religion was already on the verge of falling into disgrace before I arrived. Queen Tiy had inspired Egypt for too long. The religion of the Aton Disc has always been identified with Tiy, Mother of Egypt."

"This is all true," Ai nodded. Respectfully, he continued. "But these facts are no guarantee of lasting popularity. The masses, even the peasants, seldom faced actual starvation. Little has changed for them. There are no beggars on the public streets, that is all. Loyalties can shift and humans are amazingly volatile, O King. They can take abundance for granted. The strangeness of an alien king can suddenly look like nothing more than gross ugliness and deformity. And rebellion among human tribes can be sparked by innocuous events and burst into fire suddenly."

The king pondered these words silently, then answered somberly. "I hear your words, Honorable One, and I fear that what you say is true. I feared these things before I came here. I risk incurring the wrath of Egyptians by what I do, though I direct my actions against Amen, not his followers. The fact that I have hurt the followers of Amen is incidental to what I have done, and I have hurt them only intellectually, not physically."

"This is true, but look at one of the effects! Your wrath against the Hidden One has aroused an unhealthy and unnatural interest in him. He has not been discredited completely. Most nobles still prefer to worship Amen over Aton because of the treasures that foreign wars bring to Egypt. Now all that has ended. Treasures have been flowing to you! So, the nobles ask, what is the difference? Your popularity, O King, is most avid among the homeless and poor. But the workers, nobles, and officials are becoming very critical of you, and your attacks on the remaining temples has not helped. Pardon my words, O King, but I felt that you should know that in my opinion there are dangers ahead."

"I have heard and respect your words, Honorable Priest. I thank thee."

Ai bowed his head and did not discuss his skepticism again for a long time.

Nefertiti was angry. "In your pronouncements you said women would exert equal influence in advising you as any man in court. Yet I, your queen, have less to say in all matters than anyone in your palace."

"Do you really mean those words?" Amenhotep IV was surprised and concerned. "Is this how you perceive yourself in my estimation?"

"Yes. Ai and Parannefer agree with every word you say. I do not. So you avoid dialogue with me."

"That is not true. Ai voiced disagreements with me only this morning."

"Is that so? I am relieved to know that *someone* is standing up to you."

"You seem to think that I disregard you completely, Nefertiti. Is this so?"

"Tiy has been Queen of Egypt for over twenty years. She is the only woman to whom you listen and turn to for advice. You have avoided me on several occasions. This is not fair."

"Your words are true. I have avoided you because I sought shelter from your anger. I admit that I have provoked your temper a number of times."

"I am not as old or wise as Tiy, but I have lived among the Egyptian people for twenty years of my own life. Compared with the only year you have spent among us, where is your experience in dealing with people? You have none, and it shows in your mishandling of the Amenist religion."

"I must consider this. Twice today I have been told the same words."

Later that night Amenhotep IV meditated in telepathic union with Yod, the vast energy body aboard the starship *Aton*.

I have been warned about the volatility and rebelliousness of the human race, even among the sedentary and peaceful Egyptians. Although Egyptians loathe war and being sent to fight in foreign lands, there is a greater fear of these accelerated and permanent changes shaking up their lives. It is this fear of radical change that I have been warned about twice today. I must take these warnings to heart.

But even to risk the political and social rebellion of all Egypt is less grave than risking anonymity. It is mainly a record of the strangeness of my body and the method by which I created a new race of humans that I wish to preserve within the Egyptian records of historical time. The record of my life and family must be a time capsule. It must remain unintelligible to the masses, even to the scribes who will keep the memory of me alive throughout Egyptian history until —

Until the significance of my anatomy, inherited by specific members of my immediate family, will become apparent to the minds of the people to whom the world will be known to be not flat but round, and the sun will be known as a star among stars, in a vast sky rich with potential for life and consciousness.

It is this body, and the heads and bodies of the race that I will build, that must be recorded. The record must survive at all cost. It is not an act of creation, but a specific recorded signature on the greater act of creation of Earth humanity. It is a signature that will grow more and more legible with time.

Nefertiti was again told that she was to enter the bridal chamber with her husband. She stifled the urge to rebel and consented. Tiy had gone the night before her to "prepare the way to the Amentt" for her. In reality the mother queen had contributed another ovum cell. Its nucleus had been extracted, oncogenes removed, and recessive genes replaced with dominant genes bearing healthy traits.

On the appointed night, Nefertiti accompanied both Tiy and Amenhotep IV to the bridal altar under the circular opening beneath the starry sky.

The *Sektet* arrived and descended toward the temple. It filled the bridal chamber with brilliant rays and bathed the three figures in light. When it departed, the stone altar was bare.

The shuttlecraft swiftly shot out of the atmosphere and carried Geb and Tem, plus the king and two queens, into the airlock in the belly of the immense starship. The occupants were quickly removed to the laboratory, Nefertiti in hypersleep and dreaming of the rapture of her Pharaoic lover's arms.

Conception was accomplished in a microscopic glass sphere. A thin tendril deposited the fertilized egg inside Nefertiti's uterus. A brief scan revealed that the egg adhered to the uterine wall and was taking nourishment. The queen was pregnant once again.

The pregnancy was monitored every night for a week. Nefertiti dreamed strange and beautiful dreams of the light-filled world of the Amentt. She met her newest child, a little girl spirit, and dreamed every night of being with her. The egg developed into an embryo and from an embryo to a fetus. The forming baby appeared healthy and strong, although not as strong as the twins had been. Amenhotep IV seemed concerned, but never showed his trepidation.

During Nefertiti's third pregnancy, the king resumed his attacks on the temples of Amen. His soldiers uncovered secret worshippers of Amen in temples in outlying regions. Several times he ordered Amenists to be driven from their temples, although he ordered none imprisoned nor fined.

Icons of Amen were destroyed in public, often on the steps of the temples themselves. All renderings of Amen were defaced. The name of the war god was scratched from the walls of the temples built in his name. The statuary and frescoes created to honor him were shattered in front of astonished and often disapproving crowds.

At night strange lights were seen above the Temple of Aton in Thebes. Only Ai, Parannefer, and the king himself knew why the sky was frequently pierced with rotating multicolored beams.

Sounds issued from the Temple of Aton late at night. Strangely melodious sustains blended over oscillating harmonies. The Thebans said the temple was singing.

Inside the temple vast quantities of copper were being melted by strange devices brought to the temple by the sky-boats. It was being liquefied and turned into endless strands of wire which was plated with a thin coating of gold. Thus, enormous cables of the sacred metal *tcham* were created in the temple and coiled around a vast stone obelisk with a huge crystal set in its tip.

Experiments were being conducted inside the temple, the nature and strangeness of which were not known to the change-fearing Egyptian people. Electrified, the coil of tcham cable emitted brilliant sparks of lightning and flashes of light. It also rang with eerie whines and long notes of music.

Nefertiti watched anxiously and often silently as the events proceeded around her, unaffected by her, and she hoped without influencing her. Despite the security of the palace, she sensed in the tightness of her guts the approach of disaster. She withdrew and graced only her own domicile until the king announced a new pageant, a new celebration. He was going to give immense riches to the peasants of Egypt. He was about to give away a great portion of his personal treasures as well as the confiscated riches of the temples of Amen.

This news was well-received by the populace but treated with suspicion by the royalty. They feared that he might confiscate their personal fortunes and the thought of gold and diamonds falling into the hands of the peasants was disgusting to them.

Nefertiti held her breath and waited for the pageant.

The pageant was spectacular. Once again the Egyptian people were granted a view of their two beloved queens and the huge weird king who astonished them with his behavior as well as his body. Once again they were treated to three days of feasting and drinking, and encouraged to celebrate as men and women in those ways that the sexes were created to celebrate. The fears and doubts of the Egyptians were temporarily alleviated. Nefertiti's own spirit was lifted. There was nothing that she loved as much as the bliss from the knowledge that all Egyptians everywhere loved and adored her.

On the fourth night after the pageant Amenhotep IV returned with Ai and Parannefer to the Temple of Aton. Many Egyptians were awake, even at late hours. Many of the citizens of Thebes saw the lighted disc descend into the vast temple. They saw it merge with the erratic flashes that backlit the pillared facades.

Inside the temple, the energy-bright machines melted the copper into coils of thick wire. The obelisk was wrapped deeper and deeper in a cocoon of copper plated with gold.

A few Egyptians saw the illuminated disc depart a few hours before sunrise. The strange flashing lights continued until the sun approached the horizon and the oscillating whines continued to wail long after dawn. The citizens of Thebes were becoming accustomed to such displays in spite of their resistance to that which they did not understand.

Meritaton and Smenkhara inherited their father's physical traits but not his strange metabolism. They weaned themselves after only three months of nursing and developed omnivorous appetites, not limited to eating only meat like their father was.

This limited fare manifested another strange aspect of the king's behavior. He insisted on killing all of the warm-blooded animals he ate himself: goats and sheep and occasionally cattle. He would spend a short time alone with the animal. Then, he would be seen sitting beside or in front of the animal, stroking it as it lay curled up on the straw. The first time Ai and Horemheb saw Amenhotep IV with a young goat, they presumed that the animal was asleep, it appeared so peaceful. . . .

"If I am to eat only flesh so that my descendants may survive another time of desolation," said the king, "then I must see to it that the animal dies in peace."

"How do you kill them?"

"I meditate with the animal until it becomes telepathic with me. I do this through love. When the animal and I love each other so much that the animal wants to become me, then I admit its little mind into my own mind and we become one mind together. Then the animal and I rejoice at the joining of his old body with that of his new body, which is also me."

"I think I understand," said Ai.

"I do not understand at all," General Horemheb said, "but I assume that it must be so, since you speak it and I have seen it."

"Come," the king said, standing up uneasily in the bed of straw. "Bring with you the body of the little one and prepare it for our feast."

This had happened a long time ago, but it served to underscore the strangeness of the man among them. Everything about him was different from ordinary humanity, what he ate, how he appeared in face and body, how he walked, what he said and did. With every pageant, every time he appeared in public, each time he presented himself at his balcony, more Egyptians realized that another race, different from human, did indeed exist and could live among mortal men and women.

Adored by all of Egypt, Nefertiti spent most of her second fulfilled pregnancy seated before her beloved citizens on a throne held high in pageants or else in view on the palace balcony, either with her strange husband or alone, before the feasting celebrants.

Amenhotep IV honored his promise: at each festival he scattered riches, gold coins and jewels, to the peasants of Egypt. The first treasures he offered were those he had inherited as king.

Chapter Eighteen

Tutmose completed a towering statue of the space king. He was very pleased with it. Amenhotep IV received the news gladly, for Tutmose had been "nearly finished" with the work for three days. After his breakfast of river perch baked without garnishes, the king visited the studio. There, in the center of the room stood the life-sized statue.

Tutmose the artist at once rushed to it, fell folded onto the floor at the foot of it, one arm over his back in abject humility.

Amenhotep IV walked slowly toward the magnificent work. His face glowed with admiration. As his great long eyes studied every part of it, detail to detail, his smile broadened. At last he stood directly before the statue and nodded with approval.

Tutmose had smoothed out the acute angles of the cheekbones and rounded the curve of the jaw slightly, to conform to what the king himself had taught as rules of proportion for human realism. The applications worked. The likeness of the king was doubly admirable, considering the nonhuman quality of the face the artist had tried to render. The statue, with the royal crown, the plaited beard, the scepter and the flail crossed over his chest, comprised a double-image: an Egyptian king imposed onto the elongated face and head of an extraterrestrial humanoid. This effect, even modified to favor human contours, was striking.

"That is admirable," Amenhotep IV said at last.

Tutmose stood very slowly, breathing excitedly. "I know that I still have not curved the line of your jaw just right," he apologized, "but yours is, please pardon me, is such an…unusual countenance to depict. Pardon me, O King, for reminding you of that so ceaselessly."

"I am pleased that you took such great care to render my visage as it is, instead of with such flattery as others have extended to the Pharaohs they were commissioned to portray. This, Tutmose, is a true masterpiece. You have created the first honest attempt to depict me the way I am, for posterity."

"I have known for long that this is what you wanted, O King. That, and that you shun depictions of yourself as a warrior. How shall we depict you, now that many of us, Cato and Suti and Bek especially, are becoming more adept at this new tradition you wish us to innovate? What activities do you wish us to depict you engaging in? What, if not war and the hunting of lions?"

The king laughed. "I have a son and a daughter now! I rejoice that another child of mine will soon manifest in this world. So depict me as I am, sitting beside my wife and my mother, with my children on my knees!"

The sculptor bowed and then reached up and embraced the tall king. Affection was encouraged in his court because the king himself had declared that showing love was a virtue.

It was also during these months of Nefertiti's pregnancy that Amenhotep IV decided to modify the symbol of the Aton Disc. Since ancient times, Aton had been depicted as a disc, broad side facing full, with a cobra encircling the edge. The head of the cobra turned abruptly at the neck in some renditions, facing the viewer with an open mouth, or else it was clutching its own tail in its teeth.

Amenhotep called his artisans to him.

"The cobra is reminiscent of Amen's Uraeus, symbolizing quick death and the vulture representing the feast for the carrion-eaters that is the battlefield. These rays in the new symbol of Aton represent the multicolored beams of white light that are seen around the disc by night. And the hands that are holding the ankhs — they mean the living, intelligent knowledge that certain of those rays impart."

"I think I understand," said Tutmose.

"The ankh represents much, much more than just Life. There are many orders of life. That which we call consciousness, or Mind, is also varied and diverse. Thus, ankh can be life as well as all living things, the life force in general as it manifests through all things. And it can be the gift of living knowledge that is received through the eyes of those who look upon the disc."

"I have never received this knowledge, but I know some who say they have."

"You know many who make this claim."

"Yes, many among the priests and priestesses of Aton. Queen Tiy of course, and Ai. And some of the priestesses of Bast. They said the Aton Disc hovered over their temple two generations ago and that some of the priestesses watching, and some of the cats as well, received visions of knowledge from the disc of light."

"So they have. I was myself within the Aton Disc when each one received through their eyes knowledge that is living and compassionate."

"Then it is true."

The months of Nefertiti's pregnancy progressed toward the ninth. Amenhotep IV, who had emptied and closed every temple of Amen throughout Egypt, effectively banning the entire religion, relaxed with Nefertiti and enjoyed the benefits of his high office. He commissioned much artwork: statues and drawings of himself and his royal family. No battle scenes; all family portraits. Nefertiti was alive in the center of peace.

☥ ☥ ☥

The twins learned to speak very early. Although articulate, they were not disposed to prattling nor chatter. Meritaton learned to walk when she was nine months old.

She surprised everyone when she tediously, prodigiously balanced her huge head atop her long neck while slowly standing up in the middle of her nursery. Her tiny legs wobbled and the tendons at the sides of her neck strained. She straightened her knees and stood erect, victorious over gravity. She took three steps and toppled to the floor just a few feet from Grandmother Tiy, who caught her. Determined not to stop with one successful try, Meritaton mastered walking that very afternoon. She was jubilant and hobbled from one room of the palace to the next, announcing herself at each doorway. "See me! See me!"

Her father strode in his ungainly gait down a hallway to see what Meritaton was announcing. She plunged into the hallway, took a few steps and fell down, then picked herself up again, her head tipping precariously on her neck. She staggered to her father, arms outstretched. Queen Tiy appeared in the doorway behind her, grinning. Nefertiti was suddenly smiling over the smaller queen's shoulder, enjoying the child's breakthrough.

Meritaton, the tiny girl with the huge head, was walking.

Amenhotep IV received her with open arms. He hugged his tiny daughter.

She said: "Did you see me? I love you, father."

"Yes, I saw, my daughter. You are quite agile on your feet already."

Behind them, Smenkhara struggled on his back on a blanket on the floor. Though he kicked and flailed his legs furiously, he could barely crawl.

He was a fully articulate child. Like Meritaton, he was quiet, but while her quietude was the result of serenity, his seemed to be of reticence. He sometimes complained of pain in his legs, especially when he struggled to crawl or stand. He also had stomach problems. In all, his mental attitude was one of unhappiness.

His father paid him much attention and attempted to demonstrate great affection for the boy, but Smenkhara would have none of it. He was no longer afraid of his father's huge face, but retained his aversion to it. He thought of himself as a victim of his father's weird anatomy.

He resented the excitement just outside of his door. He knew that Meritaton was walking. He did not care to learn of anything she did. Their father's deep, booming voice only reminded him harshly of his own physical shortcomings.

At night Amenhotep IV often meditated beside Nefertiti's bed or joined Ai and Parannefer in the Temple of Aton. They continued turning copper and gold into the continuous coil of tcham wire wound around the stone and crystal-tipped obelisk. Occasionally an illuminated skyboat came to the temple. Then electrical discharges illuminated the sky and weird music sang long notes to the rising dawn.

Nefertiti remembered these visitations as celestial communion with her unborn daughter. One day in her eighth month, Nefertiti felt the pangs of labor. She had false labor before, but these contractions were strong. She was bathing in the sunshine pool when her waters broke and blood flowed forth.

Taking great care not to let any bathwater enter her body, Nefertiti's handmaidens raised her from the pool and escorted her to the room prepared for her and lay her on a sofa. Queen Tiy and Amenhotep IV entered, soon joined by Ai.

The room swiftly acquired a glow that obscured forms and colors. She felt a woman's hand lift her by the arm. She gazed into the face of that strange and beautiful midwife who had assisted with her birth of the twins a year before: the smiling woman with the huge head who was one of the Amentii. Nefertiti fell unconscious into the woman's smile.

When she awoke, her consciousness was afloat in a strange room, hovering over her own body. Her arms and legs were being supported by Tiy and Amenhotep IV, and Ai held up her back. The long-headed midwife was presiding over the birth, somehow assisting the muscles of Nefertiti's body to push harder with each contraction. As before, the mind of Nefertiti remained aloft, distant from her body.

The baby's crown appeared. The blue scalp parted the labia and bulged out. The head and diminutive body followed and the baby was born, another infant who had inherited the fantastic cranium of her father. By comparison her body seemed tiny. Two tiny eyes popped open. She squirmed, wreathed in the blue umbilical cord. The midwife deftly tied it as Nefertiti's body contracted again. The cord was cut just as the afterbirth was delivered.

Lightly washed with sterile towels and placed upon Nefertiti's belly, the little girl struggled toward a milk-swollen breast and immediately suckled.

The mind of Nefertiti suddenly ascended away from the event that was taking place in one world, happening only to her body. She felt herself falling upward into a source of brilliant light which soothed and embraced her and caused her to sleep.

Maketaton was born three weeks prematurely, her body unnaturally small. She nursed and slept, nursed and slept, waking often to murmur complaints of colic.

Her name meant "Protected by the Aton".

The Beast knew that sometimes the king haunted the abandoned halls of Karnak at night. Although the king made no psychoholographic projections of his image into The Beast's domain, the Hidden One felt the powerful empathic presence of the extraterrestrial man,

In the year that followed the final abolition of the religion of Amen, The Beast sat in his chamber in silence and plotted. He was very good at planning; strategy

was his forte. The Beast was also very patient. He had twenty years in which to make a move and much could happen in twenty years.

He still had one potential victim whom he could feast upon before those years were gone, for the Temple of Karnak was not quite empty: in the adjacent cell was Amenhotep, Son of Hapu, the blind seer, his captive. One more living brain, a potent, psychic brain, containing one last living pineal gland. At his present rate of decay, The Beast calculated he could count on another ten years, twenty at most. Then he would have to gorge on a veritable orgy of sacrificial victims.

He knew he would have to revive his cult of worshippers somewhere else, with some other human tribe. But he had done that before. Nubia was promising. The Nubians were very excitable people, easy to arouse into states of hate and bloodlust. In the past Nubia had been a second home to The Beast.

If worse came to worse, he might cannibalize the pineal glands of his own Twelve Chosen. But he was uncertain of the effects of performing the Obscene Rite on the brain of another addict of the life-prolonging process. The thought disturbed him. But he had Amenhotep, Son of Hapu as his pet still, and much depended upon whether Egypt and the new king found each other compatible. The Beast guessed they would not.

At any time The Beast could have used the maze of intricate passageways to flee the Temple of Karnak and strike out for his freedom, clothed in nocturnal anonymity. Kahotep might be able to make his way out of Thebes, out of Egypt, and into Nubia or Ethiopia. He considered this often.

On the other hand, there was little Amenhotep IV would do if The Beast remained in Egypt, assuming the king adhered to his own new law, which, Kahotep reasoned, he no doubt would. As a pacifist, there was nothing Amenhotep would do if he caught Kahotep, except imprison him. Kahotep feared imprisonment.

The collapse of the tunnel that linked the temples of Luxor and Karnak had been a largely symbolic blow to The Beast. The new foundation for the Temple of Aton intersected the secret tunnel. Kahotep himself had triggered the hydraulic mechanisms so that now both tunnels to the temples of Amen were sealed with immense stone slabs. Even as a symbolic blow, it had been effective.

Leading from the inner sanctum beneath Karnak were dozens of tunnels that led to the *mastabas* of the royalty of Thebes. Daily food offerings were brought to mummified ancestors to feed the *ka* to keep alive the *ba* alive in Heaven. Kahotep visited these mastabas to steal the fresh fruits and nuts so that he, his captive and his Twelve Chosen could stay alive. These same tunnels could give him easy access to anonymity of the streets of Thebes, thence anywhere in Egypt.

How good was the king at anticipating stealth? Propably not good at all, an ethical philosopher and big-hearted empath, not experienced at battle plans, tactics, or strategies. These Kahotep considered his own domain. The new king would miscalculate the Egyptian temperament and his demise would soon follow. Kahotep believed he knew Egyptians best. The Beast would wait for this inexperienced and fanatical king to stage his own downfall.

Amenhotep IV had already gone too far.

AKHETATON

𓅓𓏲𓇋𓂀𓏏𓆤𓇳 𓅓𓏲𓇋𓂀𓏏𓆤𓇳 𓅓𓏲𓇋𓂀𓏏𓆤𓇳 𓅓𓏲𓇋𓂀𓏏𓆤𓇳

Chapter Nineteen

At the end of his second year as king, Amenhotep IV was informed that many of the temples of Amen in the distant cities and rural regions had withheld some of their temple treasures. General Horemheb was ordered to capture every secret cache of holy artifacts and magickal tools.

The king himself made pilgrimages to remote temples and resumed his desecration of the names of the Hidden One. He visited dozens of temples on five separate journeys and left each building empty. All art objects were carefully removed, the less ornate furnishings were toppled and the name of Amen was chiseled to dust whenever it appeared among the mural hieroglyphs.

In this way the telepathic force field triggered by the name or image of Amen was quantitatively diminished. This weakened the clairvoyance and telepathy exerted by Kahotep on the unconscious minds of his followers.

At the beginning of his third year, Amenhotep IV had completed seven personal attacks against the temples of Amen in the rural regions of Lower Egypt. Although the treasures confiscated were meager compared to the riches captured in the years before, his intention was obviously harassment: the defacement of Amen's stone murals and icons and erasure of the name of the abolished god.

At the end of his seventh campaign he was received by the indifference, then coldness, then anger of Nefertiti. He was beset by the warnings of both Tiy and Ai: "You must cease!" "You have gone too far!" Amenhotep IV resolved to refrain from another campaign against the temples and remain in Thebes for a while to pay more attention to his three children and his two queens. He designed a colossus to be built of limestone. It would show him the way he really looked, sitting between his two queens. It would be a monument to intimidate time.

Nefertiti was relieved. He had not even spoken to any of his family during the brief returns between his excursions to the temple sites. Nefertiti faced this terrible contradiction with stony rage, preventing the communication they needed to reach understanding.

When they commenced the first of their sittings for Bek and his sculptors, Nefertiti relaxed, as if things were back to normal. She forced herself to forget that the attacks against the temples of Amen had ever taken place. Amenhotep IV knew that his antagonism toward the cult of Amen bothered her, and resolved to talk to her about it after one of the prolonged sittings. When the opportunity arose, he suggested they discuss their differences, either in private or in the presence of Queen Tiy, whichever she preferred.

Nefertiti refused the offer entirely at first. She dismissed the temple attacks with the words: "What is there to discuss?"

The king would have let the subject drop, but Nefertiti yielded to the impulse to confide, to release her feelings in words. After their dinner she sent her hand-maidens from her chamber and met the king for a discussion of political matters.

"I think your demonstrations against Amen have had a bad effect on your own religion," the Queen of Egypt spoke cautiously to her king. "I know we have discussed this before…"

"Yes," said Amenhotep IV. "We have talked about that before, in depth more than once and peripherally many times. I am well aware of your views and I believe that there is truth in them.

"My persecution of the religion of Amen is keeping an interest in the religion alive. But there are no new converts to Amenism. Everyone wants to talk about the persecuted religion but nobody wants to join it."

"That is true, but the religion itself has hardly been abolished." Nefertiti was growing more relaxed. She lost her doubts and reticence. "The Priesthood of Amen has been shattered, but even now the factions attempt to draw together and reassemble."

"Yes, and no doubt they have already sent their spies to the beer shops where the peasants gather to drink at the end of their daily toil. Yes, I have not eliminated work, only starvation as well as much of Egypt's surplus. Still, two fine autumn harvests have been attributed to me and the peasants do not believe that Egypt has fallen out of favor with the gods."

"That is true. You, as king, are more popular among the peasants than the god you have denounced."

"On my last seven excursions, which were completed in rapid succession so that the priests of Amen would not know where I was going to appear next, I gave most of the jewels and ornaments directly to the peasants. Again I searched among the peasantry for nomarchs and governors to replace officials I determined had abused their power and mistreated their subjects. I replaced them with men and women whose auras gave me empathic assurance that they were averse to inflicting harm on other people."

"Do I detect a hint of vanity?" Nefertiti chided.

Amenhotep IV laughed softly. "Yes, perhaps my own quest for posterity does look hypocritical to you. It is not vanity. I am immortalizing this body and the bodies of my children and I can only do this by…"

"'…drawing much attention to myself and commissioning much statuary and blah, blah, blah!'" She mocked him. She had heard these words many times.

"That is very important, Nefertiti. It comprises my entire reason for being among you here and now in Egypt."

The queen continued to chuckle and prod the king until he, too, was laughing. Still laughing, they fell together and embraced. They held each other for a long time. Then, Nefertiti kissed him playfully and announced:

"It sounds like you want the Priests of Amen themselves to preserve this vast record of yourself that you are creating."

"Yes, that is what I have been telling you all along! I want the Priests of Amen to do just that: preserve all memory of you and me and our royal family and our strange-looking children for all time."

Nefertiti realized fully for the first time that although his attacks upon Amenism looked so angry to outsiders, in reality they were theatrics. Everything he had done had been a performance. His entrance, naked, through the gates of the city of Thebes. The changes in the coronation ritual. His pronouncements against the death penalty and ritual murder. His liberation of slaves. The attacks against the temples. The feeding of the poor. The erasure of his father's name from temple walls and statuary. All of it had been staged. Probably rehearsed. Definitely planned by people in another world. Performed for an audience who did not know that their king was only acting out a drama—or perhaps a ritual. Now she understood why Ai was always laughing.

"Do you not see the night sky differently now?" Amenhotep IV asked. "Have not the visits to the Amentt, where we celebrate our union and you are given these celestial children, has this not left you with new knowledge of the Heavens?"

"Yes, my husband," Nefertiti said after a long time. "I no longer see stars in the night sky. I see worlds instead."

"Would you like to see the worlds with me, Lovely One? The night is clear and the stars are shining, my Queen."

They walked arm-in-arm to the highest balcony and spent hours sitting, he on a cushioned throne, she on his lap, viewing the starry black infinity that surrounded them in space.

The immense wooden wall plaque had been painted white and inscribed with the lyrics of an ancient drinking song which had been incorporated into the *Precepts of Ani,* a lengthy poem by an ancient and probably legendary royal scribe. The message that loomed over the beer shop was taken in good cheer by the drinkers who sometimes bellowed its verses while violating its warning:

"Make not thyself helpless in drinking in the beer shop.

"For will not the words of thy report repeated slip out from thy mouth without thy knowing that thou hast uttered them?

"Falling down, thy limbs will be broken and no one will give thee a hand to help thee up.

"As for thy companions in the swilling of beer, they will get up and say, 'outside with this drunkard!'"

At the end of each round of singing, another of beer was poured and musicians would resume playing.

But this was not an elegant beer parlor. No musicians played spinning drums and stringed instruments. There were few tables and those were wine kegs, broken in half, turned flat end up and set into the dirt floor. Candles dripped wax from wooden perches among the few oil lamps Drunkards who passed out were evicted violently by huge bald-shorn men. There were many large pillows in the corners and the dust stank of urine.

The drinkers of the sour-tasting beer were men grumbling with discontent. Brawling and stupid, many were toothless and some obviously diseased. They drank their beer at the end of the day, sometimes fought, acquired scars and discarded fingers. They bullied each other for sport. It was in such pits that the Priests of Amen had long ago learned to recruit their soldiers.

There was a man who was everybody's drinking partner. He had been everybody's special friend for years, a fixture in the tavern for as long as anyone could remember. The patrons liked him, even though he never drank nearly as much beer as they did. Of all the men who visited that beer shop, he was the only one not routinely challenged to a fight.

He was not a man to be antagonized.

He was talking tonight to his fellow drinkers about the changes that the new king had brought upon them, and whether or not they thought these changes were good, after three years of Atonist rule. From the back of the room bellowed the gutteral voice of Anpu. He was shriveled and brown. He called out:

"The king's new laws have not brought me any favor!"

The drinkers fell silent.

Cautiously, the man in the center of the room at the barrel-table spoke out:

"With what do you not find favor in the laws of this new king?"

"His new laws cost me my wife!"

"Your wife?"

"Anpu," one of the men serving the cake-ale shouted, "you used to beat your wife senseless. No wonder she left you."

"She *never* did what I told her to do. Under Amen it was different. Amen would not tolerate foolishness and *pride* in women!"

"Here!" "Yes!" "Say it! Say it!" Voices echoed through the crowded, dim, shadowy room. The few women who lounged about in the darkness were prostitutes. They were silent. Women were not allowed in most of the drinking rooms in Egypt. Only the lowest classes, who swallowed beer that was sour and cheap, drank in places

172

where women, always prostitutes, were allowed to sit with the men. The prostitutes in such taverns willingly suffered abuse and torment from violent men. Still, shrunken, brown Anpu had been unable to procure for himself the favors of any of these prostitutes for years, so harsh was his reputation.

He clung bitterly to his story. His wife was irresponsible and wept too much. When the king granted women right to bring harassment and assault by a man, even her husband, up before a judge, Anpu had to admit that his wife had left him.

"You think this is unfair?" asked the friendly man at the center table.

"Of course it is!"

"And you say things were different under Amen? I recall that they were. Amenhotep III was a war-priest of Amen, that is true. And yet, he treated Queen Tiy with royal respect."

"That is true! But she was *queen.* She was not like other women. Tiy is a goddess."

"So her son is a god?"

"He must be. But he does not know us men. He does not understand us and he is turning our society upside down."

"Why do you think this is so?" asked the friendly man in the white robe. "If, indeed, Amenhotep IV is a real god?"

"Of course he is!" Anpu leaned forward out of the darkness. "I have heard that his body is tall and weird, half man and half woman—but with a man's penis! And they say his head is huge. It is bigger than a melon. Egypt has been favored by another god-king, but this king has spent too much time among the Amentii."

"Yes!" "This is true!" "Tell more! Tell more!" echoed the other men.

"He thinks that all women are like his two queens, Great Mother Tiy and the Goddess Nefertiti. But they are not!"

The men in the tavern burst into hostile chaos, bellowing threats of torture and murder to all women who were not Queen Tiy or Queen Nefertiti.

The friendly questioner at the center table listened to all of this with interest. When the shouting subsided, he offered to buy everyone in the shop another round of yellow beer.

Chapter Twenty

Early in the third year of Amenhotep IV's reign, the Priestesses of Isis sent a delegation. Outwardly they were to dance before the king and bring him gifts of art and jewelry sacred to their religion. Secretly the Priestesses of Isis and the Priests of Osiris conspired to find out whether this seemingly very angry king would find disfavor with their respective priestcrafts.

Three of the musicians were men, priests of Osiris and introduced as such. The king received this lively entourage with enthusiasm. He enjoyed their performance of ceremonial songs and sacred mime-dances. When the dancers brought out their sistrums and played their Dance of Circles in Unison to Mayet, the Goddess of Cosmic order, the big, unearthly man wearing the woven beard was absorbed in rapture.

It was then that Nefertiti, seated beside him, saw how deeply he loved these innocent young people who had come before him. She knew that he would do their religions of Isis and Osiris any harm. She saw again that quality she had observed upon first meeting him. She clutched that first impression to her heart and saw his eyes fill with tears at the sight of Egyptian dancers.

When the priestesses finished their final dance, a ritual mime which surprised Nefertiti because she knew that it was usually revealed only to the advanced initiates of their priestcraft, the queen saw on her husband's face a look of adoration that told her they had won his total, loving appreciation.

"You have pleased me mightily!" the king announced. "I have never been so greatly impressed by grace and creativity. You have much to bless your people with. You have my blessing upon you."

"We, the Priestesses of Isis, bestow our blessings upon the Aton Disc!"

"We, the Priests of Osiris, bestow our blessings upon the Aton Disc!"

The priest and priestess who spoke for the others stepped forward and bowed. The king saw by the expressions in their eyes that they wanted something from him. He guessed that they wanted reassurance that their religions would not be banished like Amenism had been. He did not know what words to choose, so he offered them a dinner invitation instead, which the young priests and priestesses eagerly accepted.

At the feasting table they noticed that he ate only meat, though they felt obliged not to comment upon anything that might acknowledge his relative strangeness to them. They concentrated instead on talking about philosophical topics, especially the relationship, if any, between Aton, a very old god, and Isis and Osiris, also among the oldest of deities.

"Of course," the king announced. "Have you ever visited the old temples? The very old temples of Horus or Isis or Osiris?"

Some said they had.

"Then you must know that Osiris and Isis returned to Heaven together, to a new home near Sothis, the Dog-Star, by way of the Aton Disc.'"

"Then Aton is like a raft or a ship," said one young woman.

"Yes. And Isis and Osiris are inside this ship."

"Then Aton is not exactly a god," the young priestess ventured cautiously.

"There is One True God," said Amenhotep IV emphatically. "This One is Ptah, the Universe, Who is the Mind of the Universe. Ptah is the highest consciousness there is. Ptah is *so much the Universe, so much the Mind of the Universe,* that Ptah sends to this world a *material disc* from out of the Universe. This is the only part of the Universe we need to acknowledge. Things are as they were written in the Old Kingdom: Isis and Osiris boarded the Aton Disc and rode to Sothis III, the dark star-gate that circles the two stars that make the Dog-Star so bright. And know this: the Aton Disc never inspired a religion until your grandmother's time, when she was a girl. The religion of Aton is as old as Thuya, mother of Queen Tiy."

The young priestesses and priests were impressed.

"Let it be known that I have spoken to, and conversed with both Isis and Osiris in their bodies even as Nefertiti was preparing to give birth to Maketaton."

"You seem to be saying that you are a personal friend of both Isis and Osiris," said the precocious young woman.

"That is true," said Amenhotep IV.

Mother Tiy sat smiling, very mysteriously.

Amenhotep IV announced that he was arranging to have a royal caravan escort himself in the company of the royal family down the Nile River to Memphis. This was the king's first visit to Lower Egypt to the north.

When they reached Memphis after seven days of feasting and song on royal barges, they had no sooner settled into their accommodations than Amenhotep IV set about inspecting the temples of Amen to see that proper erasures of the name of Amen had been made. The guards were questioned about secret worship in Memphis or anywhere else in Lower Egypt. A few nervously reported knowledge of such practices.

Within days Amenist temples were closed down and ritual tools confiscated. Jewels were thrown to the peasants, gold and copper were taken away to the south by the soldiers, silver was given away along with the precious stones.

Overseeing all of this were Nefertiti and Tiy. Both queens smiled in amusement.

The guards, the offended priests and the peasants begging for the jewels were all like comical children to them. The king himself was like a cosmic clown, instigating the whole dramatic game and controlling it with his melodramatic actions. Nefertiti saw him as a grand puppeteer. The result was both awesome and grotesque.

"I proclaim this temple to be closed!"

The dark looks of scorn from the defrocked priests, the royal guards pushing the mob back with staves, and the grasping, ceaselessly groping arms of beggars, surrounded the royal caravan in a gnawing, shuffling ocean of arms, legs, rags and dirty faces. In the center of this, atop a towering platform, sat the king and two queens. Sixteen men carried it from wooden shafts at the bottom. At the top the king stood abruptly, reciting more official pronouncements banishing from this temple the Priests of Amen.

Nefertiti watched this same scene at temple after temple, now participating in the "attacks" with the smug delight of a practical joke. She saw the same comical elements repeated at each reenactment, improvised on the steps of temple after temple. The guards acted the same. The priests all wore leopard robes and strutted about in frustrated rage. The beggars looked the same, reminding Nefertiti of pigs feeding out of a small trough in a crowded sty.

At night when they returned to their accommodations in the Temple of Aton in Memphis, Nefertiti heard her husband moaning in misery in the privacy of his meditation chamber. She heard his voice clearly speak:

"Father Tem and Lord of Light Yod, hear me! The pain in my thighs and leg bones is insignificant compared to the misery in which the children of Egypt live. More than that, the misery to which they have become accustomed!

"Greed is everywhere. It controls the hungry by their stomachs and it fascinates the affluent and those of royal birth who will never fear hunger. Greed obsesses minds of those who should be occupied with loftier things.

"I am hurting inside, O Yod, of whom I am an emissary. I am doing my best to impress my appearance in Egypt onto the future of these people, but my heart aches with the empathy I have shared with the hungry, the afflicted. Even Nefertiti thinks my actions are extreme, but she does not know the pain in the pit of my stomach that stabs me when I see eye-to-eye people who feared starvation only three years ago and see in me some sort of living deity. This pain of pathos I cannot long endure..."

With that, his words ended and his voice trailed into an agonized wail. Nefertiti was stricken with tears. She raced down the hallway.

Shortly after their return from Memphis by an overland caravan, Nefertiti was accompanied by her husband and Queen Tiy to the bridal chamber of the Temple of Aton. There she was admitted into the Amentt again to enjoy the sexual rapture of communion with the astral body of her stellar husband. The outcome of this night was another conception. Again it was the combination of genetically manicured ova contributed by Tiy with the most compatible of Amenhotep IV's sperm. The object of this pregnancy would be to again produce twins.

The royal household received with delight the news that the queen was again pregnant. Tiy and Ai rejoiced when the king made his official announcement. Nefertiti herself was pleased. She had come to love her two large-headed daughters and her crippled son. Smenkhara, however, turned a cold ear to his father's voice, slipped from his stool and crawled painfully away.

"Smenkhara!" his mother cried, standing and following him.

"No, mother," the boy called over his shoulder. He could not walk, even using the staff his father had given him.

"Please, Smenkhara!" Nefertiti scooped up the crippled boy. She cradled him in his arms, although he struggled against her, finally submitting to her embrace.

"Are you not happy to hear this wonderful news?" Nefertiti looked pleadingly into his eyes.

"How can I be glad about another's birth when I regret my own?" demanded Smenkhara.

"Is that true?" asked the king.

Smenkhara turned away from his father and struggled to get to the floor.

"Is that true, Smenkhara?" Nefertiti repeated.

"It is true that I have an unnatural father!" cried Smenkhara. He twisted out of his mother's grip and fell roughly on the tiled floor.

Amenhotep IV stood and walked akwardly toward the rebellious child.

"No! No! Do not touch me! Do not let him touch me, do not let him touch me, Grandmother Tiy, do not let..."

The king reached out to the boy, who huddled in a corner beside the entrance into the main hallway of the palace. Instead of fleeing the outstretched hand, the crying, bitter child lunged forward and bit his father's thumb.

The king withdrew his bleeding hand silently.

Smenkhara scurried down the hall on his hands and knees. His father remained unmoving with tears in his eyes. Nefertiti followed Smenkhara, while Tiy examined the wound.

Later that night, Amenhotep IV sat with his two daughters at a table. He was silent for a long time. There was pain in his eyes.

"Any other king would have punished such a boy," Tiy said at last, "but you will not. And yet he hates you even more intensely for refusing to have him reprimanded for the things he does to you."

"Any other king, yes. Other kings preferred being remembered as killers in wars. I have been portrayed as a good father to my children. And a good father I fully intend to be."

"Does a good father suffer abuse from his son?"

"If he needs to show how pointless such abuse is, yes, he suffers it indeed."

In the months that followed, the colossus that the king commissioned of Bek and his sculptors was completed. It was thirty-three feet tall and painted with colored waxes to resemble the skin and clothing of the king and his two queens. Not only did the statue violate the tradition by showing the Pharaoh exactly the way he looked, without the flattery of convention that had been customary, but the queens were rendered as seated on elevated thrones with their heads exactly level with his.

These departures from rigid custom pleased the king, who bestowed many gifts on Bek, Tutmose, and Suti. Auta, as Chief Vivifier, ceremoniously breathed life into the giant statues during their completion ceremony.

Pageants and unscheduled feasts commemorated many events during Amenhotep IV's third year of rule and throughout the months of Nefertiti's pregnancy. Although the king ritually scoffed at the name of Amen, his direct attacks upon the temples had ceased. Another good harvest blessed Egypt in the autumn months and the people were for the most part very happy.

Word spread through the land that the new king's two daughters were distinctly of his race and not human. People who had seen them seated upon the royal float at pageants described them as long-headed and unnatural. People who were remotely connected with the palace uttered strange stories about the silent girls. They whispered secrets about the flashes of light that still emanated from the Temple of Aton late at night.

The Pharaoh's bitten hand healed amazingly fast. It was apparent to Tiy and Nefertiti that, like his son, the huge man had difficulty moving about, though the younger queen did not know why.

Among the guests they received during the months of her third full-term pregnancy was a second delegation of the Priestesses of Isis, including some of the members of the first entourage. They had been sent to demonstrate their gratitude to the king for the friendliness that the religion of Aton had extended toward the Priestcraft of Isis and Osiris.

A dinner and a sitting with the king were held in their honor, during which philosophical rather than political matters were discussed. The group of young priestesses departed following a brief exchange of gifts. The king had written each of them beautiful poems about love and nature and inscribed these words in colorful hieroglyphs on papyrus scrolls.

The priestesses were very impressed and praised the king's inspired verse. Each poem suggested that many beings of different kinds comprised all of nature. It implied that the many celestial beings comprised a vast Divine Family. Apparently this new king sought only to exclude one from the company of the Divine Family. That sole entity was Amen.

Early in Nefertiti's pregnancy came a vision in which the young queen met not one soul but two, both destined to come through her body as her children. As the first time, the young souls were of a boy and a girl. This turned out to be true. After a relatively easy pregnancy, the queen entered labor and gave birth. The girl was named Ankhasenpaaton and the boy Tutankhaton. Both children looked completely normal by human standards. Neither had inherited the distorted anatomy of their father.

When Smenkhara found out that he had two completely normal siblings, his resentment grew ever more intense. It made him more certain that his own crippled pelvis was by design and not by accident. He believed himself to be a victim of his father's cruel heredity. His useless legs and protruding belly were things that did not need to be.

Try as she did, Nefertiti could not bridge the abyss that separated the king from his tormented son. She went to bed one night in tears after a long and bitter argument with Smenkhara, who was now three years old and still unable to walk. Even the gentle hand of the king himself did nothing to alleviate the stinging of Nefertiti's tears. She wept, her husband caressed her, and still she wept more.

Amenhotep IV had refused to acquire concubines. When he received several letters from the King of Mitanni offering him daughters to take as concubines, Amenhotep IV had politely declined, using that opportunity to make a public pronouncement that he, as King of Egypt, was a happily married man and intended to stay faithful to his one wife. He would not acquire a harem.

Although it was another of the king's professional heresies, it was minor compared to the precedents he had already set. It impressed the Egyptian people very much, especially the women, that a king with the power and legal right to acquire women as property chose instead to treat his one wife with singular devotion.

This also impressed Nefertiti. She had learned to love the strange man in spite of his grotesque appearance. The nights of mystical communion with him in the Amentt were the only sex she had ever known and it had given her her babies as well. She realized as her husband read his pronouncement that she would never have to discover to what extent she would be jealous of another woman, or women.

He was not like any king Egypt had ever had.

His courtship of his queen's heart began with their coronation and wedding ritual.

It was a tender story of love poems composed to praise her beauty and eulogize the inner spirit of her heart and almost incessant gifts presented to her, including the best treasures of the temples of Luxor and Karnak. Only these did she refuse to accept from him.

The poetry moved her the most, and he composed much of it and eventually he stopped giving her jewels altogether. Until she would drop a few hints that she liked a particular scarab or a specific jeweled ankh. Then he would surround her with such adornments.

The only source of grief in Queen Nefertiti's life was the inability of her son to accept and love his father. This worsened as Tutankhaton and Ankhasenpaaton quickly grew, learned to talk, crawl, and stagger to their feet for the first time. By then Smenkhara was almost four years old and finally gaining the strength to take his first steps with the help of his walking staff.

His father stood in the hallway and repeated in controlled tones of voice, "Why do you not speak to me? Why do you not speak to me?"

Smenkhara sought the nearest empty room to escape, shuffling with one shoulder against the hallway and his walking stick braced under his arm. When he reached the doorway, he tumbled inside. He struck the floor and cried out in pain. His father reached him just as Ai and Parannefer entered the doorway behind him.

Smenkhara said the first words he had ever said directly to his father: "I hope you are amused that I would rather fall on my face on a hard cold floor than talk to you at opposite ends of a long hallway."

"Is that truly how you feel, my son?"

"Yes."

The strained silence was quickly shattered by one word:

"Why?"

"Because you...you...you..." Smenkhara doubled up in agony on the white limestone tiles. "Y-y-y-you put me in a body that I hate!"

"Do you really hate your body this much?"

"Yes!"

The king's mouth opened and his huge eyes winced with terrible heartache. He knew it was true and that he was fully responsible. He had known it all along. He saw no chance that Smenkhara would ever accept the reality or the strange purpose of his unnatural pelvis. This meant almost certainly that Smenkhara would refuse to accept, to love, to forgive his father for the crime of having cursed his own son with a prison of cruel anatomy.

As the boy lay glaring hotly up at his father, the Priest of Aton and the Servant with Clean Hands stood helpless, unable to even comfort the snarling, gnashing little figure. The king felt a surge of grief fill his heart like no pain he had ever felt before. It was then that he raised his right hand, pointed two fingers to the sky, and said the words:

"Ankh em Ma'at."

Ai and Parannefer gasped, then bowed their heads. Smenkhara froze and stopped thrashing about.

The king lowered his head and stepped out of the room.

☥ 🦉 ☽

To an ancient Egyptian the word *ankh* meant more than just "life." It was something akin to "the life force" or "the force of life." It was a word that acknowledged the relationship between life and mind, but also accentuated the interrelationships between living things, as though *ankh* referred to a psychic force field emanating from everything that is alive, and interconnecting all life invisibly but manifestly.

To the thinking modes and belief systems of other and later civilizations, like the intellectual Athenians during the golden age that would someday dawn upon Greece, or long after that when Florentine scholars near Rome reshaped the knowledge of the time during Europe's great Renaissance, the concept of consciousness as a psychic field would be questioned by many and rejected by quite a few. But to the Egyptians, the existence of a universal life force that was fully conscious and both external and internal to evey living organism, was a theory that no one had ever questioned. *Ankh* not only meant life, it meant universal life.

Em is an elusive word. It could mean "into" or "in," or it could mean "as." It depended upon context for meaning.

Ma'at concluded the short sentence. *Ma* is a universal syllable. It means the Great Mother. She was the omnipresent, very feminine side of the androgynous Ptah. She was personified as all of Nature Herself, the Mother aspect of the Living Land. But even the early Egyptians knew that she meant something else besides, although their limited cosmological notions prevented them from knowing anything about black holes that swallowed both light and time and existed as corridors to other Universes.

At referred to something that was also omnipresent and alive. This was the energy of life, the motive power behind green growing plants and grazing cattle and predators killing against starvation. It was also the essence of the life field itself. *At* was a vast energetic male principle that made time move throughout the world of matter. *At* was the original Father God.

Ptah had two manifestations, *Ma* and *At*. The interdependence of *Ma'at* was symbolized by two feathers, the *Suti*. The reason that feathers symbolized the union of the great God and Goddess was simple: when seated before Osiris, the god who holds the promise of rebirth following death, the heart of the departed soul must be weighed against the great Truth that the material Universe, which the soul has just left behind, is the product of a god-goddess, male-female union which formed the truth behind the entire Universe. The union was good in principle. For the union

181

to be fulfilled, life must be lived happily, joyously, lightly. Enlightenment, therefore, meant living life as lightly as a feather in the wind.

The heart of the living soul, at the end of life in the material, male-female Universe, was weighed against the two feathers of the *Suti,* the goddess-plume of *Ma* and the god-plume of *At.*

Enlightenment truly means living lightly, as any being who has ever passed through the event horizon of a black hole knows. To attempt this ultimate transition into universal consciousness meant eons of preparation, especially much meditation in world-created paradises. These were environments orbiting black holes in concentric rings. Most humanoids required long lives and extensive training before attempting black hole translation. Of all the anatomical variants throughout the galaxy, humanoids were most common. The humanoid races had contributed most to timespace engineering, probability restructuring, the terraforming of countless worlds and the cultivation of humanoid life forms throughout multitudes of star systems, throughout myriads of galaxies of all Universes of timespace quanta.

The king's words, *"Ankh em Ma'at,"* referred to the interconnected wholeness of the field of life, and how the many parts emanating that field co-created everything that would ever manifest on that life-field. Therefore, by living life lightly, life itself, the living field all life emanated, would be simultaneously "en-lightened."

He remembered passing the rings of Saturn many times. He had gazed past the crystalline wastes of the colonized moons of Jupiter to the giant planet's gaseous red and orange bands. He had also witnessed the destruction of the planet that had exploded into nuclear fire and left behind a band of rocky asteroids and icy remnants scattered throughout the Ra system.

Chapter Twenty-One

The three oldest children were as different from each other as they were all different from ordinary children. Except for Smenkhara, they learned to crawl early. They learned to speak when barely out of infancy, but after mastering words, they became inexplicably quiet.

Smenkhara was fully articulate by his fifth month of life. The least quiet of the children, he complained of stomach problems until he was two years old. He cried often but resented sympathy. The king tried to comfort his oldest son, but Smenkhara never overcame the horror he felt at the sight of his father's face.

The sympathy and love that often drew Meritaton to her father's lap was viewed by Smenkhara as a bond he could not share. Although the loving father tried to avoid favoritism, he developed a strong rapport with his daughter. Meritaton's vastly elongated head teetered in precarious balance atop her neck whether she walked, sat or stood. The fact that she was at all agile amazed her family, who observed that her head remained perfectly level however she moved.

She was a happy child. She was energetic and slept very little, viewing the world with wide, alert eyes. Butterflies loved her. They gathered about her whenever she sat in the sun on the porch of her balcony. Moths sought her company at night. She seldom laughed or cried and nearly always smiled.

Meritaton frequently asked her elders about nature. Her curiosity extended to flowers; she asked why some blossomed at some times while others blossomed at other times. As her father or Ai explained about seasonal cycles she would listen with huge eyes, her full attention upon her teachers. She understood every word and remembered much, always eager to repeat each lesson to her mother, Nefertiti.

Little Maketaton lacked the vitality of the other four children. She slept often and grunted and groaned from colic like Smenkhara had. Her large eyes lacked the alertness of Meritaton's gaze, lacking also the fiery rebellion in Smenkhara's glare. In fact, the spark in Maketaton's eyes was dim. Her father resolved to have the child watched constantly by her family and prayed that the meaning of her name would hold true: 'Protected by the Aton.'

The king failed to develop a rapport with Maketaton. Several times the child ascended with him into the *Aton*. She was scanned and a slight chemical imbalance in her brain was detected, though no specific cause was apparent. A genetic analog of her was cloned and grown *in vitro* aboard starship and studied for deficiencies.

After the birth of the second set of twins, Smenkhara directed his rage more intensely at his father. He also lost his affection for sleepy Maketaton. Nefertiti tried to comfort her son and sometimes he let her console him and sometimes he rejected her utterly. The queen loved all of her children equally. Through love for her children she held love in her heart for her husband.

As the first months of the lives of Ankhasenpaaton and Tutankhaton proceeded, it was obvious how precocious and unique were their personalities. Both learned to speak at four or five months and Ankhasenpaaton immediately became talkative. She was a happy girl with a normal-looking head. In a female body, her wide pelvis looked natural. At one year old she taught herself to sing songs. She walked about the gardens of the immense courtyard, adorning the sunny breezes with her melodies. The birds seemed to respond to the presence of Ankhasenpaaton.

Tutankhaton was equally precocious and normal in appearance, but he was not talkative. Also a happy child, his eyes were wide with alertness and his smile was truly innocent. He seemed to be incapable of feeling anything but love. Tutankhaton enjoyed listening to his father whenever the king spoke. The boy stood at attention whether the royal father was addressing a dignitary or holding a philosophical discussion. Often the king turned such periods of rapt attention to storytelling sessions or moments of poetic inspiration.

The boy asked many questions about nature. He was fascinated by insects, reptiles and small mammals. He was interested in the stars. He questioned his father about the River Nile and inquired about the phases of the moon. He would listen, his vision transfixed, memorizing the rhythm of seasonal changes and blossoming buds, the spawning of fishes, the nesting of mother crocodiles. When the king questioned Tutankhaton, the young prince would eagerly recite what he remembered, which was always a great deal.

At last Smenkhara could walk. He might never be able to walk unassisted and he knew he would never be able to run, but the fact that he could finally walk at all alleviated much of his suffering. Even so, his strange pride and furious hatred for his father would not let old wounds heal completely. Smenkhara let it be known that he was sympathetic to the priesthood his father persecuted. Although he never spoke to his father directly, he interjected rude comments loudly into discussions. He tried in every way to evoke his father's grief.

Discontent spread through the land. The complaint shared by men was that they had enjoyed their traditional mastery over women. Men had been free from laws prohibiting infidelity, but women were punished severely for slight transgressions.

Marital customs far older than the Theban revolution and Amenism forbade sex outside of marriage, with tolerance extended to unmarried lovers. But if either lover was married, the woman was declared guilty of adultery and sentenced to death by a pelting of stones. Any married man could claim to have been seduced by any woman, and, if accused, that woman was routinely tried and convicted and stoned.

Rich men had been encouraged to buy or take women for their harems as a sign of virility, wealth and political power. Under the new king, harems were restricted to voluntary unions between wives and husbands. Many concubines went free, fully liberated from being mere property.

The new laws did away with many inequalities. Marriages broke up because wives complained of brutality. Women were no longer stoned to death for seducing married men and women could even complain of rape and often men so accused were ostracized, if only by angry women.

The complaints of the men abandoned by their wives and concubines were voiced in the places where the feelings in the guts of men are finally spoken: in words growled over ale cups in the beer shops.

The guards posted to keep priests from returning to their sacked, abandoned temples suffered from demoralizing fatigue. Stories of secret meetings of Amenist priests which would once have sparked immediate investigations now were treated as mere rumors, easy to ignore.

Amenhotep IV became concerned when rumor of an Amenist rebellion in Lower Egypt was announced to him by Ai. A messenger was dispatched to Memphis, instructed to return with news of the situation. When the youth returned with no report, the king sent Horemheb to investigate. The general returned with word that guards had abandoned their temple posts in Memphis and outlying cities and the Priests of Amen were conducting rites in the temples and remote hills.

Amenhotep IV ordered seizure of all religious and magickal items from the thrice-dethroned priests as well as permanent closure of all temples of Amen. The Pharaoh's army poured out of Thebes, travelling north to Lower Egypt. The invasion lasted three months. They systematically sacked and blockaded all temples of Amen, from rural nomes to the villages and city centers. It was accomplished without violence, but with much intimidation.

After the third month of harassment, the Priests of Amen, who had been taught that the Pharaoh's army were the king's own arms and legs, questioned whether this king who had abolished the death penalty would maintain his closure of the temples if it meant killing a few priests to do so. So, as the army withdrew, leaving only re-inforced guard outposts, a riot flared near an unimportant little temple in a rural village. The king had departed days before, but General Horemheb had not and was summoned immediately from Memphis. He arrived and was informed that several priests had been taken captive but not harmed. However, one had killed himself in a makeshift jail cell.

The Priests of Amen demanded to know how the king justified such violent suppression of their rights. The king responded by sending a list of violations of human rights which he accused the Religion of Amen of innovating and perpetuating. He also accused the Priests of Amen of inciting the violence. It was in the spirit of Amenism, the king wrote, to incite a life-fearing priest to commit suicide, then blame the death on the king. He denounced the god as a superstition and emphasized his legal and official banishment of the religion. The king assured the angry priests that none would be imprisoned nor executed for practicing their outlawed religion. They would simply have their religious implements taken from them and, if necessary, be dragged from their temples.

Another riot followed Horemheb's departure. On his immediate return he discovered three guards had been injured by rampaging temple priests. Two of the priests had been killed at spearpoint. The soldiers claimed self-defense. The Priests of Amen insisted the rioters were not temple priests at all but beggars who came seeking handouts from the king and who rioted when they did not find him. The two priests who had been killed had unfortunately gotten in the way, they explained.

Amenhotep IV responded in a letter that the Amenist claims were lies and that the temple priests, not beggars, had rioted. Nothing could be proven. Unless the king either imprisoned or executed the Priesthood of Amen, they would be free to riot against the guards.

"This is a dangerous situation," said Amenhotep IV to Ai and Horemheb.

Apy, the scribe, sat at the meeting table recording everything with his ink brush.

"It is inestimably dangerous," agreed Horemheb. "The war god Amen will not lose his throne without a fight."

"If the temple priests are determined to incite riot," said the king. "I cannot effectively forbid this. Still, there are not many of them. The followers among the peasants are not numerous, either. Who are the remaining priests of Amen? How are initiates enlisted?"

"My informants who frequent the beer-halls tell me that there is much discomfort among men, especially peasant men whose wives have left them."

"Have many marriages broken up because of my protection of the recourse of women?"

"Apparently…many marriages."

"I understand. It is easy for a woman to leave her husband now. All she needs to do is convince a judge that her husband has beaten and abused her and she can leave him. She could not do this before. I understand something else: violent men hate the new laws. How can violent men whose wives have left them be so well organized?"

Said Horemheb: "The Priests of Amen are excellent at coordinating vast secret plans."

"Then this should be countered by a sign," said the king. "A celestial manifestation. Something that will impress upon the minds of all Egyptians that there is a world more vast and important than their little lives and petty disputes. It should be demonstrated in a way that will leave no doubt of the heavenly origins of Aton, and convince all that the words of this king should be heard and obeyed at all cost."

"Your own followers have been waiting long for such a sign," said Horemheb. "They repeat tales of when their grandparents saw a flying disc in the night sky or when a priestess they once might have known was seduced by a god and bore a special child. But these events are all in the past, all just stories now. It is true that the people have a strange-looking king who rules them and who claims much about himself, especially that he is the son of a sky-god—claims that have been made by previous kings, including Amenhotep III. To them, this new king behaves in ways too eccentric to understand. With all respect, O King, a sign, a powerful omen, would be what all Egypt needs!"

With these words, the king laughed. A smile of contemplation spread across his face. "I will arrange for a manifestation that will unify all of Egypt under the Aton Disc," he said at last. "Not an eye will fail to see."

Lately, Smenkhara spoke occasionally to his father, if only to irritate and annoy him.

"You are a hypocrite," the boy said from the doorway, leaning forward on his staff. "You have erased the name of Amenhotep III, defiled the name of Amen, and yet you still wear the name of Amen, the god you hate, *in your own name!* Amenhotep III, Amenhotep IV—Amen, Amen, *Amen!*"

"That is a point well taken," allowed the king calmly.

"Hypocrite! 'Amen is Fulfilled.' So be it! By persecuting the priests of Amen, you might fulfill their destiny: uniting against Aton!"

"I have thought of that," the king replied evenly.

"I will believe that when you stop raiding their temples! I will believe it when you stop seizing their riches! By doing these things you arouse their anger."

"My son, you have a vast wealth of observations for one your age."

"I am four years old, Father, and all my life you and Mother have argued these things in front of me."

The king nodded. "That is true. You are a remarkably precocious young boy, and we have not concealed our disagreements from you."

"You cannot hide anything from me, Father."

"I have never tried, Smenkhara."

"You even love Meritaton more than me. You do not hide that, either."

"That is not true, Smenkhara. I admit I am more compatible with her than I am with you, but that is halfway up to you, and you plainly hate me."

"*You* gave me a crippled body!"

"You can mend it, Smenkhara," sang a little flutelike voice from just beyond the hall door. Meritaton peeked around the corner, her elongated head partially hidden by the edge of the doorway. "You should be thankful that you can at least walk!"

"You have not suffered as much as I have!" Smenkhara shouted. "You do not know what it has been like, Meritaton!"

"You do not know what life has been like for me, either, my brother. I remember the first time Father explained to me why my head was so hard to hold up and why it hurt my neck so much. I accepted what he said and knew it would become easier. I had faith that I would be able to do wonderful things with my large head. Soon after that my neck muscles strengthened. I have been learning the arts and sciences of the new cosmology, preparing for the times Father says are soon to come."

"You really believe these things he says!" Smenkhara was furious. "If Aton is coming to make everything right again, then will Aton heal my curved legs?"

The king spoke. "Not your body, no. But you can acquire other bodies! You may live to see the day when you are not limited to just one body. Smenkhara? You are not listening."

Prince Smenkhara glared silently at his father, stung by the words.

"You have existed for only four years and already you know more than I do."

Smenkhara pushed Meritaton aside and stumbled down the hall. clacking his walking staff loudly against the stone floor.

𓂀

The king was preparing an important proclamation. Only Ai and General Horemheb knew the content of the message and Horemheb knew less than he thought. He knew the king would stage a brief second coronation ritual: Amenhotep IV was changing his name.

Egyptians from provinces to the south and north were gathering to hear the pronouncement, driven by curiosity inflamed by nearly five years of controversy. Everything the strange new king had said and done had delivered blows to rigid traditions which had hardened into institutions and crystallized into oppressive social machines, from slavery to human sacrifice. Because of this strange new king, everything was changing.

𓂀

The first part of the ritual was performed on the top of the pyramidal stage. The king, seated between his two queens, rose on cue and faced Ai and Suti, who were costumed as Horus and Osiris. They greeted the king with hands upraised and presented to him an ankh and a double-plumed Ma'at. The king accepted them and

188

crossed them over his chest in place of the scepter and flail, then placed them on the low circular table by his knees.

Addressing the crowd, he announced that disfavor had been shown to him by his family and his conscience because he carried the name of Amen in his own name. Therefore, he was compelled to change his name. He hereby assumed the Horus name "The seed which blooms with human flowers." He also chose a Nebty name "Lover of Earth who art in Heaven." His new Golden Horus name referred to "Messenger from the Horus-Winged Disc of the Sun." His Nesu bat name was "Son of my mother who was my wife in the Amentt." His official noumen was "Radiant Rays of the Aton Disc."

This last name, his new name, was pronounced *Akhunaton*.

After an appropriate silence, King Akhunaton spoke:

"My heritage is celestial.

"I shall reveal my stellar origin on the last day of the month of Khoiak. All of Egypt will see signs in the sky on that day. The next day, the first day of spring, in the fifth year of my reign, these signs will again be seen. By daylight, two boats of the sky, the *Atet* and the *Sektet*, will dance under the sun over Thebes. They will be visible from Karnak to Luxor and beyond.

"If the people are pleased only by miracles," said King Akhunaton, "then they shall have miracles."

Horemheb grinned. That was the announcement he waited for.

The last day of Khoiak and the first day of Tobi were one week away. Notification that signs would be seen in the sky were being sent to temples of Aton throughout the land. On the elevated stage the king concluded that he intended to spend his remaining years ignoring the religion of Amen—unless they again attempted to restore their priesthood.

"Oh, so now you have changed your name," challenged little Smenkhara. "What wonders a little criticism can accomplish!"

"You were right, my son. I was hypocritical to have gone by that name for five years. Do you like my new name?"

"'The Glow of the Aton.' You compare yourself to a glow, a radiance, do you? That is arrogant."

"I do not *look* like that glow. But there will soon be a connection between the glow of the sky-boats and my new name in the minds of all Egyptians."

"And how do you propose to establish paradise on Earth?"

"I have already started it. You shall see the result."

"I await it eagerly," the boy snarled.

"I am saddened that you mock me. I hope paradise does not arrive with you remaining too blind to see it manifest."

When he heard those words, Smenkhara threw his staff at his father and collapsed on the floor, snarling and gnashing his teeth. He doubled up painfully and wept while his father slowly bent to caress his neck and shoulders.

Smenkhara did not fight, he only wailed in internal agony. He feared the inevitable. His stomach no longer gave him pain and his legs were strong enough to walk on. The only pain he felt was the pain he continued to cling to. His father caressed him and he submitted to it. Finally, he pulled himself into Akhunaton's lap. The king sat with his legs crossed, holding the whimpering boy until Smenkhara fell asleep in his father's arms.

The message was passed from the palace to the temples of Aton by swarms of messengers. At each temple it was posted in a public place and cuneiform copies were distributed to other messengers, who ran to the outlying temples.

The king was summoning the boats of the sky, the boats the gods themselves rode in when they departed from the Aton Disc! The *Atet* and the *Sektet* would appear in the skies during the last days of winter. They would be in the skies over Thebes on the first day of spring, five and one half years after the return of the only son of Queen Tiy, Mother of Egypt. Five and one half years after the appearance of the man who now called himself Akhunaton.

Papyrus parchment scrolls carried the announcement of the manifestation, the event and the date, scrawled first in hieratic ink strokes and posted in public places, then copied in the demotic script of the common folk. Elegant hieroglyphics foreswore the announcement upon temple columns. In all corners of the land the magical date was repeated, until no one had escaped the news.

As the days passed and the final week of winter ended, the manifestation of the sky boats that the king had promised became all that Egyptians could talk about.

Chapter Twenty-Two

The first messengers arrived at the palace by afternon of the last day of Khoiak, bearing word of rural sightings. It was the day before the sky boats were expected to return to Thebes.

The king took the news nonchalantly. Tiy dismissed the messengers with her soft smile. Nefertiti was excited. She had prayed for a sign, begging the gods on behalf of her beloved Egyptians—and for herself—to confirm her faith.

She had seen the Aton Disc during its descents into the bridal chamber of the Temple of Aton. To her the boats of the sky were like stars that brightened until her eyes were filled with light and she was mysteriously teleported to the Amentt. This would be different, the king assured her.

By dinner the family could talk of nothing else but the stories brought by no fewer than three dozen messengers. They had come from all parts of the countryside to tell of the return of the disc.

Smenkhara sat in silence, eating little. He excused himself early and hobbled sullenly down the vast hall.

"His pride has been hurt by this," said Nefertiti.

"His arrogance has been damaged," agreed the king. "Pride is different from hubris, though one often leads to the other. It is no sin to love yourself or be happy when you have done or created something beautiful. But self-love is not the cause of Smenkhara's suffering. He suffers from the lack of self-love."

"Do not punish him with your words," implored Nefertiti.

"He punishes himself with the words the messengers bring."

"That is true," Nefertiti said thoughtfully. "We cannot prevent him from feeling this."

Tiy shrugged. "If he wants to storm out of the room in scorn, he cannot be stopped. He wants and needs help, but he must discover that for himself before we can reach him."

"Exactly," said Akhunaton. "He is letting us know that he still rejects our good intentions. He may never resolve that which afflicts him inside."

"You cannot just remain silent toward him!" said Nefertiti. "You promised that tomorrow all of Thebes will see the boats of the sky. Smenkhara will, too. He has been predicting your downfall for most of his short life. He will suffer much if he does not face the source of his anger before then."

"I will speak to him," said Akhunaton. "…if he will listen to me."

"Make yourself available to him," said Nefertiti.

"I will. But he, too, must make himself accessible to me."

The king tapped his walking staff on the open bedroom door. Smenkhara looked up from his bedroll and the pillows on the floor. When he saw his father, he turned his back and curled up.

"I, too, prefer walking with a staff," said Akhunaton. "…and I shall never make this body run."

"Go. Go away from here!"

"I do not understand why news of the reappearance of the sky disc affects you so adversely. Is it because I predicted it? Is it because you knew and feared that I could arrange for such a display?"

"Go away!"

"Your greatest fear, Smenkhara, is that you will have to face the fact that you are not a cripple."

"Leave me alone!"

"You are a celestial child by birth. All people are arising to claim the stars. You will see this in the sky tomorrow. Prepare yourself tonight. You do not have much time to discard all of your attitudes."

Smenkhara did not have a chance to reply. Once the king had spoken, he disappeared from the doorway. Smenkhara wailed in emotional anguish. His voice echoed out of the room and down the hall.

He could still hear the tapping of his father's walking stick. Then he burst into sobs and stibium-stained tears.

The king and his two queens were seated on their thrones atop the steps of the Temple of Aton. Before them were their five children, two sons and three daughters. The oldest son sat with his lower lip jutting out, his head tilted back and his eyes half closed. Neither son had inherited his father's strange head, but the multitudes who had assembled before the temple to view the appearance of the sky boats also marvelled at the huge heads of the oldest two daughters. The youngest daughter's head was normal, and so was her twin brother's.

As the sun drew to its zenith, two flecks of light descended in swirling dances through the vastness of the sky. The discs were metallic, shiny and they spun in the light of the sun.

Masses of people gasped and sighed in awe. Hush after hush stilled the voices as the sky discs swirled, streaked, soared in the blue. They circled the Temple of Aton, then flew directly over the heads of the people who had assembled to witness the sign the king had promised.

Smenkhara sat frozen, held by his own rigidity, as he gripped the armrests of his throne. In front of him were the Egyptian people. Beside him were his mother, grandmother, sisters and little brother. Behind him sat his much-loathed father. But Smenkhara could not take his squinting eyes off the spinning metal hulls. He could not look away even when they circled overhead, their lights spinning. When rays washed over the upturned faces, Smenkhara swallowed hard and clenched his teeth. When the discs swooped up and over the temple, reappearing on the other side, multitudes of Thebans voiced their awe and Smenkhara breathed slowly, still struggling with himself to look away. He could not.

For hours the astonished populace of Thebes stood transfixed with wonder. Every eye saw the miracle. The rays that emanated from the underside of the discs were perceived by the blind. Some recovered their sight immediately; others would wake up the next day with living eyes. People who had begged all their lives for miracles found crippled arms and legs responsive again. Lepers, victims of wars, diseased and discarded humans felt tingling warmth caress their bodies. As the discs flew over, their afflictions began to heal.

When the two discs finally rocketed back into the heavens, Smenkhara stood up easily. He walked back to the palace. He noticed to his surprise that he was carrying his staff at his side.

At dinner the royal family talked exuberantly about the manifestation of the *Atet* and the *Sektet*. Meritaton gazed upon her father with awe. Queen Tiy spoke breathlessly of the first times when she, too, was a little girl and saw the Aton Disc. Maketaton and little Ankhasenpaaton listened raptly. Nefertiti grinned incessantly. She, too, looked upon her king with renewed awe.

Smenkhara was absent from the table.

"Where is my oldest boy?" Akhunaton asked. "Where is Smenkhara?"

"He is in his room, Father," answered Tutankhaton.

"Thank you, my son," said the king. Tutankhaton's simple and pleasant disposition offered only eagerness to please.

"He fears seeing you," said Meritaton.

"Why does he continue to punish himself?" With difficulty, Akhunaton rose from the low table. Tiy and Nefertiti tried to detain him but could not. He walked around the table with his staff clicking on the stone floor.

"Do not go," Nefertiti pleaded. "There is much he needs to think about. If you invade his private domain, he will hate you forever. If you let him breathe, let him think, you will cultivate your only chance to be his friend."

Akhunaton pondered this, then returned to his place between his two queens. "I want very much to understand Smenkhara."

Meritaton looked at him and for an instant her eyes held a distant, faraway sadness.

"Good evening, Father."

Everyone turned. Akhunaton smiled.

Smenkhara walked through the doorway and took his place between Meritaton and Maketaton. A servant brought him bowls of cooked grains and a dish of roasted lamb. He bowed his head in acceptance.

The family ate in silence.

Smenkhara suddenly spoke. "That was very impressive. I have now seen the sky boats. I truly have."

"Yes, you have seen the *Atet* and the *Sektet.* Someday you will see the Aton Disc itself."

"I hope I will, Father."

"I love you, Smenkhara. I hope you will live in a better world than any that your dreams have yet envisioned."

"That is quite a big wish, Father." Smenkhara nibbled at the meat and grains. "You meant it when you said you intended to make Heaven manifest on Earth."

"I intend to. Beginning with today."

"I guess you know...it does not hurt when I walk now."

"I know that. The rays from the sky vessels are harmonics of the visible colors of light. These can mend flesh and nerves by healing the finest tissues and purifying the blood. It is very complicated to explain. Someday I will show you views of very tiny things through crystal lenses."

Meritaton looked up eagerly. "There has been a healing in this family. I am so grateful."

Smenkhara looked deeply into his father's eyes and for the first time a look of gratitude appeared. "You truly do know sciences that are older than all of Egypt. You know the sciences practised in the Hidden World."

Akhunaton nodded. "I wish to teach you about the many worlds. I wish to teach you much about this world especially. I am so glad your hips and thighs no longer hurt you."

"It is amazing! I still prefer to have my staff...but the pain is gone entirely!"

Akhunaton said: "There are invisible colors, beyond the red of the rainbow and beyond the purple. Sometimes these invisible hues can heal. Life wants to heal. Sometimes all it takes is proof, some kind of assurance, a sign for Life to recognize. That is all."

"Are you saying that because your prediction came true I healed myself? That is like taking credit for something because something else happened the way you said it would."

"Please do not be defensive! I merely meant that Life is constantly pushing hard to improve its form, its surroundings, including the body Life is in. When wounded, Life heals, like a lizard can regrow a tail. The healing spirit of the discs of the sky would have had no effect upon you unless you had wanted to overcome the pain of walking. The healing rays gave you a chance."

Smenkhara nodded. "Is that what you have been saying lately about the life force around us? When you say those words 'Ankh em Ma'at'?"

The king nodded, a joyous smile upon his lips. "That is what I mean. What did you feel in your heart as the rays passed through your body?"

"I felt...happy. Like I was truly with friends."

"Like the Universe itself would take care of you, perhaps?"

"Yes, and I felt like I had always known that."

"You could have weighed your heart against a feather just then."

"Yes. I see what you mean. I was ready...to meet Osiris on one of those sky boats."

"Osiris may have been aboard one of those sky boats." Nefertiti gasped. "It is true, my wife. Isis and Osiris live aboard the *Aton*. It is very possible Osiris wanted to return to Egypt. It would be quite perfect for him. You understand," Akhunaton turned directly to Smenkhara, "Osiris has hips like yours and mine, my son. He, too, has trouble walking. It would be so convenient for him to fly low over the desert hills and the temples and the citadels. I hope he took the chance to do that today."

"Osiris has trouble walking?" Smenkhara gasped in disbelief.

Akhunaton nodded. "You might meet Osiris, my son, without having to die first. Ankh em Ma'at."

The establishment of Heaven on Earth commenced the day after the aerial demonstration. Akhunaton assembled his scribes and dictated a lengthy and poetic invitation to the Priestesses of Isis to dance in the courtyards of all the temples of Aton throughout the land. He instructed the temples to receive visitors with open arms. Musicians were summoned from among the Priests of Osiris.

When the caravans and nomads reached Memphis or Thebes, they were told that the sky disc had something to do with the king's change of name. They were also told that the temples of Aton were seeking musicians, dancers, poets and artists. But especially musicians. Caravan folk played drums in their campfire circles at night. Young men who reached courtship age learned to play one of the many variations of Egyptian lutes, which they used to serenade young women.

Within days, dancers and drummers were sending colorful drumbeats into the sky from the steps of the temples of the sun disc. The courtyards and temple grounds twirled with dancers. As the numbers swelled, Akhunaton himself supervised the food distribution and appointed teams of priests and laborers to coordinate the digging of trenches to divert water and bury waste.

The peasants and nomads were easily received. Accommodations for the musical troupes and nomadic clans had been organized by Akhunaton and Horemheb and carried out by a very industrious peasant named Aper-El. Later, Aper-El was appointed to be Minister to the North, his homeland. Literate and quick with arithmetic, Aper-El received communications the king sent to Memphis to keep the vast Egyptian empire functioning.

After a few days, their curiosity satisfied, the caravans returned to the deserts, the pilgrims to their homelands. Many musicians remained in the townships and cities. The temples of Isis, of Osiris and of Aton stayed open as sanctuaries to traveling artists, artisans and musicians.

Music resounded through Thebes.

After Aper-El's departure and the ceremonial dispersal of coins and jewels to the peasants, Akhunaton retired to a dinner of roasted pheasant in the company of his family. He and Smenkhara conversed amiably, though Akhunaton sensed that his son was withholding his love from expression.

When he heals he will open his heart to me, thought the king. *Until then, all I can do is keep my heart open to him.*

Smenkhara ate in silence, as did Akhunaton. Ankhasenpaaton chatted with Tiy and Nefertiti and Meritaton talked with little Tutankhaton. After a short while quiet little Maketaton excused herself from the table, complaining of a headache.

"I am worried about her," said Nefertiti. "She had another headache this month. She was not feeling well after the pageant, either."

"That is true," the king said thoughtfully. "I think I should teach her some mental exercises. She should utilize the power of her immense brain. She needs extra attention from me, perhaps."

"Perhaps she needs a healing," Nefertiti suggested.

"Perhaps I can arrange for that," said the Pharaoh.

"I hope you can. I worry over her."

"Perhaps you worry over much. Life lives through us, my dear queen. Without us Life itself would have no expression in this realm. Please have faith that her living energy, her ankh, can be generated, so she can heal herself."

"Well, try whatever you wish. A healing, mind-exercises, whatever you will." Nefertiti glided to her feet. "I wish to be with my daughter. I feel something might be wrong."

She left the room swiftly. A long silence remained in her wake.

Meritaton broke it. "I agree with Mother, O Father. My little sister had a headache after the pageant. She felt fine during the display of the *Atet* and the *Sektet* but after the pageant the next day she felt fatigued."

"Were you not also tired?"

"Yes, but I felt good afterward. Maketaton did not. She hates being seated for hours in front of crowds. It hurts something inside of her."

"I understand. Perhaps with mental discipline…"

"I do not think that will help," Smenkhara said suddenly.

"What do you know of your sister's affliction? Has she confided in you?"

"Yes. When she was little, she was special to me."

"What did she say to you?"

"She said she heard voices in her head sometimes."

"That is good. That is *very* good. Did she tell you anything else?"

"Yes. She was sleepy a lot."

"Is that all?"

"No. She said she had headaches. Little ones. Up behind her ear, sometimes both ears. Most just lasted for a moment, she said. Then they would go away."

"I see. Why did she not tell me these things?"

"You were away, tending to the affairs of state—mostly discrediting the priests of Amen and sacking their temples. Or else posing for statues or holding pageants. Sometimes she told you she had headaches, but she usually had them when you were not present. She forgets much and she never bothered to talk about them when she saw you. She says little and when she talks she likes to talk about flowers and seashells and things. Not headaches…"

"I see." The king pondered. His eyes narrowed and the corners of his mouth turned down. Finally, he looked up and said in a grim voice, "I do not have the personal contact with you children that I should have. I am deeply sorry. You resent me for this personally, Smenkhara. I know you do. I will devote my time to all of you. I will live the life that a good father lives, not just a king.'"

"I would like that," Smenkhara said. He was looking directly into Akhunaton's eyes.

"I believe you, Smenkhara."

"For me, O Father, Heaven on Earth is not music as much as it is having a *real* father."

A great silence elapsed. One by one, the children finished and left the dinner table. Smenkhara departed first.

When the children were gone, Akhunaton talked long with Tiy about his fatherhood. Though their dialogue consisted of short, terse statements, it concluded with Tiy's advice:

"You cannot be a good father to Egypt unless you are a good father to your own children. If you can be a good father to Smenkhara, then you will be a good king for all of Egypt."

Again Nefertiti was invited to visit the bridal chamber in the Temple of Aton. This time when she viewed the moving star that brightened and descended, she understood what it was. When the flickering white rays separated into rings of rotating lights, her eyes discerned the silhouetted shape and she remembered the spinning metal discs that had descended the day of the visitation.

She was alone with Akhunaton this time. The temple filled with a glare that was warm and tingled throughout her skin. Fountains of colored light burst across her vision and she felt the hardness of the altar slab under her spine dissolve into prickles of warmth. She felt bathed in hot, bubbling water. Her vision was replaced by fiery sparks. She felt the reassurance of his hand holding her forearm. She did not know how she knew, but she knew in her heart that it was his hand.

When her vision cleared she was lying on a cushioned table inside the *Atet*, gazing up at shifting rows of living lights. She could still feel Akhunaton's hand gently gripping her arm. Turning her eyes only, she saw him standing beside her.

He was smiling. Beside him stood the woman with the wide lips and small chin: the goddess Isis. A human woman, smiling back. Standing next to Isis was a man who looked much like Akhunaton: Osiris. He, too, was of the race among the Amentii capable of marrying human women.

Osiris touched Nefertiti gently on the shoulder. He stroked her arm and neck. His lips were not as thick as Akhunaton's, but his eyes were larger, and his head. Horus was his son and son of Isis, Akhunaton's last incarnation…

Nefertiti thought: *I have been told that the children of Aton, the god-kings who are people like us, incarnate differently from ordinary souls. They remember their former incarnations in other bodies. The incarnations we women of Egypt are chosen to marry is, to them, only a part of something much older.*

Except when bridged by the love between Isis and Osiris. He lives in his Egyptian body to please her. She, too, has acquired many bodies of Amentii races and they have lived lifetimes together on many worlds in order to perform the courtship rites and lovestyles of those native races.

Or so I have been told. Can it ever be that way for me?

𓂀

Later, in the Amentt, wrapped in garments of foggy light, embraced by the ideal human form of her astral lover-husband, Nefertiti received another child. One cell, fertilized before and frozen in a time-stasis, awaiting the queen, was implanted in her womb at the peak of her visionary ecstacy.

𓂀

The summer months shimmered with mirages under the Sahara sun. The surplus of the autumn harvest showed no threat of diminishing, so the festivals continued. Another harvest pushed sunward its green flourishes, and Ra was contributing generously to the growing gift of life.

The summer sky contributed many brief respites from the scorching magnanimity of Ra. Often in the evenings little black clouds would race across the afterglow and mass together in the purple sky, then pitch down leaping arcs of lightning that thrilled the Pharaoh's children. Under the crashing concussions of thunder, Meritaton, Smenkhara, Maketaton, and the younger twins Ankhasenpaaton and Tutankhaton would peer off the balconies into the black winds, waiting with huge eyes for the next flash. Such thundershowers would bring cool rains and disperse by morning.

Akhunaton meditated for hours in the hot sun. He encouraged his family to do this, especially little Maketaton, whose lack of vitality he hoped to remedy. He instructed her to focus her attention on ancient mantras, the syllable names of goddesses and gods, and to meditate while gazing into reflections in water or in the sun. He taught her how to visualize images and sustain them in detail in her mind, and how to turn the feeling of mild pain into another sense perception, like the scent of spices or the color red.

Sometimes Akhunaton would spend his days in conversation with Ai or Parannefer or his other courtiers. Ani and Pa-nehsi liked to discuss politics. Suti and Nakht, his vizier, were interested in mathematics and astronomy and often debated with him the validity of astrology or expounded ideas of logic to beauty.

It was during this season that he started appearing naked before crowds on the hills beyond his balcony. Although he himself occasionally wore a tunic or transparent cotton robe, most often he was naked. He insisted on receiving all of his visitors naked. Visiting peasants agreed to disrobe gladly, though nobles and aristocrats who sought to meet him were sometimes offended. Some refused to undress and returned to their palaces in a huff. Others complied, but with much bewilderment. Surely the king's customs were more accepted by the Amentii than the Egyptians!

Smenkhara suspected that his father was cautious of weapons concealed by clothing and that was why the king greeted his guests nude. Akhunaton insisted that this was not so, but that he enjoyed sensing a person's total aura, unobstructed by clothing. Smenkhara asked why he himself could not sense auras. His father replied that it was because he was still too angry to see the subtle rays.

In the late summer month of Mesore, Akhunaton received word that the temples of Amen, Mut and Kenshu in the North had withheld their treasures from the Pharaoic Guard and that soldiers had refused to erase the names of Amen or Amenhotep III. Secret rites had been observed in the temple and captives may have been hidden somewhere. Immediately, and to Smenkhara's wrath, Akhunaton departed for the northern provinces.

Akhunaton discovered that the temple treasures withheld were small compared to what had already been taken and that the rites were unimportant and had been observed elsewhere, not in the temple itself. However, the name of the false god Amen and the pharaoh who was not Akhunaton's father were stricken from the temple walls with a mallet and cold chisel.

Akhunaton returned to tell Nefertiti how beautiful the north of Egypt was and how he had been well-received in Memphis. The family rejoiced to hear this news. Plans were made to journey to Memphis in the fall.

Nefertiti spent the night in the central chamber of the Temple of Aton. In her light-filled visions she dreamed of a girl-child who befriended her and asked to dwell in her womb. Nefertiti agreed, and the spirit-girl curled up in a little ring and slept in the queen's belly. Awakening in the morning in her own chamber, Nefertiti still felt the girl-spirit sleeping in her womb.

The Egyptian calendar contained three seasons of four months. The first season

of autumn was Thoth. The festival of Thoth celebrated the early harvest. Shortly after this pageant and feast, the royal family departed for Memphis.

The royal barge escorted by a flotilla drifted down the lazy Nile. Sun and cloud-bursts gave weather to the days; the nights were usually clear. Musicians played to twirling dancers on the decks and colored lanterns cast sparkling reflections in the water.

The king's reception in Memphis was difficult, beset by throngs of peasants who flocked to see the alien king. He was greeted by a few nobles, but many had been snubbed, so they said, on the king's previous visit. When they presented him with lavish gifts, expecting riches in return, Akhunaton responded with hand-painted poems on papyrus parchment. The king's esoteric comments about the Universe were not the sort of gifts nobles had expected.

The king and his family took up residence near the minister of the north, Aper-El. A palace was created in the Temple of Aton northwest of Memphis, overlooking the three Great Pyramids. The king's days were spent with his children, receiving visitors from among the peasantry, and listening to music while dancers flashed their colorful scarves in the sunlight.

They stayed for three idyllic weeks. During their sojourn to Memphis the royal family watched over Maketaton's health scrupulously. Akhunaton was with her every minute of the day, empathically sensing her feelings and teaching her breathing exercises and meditation. Maketaton did not suffer headaches and her lethargy was replaced by energy.

After the journey home, Akhunaton carefully watched his daughter for signs of stress. He continued to train her in controlling her consciousness and attaining visionary states of creativity.

The nighttime experiments in the Temple of Aton neared completion. The eerie whines had been replaced by celestial melodies. The brilliant lightninglike flashes no longer lit the sky except occasionally, on nights that were particularly clear or else heavy with static electricity during the approach of a storm. Sometimes a bluish-violet ray could be seen beaming from the open dome of the temple to the center of the sky.

Inside the open sanctuary in the center of the temple, the crystal-tipped obelisk, now completely wrapped in *tcham* wire, stood surrounded by panels of very thin hardwood sheets pressed between huge squares of gold foil. They encircled the obelisk like the petals of a flower. Imperceptible waves of energy, the invisible colors of light of which the king spoke so often, caused the panels to vibrate, producing the harmonious, slowly evolving melodies.

Thus the first of the singing temples was activated and sang the chorus of the music of the stars.

⟡

During his exile to the deep tunnels and chambers beneath the temple of Karnak, The Beast waited for a chance to escape. His time was not idle. Sometimes he would interrogate Amenhotep, Son of Hapu, the blind seer. The clairvoyant prisoner would respond by taunting his captor or bursting into uncontrolled hysterics. Amenhotep, Son of Hapu, was rapidly losing his mind.

The Beast conducted many experiments in his underground laboratories. He bred molds and fungi in carefully sterilized dishes. He experimented with diseases. He refined strong solvents for complex distillation processes. He had experimented with everything from poisons to drugs to explosives.

Every day he made a long and solitary journey by tunnel to one of the many *mastabas* in which the long-dead (and vacated) mummies of the aristocratic houses had been buried, but whose surviving descendants still placed offerings of fresh food and beer to the dead man's *ka,* or earthly ghost. Egyptians believed that the *ka* got hungry and that since fresh fruits and uncooked vegetables contained a *ka* of their own, the *ka* of the nobleman (always a man, for women did not have souls) should always have food to eat near the mummy the *ka* was anchored to. Thus, the living of various houses of nobility, innocently performing services to dead ancestors, were serving offerings of food to The Beast daily.

Knowing this and choosing not to prevent it, Akhunaton contented himself with posting permanent guards in the Temple of Karnak to see that the halls remained empty. None were informed of the presence of the once-human soul parasite who haunted the caverns beneath the temple, nor of his psychic hostage, nor of the Circle of Twelve, which included Egypt's most infamous Pharaoic figures, all controlled by demons created in the mind of the ancient priest.

Kahotep rehearsed the cannibalization of the blind seer's pineal gland. He plotted the murder of his own Inner Circle and visualized his escape through one of his tomb-tunnels. He became obsessed with his strategy to recapture control of Egypt.

Kahotep felt certain that Akhunaton was a pacifist. He sat, thinking feverishly in the subterranean darkness of his inner sanctum. *This king has ruled for nearly six years. I live. He has let my captives out of their cages. He has allowed me not to starve—he surely must know how I reach through secret openings underneath the mastabas to steal my food! He lets me live, yet he forces me to face age and death. Will he defend himself against his own death? Danger to his family? He has children, strange and ugly children in the eyes of my winged watchers. The children of the star-kings. Big-headed…*

Kahotep had taken centuries of ritual slaughter, prearranged invasions, fear of angry war gods and fear of death, to trick Egyptians into believing that contact with mysterious beings was evil. He had tried but could not banish altogether the notion that people lived in a friendly Universe full of magical entities. He knew that it was important to the preservation of himself as a deity that a theology of special creation, of aloneness in the Universe, of a sky that was nothing more than the belly of a cow, be accepted by enough people to constitute a moveable, disciplined military body.

The military was—there, but at the command of a star-king who fully understood the nature and origin of The Beast.

The move to Lower Egypt was an arduous task that took months to plan and coordinate. Memphis was visited again by the Pharaoh and his entourage and rejected as a new location for the capital of Egypt. The king led an expedition along the Nile using methods of advanced geomancy, sighting conical peaks on the horizon with tube-shaped devices mounted on stilted legs. Finally he chose a location to the south and west of Memphis on the east bank of the Nile. After a journey of less than a hundred miles, in a fertile green valley surrounded by rolling hills, in a district of fields tended by prosperous peasants, the king chose his site for Paradise on Earth.

"All who journey to this place must abandon despair and futility and pain and hate and fear. It will be like filth washed back into the soil before entering a temple of light. At this place, with no gates nor walls to surround us, we will stand together naked and loving and fulfill our free, happy destiny. A new human race will be born. Ankh em Ma'at."

☯

Smenkhara became quieter and gentler toward his family, especially his sisters. His jealousy toward Tutankhaton dissolved. He looked forward to the move to Lower Egypt, wherever the new home might be.

When Akhunaton returned from his preparatory expedition, he announced that a location had been tentatively chosen. His invited his family to journey to the site, but Nefertiti was seven months pregnant and preferred to remain in Thebes, as did the children. The decision fell to Akhunaton: in that valley on the east bank of the Nile the new city would be built.

"Have you thought about what to call it?" asked Tiy.

"It should have a scientific meaning. Something descriptive about Aton's nature."

"Your own name refers to the radiant energy the Aton Disc emanates."

"Yes. A similar quality should be invoked, referring to the nature of the new city in relation to the visiting Aton Disc."

Akhunaton conferred daily with Bek and Suti to plan the place, temple complexes and vast areas of comfortable living spaces for a city-to-be.

☯

Maketaton was to be taken into the Aton Disc. Although she had not had a headache for almost a year, Nefertiti worried about her child. To allay her fears, Akhunaton promised to arrange for her to board the starship and be examined for unseen infirmities.

After eating only a small dinner, the little girl was led into the central chamber in the Temple of Aton by her father. She reclined against the stone block underneath the wide circle in the ceiling that opened to a view of the starry sky. Maketaton became relaxed and calm as she lay next to her father, Akhunaton, who sat beside her and held her hand.

The *Atet* appeared. It showed first as a speck of light among the stars. Then rings of rotating bands descended and rays filled the chamber with blurry light. Maketaton found herself teleported to a brilliant realm where she could see only her father standing beside her silhouetted against the glare.

The shuttledisc ascended through the atmosphere and entered the vast airlock in the hull of the starship. Again Maketaton was transported in clouds of light, supported by gentle hands and carefully guided to walk on her own. She was not afraid. She was assisted to recline on a cushioned table. A great silver ball at the end of a shaft of woven crystals was lowered toward her by a tall being in robes. The being had a head similar in shape to her own.

The being was Tem, pilot of the starship *Aton*. He scanned Maketaton's body, especially her head, with electromagnetic sensory beams. He painlessly extracted blood and skin samples from her body with a clear tube that moved as if it were alive.

When the tests, cellular samples and sensory scans were completed, Tem and Akhunaton joined eye contact and engaged in a direct telepathic exchange. Tem informed Akhunaton that though not all information was available, the scans showed no morphological irregularities.

Akhunaton escorted his daughter on the moving table down a lighted corridor. A beautiful woman with a strong forehead, wide lips, a small chin and large, expressive eyes, appeared beside Maketaton. The woman looked into Maketaton's eyes and smiled. Maketaton felt her love.

Maketaton whispered: "Isis."

The bright light enveloped her again and only her father's tall form remained solid against the blurry glow. Maketaton was again lifted from the table by strong hands and supported by her arms as she walked into the luminous fog. Her consciousness broke free from her body with a tingling flurry of sparks and she briefly looked down on her own figure supported by many arms reaching through the glare. Her body fell far below.

High above she saw the Aton Disc. It was vast, ring-shaped, and it rotated slowly. Bands of tiny multicolored lights pulsated in waves over the curved metal hull. Underneath shined huge beams of white light. The Aton Disc seemed to be made out of brilliant rays.

Maketaton saw and beheld what the *Aton* was: a ship. A ship that crossed the skies the way a barge crossed the Nile.

The *Aton* descended through the deepening blue, into the atmosphere, toward Egypt. *My body is in that disc of light,* Maketaton thought. Her consciousness watched the descent silently from space.

The next night Akhunaton went aboard the *Atet* into the bay of the starship *Aton*. He was met by Tem. They walked quietly out of the immense airlock and down a corridor to a small holographic laboratory. There, in the lighted chamber, Akhunaton saw the results of the scans.

Maketaton's seven chakras, centers of consciousness aligned with her spinal column, radiated health. Each emanated a different color and all emanated strong, vibrant light. The electromagnetic haze of the neural auras looked resonant and vital. All the minor chakras looked balanced, throughout her body.

"This is what our ultraviolet scan showed," Tem said, reaching toward the top of the light chamber. Immediately the body of clear light changed to blue and in the field of Maketaton's immense head appeared a single pinpoint of darkness.

"I do not know what it means." Tem let a pause slip by. "We have studied her genes, dismantled and reassembled chromosomes to find structural defects. We have holographically rendered a complete clone based on her genes and we find nothing anomalous. Yet here, in this image of her, we see a tiny dark spot in the deep inside of her right temporal lobe. It shows up in the ultraviolet wavelength of her aura, approximately where she says her headaches originate."

"This is most disturbing."

"Yes," Tem agreed, "it is."

"I need a minimum of seven females to two males for another seed race to continue. I am working with a minimum of two generations before interbreeding will be feasible."

"Then we must consider impregnating Tiy herself during one of Nefertiti's pregnancies, or impregnating one of your daughters when they mature sexually."

"The Egyptians accept the fact that my family is of a different race and that our descendants will follow the plan of sacred incest prescribed to all Pharaoic families."

"Does Smenkhara accept this? That he might father a child by every one of his sisters and marry his twin, Meritaton?"

"Yes. He is quite fond of the idea, intellectually. It is the only aspect of his future that he appreciates." There was gentle laughter aboard the starship and Akhunaton paused, smiling. "I hope his fascination is entirely intellectual; artificial fertilization enhanced by dreams of rapture can translate into unhealthy fantasies unless the dreamer's consciousness is centered in the higher chakras."

"Destructive fantasies can translate into daily behavior when realized in a visionary form."

"Tutankhaton is better suited psychologically for this genetic exchange. He has a more passive, receptive personality. Yet, he alone cannot provide enough genetic variables among his sperm to perpetuate his family. We need the variations Smenkhara can contribute to cultivate another generation."

"One more generation will stabilize?"

"Yes, and the generation after that will be ready to interbreed safely."

"You need seven daughters and two sons."

"Yes, Tem, at all cost."

Chapter Twenty-Three

Neferneferuaton the Little was born aboard the *Aton* Disc at the end of a four-hour labor. The birth came early in Nefertiti's eighth month of pregnancy. The labor went well because the baby was so small and Nefertiti's pelvis was accommodatingly large for the baby's head.

Dozing in the Realm of Light, Nefertiti felt a snuggling little body creep to her nipple and begin nursing mightily. The tiny infant was very strong.

She awoke to a new day in her royal chambers. Akhunaton was still beside her. Her handmaidens were bringing towels and blankets, placing them all about her. The little baby with the long head slept in her arms. Content, Nefertiti returned to sleep.

"Smenkhara, I, too, prefer walking with the aid of a staff," said the King of Egypt to his son. They stood upon the high terrace overlooking the courtyards. Leaning back against a pillar, his staff held for balance, he faced Smenkhara.

Smenkhara stood with his back pressed against the next pillar in the row as he gazed out over Thebes. A mutual awareness dawned on them as to how similar their poses were. Smenkhara glanced at his father, then shuffled his feet and stood leaning heavily on his staff.

"Why did you change your position to one less comfortable?" Akhunaton asked.

Smenkhara started to feel resentful. "I-I do not know! When I saw that we were both standing in the same position…!"

"You had to stop standing the way I stood. You want to be different. You want to assert yourself."

Smenkhara bristled. "Why do you care?"

"It is good! Assert yourself! I think it is wonderful!"

"Then why did you reprimand me for it?"

"I did not reprimand you for it, Smenkhara, I merely pointed it out to you. Everything you do to be different from me. I encourage you. You will soon grow tired of trying to be different from me. It is then that you will begin to be yourself, unaffected by what I look like or do."

The boy looked at his father with discouraged eyes. Then he shook his head, confused.

Akhunaton said: "When I first walked out of the desert it is said that I walked very fast. This has, no doubt, puzzled you."

"Yes," Smenkhara said, his tone severe.

"I had assistance from above by the Aton Disc."

The boy's eyes widened. "Is that so?"

"Yes. It is so. I could not have walked from the desert all the way to Thebes on my legs without assistance."

Smenkhara nodded. He remembered the spinning, hovering metal discs. He was beginning to understand.

"I had much assistance from Aton in those days. I had long distances to walk swiftly. At night I frequently strode from Karnak to Luxor along the Avenue of the Sphinxes. Shimmering rays of light could be glimpsed going up from my body into the sky."

Smenkhara nodded.

"I do not get their assistance any more! I no longer have such distances to walk, no temples to desecrate…" He laughed at his own words; reluctantly, Smenkhara laughed, too. "…riches to confiscate. You remember. You were there."

Smenkhara laughed aloud against his will. He tried to suppress his giggles but only twisted his face up while chortling through his nostrils. When he regained his composure, he said:

"How is it that you came to do all those acts and appearances during your first few years? You must have been in great pain."

"I was, Smenkhara, but I practised those same psychic disciplines that I am teaching to your sisters, especially Maketaton. The technique for the transmutation of pain seems to be working for her."

"I see. Perhaps…I should listen to you when you talk to my sisters about such things."

"Yes, I think you should. Tell me, Smenkhara, what was your favorite temple which I closed down?"

With those words, Smenkhara burst again into fits of laughter. He tumbled into a heap on the tiles and rolled to the feet of the king. Finally, he drew himself up and stood, wobbling with his weight on his unsteady staff.

"You are learning Ai's secret," said Akhunaton, "the reason he laughs all the time."

Smenkhara caught and held his breath, then steadied himself and leaned back against the pillar. "I remember — it was on the only temple-sacking caravan we ever went on, Father. My sisters and little brother and I mostly stayed in the temples of Aton, you recall, while you went off with the soldiers and sometimes Grandmother Tiy and Mother Nefertiti. You came back all full of laughter, as though it had been funny. Then, when everyone decided it was safe, we children saw one temple to Amen closed. We watched it from the throne room of one of the governors, and it *was* funny! The jewels were tossed to the beggars and the priests paced back and forth in rage. They were all pushed by crowds of curious onlookers, trying to see everything.

"So it was not so appalling, was it?"

"Oh, but it was! That temple had been there as long as anyone could have remembered, and those priests had sung their hymns and chanted their war-poems as long as anyone knew. So what you were doing really was appalling, Father."

"I intended it to be," said the king.

"But why?"

"Because people in another age will witness the return of the metal discs from the sky. I want to leave a great indication out of time to those witnesses as to what these discs are, who flies in them, and *what they come to this world for!*"

"That is what you tell us all the time. I still do not understand."

"Do not think too much about it. Just look about you. Listen: you can hear, even now, drums and voices throughout the hills. At night the Temple of Aton sings sweet melodies from the stars. Listen and watch all around you, Smenkhara, for as the false ideas about the real world crumble before the people, a new world, more real, will manifest before the eyes and ears of everyone."

The sound of music, laughter, festivity splashed and echoed far below the palace colonnade. Colorful encampments were tucked between acacia and palm trees. The sound of drums, flutes, and lyres could be heard everywhere.

As Neferneferuaton the Little rapidly grew during her first few months of life, construction on Egypt's new capital city began. The little girl saw her father sporadically, between his weeks-long caravans to the city site, when he would spend his days in his palace in Thebes and meditate in the sun with his children, enjoying the company of his family and courtiers.

Neferneferuaton the Little was a strong, healthy baby despite her premature birth and small size. She slept little and remained alert, like Meritaton and Ankhasenpaaton had when they were newborns.

The royal family was also impressed by how much Smenkhara had turned away from the surliness of his first four years of life. After the manifestation of the sky boats, the boy had opened his heart to his father and his father had received him with love.

As the new city reached completion, Smenkhara dreaded moving away from Thebes. His family sensed this and both Tiy and Nefertiti tried to coax him into expressing himself about the matter, but he remained reticent. His father knew that if and when he was ready, Smenkhara would talk about his feelings.

The city of Akhetaton consisted of three separate complexes. A fourth and fifth building were under construction to the north. The central palace, which was reserved for the king, his children and Queen Tiy. The building to the north was Nefertiti's palace. She announced after the birth of Neferneferuaton the Little that she would not live with Akhunaton in the new city. The king endorsed her decision and promised to build her a palace of immense size.

In truth, Nefertiti enjoyed her relationship with Akhunaton as much as ever, but after having given birth to so many children in so short a period of years, a great urge was on her to live her life in privacy and to search within herself to discover the lost soul of Nefertiti.

The king advocated that all young people seek to find themselves. Nefertiti knew that great age and vast memories separated his consciousness from hers, so she listened to him, thinking he meant well but was a bit condescending. His promise of her own palace, a very spacious one at that, appealed to her. She was eager to move to the new city.

Akhunaton disembarked on another royal caravan to see how the construction had gone. Upon arriving he found that building sites were graded and foundations poured in the ancient tradition of stone chemistry. Many walls had already been erected in the same way.

The excavators worked by day, clearing foundations for every district from the North Suburbs to the South City. The builders worked at night, taking advantage of the cool air and dark sky for precise geochemical reactions.

After six weeks of supervision, the Pharaoh looked back on great progress. The real achievement was not the erection of huge walls or stone superstructures. It lay in the happy songs of the work crews, in the abundance of crops harvested by the peasantry, and in the laughter that followed the work days when the music got louder and the dancers spun in the firelight.

The royal city would have a singing temple, far to the south, to be called Maruaton. There would be others. A royal temple would adjoin the king's house to the south. Other singing temples would be built all over Egypt: at Abydos, Memphis, Onn. Everywhere.

When he returned for the last time to Thebes, he was received into the open arms of his children. They gave him gifts and he gave them treasures he had aquired along the way.

Smenkhara was glad to see him, at first, but before an intimate exchange could occur between them, the young prince remembered that his father had returned from overseeing their drastic move away from Thebes! Smenkhara immediately fell into angry solitude.

Akhunaton was too busy to bother about the boy. Smenkhara's gifts from his father lay in a heap at the entrance to his room A nurse tried to comfort him, but his hostility repelled her.

The dinner that welcomed Akhunaton was a feast of great extravagance. The royal family and courtiers dined together in the great hall where dancers undulated to the sweet melodies of lyres and flutes. Guests from the temples of Aton were attending the dinner feast to show their love for the king upon his return.

֍

Nefertiti and Neferneferuaton the Little ascended into the starship *Aton*. The growth of the infant was being closely monitored by the Amentii.

Experiencing the starship as a vision, Nefertiti felt closer still to the Other World, which she now thought of as many worlds—as many as the stars…but Nefertiti was not predisposed to think about cosmological matters at all during her daily life as Queen of Egypt. She was content chatting with her handmaidens, two of whom, Henttaneb and Sitamen, were daughters of Amenhotep III and understood how a king could be.

But neither of them had known any man like Akhunaton. They agreed with Nefertiti that Akhunaton, as eccentric as he was, was a far easier man to live with than naive, temperamental Amenhotep III had been.

Ast, Amenhotep III's eldest daughter, no longer resided at the palace but lived with a nobleman in a palace in the countryside. She, too, befriended Nefertiti shortly after she ascended to the throne. Nefertiti would miss Ast, as well as many other friends, who would remain rooted in their estates and palaces in and near Thebes.

𓅃

Where the beer tasted rich and good, the peasants who drank it were happy. Where the beer was cheap and diluted, and brought with it unhappy mornings, the men who drank were surly and dissatisfied.

The bitter and cynical in Egypt were few in number after the appearance of the *Atet* and the *Sektet* in the skies. But some dissatisfaction remained and it settled in the dark ale dens. In one such place, a man named Anpu boasted to his dour-faced companions that he had helped to incite a riot at the closure of one of the temples of Amen. His drinking companions were listening with lukewarm interest. Almost everybody had heard the story before.

"I cannot understand," said a young man, out of place among his battle-scarred elders, "I do not understand why you have such fierce animosity toward the Atonist king. Are you a worshipper of Amen?"

"I was not! No, when he came out of hell to haunt this land, then I was not. I lost my wife because of him."

"You lost your wife? Did he take her? Did he kill her?"

"No. She left me…under the new laws."

"Oh?" The man guffawed. "Why would she leave such a wonderful man as you?" The patrons of the beer shop burst into laughter.

Anpu was furious. He kept his distance from the young man, who was much bigger than he was, but the man with the burn scar on his face continued taunting:

211

"So, two people were killed and soldiers of the king suffered injury. Yet you, Anpu, if that is your name, you look intact. How is that?"

"Yes, how is that?" someone cried out.

Anpu backed into a corner draped with shadow. "I was…lucky. One spear came quite close to me."

"We had a friend who came here until not long ago," said one patron, "but that man does not come here anymore. He was a Priest of Amen. He does not come here anymore, and the king was not overthrown."

"Egypt is in darkness," Anpu cursed from the shadow.

Several other voices called out in agreement.

"The new king is a demon," said Anpu.

"I have seen the Boats of the Sky. I do not think they are demons and dragons."

"I have seen them, too!" Anpu screamed. "They are unnatural, as is that unholy king. Ugh! Why, the first time I saw him, I felt ill! His head was *huge!* He was so dreadfully unnatural. I knew he had been born in *hell!*"

"No, he does not come from *sheoll*," spoke the young man, using a nomadic dialect. "*Sheoll* once meant the Unseen World. That is what the desert people say it is. They say it is different from what the Priests of Amen say it is. I saw the sky boats, and the pain of this scar subsided. I feel healed."

"So—that is it! You received an evil trick and feel the benefits of a false miracle! That made a believer out of you!"

"Yes, it did. And your bitter scorn makes me feel justified in my beliefs. You have convinced me to go to the new city and work as a builder. I can get work there in my trade, and everyone has been promised their own courtyard and garden. What can be better than this? And this years's harvest was amazing even compared to last year! No, the new king is not a demon and the Boats of the Sky are not dragons. But poor Anpu! If anything has a dragon or a demon, your body is its house!"

The beer drinkers in the dark hovel laughed. The young man stood, paid his bill, and left for the streets in the night.

Chapter Twenty-Four

Akhetaton was unlike any other city ever built. The name meant "Home Horizon of the Aton" and the designs of the buildings, especially the vast sanctuaries, emphasized this theme: the central temple consisted of decorated walls without pillars, open wide to the sun. The many government buildings lacked ornate decorations and deceived the eye into not fully appreciating their heights. Their lines were long, sweeping, minimizing pillars and peaked roofs. But the city seemed to hug the ground, for from atop the highest colonnades the overall effect was that the buildings were trying not to obstruct the view. They comprised the city that the Material Disc would view upon returning to Egypt.

The singing temple in Maruaton dominated the grounds of the immense pleasure palace. It was a vast garden of fruit trees and beds of scented herbs. Fountains, ponds and streams were sculpted into the gentle land. The singing temple was activated upon the arrival of the king and melodious strains poured forth at night to accompany drumbeats and dancers.

Though the city centers were adequate to insure comfortable occupation, the northern suburbs were still being built and the workers resided in spacious one-level homes surrounded by lavish gardens and connected by tree-shaded avenues.

Nefertiti's private palace loomed above the Nile, elevated at the foot of the cliffs that enclosed the western edge of the new city. The queen marveled over the vast northern palace. She strode through the immense hallways between rows of pillars. It was one of the rare sky-reaching buildings in the City of the Horizon of the Aton. Queen Tiy and her handmaidens occupied the rooms designated as the elder queen's domicile. The children shared a common nursery that joined terraces open to the sun. The facade of pillars supported a flat stone slab level with the western horizon.

Akhetaton was an idyllic place for a meeting point between Heaven and Earth. With rows of fruit trees between every public building, potted gardens on high terraces and towering dual facades in front of the sun temples only, Akhetaton lay between limestone cliffs and a bend in the Nile. This was a city of seekers; a city of musicians and poets and hopefuls; of self-exiled pilgrims and hermits as well as disenchanted refugees from big cities.

Akhetaton was a city of costumes as well. Loose-fitting semi-transparent robes was the fashion and nudity became common in the city. The king began his occupancy of the city with a series of nude appearances, including the reception pageant in which he, Queen Tiy, and Queen Nefertiti presented themselves on the royal float in the nude. Few who viewed the royal family were at all disconcerted; most appreciated their nakedness. Men and women alike were awed by Nefertiti's immeasurable beauty and all were impressed with the physical loveliness of Mother Tiy, who was still a young woman, barely four decades removed from her birth. The children also displayed their bodies naked before the citizens of Akhetaton, who were overwhelmed by the tall, weird body, the huge head and face of their king as he stood atop the float not even wearing his crown.

In time, many abandoned the ethic that clothing must be worn to hide the sexual organs. They wore only jewels or scarves or nothing at all. The pageant signalled the beginning of a new age in Egypt, a time like no other for the twenty centuries since the departure of Horus, the last of the star-kings.

Smenkhara's spirit relapsed into inward rebellion. He tried to concentrate on his father's psychic instruction of Meritaton and Maketaton. He joined them when Akhunaton taught them concentration and thought control, but after a few days under the hot sun on the bright stone terraces, Smenkhara tired of it and spent his days indoors, brooding about having left Thebes.

Nefertiti was not present to notice the darkness that overshadowed the young prince again and Queen Tiy was occupied governing Egypt, which she loved to do. She took charge of the food distribution throughout the city, stabilized the local economy and resolved disputes whenever they erupted. Always known as the "Solver of Problems," the political affairs of the land became milder and easier for Egypt's Great Mother to manage now that the king had retired from the art of theatrical temple-sacking,

Smenkhara's nurses reported his son's volatile moods to the king. Ai looked after the boy during his most hostile tempers, though Smenkhara stopped short of ever actually demonstrating his anger. When asked by Ai or his father if he wanted to talk, if anything was wrong, to tell them what was bothering him, he would say that nothing was wrong and that there was nothing to talk about.

So it went. Anticipating a violent tantrum, like a storm approaching that massed in the sky without bursting, Akhunaton approached Smenkhara, testing his disposition from day to day, keeping open an invitation to talk which Smenkhara nonchalantly rebuffed.

Akhunaton spent his mornings in the sun, alone at first, then with his daughters, whom he tutored in meditation and natural science. Ankhasenpaaton and Tutankhaton were too young to participate fully, but they were beginning to take interest.

Akhunaton began to emphasize memory. "Training your memory is essential to developing your mind power," he told them. "One way to do this is to take turns writing and memorizing poetry."

"You have told us to write poetry about nature," said Meritaton. "I have written many little poems about flowers and butterflies, about the plant spirits."

"That is good. You have written many beautiful poems, Meritaton."

"Thank you, Father."

"I have sung little melodies to nature," said Maketaton, "but nothing I could write down."

"You will develop these talents in time, I am sure."

"It is hard to visualize an image for long," said Maketaton, closing her eyes in concentration.

"Focus and let the image form itself. Then sustain the image by keeping your mind clear."

"I...I keep trying, Father."

"It takes practise, my sweet daughter." Akhunaton drew a scroll from his robe. "I have written a poem about the Aton Disc. It is a metaphor about how the Aton Disc, in visiting this horizon, cultivates life on Earth. This is my hymn:

"'A hymn of praise to the Living Horus of the Two Horizons, who rejoiceth in the horizon in his name of Shu-who-is-in-the-disc, the giver of life forever and ever, by the King who Liveth in Truth, the Lord of the Two Lands, Nefer-kheperu-Ra Ua-en-Ra, Son of Ra, who Liveth in Truth, Lord of the Two Crowns, Akhunaton, Great in Longevity and Giver of Eternal Life, has written:

"'Thou risest gloriously, O thou Living Aton, Lord of Eternity! Thou art sparkling with beautiful colors and mighty rays of light. Thy love is mighty and great. Thy multicolored rays hypnotize at a glance. Thy metallic skin shineth brightly to make all hearts want to live. Thou fillest the Two Lands with thy love, O thou god, who didst build thyself.

"'Maker of every land and creator of whatsoever there is upon it, men and women, cattle, beasts of every kind, and trees of every kind that grow upon the land. They live when thou shinest upon them. Thou art both mother and father of what thou hast created; the eyes of thy creations, when thou rises, turn up their gaze upon thee. Thy rays can light up the earth like dawn. Every heart beateth at the sight of thee, for thou risest as their Lord.

"'Thou settest in the western horizon of Heaven; they lie down in the same way as those who are dead. Their heads are encased completely and nostrils are blocked, until they reemerge at dawn in the eastern horizon of Heaven. Their hands are lifted up in adoration of thy *Ka;* thou fillest hearts with life with thy generosity, which is Life itself. Descending, thou shinest powerful beams upon every land and joyous festivals proceed. Singing men and singing women, choruses of men make joyful laughter in the Hall of the House of the Benben Obelisk, and in all the singing temples, especially in Akhetaton, Seat of Truth, Horizon of the Aton..

"'Thy son is sanctified to perform the will of Aton, and will perform each task in the appointed succession.

"'Every creature thou hast made skippeth toward thee, thy honored son rejoiceth, heart filled with gladness, O Thou Living Aton who exists every day in Heaven. He hath brought forth his honored son, Ua-en-Ra, like his own form, never ceasing to do so. The son of Ra supporteth his generosities.

"'Nefer-kheperu-Ra Ua-en-Ra saith:

"'I am thy son, I will manifest thy will and exalt thy name. Thy strength and power are established in my heart. Thou art the Living Disc, eternity emanates from thee. Thou hast made the Heavens afar and gaze upon everything thou hast made. Thou thyself art unique, but there are millions of living forms within thee to make all creatures live. Breath of life it is to their nostrils when they see thy beams. Buds hurry to bloom and thy rays make plants grow out of desert wastelands. They drink themselves drunk at thy appearance. All the beasts frisk about on their feet in excitement. Thy birds fly from their nests and flap their wings with joy, circling around in praise of the Living Aton.'"

The king stood, lowered the papyrus scroll and smiled over his two daughters. Meritaton sat upright, rapt attention in her eyes, while Maketaton looked about, pinching her eyebrows together in the middle of her forehead in concentration.

"It is a funny poem," Meritaton said. "At first you use all your sacred names to announce that you are about to sing a hymn, then, just when the hymn forms a fit description of the Aton Disc, with its gleaming rays and metallic shine, what does the Disc of Aton do? It brings forth you, the Honored Son, who then goes on to make a pronouncement of praise to the Aton Disc! The poem goes in a circle!"

The king laughed. "That is a very good observation, Meritaton. The poem goes in a circle to demonstrate the circular nature of things. Consider this: 'Thy multi-colored rays hypnotize at a glance.' That describes how rays from the Aton Disc can read minds and even control a living body at a distance. The rays can also impart visionary knowledge through the eye. I reassure you that the Aton Disc is filled with love and that it is artificial, not a natural construction. 'Who didst build thyself' was my choice of words, for the builders of the starships and the wheelworlds were beings from out of time and space, not of this world nor of this Universe. In a sense, they were self-created, coming from so far beyond all known time and space.

"This is why I stressed the 'Horizons of Heaven,' for there is a horizon in Heaven that does to all of space and time what the horizon of the land does to the light of day after the sun descends. To journey through that dark horizon a traveler must be clothed the way the dead themselves are clothed, with their heads and bodies wrapped, nostrils plugged and eyes covered. They enter a horizon in Heaven and exit through another horizon in Heaven, then come to this worldly horizon, Akhetaton, where hands clap and voices laugh and a festival rejoices to see the Disc return. Remember, the two principal symbols of the poem are rays of light that can hypnotize, impart knowledge and impart life itself, and a journey through the horizons of Heaven, for which one is clothed as in death, at the end of which there is this world to rejoice upon."

"Tell me more about this 'horizon in Heaven'," said Meritaton.

"The horizons in Heaven are places in the vast, starry sky where time and space are like day and these regions are like night. It is impossible to describe them. Inside them exists a constant state of time colliding with space and imploding endlessly. You cannot experience it and live.

"But you can make the journey between the dark horizon and the light horizon and live. If you do this, you have a chance to briefly master all of space and time. If you can avoid that point of greatest collision, where space and time implode upon themselves forever, you can circumvent that crushing vortex and journey out of the realm of time and space and into any realm you wish. To this world again perhaps, but with all time, past and future, and any of the other portal-horizons to return through. These horizons in Heaven are gateways to all of the Possible Universes."

"Is this how you enter the Amentt?" Meritaton asked brightly.

"Yes, that is the true Amentt, the real Hidden World. We called it that, long before the false god Amen arose, because the blackness that surounds these portal-horizons hides everything. Even the very principle of light is snatched out of existence in close proximity to them.

"However, the worlds that the Amentii come from can be seen clearly in two directions. One is up, into the sky at night when the stars are visible, and the other is anytime. Just look down at the ground. The Earth. That is another world the Amentii come from."

"How can that be?"

"There have been previous evolutions of life on this world, also guided, cultivated by visitations from the Aton Disc. Some of the previous evolutions produced human races and, of these, quite a few now occupy places among the Many Worlds. Also, the people of this present new emergence will not be the last. Other human races, yet unborn, will leave this world through those portal-horizons and gain access to past and future throughout this and the many Possible Universes. Those unborn races have access to this time, and may return to it to observe and participate in the cultivation of life here, in this cycle.

"But, Meritaton, travel in artificial, self-built discs is an uncommon method of timespace translation. There is a simpler method for journeys outside of the continuous Universe. It is a technique called wave-shifting, which is purely mental. It can be mastered only by perfecting the power of internal visualization and external manifestation.

"We will work on those methods. By these exercises which I am teaching you and your sister, you will both master wave-shifting. You will learn to control a limited access to the timestream and this will free you from the physical Universe momentarily."

Meritaton's eyes were wide as her father spoke. She listened intently.

Akhunaton smiled. "I will speak to you further of these things. Let us sit and face the sun in meditation."

The days passed. Nefertiti posed for Tutmose, who sculpted a bust of her in limestone. The visage was so perfectly real that when it was painted, it looked alive.

Akhunaton posed for murals of himself to be painted in motifs no other Pharaoh had ever chosen: instead of warrior, he chose to be rendered as a good father, with his children on his lap. Instead of smasher-of-foreheads, he was painted with his arms open to all of nature, from river scenes with crocodiles and hippopotami to landscapes of grassy plains dotted with buffalo and wildebeest. Instead of riding a chariot hunting lions, he was shown praising and blessing them.

The king spent the noon hours with his children. He was teaching Maketaton how to use the rays of the sun as a source of psychic power. His own body was designed to thrive in the heat and he knew the day would come when the tribe which inherited his seed would have to live for a time in a world laid bare by interplanetary disaster. But his body would not survive to see that era. His children might, providing they learned the techniques he was teaching them. He had so little time…

They memorized his long poem, stanza by stanza. Because of the vast symbolic imagery of the Egyptian religions, the poems imparted great meaning to the children, precocious as they were. Meritaton and Smenkhara were almost five and Maketaton was four, Ankhasenpaaton and Tutankhaton were two years and two seasons old. All but the youngest were fully articulate, and the younger pair of twins were reading hieroglyphics.

Maketaton continued to have difficulty sustaining her attention, even on her father's voice as he spoke to her. She could not memorize even the first few lines of his poem. Empathically, he could pinpoint no source of pain nor specific cause for her lack of focus. Her headaches had ceased; she had not suffered one in more than a year. Akhunaton was discouraged and, during his nocturnal telepathic communion with the occupants of the *Aton*, he arranged to have Maketaton taken aboard the following night for another energy scan and a complete body examination.

Ramose visited him briefly before breakfast to inquire of Akhunaton's health ("Excellent!") and to discuss daily business ("You have an afternoon of portrait-sitting. In the evening you greet some people from a caravan whom you invited to dinner. Some musicians and dancers wish to perform before you then."). After a breakfast of river perch (the only food he ever ate for breakfast), Akhunaton meditated alone facing the sunrise and then summoned his two oldest daughters, Meritaton and Maketaton.

Meritaton had memorized the entire poem and was eager to recite it for her father. Akhunaton listened with a pleasant smile, then dismissed her to spend an hour meditating and focusing on mental images of solar energy, as he had taught her. Then, he went with Maketaton to the upper colonnade atop his palace and meditated beside her, facing into the morning sun.

Hours passed. The sun was bright and warm, the sky devoid of clouds. The blue air was clear, illuminated by one powerful source: Ra. With green hills below them, the vast Nile River before them, and the awesome cliffs above them, the two figures absorbed the hot impact of the desert sun with their eyes half-closed and legs folded, facing toward the solar furnace, staring into the glare.

Then, without warning, Maketaton fell forward onto the stone terrace. Her face was twisted tightly with intense pain. Her eyes were clamped shut and her mouth was open, silently gasping for breath. She crawled away from her astonished father.

"What is wrong, my daughter?" the king asked, reaching out to touch her tiny shoulder.

The girl writhed and twisted, but did not utter a word.

"I can feel your pain. Did it come on suddenly? Is it coming from here, in this part of your head?" Akhunaton touched where the tiny dark spot had appeared in in the last energy scan.

Maketaton turned and twisted and did not open her eyes. She did not answer. She did not cry or scream. She did not utter a sound.

She simply died.

Akhunaton was stunned. He felt her living essence depart from her body. Her consciousness was whisked away silently, invisibly, and was gone. The body of Maketaton was suddenly still, curled in a fetal position, the same as when she had entered the world, with her knees touching her forehead.

Nefertiti had chosen just that moment to leave her palace. She walked to her stables and commanded that her horse be bridled and fitted to her chariot. An escort was summoned for her journey to the Central City.

When she arrived at her husband's house, she heard his deep, agonized moans resounding throughout the palace. She hurried through the deserted reception chamber, through the empty rooms and the corridor to the rooftop terrace. There, at the top of the stairs, on the edge of the sunlight and shadow, the king kneeled, clutching the lifeless body of his daughter to his chest and casting great moans and wails into the hot air.

Chapter Twenty-Five

The queen was furious. Her grief leaped up like a great storm wave. When the wave broke, her grief became anger which thundered against her husband, the strange and alien king.

"What have you done?" Nefertiti wailed with the voice of a wounded lioness. She streaked up the stairs to Akhunaton and tried to wrestle the limp figure from his arms. He drew back. Intense pain flared in his huge eyes, which overflowed with tears and melted the stibium eyepaint into black rivers that ran down his cheeks.

Standing, Akhunaton moaned again in great pain and cried out, "What do you want?"

"What have you done to her? What have you done?"

Akhunaton turned suddenly and strode past Nefertiti into the shadow of his house. He walked placed Maketaton's body on a golden couch with pillar legs and lion heads. The little girl appeared to be sleeping.

"She must have died of sunstroke," Nefertiti moaned. "You! You gave her her name 'Protected by the Aton Disc.' What irony! My daughter was unprotected by Aton!"

Akhunaton was silent.

"She died of sunstroke! My little daughter died of sunstroke. Meritaton tells me you have her and Maketaton sit in the sun for hours. She died of sunstroke!"

"You do not know that, Nefertiti. You do not know that with certainty."

Nefertiti backed away, grief-stricken and angry. "Your breathing exercises, your concentration games, they did not work! Now she is dead. Meditation—it did not work. She is dead. You! You have been irresponsible with my children!"

"It could not have been sunstroke! We were not in the sun for long. The sun is not hot yet…"

"It is a very hot day! When did this happen? An hour ago—or just this minute? She is still so hot, she is so white, so pale…!" Nefertiti glared at Akhunaton and cried out, "You named her 'Protected by the Aton.' What kind of a protector is your god?"

Nefertiti fled from the chamber to the balcony. Akhunaton followed her in his slow, angular walk.

Mother Tiy appeared at an archway. "What is wrong?"

Nefertiti cried in mourning. Tiy ran toward Akhunaton, who stood helplessly, moaning in bottomless pain.

"What is the *matter*?" Tiy demanded, halting at the top of the stairs and peering down at Nefertiti.

The king threw back his massive head and closed his eyes. He breathed deeply several times, then lowered his head and looked into his Earthly mother's eyes.

"Maketaton is dead. Nefertiti blames me. She says sunstroke killed the little one. She died in my presence. I could do nothing."

"Oh dear Lord Ptah! Where does she lie?"

"This way." Akhunaton led Tiy to the room in which a tiny body lay on the royal couch, still curled in a fetal pose. The little girl's head was so large she looked like a baby unborn. Mother Tiy bent over Maketaton and, weeping, embraced her for a long time.

She left the still figure and clutched the huge body of the artificial man who was her son. They walked arm-in-arm to the reception hall, where they met Nakht and Ai returning from a stroll through the orchards and gardens. Both were shocked and grief-stricken on hearing the sad news.

Ai and Parennefer removed Maketaton's body into the inner chambers of the palace, where they wrapped it and prepared to take it to the Royal Temple, across from the Pharaoh's Palace.

Akhunaton returned to the courtyard to comfort Nefertiti, but she pushed him away and fled down the stairs to where her chariot waited. Her guards begged to know what caused her tears and tried to comfort her, but she ordered them to drive her swiftly back to her palace.

She arrived and was received by her handmaidens. They insisted that she confide in them. Nefertiti wept in their arms and told them of the death of little Maketaton.

Inside the laboratory complex of the starship *Aton*, the body of Maketaton was laid on a cushionless table where it was scanned with energy sensors. A clear strand from a neural probe flowed from the crystalline cube and entered Maketaton's right eyelid. It slipped along the optic nerve and into her brain. As the microscopic eye illuminated the dark tissues it explored, the webs and draperies of brain appeared on a holographic screen overhead. All aboard the *Aton* viewed what the probe revealed.

When it reached the area that had shown up as a black spot on Maketaton's ultraviolet scan, the probe revealed a row of microscopic hemorrhages following a web of capillaries converging at a vital junction of neurons. So fragile was her mutant brain, little Maketaton had died of a stroke,

"That defect did not appear in Maketaton's clone," said Pilot Tem, pointing to the flurry of red cells still swarming from the microscopic ruptures. "That defect was not genetic. It was structural."

"The result of a bad bump or a birth injury, perhaps?"

"Perhaps, Shu."

"It was a relatively easy birth. I know of no such injury."

"It might have been a prenatal cellular disruption."

"That is more likely. A failure in cell reproduction that resulted in a multicellular structural defect. A tragic loss."

Tem placed a hand on the shoulder of Shu-in-Akhunaton. They looked from the screen to the limp body of the little girl with the huge head. Wordlessly, Shu-in-Akhunaton lifted his daughter's still body off the table and walked to the corridor that led to the docking bay and the two landing discs. There, with Tefnut and Geb, he boarded the *Atet* and departed for Egypt, far below.

※※※

"So! Meditation did not save Maketaton," Smenkhara said flippantly, leaning in his father's doorway.

Akhunaton slowly returned from a state of deep internal meditation. The morning sun fell on the side of his face.

"You! You!" Ramose was running down the hall. "Get out of there!"

Smenkhara looked casually over his shoulder. "I wanted to see him. I knew it would still be early enough to catch him in his chamber. I did not want to wait until he was busy with his daily schedule."

Ramose had reached the doorway and was about to drag Smenkhara away when Akhunaton said, "He has an open invitation to speak to me whenever he wants about anything he chooses. Speak to me, Smenkhara, for I welcome your derision over your silence."

That shattered the boy. He pointed his walking stick at his father and bellowed, "You are not a holy man! You feign superior consciousness but you do not really have it. You sat my sister in the hot sun until she died! Did meditation save her? Did memorizing poetry prolong her life? No! You are not a holy man, and yet, sitting there, being so self-righteous, you say you prefer my insults to silence! Then you shall have my silence again!"

With that, Smenkhara stomped down the hallway, his walking stick clacking loudly on the stone.

"Let him go," Akhunaton said to Ramose, who stood, mouth agape, staring after the boy.

That day Smenkhara left the king's palace to live with Nefertiti. Although he did not speak much with his mother, they shared the opinion that Akhunaton's carelessness and insensitivity had killed Maketaton. Neither would hear what the king had to say. The queen's palace received several communiques from him, but sent back only one, a general refusal to meet with him and hear what he had learned aboard the Aton Disc.

222

Queen Tiy listened. She and Ai met with Akhunaton, fasting in mourning. They spoke gravely of the girl's death, then sat together in a silence that ended in peace, their grief transformed by the sounds of many birdcalls sprinkled over the summer winds.

"Is this certain?" Tiy wanted no doubt.

"Mother Tiy, I can state yes with absolute certainty." The king leaned forward, his huge eyes narrowed. "Tem is in the process of carefully studying the defect. We know that it was not a genetic defect, but caused by imperfect cellular reproduction during the first three months of gestation."

Ai rocked back on his feet, his arms folded behind his back.

Tiy thought deeply. She closed her eyes. Finally she looked up and put her hand on her son's forearm. "I will talk to Nefertiti, but I will let a few days pass. She needs to vent her rage and despair. She knew no grief until her marriage to you."

"You intend your words to include other, less intense heartbreaks."

"Oh, yes! Everything she lived until the very day you arrived and took her as your queen, everything she had experienced as a priestess was very different from the life she has known with you."

"I understand," Akhunaton said sadly.

"She had been so hopeful and now that her hopes and dreams have been realized, she has found them not of her liking. She may blame...I fear to think it. I will talk to her, but after a time has passed."

"Thank you, Mother Tiy. I know that much of what you say about her is true. Even seeing me the first time was a heartbreak for her. Neither Egypt nor Nefertiti had ever seen anything like my body before."

Ai laughed first, then Tiy chuckled and Akhunaton himself smiled.

"That is why I built her a palace of her own. I know she needs personal privacy now, and especially distance from me. I knew it would be this way with her when first I met her. She is lovely both in spirit and in form, and I have a high estimation of her talents and intelligence. I would respect her less if she was less independent and assertive."

"That she has difficulty believing, given the way you excluded her opinions from your actions against the temples of Amen."

"I know. I had my reasons for attacking the temples, as you and Ai well know."

Tiy nodded. "Still, it was unfair. You gave her one token hearing and dismissed her words by so eloquently stating that you knew more than she did and therefore did not need to explain your actions."

The king pondered this for a long time, then slowly nodded and said, "I have been unfair."

"Yes, you have. And insensitive."

"Yes, I can see that now."

"What did you feel at the time?"

Akhunaton thought. "Boredom. A feeling of too many rehearsals."

"So your heart was not in the performance."

"Not in that vital way it needed to be."

"It showed."

A look of gigantic agony stabbed the long, angular face. The huge eyes shut hard and the immense mouth pulled downward in a seizure of grief. Finally, Akhunaton said, "It is true."

"What was in the deepest part of your heart? It is a dangerous game you are playing. You are among hostile and primitive men. What was really in the pit of your stomach, where the power center dwells? Do not tell me what was in your heart; you already have: you view us as children and our games bore you. What was in your third chakra while you caravaned from one temple to the other with your crook and flail, your mallet and chisel? What did your guts feel?"

The huge eyes closed once again and when they opened, Akhunaton said, "Contempt. I suppressed it with a layer of indifference."

"But it was contempt."

"Not toward the people! I love even the soldiers and the deluded priests. I hate— I admit, I hate that cruel one you and Ai saw a vision of when you received the cosmological knowledge."

Tiy nodded. "Nefertiti did not receive knowledge of these things. She knows only celestial rapture."

"She has declined it." Akhunaton shook his head. "She tells me she is not ready for visionary knowledge and I fear she is correct."

"That is true, Akhunaton. Visions of the type Ai and I have had would devastate her. I was so young then, the return of Aton was like a sign pointing to water in the desert. When my parents were young they were very open to such revelations. Aton had returned! Aton had returned! Aton might impart visions and prophecies! Yes, this turned out to be true, and we were open to new knowledge.

"But this is now! New knowledge becomes old knowledge, even the face of a strange new king has become mundane. People grow accustomed to things in the sky. Times change, sometimes suddenly. The people live, they adjust, and life goes on."

Akhunaton nodded. "In times of long and slow transition, when the life is tedious, miracles can make the mundane more difficult to endure."

"This is true. People like Nefertiti, all men and women, from nobles to peasants, are clinging to the ordinary and cherishing the mundane. It is all that does not change for them, the only aspect of life that does not seem threatening."

"Humanity fears sudden change, is that right?"

"Yes. Just as the mind fears oblivion, as life fears death, so do the people of

Egypt—people everywhere—fear interruption in their lives, sudden conditions they are not prepared for."

"I understand. It is too bad. The static and sedentary has stagnated into foulness. Like a stream diverted to clean bad water out of a pond, so the essence of change must sweep the human world."

"O King, the metaphors you use to describe us betray a strange inner contradiction: you speak of us humans as though we were a disease on this living planet-body, something to be cured."

The man looked into his mother's eyes and let her see some of the fear his eyes contained. "Mother Tiy, humans are not a disease. But they may become one and infect this living planet. The potential is here, and it is strong. If this comes to pass, then the human race must be treated as an infection that must be cured."

The full impact of his words struck her. Shuddering, she said, "You do not mean Aton would exterminate its children?"

"That is why I am here. This is why I do things to make my name known for thousands of years. I cause catastrophes in Egypt to prevent global catastrophe that will hurt and kill all people."

"Aton would do this?"

"Aton cannot and does not need to do this."

"Who—or what—will kill all living people?"

"Earth! *Earth!* Nature will rebel! The mother planet will defend her fertility against this one errant creation, this one misbegotten child."

Tiy gasped, then nodded. "That was the meaning of those final visions we received! I thought that was another world, one that had destroyed itself in ways Egypt destroys herself, under the yoke of…The Beast."

"That world of towering palalces and self-driven chariots is not another world. It is Earth. Thousands of years from now, in an age when warfare becomes so violent and immense that exploding fires can thunder and strike down cities many times bigger than Memphis or Thebes."

"And that is Earth's retaliation against war and violence here and now?"

"It is only one possibility. There are many, and without an act of intervention by Aton, all are very grim. Your species seems to have an inability to conquer its own lower mind, the beast-brain in all of us. That strange inability could bring about human extinction, which is immeasurably terrible! Of all the human races to have been born by this planetary mother, this fourth mammal race of humans is by far the most creative and imaginative, the most energetic, filled with the greatest potential for celebration and joy that human beings have ever achieved on any planetary home! That is why beings from throughout the galaxy and other realms and dimensions and Universes have converged here! This fourth race of humanoids on Earth is the most precious event in this entire radius of the timespace Universe."

"Everything that happens here is of cosmic importance," Ai mused. "That is a staggering thought."

Akhunaton nodded. "What happens in this court today is of immense, cosmological import. But let us not be staggered! If my own heart had been lighter, I would not have stumbled in my dance with Nefertiti."

Tiy nodded emphatically. "You must remain uninvolved in the drama but involved in the moment," she told her son. "You taught these things to me. Now *I* must to remind *you*."

"I have no more temple-sacking to do, no more radical pronouncements. A few more heretical proclamations, but they will be minor compared to the blows I have already dealt to the sedentary Egyptian order."

Ai chuckled again. "I will never forget those days…"

Akhunaton shook his head. "I am glad they are behind me."

Tiy's talk with Nefertiti took place four days after the funeral procession.

At the procession, Nefertiti had been completely silent toward Akhunaton, preserving only the Egyptian veneer of civilized behavior, veiling the real feelings of their lives. Retreating to her palace, Nefertiti sent all except her children away. Tiy did not attempt to contact her, nor did Akhunaton, although his letter of condolences had been received. It contained a clear message of understanding and he endorsed his wife's need for complete privacy

When Queen Tiy sensed it would be right to pay Nefertiti a visit, she sent by courier a cordial note of endearment. The young queen responded with a letter of invitation. Tiy summoned an escort and departed by chariot to the palace in the north.

Nefertiti greeted Tiy in a slightly aloof manner, not unexpectedly. Tiy tugged at Nefertiti's arms, insisting on a hug. Nefertiti could not resist, and the women embraced warmly.

Stepping inside, the queens walked past the nursery where Smenkhara played idly with one of his nurses.

"I hope he likes living with you," Tiy said softly.

"He does. I love Smenkhara. We have our little disputes, but we have a deep friendship. He talks to me and I listen."

"Akhunaton wishes he had that rapport with him."

"Smenkhara will probably always resent his father. The rift between them is too great. It widened with the death of his sister."

"I see. Akhunaton thinks all things can heal, given time."

"A lifetime in Smenkhara's body would not be enough for Smenkhara."

"That is tragic. A truce needs to be drawn between them. Smenkhara will probably be Egypt's next king."

"That is between him and his father. And it is not why you came to see me, Mother Tiy."

"Of course not, Nefertiti. I came to talk to you about what I learned from your husband about Maketaton's death."

"Please—I do not want to hear it." They had walked to the interior courtyard with reflective pools and wide sky views. Nefertiti lingered in the dooorway, giving pause to Tiy's approach with a raised hand. "You and the king can discuss such things with appropriate detatchment. I...I am too deeply bound in my heart to deal with my daughter's death with mere science."

"He does not do that. He has suffered much. He will continue to grieve. But he is letting go of Maketaton. He tells me he will always retain the bright moments he shared with her, and that her essence will remain in the great memory of Ptah. She lives on, as we all will, in the heart and memory of Ptah."

"How poetic!" Nefertiti strode into the open courtyard, into the cloud-filtered sunlight. It turned the transparent sleeves and gown she wore into a cloud of blue haze. Her beaded wig was almost black and did not shimmer. "Tell me—does he say these things with loving tones in his voice, perhaps like a minstrel? Like a singer or an orator?"

"You think he is insincere as well as insensitive."

"I do. I think he and his weird race trifle with us."

"You think we are their pawns?"

"I do. I think Aton is intrusive. Aton constitutes an unnatural and dangerous intrusion into our lives."

"I see. Is that deepest in your heart, Nefertiti?"

"My heart is stung with pain, Mother Tiy! You do not feel the same way I do about Maketaton's death. I know this, I *know* it! Go now, Mother Tiy, and make your peace with your better-than-human king. You and he can progress beyond a mere death in the family to continue your discussions of politics and even bigger things: cosmology."

"I will go, Nefertiti. I bless you. I hope you swiftly heal."

☥

Akhunaton was teleported directly aboard the vast starship as it descended closer to the Earth over Akhetaton. He materialized inside the holographic chamber, in the midst of Tem, Geb, Nuit, Nephthys, Set, Isis and Osiris. The omniscient presence of Yod pervaded the air.

"The death of Princess Maketaton has created a critical situation," said Akhunaton. "Nefertiti continues to blame me for having subjected my daughter to enough solar radiation to induce fatal sunstroke. She even rejects Aton, saying that we intrude upon Earthly matters. This is true, but is it necessary? Is it moral?"

Tem replied, "The destructiveness of this latest human race is awesome in potential. It would not be so critical if it were only directed towards the species that bears the tendency. But consider the band of asteroids between Mars and Jupiter. Consider why Mars is barren, why her seas have evaporated and her atmosphere has been scorched away. There were once four life-bearing worlds in this planetary system. This, which is now the third planet from Ra, is the most idyllic of the worlds, the last living mother-world in the Ra system. Three life-bearing worlds have been annihilated because of two warlike races! How vast is the potential for chaos? Is Ptah's Universe ridden with the fatal flaw of rapid entropy and violence?"

The crew members of the starship *Aton* were silent.

Tem turned forcefully to Shu-in-the-body-of-Akhunaton and said, "Even you have soaked up your share of the animosity that festers down there, Shu. Even *you*, the empath that you are!"

Struck by self-scorn, Akhunaton-that-is-Shu breathed a heavy sigh and shook his head. "It is true. I hate and fear Kahotep, not because of what he can do to me, but because of how easily he can control masses of humanity. How obediently they destroy life at his command!"

"You must remember," Nuit sang to him in a loving falsetto melody, "that these are the people of Egypt today. They are not the people of Planet Gaia tomorrow."

Akhunaton nodded. "I must remember that, Sister Nuit."

"Heal thy heart, Brother Shu," said Pilot Tem. "You have absorbed much wrath and contempt. You have become attached to this planet and you fear that it will also be destroyed. You have let your heart sink from lightness and grace, Brother Shu. Your heart fell into worry and contempt very quickly in that world below."

Shu-in-Akhunaton nodded sadly. "That is true. And yet, I feel hypocritical. The motto I tell people is 'Ankh-em-Ma'at'."

"Then live up to it! You must inspire Smenkhara's love and trust! You must do this for Egypt today and for Earthlings in the future."

Akhunaton nodded. "We will need four more girl children to complete the experiment and create a new royal lineage."

"Three more daughters will do. The seventh is hypothetical, an odd number to create greater variations and faster assimilation by the evolving population."

"Nefertiti will not agree to another impregnation. I am sure of it."

"Give her a year, Brother Shu," said the pilot. "A lot can happen in a mother's heart, especially a mother who will live less than a century."

Akhunaton again sighed. He pitied these short-lived humans and secretly knew why theirs was such a world of pain. The awesome length of his own life and continuous memory was a gift he had learned to cherish above all else during his return to violent, primitive Earth.

✺

The next day began with Ramose's usual morning visit and recitation of the daily business: Akhunaton sat cross-legged in meditation. He opened his eyes more widely, nodded in recognition, and listened in silence. When Ramose finished, Akhunaton blessed him and dismissed him, then remained in meditation as the morning sunlight poured over the eastern clifftops and through his bedroom window.

He could hear music pulsing and spilling over the morning air. It alleviated some of his sadness. He envisioned Maketaton's smiling face, then let it fade in his mind. He envisioned Smenkhara, and retained the image of his son's smile, though Smenkhara's image had a tendency to fade from smiling into frowning.

He recalled his discussion aboard the *Aton* the night before, and fathomed wordlessly the depth of the challenge that lay ahead. He had definitely established Heaven on Earth for some people. The former victims of oppression now ceaselessly rejoiced, viewing freedom from tyranny as being equivalent to Earthly paradise. But his own oldest son still rebelled and his second daughter had died in the bosom of Utopia. Although Egypt was blessed with a bountiful harvest and peace at home and abroad, the family of the king himself was afflicted with trials of misfortune.

There was no response from Nefertiti to his letters requesting communication between them. Smenkhara refused to acknowledge his father's condolences. But Akhunaton received a visit from Meritaton that afternoon, and they chatted about her mother and brother. She left her father with reassurance but not resolution, something only time could bestow.

By evening the sky had become a playing field for spotty tufts of clouds. Sunlight hid, then peered out from behind the jagged patches with long silver beams. Music never ceased to pour from the hills. The sounds of drumming and laughter did not contradict that Egypt was in mourning for the death of a tiny princess.

The word of Maketaton's death spread quickly through Egypt. Those who deeply believed in Aton grieved, but saw an opportunity to express love in music, song and verse. In Akhetaton, the citizens danced and sang for her as the music continued. Its tonal quality changed, from festive to sonorous, then back to festive. The people of Akhetaton were praying for Nefertiti to have another child.

Outside of Akhetaton the news of Maketaton's death evoked feelings of dread and sorrow more than appreciation and contemplation, much less celebration. For some, her death and the meaning of her name cast doubt about the power of Aton to protect its children. To many who secretly feared their own deaths, who lacked the faith that they would escape Baba, the Soul-Eater, the death of Maketaton was a sign that an imperfect Heaven had been brought to Earth.

The sudden withdrawal of the Pharaoh from Thebes and his seclusion in Akhetaton had some negative effects upon the popularity of his religion. Aside from the great attention he had drawn to Amenism by banning the religion, sacking its temples and erasing the name of Amen wherever he found it (including from his own name), he had limited his persecution of the priests to symbolic measures. While he defrocked the priests and confiscated their riches, he did not imprison even one. None were tortured, none were killed on a sacrificial altar to a new god. Even after the demonstration of the Boats of the Sky, many of the men of Egypt still held a continuing fascination for Amen.

The Priests of Amen, who never considered themselves defrocked, began to reassemble and reestablish their religion. They knew that compromising with this Pharaoh was out of the question; he had made that clear. His ethics were clear: he would rely on manifestations of sky-spirits to convince the masses of the superiority of his religion while limiting his assaults against Amenism to ideological challenges, confining his attacks to vandalism and outright theft. This lenience allowed the priests of Amen to resume practice of their religion of conspiracy, assassination and war.

The guards posted at the temples of Amen were dwindling in number. Some who remained at their posts were fanatics of the cult of Aton, having seen the aerial discs and been blinded to all else. Some remained for another reason: guarding the temples of Amen put them in a position to be approached for bribery.

The Temple of Karnak was the most heavily guarded and no Amenist priest had entered it since its official closure. Attempts were made to blackmail, seduce, bribe, or intimidate the soldiers who remained there. Sometimes this resulted in public exposure and harassment of the priests, but the only punishment the king meted out was banishment from Thebes, but that was severe enough for any struggling Amenist priest.

Thebes was all but deserted. On the banks of the Nile spread abandoned houses, boxes of mud and brick, lifeless like white, discarded seashells. The Temple of Karnak was empty, as were the interconnected cities of Karnak, Luxor and Thebes. After the demonstration of the sky boats, Thebans almost unanimously embraced the religion of Aton. Then, when the king announced that he would be building himself a new capital north of Memphis, many Thebans migrated north, seeking employment under Pharaoh Akhunaton by building him a city.

The first residents there enjoyed a one-story home with a courtyard filled with spacious gardens. The continuous bounty of the harvest was shared by all and every citizen had land for a vegetable garden. Land was Egypt's great strength, shared by all Egyptians.

This made it difficult for the priests of Amen to find new recruits, except for hostile losers: government officials whose political corruption or depraved personal lives had cost them their power or men whose hatred of women had been thwarted by the king's new laws enforcing the rights of women as equal to men. The priests of Amen exploited these pools of disillusionment and contention. Their methods were swift, well-organized and not dependent upon recapturing, even if only secretly, the Temple of Karnak.

The priests of Amen did not know the true nature of their god. They viewed him as a purely supernatural being, a god made manifest in some remotely human way inside the many temples built to him. The entity who actually existed inside Karnak was as real to his priests as the entities they believed lived in Luxor or any of the other temples of Amen throughout Egypt. This belief had been carefully cultivated by The Beast, but now it worked to his detriment. None among his priesthood knew the true nature of the man who lived in the Temple of Karnak, so none knew how to rescue and resurrect their "god."

The Beast had broken all contact with the outside world shortly after the appearance of the *Atet* and the *Sektet*. He felt their presence powerfully and the visitation was confirmed by his spies among the birds of the air, though lately these birds no longer returned to the ventilation shafts of the temple to seek out The Beast's chambers.

Infrequently, he interrogated Amenhotep, Son of Hapu, to gain impressions of the outside world, though it was fruitless: the blind seer was hopelessly insane. The day was rapidly approaching when The Beast would murder his remaining Inner Circle and cannibalize the brain of the blind seer to prolong his longevity by another, slightly shortened lifespan. Then he would leave Karnak by one of the tunnels to the mastabas and infiltrate Egyptian society. He hoped his religion was in the process of reorganizing without him. He would have to make contact again, on his terms, and stage a mysterious reunion. The Beast had less than fifteen years in which to stage a coup.

To occupy his time he continued his scientific experiments in his underground, electrically-lit laboratories. He had spent six thousand years as a laboratory technician of the gods. For two thousand years and several centuries he had struggled to add to his body of knowledge. That knowledge was contained in a series of scrolls Kahotep called the Ka-Ba-Ra. He kept them in a dry vault carved into the limestone floor of one of his chambers. He intended to supplant that great body of knowledge with further experimental discoveries that would ultimately make him also into a god.

He meditated and tried to translate himself into a wave-shifter. He was unable to do so, despite his determination and eight thousand years of memory to facilitate his ability to construct perfect mental imagery. Even with these great abilities, The Beast could not infold/enfold a psychohologram and thus change his location in the timespace continuum. Psychophysical time travel and teleportation were somehow not within his grasp, although telepathy and hypnosis were, and enabled him to create and project demons eye-to-eye.

One of his last bits of information about the outside world came when, several days after the visitation by the *Atet* and the *Sektet*, he had lurked in a concealed viewpoint inside the temple walls. Overhearing two of the king's guards discussing the state of Amenism versus Atonism among the Egyptians, The Beast caught the words "Ankh em Ma'at" quoted as the king's new motto.

To weigh his heart against the Feather of Truth. To know the lightness as the key to ultimate freedom. Freedom of non-energy exchanges between time and space. Even as he sat contemplating that inevitable realization, he sought out the exceptions to the causality of mind. He wondered how he could bribe Ptah himself to to make an exception for him, one death-fearing being, in the Universe of dense matter and expanding energies.

Akhunaton remained physically distant from Nefertiti and Smenkhara for several weeks. The queen would rage against his very name, then fall into deep depressions that lasted for days. Unable to visit her, he sent poems to her written in colorful hieroglyphs. He eulogized Maketaton, offered sympathy, painted verses with images of spring buds, butterflies escaping from the chrysalis, or baby birds chipping their way out of the egg shells of sleep.

She was frequently visited by Queen Tiy, and greeted her each visit more warmly than the last. After weeks of suffering, Nefertiti broke free of depression and grief. One morning, Tiy found her to be markedly more self-composed and hopeful.

The summer was growing old. Nefertiti leaned against the huge stone column on the southern facade of her palace, gazing south. The slanted sunlight tipped down from the clifftops and lighted the side of her face and body with shining gold. She gazed silently upon the Nile, which curved into view from the west, spreading broadly into the brown and green land, parting the hills and defining the city that the people of Egypt were building for her…and for Akhunaton.

She turned to face Tiy, who stood behind her. Then she again faced the Nile and Aketaton. Her eyes caressed the toiling builders who carried liquid stone in buckets and skins up the dirt ramps. They hauled it over the scaffolding and catwalks, then poured it into earthen and wooden molds. Then they would climb down and return with another full bucket to pour another molded building block. They sang as they worked, motivated by the love of their beautiful queen.

She was a loving queen. She turned again to Tiy and said, "Take me among them."

"Is that your wish? Right now?"

"Yes. Please. Take me down there. I wish to go."

They departed immediately. Queen Tiy and her royal escort accompanied Nefertiti by chariot from her palace to the house builders of the northern suburbs. The workers stood at attention, their faces pulled wide with blissful grins of love and rapt awe. They faced her, their hearts expansive and faces streaked with tears of joy.

Tiy and Nefertiti rode their chariots down the dirt avenues between rows of fruit trees and the widely-spaced building sites. The homes were separated by large gardens and courtyards. The suburbs looked more like great parks than districts of population centers.

Under the bright desert sun, the sky seemed to shine with light reflected in all of the smiling faces. As the workers hailed their queens, Nefertiti saw living adoration in each eye. She measured the love along with the progress that stretched before her as a new city was being built, and she fell in love once again, but not with Akhunaton.

She fell in love with her role as Queen of Egypt, with the knowledge that she was the most loved woman in the land she herself loved: Egypt. She rode in her chariot beside a soldier. She did not know the man. The reins led from his hands to the mouths of four horses. The wheels rolled, clattered over rocks and dirt. Nefertiti remembered who she was.

When she returned to her palace with Queen Tiy, her smile had fully blossomed. The two Ladies of Egypt talked on friendly terms for the rest of the afternoon, mostly of family matters, though the relationship between Smenkhara and Akhunaton was avoided.

When time approached for Tiy to depart, the Mother of Egypt asked the younger queen, "Do you have anything you wish me to tell your husband?"

Nefertiti stiffened and looked away from the Royal Mother. A long silence soaked up the air between them. Tiy turned and said, "Please, Nefertiti. What did you start to say?"

"Nothing...Tell him...Tell him—I am recovering." Tiy offered her a gaze of sympathy and affection, but Nefertiti looked away. "He is unnatural. Everything about him is unnatural. I am only remaining here...for Egypt."

"Do you really mean that?"

"Yes, I do," she said without hesitation.

"Do you not believe in another side to nature? A side to this world that is not so ordinary?"

Nefertiti shook her head. Tiy's well-intended inquiry reminded Nefertiti that the old, familiar world with regular dawns and sunsets, seasons, human-looking kings and familiar skies devoid of intruders was all gone now. The world would never be the same as she remembered it, once, long ago.

"What is wrong with just nature? Does everything have to be shaped by the hands of Aton?" Nefertiti strode angrily to the southern balcony. "The green things in the spring, the the birds that come and go, all of it, from the rains to the surge of the Nile in winter to the hot, dry air of summer. What is wrong with leaving it alone?"

Tiy touched her shoulder, then stepped back. "Nefertiti, we *are* the scheme of things."

Nefertiti whirled around and glared at her. "I know that you and your son take credit for much that happens in the natural world, but his failed effort to bring

'Paradise to Earth' taught me to separate our king's claims from his results. The same must be done with all his claims, except, of course, his rightful claim to the throne."

"Nefertiti, what are you saying?"

"I do not know. Of course…he is not insane!"

"Is that what you think? That Akhunaton is insane?"

"I have thought that occasionally. No, in truth, I have thought it often, especially lately."

"Nefertiti, you would see all things differently if you opened yourself to the visionary knowledge. Think of the knowledge that came to our parents and to us, their children, when the Aton Disc returned to the sky. Remember the many children begotten by the Amentii who were born into Egypt."

"No! You have described to me those visions before. No, I do not want to receive them! I do not want to know too much about those things."

"You have always said those very words. You fear knowlege, Nefertiti, and that is why your word does not carry equal weight with mine in Akhunaton's court. You could have expanded your knowledge in visionary ways by now, and you reject the opportunity every time it manifests. You have obtained some visionary knowledge through your raptures of union with Akhunaton aboard the Aton Disc, but that is all. To receive a visionary memory of the living cosmology is the greatest blessing a living thing can have. You refuse this out of fear, Nefertiti. What you fear most is knowledge."

Nefertiti frowned. "Say what you will. I fear anything that will make me think the way he does. Yes, I am afraid such visions might make me think like Akhunaton does."

"You still believe he is insane."

"I do not know what to believe! Go, please, Mother Tiy. I cannot bear it any longer."

Tiy turned, walked to the dooorway and paused to say a blessing. Then she departed.

Smenkhara passed the time studying with his tutors, playing occasionally with his siblings or his nurses. He spent his solitary moments almost autistically, rolling up into a ball on the floor or gazing out from a palace window.

His only friend was his mother. He knew his family resented his sullenness. He exploited this as a way of getting sympathetic attention from Nefertiti. He avoided Queen Tiy and Akhunaton was never mentioned. Secluded in the northern palace, Nefertiti and Smenkhara shared an unstated understanding that they would not speak of the king.

The pain from where his legs joined his pelvis had subsided long ago. He was far less crippled than he had been before the visitation of the *Atet* and the *Sektet* over

Thebes, so Smenkhara now rejected his father by blaming him for his sister's death. He resented the move from Thebes to this new home in the north. On this he and his mother disagreed: Nefertiti liked having her own palace, isolated from Akhunaton.

❦

The Pharaoh lived in his house in the Central City of Akhetaton with his mother. Queen Tiy occupied the Women's Chambers across the bridge over the main avenue of the Central City. She saw the king daily, often immediately after his morning meditation. He consulted with her about all political matters before making decisions.

She was sitting with General Horemheb on the western balcony of the state building, looking out over the Nile, discussing the uprisings of the priests of Amen. Queen Tiy voiced disfavor with a policy of forceful suppression or imprisonment. Horemheb, who had spent three decades of his life as Egypt's General of the Army and Navy, defended the opinion that anyone caught practising the priestcraft or entering a temple of Amen should be arrested, tried, and, if found guilty, imprisoned.

Queen Tiy asserted, "We do not need to imprison anyone for breaking that law because the old priests have already lost face throughout Egypt."

"Suppose they riot like they did two years ago? Suppose one of my soldiers or a temple guard is killed? What are we to do—harass and ridicule an angry mob? Banish a riot with a proclamation? How can I disperse a rioting mob without using force?"

"There will be angry mobs if the priests are jailed! They have been mocked and humiliated. The king says to leave them alone!"

"I am familiar with his words—I wish I could accept his idealistic view! I fear that the damaged priesthood will be more dangerous than ever. And this king has made them dangerous. I sense that. I remember his father, Amenhotep III. He smashed a lot of foreheads..." Horemheb laughed at this "...but the wars were few, and I found that everything I had to settle as a military commander could usually be resolved with diplomacy, not show of arms. Do you know why we never invaded Nubia?" He laughed and nudged Tiy's forearm. "When diplomatic efforts failed, I showed up with soldiers and diplomatic methods suddenly succeeded!"

Tiy laughed at this and summoned a courtier, Mahu, to get some wine.

When he departed, Tiy said to Horemheb, "This was what Akhunaton admires about you. You are a greater diplomat than a general—and you are Egypt's greatest general, he thinks. He has praised you because of your fairness. He has noted that you have never invaded foreign territories and your diplomatic talent has also received his attention. That is why you retained your post after the disappearance of my husband. That is why you retained it after Akhunaton became king."

General Horemheb nodded thoughtfully at these words. "Tell the king I thank him for such high praise."

Queen Tiy nodded. "If a riot occurs, imprison specific people for specific crimes. Arrest those who inflict harm against a person. Do not imprison a believer for a religious ritual or a religion. If someone incites to riot, arrest them and try them in front of witnesses and neutral judges immediately."

"Suppose a soldier is killed in a skirmish?"

"Permanent exile. Take the rioters to some waterhole, some faraway oasis, and leave them there. They will survive. Make certain they have a source of water, dates and figs nearby, and lots of desert between them and Egypt."

"A fine idea. Like imprisonment."

"Except that you can make a fine beginning for yourself at a suitable oasis. You cannot in a prison."

"Some beginning!" General Horemheb chuckled. "Oh, let me stay in Egypt and know every day where the Nile is!"

Both he and Queen Tiy laughed at this. Mahu returned with the wine and two cups.

"What is your opinion about this, Mahu?" Horemheb took one cup. "How far should we go to punish rebel priests? The ones who are still trying to take over the temples?"

"Are you not having any wine?" Queen Tiy asked, noticing that the courtier had not poured a cup for himself.

"Oh, no. The king wants me to be with him for conversation this afternoon. I like to be clear of eye and mind when I speak with him."

Tiy smiled. "I am impressed. You and he have talked much about birds, have you not?"

Mahu's eyes widened. "Oh, yes! He has told me so many things about birds. Things I never knew before. He says that birds are old, very very old, older than most of the animals we know today. Not the birds themselves, but the types of birds in the world are the same many kinds that lived as long ago as the Age of Dragons."

"Oh, he has told you about the Age of Dragons, has he?" Tiy's eyes sparkled. She remembered her visions of the Age of Dragons. "Yes, the Ocean Age, the Age of Fishes, the Age of Insects, the Age of Dragons, the Age of Behemoths, and the Age of Elephants. This last age was also the Age of Ice and the Age of Humans. And this is the Fourth Age of Humans, this age, spreading out from Egypt."

"Yes, yes, Lady Tiy, the king has spoken to me at length about these things, especially the Age of Dragons and the Age of Elephants and Ice. Do you know something? The king remembers living in the world in another body when those great hairy elephants roamed the world when it became frozen. Is that not amazing?"

Queen Tiy nodded.

General Horemheb sat, gaping for an instant, slightly unnerved by the strange ideas that Akhunaton and his entourage discussed. Horemheb was a practical man. An Age of Dragons or an Age of Behemoths was something that he could not imagine. But a treaty between warring tribes, games of tactics and strategies, this was the world that General Horemheb best understood.

"General, you should talk with Akhunaton about natural science," Lady Tiy suggested, seeing that the military man was disconcerted. Returning to Mahu, she asked, "What do you think of the military matter of jailing priests of Amen who try to break into the temples or carry on their rituals in secret?"

Mahu shrugged. "Aahmes and Pa-nehsi the Negro like to discuss these matters, especially with Akhunaton. I think that I agree with the king. They have suffered enough humiliation. They should be left alone."

"Then the temples should be left unguarded?"

"Oh, General, I did not say that! I said that they should not suffer further persecution. If they worship in secret, that is their business. If they try to break into a temple or bribe a guard, *that* should be dealt with."

"How?"

"I do not know. Banishment, I guess."

"Sending them to a remote oasis?" General Horemheb laughed. "Yes, Queen Tiy and I have discussed that."

"Waterholes can be located by the Aton Disc," Tiy asserted. "Adequate desert forests can be seen from the sky that will support an exile colony quite comfortably. The main task is to keep the temples of Amen closed in Egypt. Humane provisions should be made for all people found guilty of specific crimes."

"I hope I do not lose a single soldier!"

"I hope you never do!" Tiy raised her arms. "I hope you never have to *use* a soldier! That is why we are going to follow a policy of tolerance from now on."

The general frowned questioningly. "They will take advantage of your tolerance."

"The music in the land, the bounteous harvests, these remind the old priests constantly that it is not their land anymore. It is natural for them to want it back."

"How far should I go, Lady Tiy, to keep them from getting it back?"

The queen reflected for a moment, then said, "I want you to stop short of ordering the killing of another human being."

Horemheb scowled. "I hope that I never have to make such a decision."

𓅓

I will be villain, but I will be there.

Akhunaton gazed from the top of his house into the sunset over the vast Nile. The wind blew chilly over his naked body. His immensely long eyes reflected the fiery light. He thought:

I will demonstrate the creation of a new human race from a genetic seed race. Seven females, two males. The third generation of a series of genetically engineered bodies, conceived artificially in vitro and gestated in utero. Born to a human mother.

237

The first genetically-crafted body was that of my earthly mother, Queen Tiy. The second was mine. My daughters and two sons are the third. The goal will be to produce a fourth generation that will be capable of interbreeding with humans at this stage of their evolution.

A demonstration—that will be all. Only a porion of the Egyptian population will experience genetic enhancement. The hereditary traits will be assimilated and modified so rapidly that in a century the descendants of my daughters will be indistinguishable from anyone else in Egypt.

The traits are irrelevant. I must show in art and records how it was done.

Thousands of years ago, when Thoth and Seshat were father and mother of a fourth evolution of human races, Isis and Osiris returned from Sirius in the Aton starship. Horus and Hathor have returned. Horus in a new body, betrothed to Hathor, a Hathor who has a broken heart.

We had so much more time when Thoth and Seshat were married. He beamed knowledge of the true cosmology into her eye. They were married according to her tribal codes. We spent years of genetic crafting to produce the first offspring. We have no such span of time to work with now. It will be recorded that the heads and faces of my two sons and daughters have been depicted with realism in scupture and frescoes. The story of my reign will be etched in cunieform and painted in hieroglyphics for another age to read.

The purpose of this is simple: to foreshadow our return to this world. Because it is our world.

A child does not own its parent. A child will someday leave the parent. Especially when a mother planet needs communnion with her extraplanetary Godfathers.

That time will come. We are fathers and this world is a mother. The child of our humanity will be educated from within as it grows: we will cultivate culture as we have cultivated evolution. Let the experiments at Akhetaton demonstrate how a seed race was created here.

This will be the first demonstration. There will be many others. Together, they will cause history to say:

"Expect us. We are returning!"

Chapter Twenty-Six

Autumn was a time for healing. Nefertiti and Smenkhara were quiet companions during the months of heavy skies. The queen dreamed again and again of receiving a little female soul into her belly. Glad that she had no memory of an experience aboard the Aton Disc, she recalled only dreams of reunion with this sleepy soul of a baby girl living in her belly.

Akhunaton and his other children dwelt in the king's house in the Central City. The princesses and Tutankhaton enjoyed the days with their father. They practised meditation, eidetic imagery and the asanas of yoga, and continued their lessons in natural history and physical science.

Neferneferuaton the Little was growing out of infancy and learning to crawl and utter tiny syllables. She shared the spark of alertness in her eyes that her siblings had, which had been dimmer in the eyes of Maketaton. She took more than a year to learn to walk, but by that time she spoke using a wide vocabulary of words.

Three of the five surviving children appeared normal to the casual eye: Smenkhara, in spite of his wide pelvis and protruding belly, Tutankhaton and Ankhasenpaaton. They lacked the radically elongated head that Meritaton and Neferneferuaton the Little had inherited, though Tutankhaton's head was definitely egg-shaped. It bulged in the back, where his skull molded around the extended occipital lobe of his brain.

The children posed in the afternoons for Bek and Tutmose, who carved figures of the strange assortment of head shapes with great precision, contrasting them with the normal-shaped heads of Smenkhara and Ankhasenpaaton.

Smenkhara posed only occasionally and reluctantly. Though he was depicted in scenes with his father, they had to be rendered separately as Smenkhara would not agree to sit with Akhunaton.

Once, after a year of negotiations, Smenkhara did consent to pose with Akhunaton. The sitting went poorly. A charge of tension existed between them as they sat in silence. When the king attempted conversation, Smenkhara flew into a rage, accusing his father of sham in depicting friendly terms between them.

"If we are not friends, Smenkhara, the fault does not rest with me."

"You wish to be remembered as a far better father than you really are!"

"I offer you love but you reject it. I continue to offer you love, and you continue to return hostility and rage. Now you say I want to be remembered as a better father to you, an angry boy, than any man you will ever find outside this palace. Many Egyptian fathers would have beaten you at your first childhood tantrum. Many would heve evicted you into the streets and gutters. So be not smug and self-righteous. Your mother has a palace."

With those words, Akhunaton was silent, scrutinizing his son's face. Smenkhara struggled against tears, then sat in his throne and stared straight ahead while the sculptors chiseled limestone blocks and drafted studies on papyrus.

Smenkhara consented to occasional sittings and even posed with Akhunaton several more times during the following year. One morning, at the start of a session he greeted his father with a smile.

Nefertiti gave birth to a girl in the winter. The child was healthy, alert, and had inherited her father's long head. Her name was Neferneferura and Nefertiti loved her very much.

Spring arrived late and the vernal equinox brought a generous harvest as Egypt enjoyed continuing prosperity. The summer was hot and Nefertiti sailed many times up and down the Nile on her royal barge, accompanied by Smenkhara and baby Neferneferura. Festival celebrations, as well as posing for murals and statues, frequently brought the family together.

From his new capital, Akhunaton designed many new temples for the Material Disc. They would all emanate the melodies from the stars the way that the Temple of Aton in Thebes and the main temple in Akhetaton sang at night.

During that year Akhunaton sent numerous letters to his Minister in the North, Aper-El, regading cosmological matters as well as philosophical and religious subjects. These communications were stamped in cuneiform onto clay tablets in the universal diplomatic message style of the time. Carried by relay runners to Memphis, they predicted a great natural cataclysm five hundred years from the date of Akhunaton's reign in Egypt. Many foretold a time when fiery stones would fall from the sky, tops of mountains would explode into rivers of liquid fire, and the waters would rise from the ocean banks and leap into the skies. Egypt would survive, but only by a miracle. Many cities in the east would not: the flourishing civilization on the island of Crete would perish and most of Egypt would be shaken to the hot and steaming ground. The only comfort that these terrible predictions offered was that they would occur five hundred years in the future.

Scribes were assembled in veritable armies, all sitting cross-legged in rows, tapping the clay message tablets with sticks while the king spoke. Copies were carried throughout Egypt.

Akhunaton and King Tushratta of Mitanni exchanged cordial letters. Tushratta was astounded at Akhunaton's cosmological predictions and was reassured only when the king told him that many great cities of the east would survive and prosper. The

King of Mitanni read these communications with great wonder and amazement. His curiosity was inflamed about the new king of Egypt, so Tushratta planned a journey to the new capital of Egypt.

Secluded in his city, Akhunaton watched the people from his rooftop. They enjoyed their new freedom. Dancing and music flourished everywhere and the visual arts lost the static, rigid quality that had frozen Egyptian art for millennia. Color and songs resounded throughout the land of the Nile. Frequent visits from the *Atet* and the *Sektet*, and the low-altitude flights of the *Aton*, were witnessed over Akhetaton. The people rejoiced to know a god who was accessible to their senses. Egytians knew they were living a manifestation of Paradise on Earth and they were grateful.

Hatshepsut, Teti I and Teti II, Pepi I and Pepi II were sleeping. The twelve that comprised The Beast's Inner Circle were hypnotized and kept comatose for six days of every seven, each in their own sarcophagi. They were awakened by a whispered word, fed, instructed while in trances to urinate and defecate, then commanded to returned to deep sleep for six more days.

It was easier for Kahotep to control them if they were immobilized. He gathered offerings to the dead from the many mastabas connected to Karnak. The Beast wheeled a cart through the tunnels, collecting food to keep himself and his captives alive. He occupied the balance of his time with experiments on diseases of grain. He was preparing more than an escape from Karnak. The Beast was preparing a dramatic return to the pantheon of Egypt.

Akhunaton lived a fairly idyllic life in Akhetaton, so that was how he requested his life there to be portrayed. He was gradually establishing a rapport with Smenkhara again. The safe birth of Neferneferura helped greatly, though Nefertiti felt a growing aversion to Akhunaton even as Smenkhara's hostility lessened. She refused any social contact with Akhunaton except for posing for statuary or attending pageants as a royal couple. Because the conception of her daughter Neferneferura had been completely nonsexual, she remained open to further procreation.

Akhunaton began to display more eccentric behavior than he had during his five years of persecuting the priesthood of Amen. His generosity to the poor was not extended to the aristocrats, Egyptian or foreign, who visited him. He gave jeweled scarabs to peasants, but to visiting kings he gave scrolls of papyrus parchment with simple poems written in hieroglyphics. He would toss scraps of precious gold and silver to the townspeople, then shock judges and nomarchs by greeting them naked and sending them home without gifts. He admonished the houses of wealth and power for having "sought me with favors and motives, not questions for knowledge in your hearts."

Music rang in the hills of Akhetaton and reverberated off the limestone cliffs.

Painters splashed each day with color and dancers wriggled and undulated to the drumbeats. But there was something too wild and abandoned for conservative Egyptians. Outside of Akhetaton, Egyptians toiled, then celebrated, glad to hear the music by day and the dancers by night.

Despite numerous manifestations of the sky ships, the priests of Amen managed to locate recruits among the swelling ranks of the discontented. The beer-shops and ale houses were the greatest asset the war-priests had. The discontented met and voiced their anger in the primitive taverns where fermented drinks were sold.

Devotees of Amen enacted their ancient rites in personal temples they built in their own houses. Some worshipped in caves in the hills—anywhere that could not be seen from the sky. But no oracle received their prayers, no Voice of Amen replied to their pleas. They were lost and blind except for their tradition, but they shared a common goal: every priest of Amen in Egypt was determined to seize control of the Temple of Karnak in the hundred-gated city of Thebes. Bribery slowly gained influence over the guards stationed at the Temple of Luxor. On the other side of Thebes was the Temple of Karnak, with the unfortunate Temple of Aton directly between them.

Nefertiti lay on the thin mattress, the back of her head braced by an Egyptian pillow. The bright star Sirius had just risen as she fell asleep gazing at the constellation of Canis Major in the southern sky. Her mind fell blank, then passed into a realm of soft blue impressions like floating liquids. Light was not seen but felt, as if through her heart. The world around her was familiar: it was the Amentt, the Unseen World.

She sensed a presence approaching her. The entity was warm and loving. Nefertiti responded to this living ghost-girl with immediate, natural love. The little soul, old and wise, found a home in the belly of Nefertiti.

Shu-in-the-body-of-Akhunaton arranged to have Nefertiti's sleeping, pregnant body teleported aboard the *Aton* one night in her third week of pregnancy. Sleeping under the influence of long-wavelength electromagnetic emanations, Nefertiti experienced dreams of rapture but not erotic imagery. Her sensations were expressed as empathic communion with the baby inside of her.

The energy scans revealed what the crew of the *Aton* had hoped: a healthy embryo developing rapidly into a fetus, glowing with the bioelectricity of life, living in the womb of a strong, healthy mother. Nefertiti was teleported back to her bed in her personal chamber in the center of her palace. There her dreams of rapture ended and she silently awaited morning.

Akhunaton remained aboard the starship. The other eight humanoid occupants

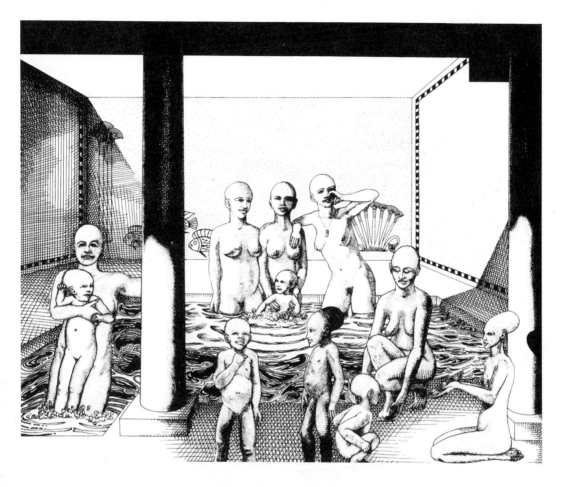

of *Aton* were silent; they knew by the residual empathic field left by Nefertiti and the pain in Akhunaton that something was drastically wrong.

Akhunaton was an empath. As such, though he secluded himself, first in a palace in Thebes, then in a city beside the Nile surrounded on three sides by towering cliffs, he absorbed awesome amounts of pain. During his years of attacking the temples of Amen, among men barely out of primitive brutality, many called upon him to pass judgements in violent disputes. Akhunaton had gradually accumulated in himself the emotional pain inflicted by the pecking order of the men.

Akhunaton tried to meditate in solitude immediately after Nefertiti's departure. His body was overcome with nausea and only by rapid breath control was he able to force the urge to subside. He communed for a time in personal rapture, then fused psychically with Yod, whose field of electromagnetic presence permeated everything. Yod resonated empathically with Shu-in-Akhunaton. The body of the earthly Pharaoh levitated in the vast illuminated chamber when the embrace of the loving energy being was complete. The two minds became one in sentient rapture. Hours elapsed and Shu's psychic wounds healed.

Awakening back in the Horus body, Shu telepathically summoned the other occupants of the starship to join him in meditation and a final discussion. On the main observation deck, under the stars of space, the nine conversed about the possibilities and alternatives that their presence had created in Egypt.

"Their primary fascination is violence," spoke Shu, relaxed in his native body. "The males of this species are worse than any of their predecessors. Their propensity for violence has increased with every generation. There is an increase in violent propaganda from many sources. The priests of Amen are only one."

"You make it sound hopeless, Brother Shu," said Tem. "Is there no room for a happy outcome? The time traffic of wave-shifters is so great on this mother-world that all of our models of probability show that this is a planet with a viable future. Even Mars, scorched and airless, can be restored to life. If this world survives this epidemic of misevolving humans, that would explain the presence of wave-shifters in festivals and seasonal ceremonies. This planet is rich with the presence of great time."

"True," said Shu, "there are many wave-shifters present on this world. Stories abound with tales of 'the Little People,' a general term applied to extraterrestrial humanoid races, most of whom are small compared to Earthlings. It also applies to wave-shifters, past and future."

"And that term is…?"

"To the Egyptians, that term is 'Amentii.'"

"Yes, Brother Shu, I wanted you to mention that because I have a point: all of these evolving humans are powerfully psychic, very telepathic, in spite of their volatile emotions. Although 'Amentii' means 'Hidden Ones' or 'inhabitants of the Hidden World,' the association is subconsciously and unconsciously clear: 'Amentii' can also mean 'of Amen.'"

"I have thought of this, Pilot Tem," said Shu. "It is another variable I have to calculate in dealing with these unpredictable human beings."

Tem said, "I have watched you respond more and more with fear at the mention of Kahotep and his use of political power to satisfy his addictive needs. I have spoken to you of this, and you have admitted to it. This causes me anticipation, Brother Shu. These next ten years will be crucial to the experiment. Absolute self-mastery will be essential on your part to achieve the positive result. It would be terrible if you caused great pain and suffering. You would simply go unremarked in the recorded procession of war-tyrants."

"I must accomplish a positive result without causing harm," said Shu. "That is the greatest challenge of all."

"Have you a plan?"

"What we have all agreed upon under the sanctity of the consciousness of Yod."

"Beware the random factor," Geb warned. "Entropy, the tendency toward chaos, is exaggerated in these beings. Alternatives to the basic plan must be formulated."

"Yod and I have rehearsed, psychoholographically, many variables. Realistic cause-effect chains have been explored," Shu explained. "I am satisfied that I have adequately prepared for difficulties to come."

"Suppose you are invaded by a reorganized army of war priests?" Nuit suggested.

"That is precisely the event I am counting upon." The circle of beings contemplated this. Shu continued, "Timing of the invasion is everything: that will be the challenge. From then on, the war priests will do all my work for me."

"Providing you have somehow banished the random factor."

"Not 'banished,'" corrected Shu. "Controlled."

"How can you control chaos?" Nuit asked.

Shu smiled. "By deception."

"You should be returning soon," Tem reminded him.

Far below, to the east, the curve of the night edge of Earth was illuminated from behind by sunrays in the high atmosphere.

"Yes, I must." Shu cast his gaze downward. His heart emanated the heaviness of dread.

Tefnut embraced him. They held each other for a long, loving time.

"Let us depart," Shu whispered to his mate. They retreated to a time dilation chamber, where they spent an eternity of rapture in loving embrace.

After this erotic farewell, Shu returned his native body to the hypersleep tank and his consciousness was transferred to the body of Akhunaton. He assured them that he was on friendly terms with Smenkhara, that Nefertiti was softening in her attitude toward him and that he was strong-hearted enough to live among barbaric humans again.

After his departure, they returned to the observation dome of the starship.

"Exposure to the violence and fear of death that still lives in that land has put a great strain on Brother Shu," observed Tem.

"Yes, I sense that mightily," agreed Tefnut. "Meditation does not purge his sensitivity to the vibration of pain. Whatever healing he does is undone when he dines with a brutal, savage tribal king or some arrogant aristocrat. Glimpses of remembered violence that some visitor recalls in the range of the king's psychic senses— that is why there is cause for concern."

Tem said, "I will enter into holographic communion with Yod and discover any variables that have not been explored along the probability chains. There is one that concerns me: if Shu himself suffers an emotional overload."

Tefnut whispered, "We will have to watch him carefully from now on."

The Beast had not executed his plan to murder his Inner Circle nor Amenhotep, Son of Hapu. He had merely drawn his food cart through the tunnel to the royal cemetery, every night, to pick through the offerings left for the dead. He unsealed a passage built into the wall of a particularly deep tomb, the serdab beneath the mastaba of a Theban nomarch. In the wall of every sedab was a false door, a rectangular indentation cut into the stone facade overlooking the tomb. The purpose was to admit the soul into Eternity when the body and soul were reunited. This false door slid open, then shut as a figure dressed in veils and black robes stepped into the tomb. It flew like a shadow and vanished up the stairs. Moments later the metal door of the mastaba creaked open and clanged shut. The figure escaped into the night. The Beast had escaped temporarily, disguised as a widow in mourning.

The following day Kahotep learned much about Akhunaton. He visited the marketplace, eavesdropping on passers-by, listening to what was being said around him, eyes lowered, as if paying no attention to external things. Sometimes, in a soft voice, he would ask questions. He spoke mainly to the women and got their opinions about many things.

He learned that the skies over Thebes had been visited by silver discs, exactly as the king had predicted. He learned that the king had left Thebes for a new city to the north two years before. He took delight that the king's daughter had died of mysterious causes, that Nefertiti lived by herself, and that the king had relaxed his stranglehold on the Priesthood of Amen.

This seemed too good to be true. Things were not going well for King Akhunaton: problems, difficulties, unexpected tragedy. All of this placed great advantage in the hands of The Beast. The Beast retired to the underground chambers of Karnak with the information he had sought as well as a new confidence in his ability to leave the tunnels and travel undetected among the people.

Akhunaton always insisted that his court officials confer with him naked, as was customary in the court of Aton. Mahu, the chief of police throughout Egypt, and Sutau, the king's treasurer, had been summoned to discuss political affairs. General Horemheb, commander of the military, was also present with his chief executive, Paatonemheb. They met on the king's private terrace, under the hot summer afternoon sun.

The king spoke after a formal meditation. "I have given the matter much consideration and I believe Egypt is in no danger of attack nor invasion. Now I must give time to dissenting opinions. Paatonemheb? Horemheb? What say you on this?"

Horemheb cleared his throat. "O King, our colonies to the south murmur with restlessness. Your laws that abolish slavery and elevate Negro people to the status of human have given rise to ideological questions regarding the use of force in managing a colony…"

"*Never* use force in managing a colony!"

"But…you do not understand. Are black-skinned Nubians fully human, too? With rights? How do we deal with Nubians in our colonies on the borders of Nubia? People are voicing dissatisfaction with our presence there. How do we handle them without force?"

"Find out the source of their dissatisfaction, then remedy it."

"They want us to leave our encampments and march north, back past the Second Cataract, past the First Cataract of the Nile! *That* is what they want."

Akhunaton laughed. "I thought so! What is the source of this animosity? I have elevated their status to that of citizens, if the Nubian people recall. Do eight years dim the memory that much? I do not believe it!"

"They call us invaders, O King."

"That is correct," said Horemheb. "The resentment persists, even though the Nubians can claim greater status than ever before."

Akhunaton nodded. "The borders between Egypt and Nubia have shifted constantly over the centuries."

"We need a safety zone between their land and ours." Horemheb gestured with clutching hands. "They are invaders! Remember Egypt's sacred history: how their invasion caused the fall of our First Kingdom, how all through the Second Kingdom we fought wars along our southern borders. The Nubians invaded repeatedly, in hordes so vast we often thought we had slain them all when suddenly more, more, more flooded the deserts, shrieking and hurling spears! O King, I truly believe we adopted slavery only to employ the surplus of war captives! That is my opinion."

The king looked thoughtfully at his general, then to Paatonemheb. The younger man nodded.

"Well, of course we cannot withdraw all Egyptian citizens north of the First Cataract." The men at the table laughed. "If the Nubians wish this, they are being far too optimistic. From what you have told me, Horemheb, they would like to see all Egyptians march north and not stop at the tip of the Nile Delta!"

"That is true!" Horemheb laughed.

"We must avoid such a march at all costs!" the king joked. "But what is Egypt and what is Nubia? Napata is Egyptian, and it is far to the south of the First Cataract, well into the Nubian desert."

"Egypt owns the Nile to the south of the Fifth Cataract," said Horemheb. "It is the only land where humans can survive in that desert."

"Where do the Nubians live if Egypt claims the banks of the Nile?"

"They live in the desert and now along the river. Until recently it was illegal for

them to live on the Nile and we fought them over it. Now they have returned in greater and greater numbers."

"Horemheb, these vast hordes of Nubians must be making a pretty good livelihood. 'Day and night they came,' you once told me, but then admitted that they inhabit only desert, while soldiers defend the banks of the Nile. How far south? That must be hundreds of miles into Nubia proper!"

Horemheb lowered his eyes and shook his head. "It is our sacred history, my king."

"I know that. It was written down by scribes who were far removed from the battlefields, as told to them by survivors. I think that, in the bloody, violent distraction of the battle, the numbers became exaggerated, Horemheb."

The general clenched his teeth. The king's words again bordered on heresy. Horemheb merely shrugged and shook his head. "Whatever you say, O King."

"In the future, fight to defend Egyptian lives only. Do not displace Nubians living along the banks of the Nile. Do not intimidate the population with soldiers or military marches. Invite Nubians to join the festivities of the religion of Aton. Entice them to seek pleasure. And exemplify kindness in their eyes, so that their resentment will have no basis."

"How can I order my soldiers to 'exemplify kindness,' O King?"

"By reminding them of the true story of how Osiris united Lower and Upper Egypt with an army of philosophers, poets, and above all, musicians and dancers! You, yourself, Horemheb, were impressed by that story. I have been told that while you served under Amenhotep III and later Queen Tiy, you relied more on diplomacy than show of arms. That, for a military man, is the greatest genius."

Horemheb scowled, then buried his look under a huge, beaming smile. "Thank you, my king."

"Please circulate that information among your soldiers. I will greatly appreciate it."

Horemheb nodded.

"The next matter for consideration is the continued closure of the temples of Amen." Akhunaton looked at Mahu, then Sutau, and continued. "As indicated, the policy of tolerance for the defrocked priests will continue, with orders to keep the temples barricaded and blockaded. Banishment is recommended for priests attempting to revive the forbidden practices."

"This borders on contradiction!" Mahu objected. "*All* the priests of Amen seek to reunify! They try to bribe or blackmail their way into the temples. Their recruiting officers haunt the beer shops and infiltrate the brothels. They have been overheard plotting your murder, O King!"

Akhunaton raised an eyebrow and smiled. "Why do you think I have abolished their war cult? It reeks of treachery! I fully understand that they are capable of inflicting the kind of vengeance they conspire to."

Mahu nodded vigorously. "Remember the assassination attempt made by their pawn, Xepuru-Ra? It did result in death: in suicide!"

"I remember," said Akhunaton.

Sutau interjected, "I think Mahu is saying that our policy of tolerance toward the priests is risky. They and their recruits will not listen to sensitive poets nor respond lovingly to dancing priestesses."

Again Akhunaton nodded.

"I guard the treasury," Sutau continued. "They steal back the sacred relics you confiscated and use these to bribe the treasury guards so that they can remove more riches."

"That is illegal. Arrest anyone attempting to bribe a guard and give him a trial. If found guilty, have him removed to exile."

"They have robbed and murdered some of the peasants you gave gold! We purged the disloyal guards, as you surely know, but the treasury is still in disarray, and we cannot really be sure of who to trust anymore. We take inventory, but this is not enough. What has become of the great portion of the gold and copper you seized? You keep sending orders to have it sent to the temples of Aton here and in Memphis. Why? What is being done with so much gold and copper?"

"It makes the temples of Aton sing."

Sutau and Mahu opened their eyes wide. Sutau ventured, "It must be the sacred metal *tcham* which gives the temples their voices, then!"

"Yes. At the two temples, I have taught my metalworkers techniques for turning the copper into long strands coated with gold! These are wrapped around a crystal-tipped obelisk."

"Flat pieces of hardwoods are also coated with thin layers of gold and shipped by caravan to new temples that need a voice. You are correct, Sutau: this has diminished the gold in the treasury by much."

"This makes so it hard for us to take inventory! We have scribes working night and day to account for what is there, but so much gets sent....They say the temples light the sky every night with lightning bolts!"

The discussion progressed into a philosophical conversation, as did many with Akhunaton. Matters entirely unrelated to politics were debated in a friendly way. Unnoticed, Paatonemheb and Horemheb abstained from these intellectual tangents. The two military men shared a common fear: that of a Nubian invasion.

Tutmose was summoned by Nefertiti. She greeted the tall, thin man by the pillars of her southern terrace. She was naked, seven months pregnant and the skin of her belly and breasts was tight and smooth. Her whole body was filled with living motherhood.

"How may I serve you, O Queen?" Tutmose asked, gesturing expansively.

"I wish you to sculpt me in my pregnant state, my dear friend. This will be my last child, I have decided. I wish to be rendered by you as I am, ready to give birth and...there is something else."

"Anything, my queen."

She was seated on a stone bench by a lotus pillar. He moved to her side. She silently placed his hand on her throbbing belly. He was reluctant to embrace her, but he felt how she needed his human touch. He caressed her and put his head on her shoulder, his cheek resting above her breast.

"Love me," she whispered.

With an unborn child inside her and milk filling her brown breasts, Nefertiti received her first erotic touch from a mortal human being.

While Tutmose completed drawing after drawing, clay models and preliminary sculptures of Nefertiti, Akhunaton sent another volley of letters to Aper-El in

Memphis and again copied them *en masse* for distribution throughout Egypt and Mitanni. The letters comprised a manifesto describing the similarities between the gods aboard the Aton Disc and other solar pantheons. This affirmed continuing alliance between Egypt and Mitanni.

If Akhunaton was aware that Tutmose and Nefertiti had become lovers, he did not let it affect his actions. He still refrained from seeing her except in preparation for pageants and during the few times they posed together for Tutmose and the other artists. He spent his days with his children and remained on good terms with Smenkhara for much of the time.

During his ninth year as Pharaoh, his daughter Setepenra was born. Akhunaton watched over the baby as much as he could without intruding upon Nefertiti's privacy. The tiny girl was lively, alert and had her father's long skull and huge brain.

Within days of the sacred birth, mother and daughter were teleported while sleeping aboard the Aton starship. They remained asleep through energy scans and holographic examinations. Both appeared healthy and strong, full of life and were teleported back to Nefertiti's palace without awakening.

Setepenra was not given over to a wet nurse. Nefertiti insisted on nursing the tiny girl herself. When she told Akhunaton of her decision to let Setepenra be her last child, without explanation Akhunaton departed from her presence and withdrew into his house, remaining out of communication with everyone, even Ramose, for several days.

He was in telepathic communication with Yod and Tem aboard the *Aton* starcraft, trying to formulate a plan to persuade Nefertiti to have at least one more, but hopefully two more babies.

"We cannot coerce her," was the final statement that emanated from Yod. "Her free will must be respected."

Eight-year-old Smenkhara informed the king of Nefertiti's love affair with Tutmose. It was in the form of angry taunts during one of the prince's occasional tantrums.

"I expected this," Akhunaton responded casually. "She is a human woman. She needs the sexual love of a human man. That is something I am unable to give her in this body."

"But my mother is Egypt's queen! Suppose they are discovered?"

"Are they indiscreet?"

"*I* know of their union. That is partly why I no longer wish to live there."

"I see. Then you *should* live with me."

"But you act like you do not care!"

"I no longer care what Nefertiti does."

"Father, I cannot bear this! I fear she will ruin you."

"Why do you say this, Smenkhara?"

"I fear she makes love to Tutmose out of contempt for you, not affection toward him."

"Why do you say this?"

"She sometimes weeps after his visits."

"I see. That is something I cannot understand about the Egyptian people! How often they join in sexual union with partners for whom they have contempt. Although I do not think Nefertiti has contempt for Tutmose. He is a sensitive man."

"Yes, I know! Nefertiti calls him 'sensitive' and 'effeminate' behind his back."

"She does? And yet, she continues this love affair? It sounds like Nefertiti is becoming self-destructive, afflicted with self-loathing."

These words were more than Smenkhara could endure. Knowing that they were true, he took up his walking staff and clattered from the light-filled terrace into the main hallway.

Akhunaton followed him, but after a long wait. He knew his words had been clumsy, insensitive. He was dizzy, his head ached and his ears rang. His heart seemed to throb with grief. Living with his family was nearly unbearable.

"I am sorry for what I said," Akhunaton said gently, finding his son alone.

Smenkhara sobbed in the corner of the empty nursery room. "It is true. Nefertiti is very sad. Only her love for her littlest daughter gives her any happiness at all."

"Then it would be useless to tell her I love her."

"She hates you, Father! She hates you!"

"Have I been so bad?"

"She thinks her only purpose is to give birth to unnatural children."

"She is wrong! Her purpose is to be Queen of Egypt and mother to all Egyptians."

"She calls herself a 'breeding mare.'"

"She has danced before the people of Egypt many times! She has become a fertility goddess to her people! She is fooling herself if she thinks she does not enjoy the pageants, the floats, the ceremonies."

"You do not understand, father. She resents…"

"She resents the fact that being *my* queen was not what she thought being Queen of Egypt would be like, is that it?"

"Oh, Father, you do not understand us! I am your son and I am human, too. I am not of your Amentii, I am human! Look at me! I do not think with my hips and drooping belly. I think with my head, my little, round human head!"

"Please tell me what you think, Smenkhara."

"I think you do not understand even one person in this world *at all*. I do not think you understand any of us, Father!"

"I do not understand why you humans cling to ancient pain, why you fight over old hurts…"

"Because there is pain in this world, Father, and we can all feel it and it will not go away!"

"But why do you add to it?"

After a long time, Smenkhara said, "Because we cannot help it, Father."

As his son spoke those words, Akhunaton fell to his knees and burst into tears. His eerie sobs rang throughout the palace.

When Meritaton, Ankhasenpaaton and Queen Tiy rushed to his side, Akhunaton staggered to his feet and commanded them to leave him alone in his private chamber. He would be comforted by no one.

Nefertiti's love affair with Tutmose ended, at the artist's request. Although he did not fear Akhunaton's anger, he feared the king's disapproval. So Akhunaton brought it up with Tutmose, encouraging the astonished artist to "heal Nefertiti's human heart."

"I cannot do that!" Tutmose said in a hushed voice.

"She is a woman with desires, and I am not a mortal man."

"But, O King—she is the queen!"

"Do what thou wilt," said Akhunaton, and neither man said more.

Horemheb was not a man whose heart would ever weigh lightly against a feather. Egypt's top-ranking military officer for more than thirty years, he was fifty-three when he became Nefertiti's lover, his huge, body strong and hard with muscles.

A powerful man of battle, Horemheb always had mixed feelings about the king who had followed Amenhotep III. He had enjoyed serving the former Pharaoh and had been offended when Amenhotep IV, now Akhunaton, had accused his predecessor of depravity. But Horemheb was a soldier and he bit his tongue and said nothing. A devotee of Aton only by convenience, Horemheb's loyalty rested with Egypt and King, not with any god, whether abstract and unseen or visible and illuminating the sky.

He had obeyed the king's orders to confiscate the riches of the temples of Amen. He had been a soldier then, too, perfectly obedient. He had subjugated his will to that of the king. But by one act of persecution and harassment after another, the king had exaggerated the actions of a good leader and subjected the Throne of Egypt to humiliation.

Of course, this was all redeemed when the *Atet* and the *Sektet* appeared in the sky over Thebes. And the king had exhibited compassion when riots broke out in the northern townships and death followed injury. These things weighed heavily in the mind of Horemheb.

But the way that the king behaved in his personal life, his nudity, his fanatical obsession with philosophy and the arts to the exclusion of all else, and finally his failure to hear Horemheb's warning of danger from the priests of the war god and the Nubians to the south, all contributed to the erosion of the general's respect for the strange-looking king.

He does not understand people, Horemheb thought again and again. *He is not one of us. He looks different, he is different. Perhaps it is not good for the race from the stars to rule us. Perhaps it is not good for the Amentii to come into our lives and interfere with our politics…*

The thought remained. He believed that intervention from the Unseen World constituted an intrusion very close in principle to an invasion.

And now, the Queen of Egypt was his mistress. It was only a matter of time before he articulated these thoughts to Nefertiti.

The night air was hot and still. in her bedchamber they were standing, looking out the window to the west. They could see the starlight above and the deep, black Nile below. Something moved among the stars, a point of light—maybe the *Atet,* maybe the *Sektet,* or perhaps the big Aton Disc itself—journeyed like a swimmer through the black void.

Nefertiti saw it and shuddered. Horemheb put his arm around her. She clutched him. A teardrop formed in her eye.

They remained in embrace for a long time after the starship had crossed the sky. Nefertiti closed her eyes. When she looked up, Horemheb kissed her. They walked to a gilded sofa and sat together.

"The lights in the sky disturb you," Horemheb said gently.

Nefertiti shivered. "Protect me, Horemheb, from *him.*"

"Akhunaton?"

"Of course."

"Has he ever hurt you?"

"No, not physically. He has never abused me."

"You are free from him in this palace. He does not come here. Everyone knows that."

"Everyone must know that you and I are lovers, too, Horemheb."

"No!"

"I am certain that Akhunaton knows."

Horemheb held her against his chest for a long time. Then, arching his arms around her protectively, possessively, he said, "If he knows…he seems to not care."

"He does not care! He cares not for earthly pleasures. He has never made love to my natural body."

"Nefertiti!"

"It is true: only in the Amentt has he touched me. And only…to make me a mother."

"You do not need to tell me…"

"I need to speak of these things to somebody! If not you, Horemheb, then who? Who can understand what it is like, being a woman, being a mother, and having no

254

one to lie next to me at night? Baby after baby, twice twins, and no lover at all in the Earthly, human world!"

Horemheb held his queen gently. She placed her forehead against his shoulder and he caressed her face and neck with his hands.

"Nefertiti—perhaps it is not good that they rule us…"

She looked up at him, startled. Calming, she whispered, "I have thought so, too. I cannot help but think it constantly. The Amentii do not understand us. They handle us clumsily and without regard for our true feelings. Akhunaton—I will never understand his mind as long as I live!"

Horemheb looked up at the night sky. A dark scowl fell across his face like a shadow. Nefertiti had spoken. She knew the strange king best of all.

"It is not *good* that the Amentii rule us…"

"It is not good for us to rule the people of Earth." Akhunaton was aboard the starship *Aton*, in conference with its occupants. "It is not good for us to rule primitive people."

"Shu," said Pilot Tem, "you have been showing the effects of psychic strain. You cleanse yourself in communion with Yod, but it is not enough. Tell me, is living among primitive people so terrible?"

"Cruelty is a disease, Father Tem." Shu-in-Akhunaton sighed mightily. "It is contagious and infectious. It emanates from a part of the brain that reached its highest development in the mammals of this planet. It is a violent, defensive part of the brain. It exists due to fear of predators *and* it exists in all predators. It has been supplanted by the vast outer cortex in nearly all humanoid races, so this natural, primitive, animal brain is easy to subdue: all it takes is living in a noncompetitive culture.

"This human race is like all others: it could choose to create a society condusive to development of higher consciousness. But *these* humans, it seems, *prefer* to create societies based on fear. Then they behave in ways that make other societies fear them and respond defensively. I anticipated that Kahotep had corrupted the innocent, primitive Egyptians with his own violent nature. Now I see he is simply the natural exploiter of this human addiction."

"You have isolated yourself in Akhetaton," said Tem.

"It is everywhere, even among my own family members! Meritaton and Ankhasenpaaton and Neferneferuaton the Little sense this, but they have lived their short lives knowing no other vibrations. They function psychically very well, despite a constant feeling of pain that emanates from Smenkhara and Nefertiti. Ai and Queen Tiy do not emanate this pain vibration, which is why the other children besides Smenkhara have preferred to live with me. Now, even Smenkhara will not live with Nefertiti. He has even shown me love and affection in the past year or so.

"I see and speak to people every day, who bring their cruel hearts and crude ways before me: aristocrats who have become petty tyrants, corrupt judges, mayors and governors seeking favors, visiting kings who seek a share of the wealth I have taken from the temples of war.

"They are like children, but in the dark, cruel ways: hurting small animals out of curiosity, the thrill of wielding power. That is it: the males of this species are addicted to wielding power over others. Even when they see how destructive this addiction is, they still refuse to turn away."

"That is a sad truth," said Tem, "but, like all realizations, it is an analogy."

"Perhaps," said Shu, "but the most basic fact is: we cannot save this race from its own nature."

"We do not yet know what that nature is!" Tefnut quickly interjected. "Shu, you see them through your eyes. Originally you approached them with no expectations, but now you do not act and react like a man with no expectations. You have acquired some along the way."

Sadly, the extraterrestrial king replied, "This is the last life-supporting planet in the Ra system. Kahotep knows how precious this world is. He knows he cannot live forever, so he is using this planet as a hostage to force us to give him the secret of eternal life."

"How can he hold Egypt hostage? He ruled Egypt in such secrecy that removing the throne of Pharoah from his influence was easy: we just replaced a king by a very popular human Queen for less than one generation! When you returned, Kahotep found himself in exile in the basement of the Temple of Karnak."

"Sister and mate, Tefnut…my love…Kahotep has lost power for now, but I am also losing power, rapidly. The dancers and musicians keep the air afloat with happiness, but outside of Akhetaton the men are responding far less jubilantly than the women. Because the women cannot be owned as property anymore, men who feel robbed of them are estranged from the dancing, the music. They never sought erotic enjoyment, only sexual domination. Now that this is forbidden to them, they seek revenge."

"How do you know this?" Tem and Tefnut asked in unison.

"Every day I am asked to judge cases in which violence has befallen a woman due to the jealousy of a man. Such conflicts are growing in number. The priests of Amen preach a return to the old law. Any way that they can express power over women, they feel gratified."

"And that is where their violence starts," mused Tefnut.

"But it will not end there," said Shu-in-Akhunaton. "I do not know where it will end…"

Queen Nefertiti was adamant in her refusal to give birth to even one more child.

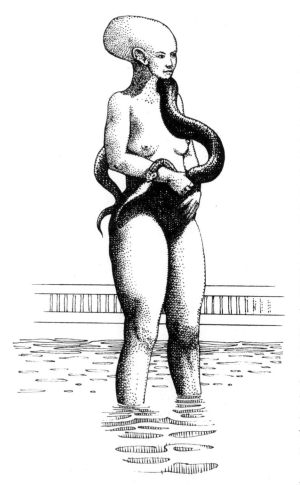

Knowing that this was her fundamental right, Akhunaton stopped trying to persuade her and devised an alternate plan.

Nefertiti had been the maternal mother of the children, but not their genetic mother. The combination of her genes with his was found to be not viable. Queen Tiy, Akhunaton's genetically-engineered mother, had contributed all of the ova which became the royal children: genetically, Tiy was their mother. Nefertiti did not know this. She had contributed her womb, her body, and her mother's milk never knowing that the babies she gave birth to were the result of a vast collaboration.

Akhunaton's plan was to produce one more child, and for this he did not need Nefertiti at all. Tiy, the genetic mother, would also be the maternal mother.

He did not propose this idea immediately to Tiy, but consulted telepathically with Yod. The result was a psychoholographic projection of two probability chains representing two possible universes influenced by the event of the the birth of a final daughter by Queen Tiy . In one model, the impregnation was done in secret and not recorded in art and journalism.

They second model recorded the event along with all other events of this dynasty. It was calculated that a more perfect Universe would proceed out of the recorded creation of a new race if Tiy completed the family. His children would then consist of two sons and six daughters. The trick of seed race genetics was the creation of a race of genetically-engineered parents representing two different races, one native, the other extraterrestrial. This process would be more fully apparent with Tiy known to be mother to the final daughter.

Akhunaton himself, Meritaton and Smenkhara, Ankhasenpaaton and Tutankhaton, Neferneferuaton the Little, Neferneferura and baby Setepenra were all fashioned from the genes of Queen Tiy. Her genes had been selected from the sperm, ova and cell nuclei of thousands of Egyptians. This first artificially fertilized ovum had been implanted into the womb of Tiy's mother, the priestess Thuya.

When Akhunaton explained his idea to Tiy, she accepted immediately.

"It is the only way to complete the experiment," she acknowledged.

"We cannot hope for a seventh daughter. A sixth will be a bare minimum to start a seed race with. The generation that these mothers will give birth to will be genetically and morphologically compatible for intermarriage with native human beings."

"Then it must be done."

"We will start making preparations for the final birth and the assimilation of this vulnerable empire."

"This will be the most dangerous part," said Ai.

"Yes. Even now our destruction is being planned."

"The rebel priest?"

"Kahotep has departed via his tunnels from Karnak at least five times. He journeys disguised as a widow in mourning. He has done little to contact his scattered priesthood; he is pleased that his religion is mending itself so nicely. He is waiting for a time and place to stage a dramatic return."

"How can this be prevented?" Tiy was concerned.

"In no way that involves violence. We are morally restricted. We must work within that. I am counting on succeeding. I base my actions around the thought that peaceful intervention will be recorded for all time, or at least until Earthlings advance in their sciences enough to decipher the importance of these events buried in their history. Contact, genetic colonization and translation are essential. We must complete this experiment as planned. The lives of all of my subjects depend upon it."

Chapter Twenty-Seven

The spinning starship descended to the elbow bend in the blue-black Nile. Hovering over the city buildings and illuminating the cliffs on the river's east bank, twirling spotlights pierced the starry night. Thousands of eyes looked up to again witness the arrival of the Material Disc, brighter than the sun. The vast dome beneath the rotating rings shot down immense beams of energy which converged and fell upon the Great Temple of Aton.

In the center of the inner sanctuary stood a circle of vertical, gold-coated hardwood panels mounted on rows of stone blocks. Walking arm in arm up the steps to the altar platform were Queen Tiy and Akhunaton. Their figures were visible for an instant as the ray that fell upon them intensified, but as the tall gold panel reflected the light, their silhouettes were lost in the glare. When the beam subsided, the king and queen were gone. The spinning, illuminated disc ascended swiftly back among the stars.

Aboard the star craft blinding light poured from the teleportation chamber. In the center of the immense room a circle of diminutive humanoids surrounded a human woman and a towering synthetic man.

They walked from the teleportation chamber to a moving corridor that led to the genetic laboratory. The woman and the man entered. Overhead a labyrinth of clear tubes wove through the lighted air and parted where scanners loomed over a cushioned silver table.

Queen Tiy sat at the edge of the table and reclined. One by one the energy scanners were lowered and their sensors passed over her body. Transparent holograms appeared beside her, rendering in colored light what the electromagnetic receptors were perceiving. The holograms revealed her to be youthful, strong and exceptionally healthy in her forty-sixth year of life. She would be a perfect mother.

Tem placed a crystalline box between Tiy's legs and a transparent serpentine tube streaked out from it and entered the folds between her labia. Tiy held Akhunaton's hand. She barely felt the thin tendril inside of her.

The elongating thread narrowed, fitting through her uterus, narrowing again to slide into a fallopian tube. A vacuole formed in the flowing tip,. It pierced the ovary. Seven ovarian cysts were ripe and the ova within them awaited ejection. The tendril sought the healthiest and strongest one and swallowed it inside the vacuole. Then the tube swiftly retreated from Tiy's body.

Tiy sat up and watched the holograms of the nucleus of her ovum projected overhead. A sperm had been chosen from the bank of sperm samples from Akhunaton's artificial body. It was being introduced to the waiting egg. Fertilization transformed the egg's sphere suddenly, and the rapid reshuffling of chromosomes scrambled strands of holographic light. Nucleic and cellular divisions followed and the sphere unfolded and looked like a growing cluster of bubbles.

Queen Tiy placed her legs on both sides of the cube and held Akhunaton's hand gently. She barely felt the slithering tube reenter her body.

The tip flowed into her womb and sought and found a patch of lining that would welcome a living, growing gift. It left the fertilized egg imbedded in the uterine wall. The living tube retreated from her body. A chemical change flowed from that spot and Queen Tiy was pregnant.

Knowing the estrangement between him and Nefertiti would be complete, and knowing as well that it needed to be recorded in the history of Egypt, Akhunaton summoned scribes and dictated a pronouncement. He and Nefertiti lived in separation, with the queen retaining her throne and equality to the king. Also, Akhunaton, the king, was now entering into a marital relationship of fidelity and companionship for the purpose of fathering one last child. The statement was copied in hieratic and demotic Egyptian and in cuneiform. The clay tablets were carried by messengers to the kingdoms of the east.

The announcement shocked the citizens of Egypt. They had long accepted the practice of incest within royal bloodlines, especially the sacred incest between brother and sister. However, incest between mother and son was strange and unheard of, even among Pharaohs.

Thus, many of the women of Egypt were estranged, though devout Atonists were unperturbed by the thought of the star-king marrying the queen they called The Wise Woman and The Mother of Egypt. Stories of miracles and healings continued to spread and the sin of the king did little to diminish the fecundity of the autumn harvest, leaving undimmed the many blessings that befell the people even while they criticized and condemned their king.

Within her palace walls, Nerfertiti was furious. She made an announcement of her own: that she refused to journey outside of her palace walls and she forbade Akhunaton from entering them. For weeks she refused to see anyone except General Horemheb and Smenkhara, who was similarly appalled by his father's announcement.

Smenkhara remained at his father's house, for he understood that his mother did not wish him to join her in her vast palace. Smenkhara wandered the palace, always seeking to be alone. He posed for murals with his father and complied with instruc-

tions to smile and pose with amiable gestures. He still spoke little to his father, even understanding that he would soon be king of Egypt. Tutankhaton looked up to Smenkhara with admiration, and the older boy appreciated that. He bcame friendlier with his sisters, especially his twin, Meritaton. He still refrained from practising meditation and his father's visualization arts.

Tiy spent the winter and spring months of her pregnancy in the seclusion of her harem. Her father, Yuia, was appointed to the post of Superintendent of the Queen's Harem and personally tended to his daughter's needs until her labor approached.

Nefertiti dictated statements to scribes who recorded them on papyrus and clay. She cast bitter aspersions on her mother-in-law, accusing her of, among other things, demonic sex.

Word of Nefertiti's estrangement spread through Egypt further waves of shock and disapproval. People uttered wild rumors. Some now turned and fled in panic when the huge disc or the small shuttlediscs appeared in the sky. In the beer shops, the brothels, and wherever the discontented in Egypt gathered, the eyes and ears of The Beast recorded what Egyptian men were saying.

$$\cap$$

In the city of Akhetaton, the news of the king's marriage to his mother was variously received with awe, peals of laughter and much happy, irony-filled gossip.

Over the years a rift had developed between the inner societies symbolized by Akhetaton and the outer world of post-Amenist Egyptians. Virtually all of the aristocrats rejected the religion of Aton, having been "snubbed" by the king who championed it. By greeting them completely naked, exchanging their precious gifts for his handwritten nature poems and abolishing their war-god, the king had estranged his nobles. Many who had witnessed nightly visitations of the *Aton* over Akhetaton or had seen the *Atet* or the *Sektet* over Thebes, now questioned whether such manifestations were divine or perhaps demonic.

Most Egyptians considered their strange-looking king to be ugly, an opinion busily reinforced by the priests of Amen. No hidden resentments, apprehensions, fears were overlooked by the secretive priests. Although they no longer controlled the throne of Egypt, they retained their age-old monopoly of beer shops and brothels.

The music played in Akhetaton. The caravans trekked, one by one, to the city which was the Second Horizon of the Aton Disc. The workers continued to build one-story mud brick buildings and plaster houses for the new arrivals and the population grew just abreast of the construction. Encampments of tents and wagons fringed the suburbs and new families participated in the building of their homes.

During his tenth departure from the underground tunnels of Karnak, The Beast learned of Akhunaton's unprecedented marital union with his mother, Queen Tiy. That told Kahotep much. Rumors that Nefertiti was estranged from her husband must certainly be true, similarly rumors of a death in the family. *To complete this seed-race they need another daughter*, Kahotep clearly understood. He wondered if Queen Tiy had been contributing the genetic material all along. Then, if Nefertiti had withdrawn entirely from family relations, in their clumsy, vain attempts to perpetuate their race, the genetic mother was now, by necessity, the natural mother! Furthermore, the inhuman king was attempting to make his marital union socially acceptable. It was clear that favor with the Atonist king and his religion was ebbing.

Returning from his tunnels, taking with him food bought at the marketplace, The Beast awakened and fed his hypnotized subjects, then commanded them to enter such deep comatose states that they would require only air to breathe for weeks. He left food for Amenhotep, Son of Hapu, enough for one week. The Beast was planning an extended excursion from the Temple of Karnak, to mingle with the populace, his eyes and ears open, in preparation for a dramatic return.

Queen Tiy's pregnancy culminated in a brief, carefully controlled labor and the birth of Akhunaton's last daughter. The girl was vivacious and wide-eyed as she nursed from the breast of her mother, the queen. They named her Beketaton. Queen Tiy gave Beketaton to a wet nurse after several weeks of enjoying mother-hood and returned to relative seclusion.

Smenkhara continued to resent his father, but accepted silently, for the most part that there was a purpose for the long heads of six of his seven sisters and for his ungainly hips. Whether he understood or not, he accepted also that another daughter was needed to complete the family circle.

Meritaton, ten years old and approaching sexual maturity, was unconcerned by the marriage of her father and grandmother and the birth of her new sister. Eight year old Tutankhaton and Ankhasenpaaton accepted both as natural. They themselves would be married brother to sister in the ancient custom of Pharaoic incest. Neferneferuaton the Little and Neferneferura celebrated quietly the enlargement of their family, while Setepenra, less than two years old, was unconcerned.

King Akhunaton remained with his mother-wife almost constantly. Two weeks after the birth, he escorted Tiy and Beketaton to the indoor courtyard of his house, a big room with a circle of pillars around a wide opening to the sky. Overhead the night sky boasted many stars. They boarded the *Sektet* and ascended into the *Aton* starship. Queen Tiy and her new daughter were scanned and complementary cellular samples were examined and duplicated. Both appeared healthy and strong.

Queen Tiy began spending more time with her aging mother and father, who had taken up residence in Akhetaton to spend their final years with her. Beketaton joined the daily routine of visualizations, art lessons and natural studies, all under the tutelage of Akhunaton.

Smenkhara had learned to read and write with his father, but cultivated few other mutual interests. He continued visiting Nefertiti and the young prince spent as much time as he could with General Horemheb. They talked about battles, wars, uprisings that had been suppressed, the days when enemies were slaughtered and captives were honored as offerings of sacrifice. Smenkhara found in these tales of death and bravado something opposite to his father's fanatical pacifism. Heroism as an antidote to heresy.

If Akhunaton was aware of Smenkhara's new father-figure or of the content of their conversations, he never commented. He never spoke to Smenkhara about how he spent his time at all and Smenkhara spoke little to his father, though they presented a facade of good relations to the Egyptians. Pageants continued to bring the family together except for Nefertiti, who refused to leave her palace for any reason.

A priest contacted the child-beater through a brothel that specialized in young boys. The priests of Amen had been preparing him for years. This disciple was a man so scorned by the women prostitutes in Thebes that he satisfied his brutal temper on children. The little man was also fascinated by fire. He was the arsonist who had sparked the riots during the final days of confiscations and closures. He had once murdered some royal emissaries and substituted false messages for the king's own communiques.

The nameless priest walked, as if in a trance, out onto the dry wash of desert mudstone. He was followed by his fearfully blubbering disciple. The priest commanded him to be silent, then walked like a somnambulist toward a black outcrop of volcanic rock, ancient and eroded. The rose-colored drops in the beer drunk as a libation before the trek began to work their hallucinogenic magic on the nervous system of the seeker of Amen. By the time the slack-jawed priest arrived at the outcrop of black boulders, the brain of the initiate sparkled with the alkaloid ergotamine.

A voice bellowed out of the rocks, "Anpu!"

The initiate heard his name echoing, as the drug stretched and dazzled his senses. He fell to his knees.

"Anpu! I command thee to address me!"

Anpu groveled and scurried back and forth on his hands and knees, moaning fearfully. Hallucinations of red and green serpents danced about him. He howled in terror.

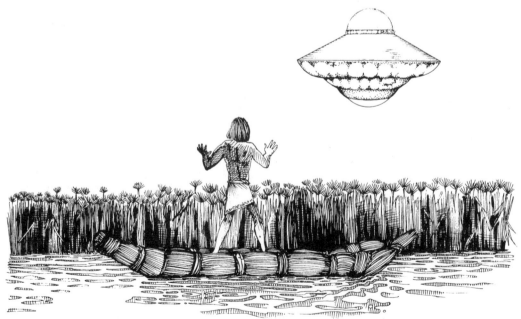

"I am your god, Amen! I command you to obey. Address me by my name at once!"

"Amen!" Anpu screamed.

"That is better. Anpu, I am the One True God, Amen of Thebes. My spirit dwells in Thebes, but as you can feel, my spirit dwells in *you* now. Do you feel my spirit within you?"

"Y-y-yyyes-s-s!" the initiate wailed, clutching his belly as his stomach cramped and his vision faded to blue.

"You know my force. It is *inner* force, Anpu, not *outer* force, like moving lights in the sky or flying discs. Mine is a power of mind."

"Y-yes, O Amen! I c-can feel my...*mind!*"

"That is good. And is it fused with my mind?"

"Y-yes, O Amen!"

"Good. You will spend the night in rapture, divine rapture, with me. I will leave you with the priest who has brought you here. I will enjoy spiritual union with you. Do you understand?"

"Y-y-yes!" Anpu shrieked. "H-h-how long?"

"Our spiritual union?"

"Y-y-yes!"

"All night—a million years, Anpu!"

"A-a-aaaaaaaaahhh!" The terrified initiate wailed. His guts cramped violently. His bowels emptied roughly into his robes and a wave of nausea washed over him without causing him to vomit.

"Is my power causing you discomfort? Does my presence within you frighten you?"

"Y-y-yyyeesssss!"

"Then remember this night and know, Anpu, that to avoid the hell of the Soul Eater in the afterlife you must obey my commands in this life!

"The priest who has brought you here will contact you again. You will be led to a cave, far from here, where my spirit also dwells. There, you will receive regular oracles and you will seek out other devotees, men who have their own reasons for wishing death upon the enemies of Amen."

"A-a-a-a a a c-cave...?" Anpu fell prostrate with fear.

"Yes, a cave! And an oracle! But do not fear these things." The ancient priest secreted behind the rocks knew that the time for coherent communication was slipping away as lysergic acid flooded Anpu's beer-soaked brain. "Remember this night, Anpu. Remember this night!"

"Y-y-yes, O Amen!"

"Remember this night!"

Anpu rolled into a fetal position and wailed in a high-pitched voice as he tumbled over the sand. Then he hurled himself to his feet and ran into the bush-tufted desert until he collapsed under the sky, where he moaned and trembled until dawn.

Horemheb knew that Nefertiti thought often about how her husband had failed her. He, too, was beginning to hate the radical, incestuous king. Yet, as a loyal servant of the king, the general kept his change of heart unspoken except to his only confidant, his lover, the queen.

The king ordered the final transfer of all gold and copper in the tax offices to Akhetaton. The tonnage was spectacular. Horemheb could not guess why the king required this massive quantity of precious metals. Though he heard the singing temples of Aton, he did not know that it was the gold and copper that gave then their voices. Horemheb was appointed to oversee the operation. It required that the general and his special troops tour all of Egypt, to every township where gold was stored. During his visit to Thebes, the notion of overthrowing the king occurred to Horemheb. Thereafter this thought followed him like a shadow; though he tried to suppress the obscene notion, he could not. Treason became a constant temptation. As he journeyed back to Akhetaton, General Horemheb knew he would have to confront Nefertiti with his plan.

Chapter Twenty-Eight

As the six daughters of Akhunaton matured they became more psychic. Ankhasenpaaton, the only daughter who lacked her father's elongated skull, and Meritaton developed a telepathic rapport with each other, communicating extensively on the nonverbal level. Those who were close to them during their eye-contact communion could feel the enveloping power of their love. Neferneferuaton the Little and Neferneferura also developed psychic bond, which merged with the bond that Meritaton and Ankhasenpaaton had established. Tutankhaton, Ankhasenpaaton's twin, frequently joined them in their group meditations and completed the psychic resonance with the masculine emanation of his presence. Thus, five of the children were linking together to form a telepathic entity.

Setepenra was still a little girl, more interested in flower blossoms and butterflies than psychic imagery or meditation. She showed the same precocious behavior as her siblings had and she complained of no discomforts indicating unseen physical defects.

Even as an infant, Beketaton was the most amazing of all the children. From the morning after her birth, she sought eye contact with everyone around her. At one month old, she squeaked out distinct syllables in attempts to speak. At two months, she was using words and pointing her fingers to communicate to those around her. By three months of age she was speaking with short complete sentences. Beketaton and Akhunaton formed an immediate psychic bond. The father gazed for hours into his infant daughter's eyes. She returned his silent communications. Their wordless exchanges filled those present with love.

At night the sky over Akhetaton was filled with electric blue flashes as Ai and Parannefer assisted the king with experiments. From the Royal Temple on the bank of the Nile or from the North Palace, between Nefertiti's Palace and the North Suburb, flashes of light and snapping, burning sounds would emanate.

Huge rectangular panels of gold-coated wood had been placed upon rows of limestone blocks in the open-sky sanctuary in the Great Temple of Aton. Cables of the sacred metal *tcham*, corrosion-proof due to the gold coating, were produced in vast lengths at the king's North Palace, where the Atet and the Sektet often visited. Coils of *tcham* embraced a towering limestone obelisk in the center of the open sanctuary. The obelisk was tipped with a massive quartz crystal which, in turn, was tipped by a huge southern diamond.

No one knew the purpose of these. Most assumed it was to produce the melodies that could be heard at night. While it was true that celestial voices did emanate from these panels, the city of Akhetaton had one singing temple, but most of the panels were in the Royal Temple. The sounds emanating from the Royal Temple could be heard all over Akhetaton—until the vast arrays of gilded panels spread before the tcham-coiled obelisk were deactivated the day of the temple's completion, when a temple priest climbed the finished scaffolding and removed the quartz and diamond crystals.

Nefertiti had witnessed the conversion of gold artifacts into gold plated panels and *tcham* wire. She considered this proof of Akhunaton's madness. The deactivation of the obelisk was further proof. She described these activities to Horemheb, who was avoiding contact with the king. He feared Akhunaton's telepathic abilities, knowing that his own heart held treason.

The dancing continued. The people sang and rejoiced every day. Festivals were celebrated on every conceivable occasion. Festivities rippled out from these centers and filled the city.

The two queens had retired from public life, but the king was making himself accessible to his people again. He spent weeks giving the last of the confiscated jewels to the peasants and he often strode among the populace naked, untouched by his adoring subjects.

He had continued to send communiques to Aper-El and King Tushratta. The Mitannian king repeatedly reminded the Egyptian king that his father had been given two Mitannian princesses as concubines, and that both had born children. A visit was arranged and Tushratta made the journey by caravan. The expedition took weeks.

On arrival, the huge, bearded, powerful king was asked, like all visitors, to undress completely before seeing the Egyptian king. Complying reluctantly, Tushratta and his men walked to the reception chamber. There they were instructed to meditate with Yuia, Queen Tiy's father, who sat with them in blissful silence.

Thus they remained for hours. Tushratta became increasingly uncomfortable. He expressed it at last with angry grumblings. Yuia merely stood and departed, returning after a few minutes to announce, "The king will see you at once."

They followed Yuia to a room with undecorated walls. There, sitting with his back propped against the wall and his feet stretched out in front of him, was the strangest living being that Tushratta had ever seen. Overcome with shock and aversion, he covered his genitals with both hands and backed up against the far wall. He stared wide-eyed at the bizarre creature that was the king of Egypt.

"Greetings, O King Tushratta," said a baritone voice.

"Dear Lord Mitra," said Tushratta, turning to his bodyguard.

"Welcome to my palace," said Akhunaton. "Please be seated. I have given my simple furnishings to some people who were in need, so do not be alarmed at the lack of stools or couches or pillows. I trust you have been well fed upon arriving this evening?"

"Y-yes," Tushratta stammered, unable to look away from the grotesque figure on the floor before him. "W-we were well f-fed…"

"I am glad. I have many gifts to give you. Personal creations of mine, far greater than the trinkets and baubles I give to the peasants. Here." He handed Tushratta a piece of parchment.

"What is this?"

"That, King Tushratta, is a poem I wrote when I heard word of your arrival. Do you read hieroglyphic Egyptian? On the back is a translation in your own language."

The King of Mitanni read the words with a puzzled look on his face. He did not understand the poem. He found no praise in the simple verses, no flattery addressed to King Tushratta of Mitanni. He let the paper flutter to the floor and continued to stare unblinking at Akhunaton.

"Did you not enjoy the verse?"

Tushratta started to speak, but his voice was lost in his throat while his lips merely trembled.

"I have written other poems to give to you. Here, here are some brush sketches I painted while awaiting your arrival. They depict the wildlife you might encounter on the Nile River. Here is a sketch of wildebeest, and here is an ink painting of a herd of zebras, which are found far to the south of Egypt."

"I-I see. Why do you give me such things?"

"Does my physical appearance make you nervous, King Tushratta?"

"Y-yes!"

"I thought so. Do not be afraid of what you see. I am as human as you are."

King Tushratta knew that this was not true. He turned to his bodyguard and spoke rapidly in his own tongue. Then to Akhunaton he forced a smile. "I, too, have brought many gifts: silver and gold. Diamonds and rubies. Emeralds, sapphires. We…hope they will please you, O King Akhunaton." Akhunaton did not respond. Finally, King Tushratta asked cautiously "Where are the jewels you have to give me?"

"I have no jewels to give to you."

"But you confiscated all the treasures of the temples of Amen!"

"I used the gold and the copper and gave the silver and the jewels to peasants who persuaded me that they appreciate such things. The priests of Osiris and priestesses of Isis use crystal jewels in their healing arts, and complained that there were few such stones available. So, I gave the jewels away."

King Tushratta stared in shocked horror at the king's nonchalant admissions. Finally, he gathered up his courage, and his greed, and asked, "Are these scraps of paper all you have to give me?"

"Yes. Are my poems and ink drawings not good enough for you?"

Akhunaton never received an answer. Tushratta and his party left the chamber indignantly. In the reception room they demanded their clothing, dressed in haste and left the king's house. Outside, their guards were commanded to gather up the treasures they had brought and, to their amazement, to depart.

Within the hour the ill-fated visit of the King of Mitanni was the cause of the greatest rage Queen Tiy had ever displayed.

☥

"I called him back! He would have nothing to do with me."

"Did you not anticipate his expectations? That he would *want* diamonds instead of poems; gold and silver instead of paintings?"

"Expectations become unfulfilled demands. This leads to sensual excesses and jaded men display violence. That was the implied theme of my poems to King Tushratta, but he apparently failed to recognize the symbolism."

"You idealistic fool! He is a *king!* He knows wealth. That, and military power, are *all* he knows. How could you read his letters and *not see* what he was hinting at, with all his reminders of the gifts he had exchanged with your predecessor, Amenhotep III?"

"That kind of diplomacy disgusts me."

Tiy argued with him for hours, but these remained his final words on the subject of "insincere generosity" and "appealing to vanity." Try as she might, Tiy could not get him to change his opinions.

Her parting words to him were, "I fear we have lost our political friendship with the empires of the east."

"The friendship was based on mutual bribery, which is greed."

"I fear we have made an enemy, Akhunaton."

"Tushratta was offended, but I doubt that he will invade Egypt."

She repeated as she walked out the door, "I fear we have lost the friendship… alienated the eastern empires. Completely."

"So be it," the king said indifferently.

When Horemheb heard of the disastrous meeting, he exploded into rage. He demanded to see Akhunaton, but was told that the king was in meditation with his daughters and would not be available. The general demanded to see Queen Tiy, but she merely added her anger to his own. The military commander rode back to headquarters and stormed about in impotent fury.

He had made a decision: he would engineer the removal of this Pharaoh from the throne of Egypt.

If Akhunaton knew that his commander of troops was conspiring to overthrow him, he did not show it. The king would not be reminded of the indignant king, so pleased was he to witness the levitation of a fiance scarab from the palm of his hand by the will of Neferneferura. Nothing could dampen the excitement of his daughter's psychic breakthrough. He assembled all his children to tell them this thing of great importance. He explained to them about the relationship between mind and matter, how mental concentration made control over the physical world possible.

Seated in their midst on his highest terrace, Akhunaton told his children, "The various forms that appear throughout the material world are contained in the *nou*, the pre-physical essence of all things, that exists in the substance of all things. The *nou* is even more ineffable than that which we call 'spirit.'

"Remember when I explained that solid matter is the pattern of a dance between the force that makes up lightning combined with tiny particles of opposite energy. In these essential particles is an image of the entire Universe. We call that positive particle a *proton*. It is feminine in nature, whereas electricity is masculine and active. These protons, each containing a picture of Ptah, the Universe, past, present and future, give order and maintain cause-effect relationships to the Universe. These images work together to keep the force that animates the Universe from dissolving back into primordial chaos.

"The images of the Universe, past, present and future inside each proton are called *holograms* in our Pangalactic language. The hologram inside the proton is an infinitesimal fractal of the Universe around you, and inside your mind, in memory and imagination.

"Remember this: when you create a mental picture, you are evoking a portion of the holograms within the multitudes of protons of your body.

"When the mental image is complete, it can be *superimposed upon reality*. The mind can then manipulate the image. For example, to cause an object to levitate, do not think a command to rise. Merely create a superior mental picture of an elevated object. To make yourself levitate, create an inner feeling of such vast, loving expansiveness that you no longer feel the gravity that weighs you down. Mental commands have nothing to do with power over materiality. The expansiveness of love and the ability to create perfect mental images — that is the secret of a power that is not power!

"The Egyptian word for hologram is *nou*. When you hear the priests of Osiris and of Aton speak of *nou*, know that it refers to forms in the potential inside the protons themselves. Know that this form is as much the mental images of your dreams and memories as it is the living shape of the rocks and trees and the sky above you. Know that *nou* is the knowledge that the particles have of how to give grace to the electrical dance of form, and give form itself solidity.

"When two or more minds are joined in telepathic union, and when the same image is projected by both minds simultaneously, the combined mental images cancel out the present appearance of physicality and the electrical dance conforms to a new description of reality. This is not one in which causality has been suspended, but one in which the description of reality that always depends on causality for order has been overridden by a new description of reality not so dependent upon habitual natural law for orderliness."

The children had been listening in rapt attention. They smiled serenely, pondering their lesson. A long pause passed. Akhunaton concluded, "Let us meditate. Ankh em Ma'at."

Rumors were spreading throughout the rural nomes south of Thebes that Amen had reappeared from hiding and was selecting priests. These were hushed murmurings, spoken by men to men. Amen had returned and was gathering forces. The Hidden One was appearing, often in caves, the limestone cliffs overlooking much of the northen Nile, extending well into the desert, where were caverns. The Hidden One was never seen, but entered the bodies of his priests and bathed their minds in rapture. The Hidden One could bounce his voice off the walls of caves, seeming to be everywhere at once. The Hidden One was still unseen, but not unnoticed.

Other troubles were stirring in the south of Egypt. The Nubians were still wondering greatly about this new Egyptian society. Many former slaves and captives, who had rejoiced at their new liberated status, now showed contempt for the Egyptians with whom they still shared their homeland. Finding that they could express their contempt and not suffer brutal retaliation, they exploited conflicts any way they could.

Irumen, Horuta, and Kagemni disembarked before sunrise from a ferry boat that nudged the west bank of the Nile opposite the city of Akhetaton. They slipped into the rushes of papyrus reeds that made the shoreline invisible and journeyed for three weeks. The young athletes covered many miles every day, living off the green land, catching fish or fowl for food, avoiding all human eyes.

When they arrived at Napata, they saw no indication of conflict. The people seemed happy and contented. Black-skinned Nubians and brown-skinned Egyptians conversed amiably everywhere. Kagemni, Horuta and Irumen saw little difference between Napata and Akhetaton, except for the lack of music and dancing. Reassured, they stayed one night and departed early in the morning.

They returned bearing news of what they had seen: peace and tranquility in the southern nomes, especially in the city of Napata. This seemed to placate Akhunaton.

Horemheb continued to be suspicious, but said nothing to his king. He was formulating his own plans, designs for one purpose: to dethrone Akhunaton.

𓏏𓏏𓂝

Shu-in-Akhunaton teleported aboard the discoidal starship and communed in rapture with Yod. Purified of psychic pain, he discussed the situation in Egypt with the other occupants of the *Aton*.

"Treachery surrounds my city," said Akhunaton. "My messengers either do not return or return mesmerized. A glamor has been cast over the southern colonies, and three of my most trusted were unable to see through it. They were hypnotized. They brought back a false impression of the reality there."

"Why do you not journey down there?" Geb suggested.

"Even now this body fails me," said Akhunaton. "My hips and pelvis ache when I stand. My joints hurt when I walk. I use a staff more than Smenkhara does—he taunts me and says it is my punishment for making him begin his life the same way, as a cripple. I fear I cannot disagree with him."

Nuit was apprehensive. "If the forces of Amen prevail. . ." She continued in a hushed voice, "You may have a million people down there singing and dancing at Akhetaton while doom gathers itself to leap over the eastern cliffs upon them."

"I fear this," said Akhunaton, "but it will not happen. To lure the innocent into slaughter is murder. I have already prepared the sanctuary of the Great Temple for mass-teleportation."

"I understand." Pilot Tem reflected Shu's enthusiasm. "A million people could journey aboard the *Aton* to Sothis III for education in the cosmological arts and sciences! They could return when, and *if*, the people of this world overcome their violent natures and discover that the many-worlds cosmology is *already open* to them."

"The humans of this wave of evolution must outgrow their struggle for dominance," said Akhunaton. "At all our festivals, wave-shifters from the far future and distant past arrive out of the night shadows to dance, gather around bonfires and commune with the human population. Cross-fertilization of human-related races has contributed to Egypt's rising birth rate. The energy of love raised every night by the drummers and dancers has reversed the effects of age and decay upon the bodies of many celebrants. Not a single person has died in this city, with the exception of my own daughter."

"The first fact is impressive, Shu," said Tem. "The second, regrettable."

Said Akhunaton, "I have already started preparing my people for translation. We cannot turn back now."

☟

Meritaton had matured into a lovely young woman and Smenkhara had overcome his sullenness. He had acquired a calm temperament as detachment replaced anger. Ankhasenpaaton and Tutankhaton approached puberty, both bright, cheerful, intelligent children. Neferneferuaton the Little was also maturing. Although her slender, nubile body looked at first much younger than ten years old, her tiny, swelling breasts indicated that she was approaching puberty. Neferneferura was eight years old and a very mystical child, always silent except when singing or reciting one of her many poems.

Setepenra was four years old. She shared her siblings' precociousness and wordless mysticism. Her greatest interests were the stars and the nature of time. When her father told her about the ancient ages of prehistoric animals, she informed him that she dreamed of the Age of Dragons and the Age of Behemoths at night. At two years of age, Beketaton was the most psychically powerful of all of Akhunaton's children. She was highly telepathic and often shared silent eye-contact conversations with Akhunaton. They sometimes joined in empathic communion with Neferneferuaton the Little.

The conversion of the last of Amen's captured gold into panels and *tcham* wire had been completed. All nocturnal experiments had ceased in the North Palace and in the Royal Temple. The children of the king spent more and more time living in the North Palace, between Nefertiti's Palace and the house of the king. They sometimes visited their mother, but only when her moods permitted.

The years seemed to be accelerating toward some unseen end.

Smenkhara was being groomed to become the next king. He was to marry his twin sister, Meritaton. They had already started to learn the love arts under the guidance of their father. One night, as the children slept, the Aton Disc descended from the sky and Smenkhara and Tutankhaton dreamed of being taken to the Hidden World, the Amentt. There they were sexually awakened and loved by the perfect astral counterparts of their twin-sister-wives. Although neither Meritaton nor Ankhasenpaaton had comparable dreams that night, their twin-brother-husbands delighted them with the news of this otherworldly communion.

In the genetic laboratory aboard the starship *Aton*, Tem and Geb scanned the newly-gathered samples and catalogued the sperm cells. Six new bodies were being designed, each a human female. The holograms were being designed and the genes selected or created to correspond with each conceptual trait. The designs of the bodies included vast modifications of the extended occipital lobe of their prospective mothers, the daughters of Akhunaton.

Chapter Twenty-Nine

Horemheb had never been a conqueror, though it was in his nature. His years as Commander-in-Chief under Amenhotep III had been peaceful. He had fought off no invaders and subdued no more than a few uprisings, one of which was merely a ploy for glory and the subject of many murals on the part of the king: the Pharaoh's only battle had been carefully staged so that he could fight and not risk his life.

Such had been the politics of the day: nothing more than a set of peaceful trade relations. Mitanni held the secret of smelting iron and supplied Egypt with iron blades and shields. In the past, when trade with Mitanni was cut off in times of war, while the Egyptians ruined their bronze swords and shields on the battlefields, the Mitannians kept returning with freshly forged iron blades.

The Nubians possessed no such secrets. Nubia was a source of gold and diamonds—and of slaves, though after the disappearance of Amenhotep III, Queen Tiy had refused to send any more slavers to Nubia. When Amenhotep IV returned and claimed the throne, he abolished slavery altogether.

Now Amenhotep IV, Akhunaton, lolled about in his capital city. The army and navy stood idly by, though their commander, Horemheb, suspected that Nubian hordes were gathering along the banks of the Nile, south of the Fourth Cataract, waiting to invade Napata and move north. The general planned a journey, travelling *incognito* out of Akhetaton and to the far south. He informed a few of his officers and arranged to be protected at all times. He was determined to learn what was really going on in Napata.

The priest of Amen had sent two new initiates to watch the king's city. They had tracked three runners departing from Akhetaton. The athletes did not go far before they were ambushed, hypnotized and guided surreptitiously on their way. Now the two studied the city from the clifftops, using a wooden tube with crystal lenses in its ends, given to them by the nameless priest of Amen. The device had great magic and distant visions of great clarity could be seen. They were watching for another secret departure.

Peser and Pewero spied on Akhetaton night and day, even watching Nefertiti when she appeared on the balconies of her immense palace. They paid very close attention when she appeared with General Horemheb under the open sky and under the illusion of complete privacy. They knew by his tenderness toward Nefertiti that he loved her. It was also apparent that Akhunaton did not care. Peser and Pewero reported regularly to a fellow initiate up in the secret hierarchy. His name was Anpu.

The king summoned his children together. He had written another poem, one which was to be copied many times and sent throughout the land; a poem which Ai would paint in hieroglyphics as a mural on the king's stable.

"This poem is dedicated to Ai," said the king, "for he has inspired it with our discussions of sacred things of nature, how we live in a world that is like the inside of an egg shell, and how that shell will break one day when the night sky is no longer seen as mere lights on a black shell. This poem is based on the words of Ai, whom I mention in the introductory lines. Ankh em Ma'at."

The eight children were seated in a semicircle before their father. Their legs were crossed, their eyes did not move. Akhunaton held up the scroll and read:

"'Thy rising is beautiful in the Horizon of Heaven, O Aton, ordainer of life. Thou dost shoot up in the horizon of the east, thou fillest every land with beneficence. Thou art beautiful and great and sparkling, and exalted above every land. Thy rays penetrate as if transparent the very ground thou hast made.

"'Thou art similar to Ra. Thou bringest people up, according to the number prepared, for thou subduest their hearts for thy beloved son. Thou thyself art far off, but thy beams illuminate the earth; thou art in the faces of all, for they admire thy visits.

"'Thou settest in the horizon of the west, the Earth is in darkness, in the form of death. Men lie down in a booth, their bodies wrapped as if in cloth, and one eye cannot see its fellow. If all their possessions, which are far below their heads, were carried away, they would not perceive it.

"'Every lion emerges from its lair, all the creeping things bite, oblivion and darkness become a retreat. The land is in silence. He who hath made all things has set in his own horizon.

"'The Earth will become like light itself; thou shootest up in the horizon, shining in the Aton as if by daylight, thou scatterest in darkness. Thou sendest out rays, the Two Worlds join in festivals, and men wake up, stand upon two feet, it is thou who hast raised them upright. Now, they bathe themselves and take up clothing to wear.

"'And they array themselves therein, their hands outstretched, in praise of thy sudden rise, throughout the land they do their works.

"'Beasts and cattle of all kinds settle down upon pastures, shrubs and vegetables flourish, the feathered fowl fly about over their marshes, their feathers praising thy earthly manifestation. All the cattle rise up on their legs, creatures that fly and insects of all kinds.

"'They spring to life when thou risest over them.

"'The boats drop down and sail up the river, likewise, every road manifests at thy sudden rise, the fish of the river swim toward thy face and thy beams penetrate even the depths of the Great Green Sea.

"'Thou makest offspring to take human form in women, creating seed in men. Thou makest the son to live in the womb of his mother, making him also to be quiet and crieth not; thou art a nurse.

"'In the womb, giving breath to vivify that which he hath made, when he droppeth from the womb, on the day of his birth, he openeth his mouth in the ordinary manner, thou providest sustenance.

"'When the fledgling in the egg chirpeth in the egg, thou givest him breath to preserve him alive. Thou makest for him a more mature form, so that he can crack the shell of the egg he is inside of. He cometh forth from this egg, learning to sing with all his might, and when he walks forth from that egg, he walketh upright on two feet.

"'Multitudinous are thy created creatures.

"'They are hidden from the face.

"'O Thou One God, like whom there is no other. Thou didst create the Earth by the will of thy heart, existing in time before all men and women, cattle, beasts of every kind that now exist, all creatures in the sky that fly with their wings, from the deserts of Syris and Kesh to the Land of Egypt.

"'Thou hast set every person in place. Thou providest their daily food, everyone having their rightful portion. Thou dost compute the duration of life. Their tongues differ, as do the colors of human skins, giving variety to the dwellers in the foreign lands.

"'Thou hast made the Nile in the Tuat, bringing it out of the Land of the Dead to make mortals live, inasmuch as thou hast made them for thyself, their Lord who dost suppose them to be uttermost, O Lord of every world, thou shinest upon them, O Aton of the day, thou great one of majesty.

"'Thou makest the life of all remote worlds. Thou settest a Nile in Heaven, which descends to these worlds.

"'It maketh a flood on the mountains like the Great Green Sea, it maketh to be watered in their fields and their villages. How beneficent are thy plans, O Lord of Eternity! A Nile in Heaven art thou for the dwellers in the remote worlds, and for all the beasts on those worlds that go upon their many legs. The Nile cometh from the Tuat where the dead dwell, to the land of Egypt. Thy beams nourish every field; thou ascendeth and they live, they germinate for thee.

"'Thou hast made the Heaven which is so remote that thou mayest shine therein, and look down upon the things which thou hast made. Thine occupants are as one being, thou shootest up into the sky and shineth down upon thy living creatures as the Living Aton, ascending suddenly, shining down, departing from afar off, returning. Thou hast made millions of previous evolutions from thy one self, as of towns and cities to villages, fields, roads, all in the river of life. All men's eyes beholdeth thee, confronting. Thou art the Aton of daylight at its zenith.

"'At the departure from the eye, thy form recedeth into Heaven. Thou didst create their faces so that their eyes mightest not see thee, in that remote Heaven. Only one was created by thee, whose eye could see in that remote Heaven. Thou art in my heart. There is no other who knoweth thee except thy son, Nefer-kheperu-Ra-Ua-en-Ra. Thou hast made him wise to understand thy plans and thy power. This world came into being by thy hand, even as thou hast created human beings upon it. Thou ascendeth, they live. Thou setteth, they die. As for thee, there is duration in thy members, life itself is in thee.

"'All eyes gaze upon thy multicolored rays until thou settest, when all labors are relinquished. Thou settest in the west, thou risest, making to flourish the living Earth for the King. Every man who standeth upright, since thou didst create the foundation of the Earth, thou hast raised up for thy son who came forth from thy body, the King of the South and North, the Living Truth. Ankh em Ma'at.'"

They meditated for a long time.

"The poem is about the evolution of human beings on the many worlds," said Akhunaton. "That is why I stressed the metaphors of flight and standing on two legs. The humanoid form is like a baby bird, in that both must stand upright on two feet before learning to fly."

"Again you state there is a horizon in Heaven," Meritaton said. "Or *two* horizons in Heaven."

"Time and space have their horizons," said Akhunaton. "This is one of the symbols I have emphasized in my poetry."

"What is the Nile in the Tuat?" asked Ankhasenpaaton, her eyes shining.

"Time behaves much like water," said Akhunaton, "and the quality that is Mind comes out of the same void that it enters after death. Time is circular. The Nile on earth represents the circular nature of time, for the rain always carries back the water of the river's future.

"But, by riding time, flowing between the worlds on currents of time alone, and carrying consciousness in it, the *Aton* and the other boats that 'drop down and sail on the river,' traverse the distances between worlds as if sailing on a river. This brings the worlds closer, and brings the seed of life to many worlds."

Neferneferuaton the Little asked, "Is it true that the Aton Disc created the multitudinous forms of life?"

"Yes. There is a library of forms, holograms of the *nou* in the Aton Disc."

"Are there other discs like Aton?" Meritaton asked.

"Yes. Multitudes of them. From multitudes of other worlds."

"And their visits have caused people to walk upright?" Neferneferura chirped.

"Yes. And take to wearing clothes and bathing."

"Was this by creating forms that are like human, and placing them in human mothers?"

"Yes, just like I wrote in the poem: 'Thou makest offspring to take human form in women, creating seed in men.' That is a description of how a body like mine came to be. I am not human in my native form but manlike, humanoid. This body was created and placed in the womb of Mother Tiy, as you know. You will all be given a first child before your dispersal into the world of humanity.

"When Osiris was carried to the Dog Star by the Aton Disc in ancient times and his penis remained, that is a way of saying that his seed, in the form of male children, remained to fertilize the wombs of native human women.

"My return to this world constitutes a final demonstration of this process, as described in this poem. It is for people of another age to read, when their own natural scientists plant the seed of life created in the wombs of animal mothers."

"This shows the power of the Aton Disc is through life and creation," said Meritaton, "and not a force out of control."

"That is right," said Akhunaton. "That is why I use such words as 'illumination' and such metaphors as light that penetrates matter and makes solid substance transparent. People of a later age will know of such rays, and my poems will suggest ways of perceiving such rays from a vantage point in the remote heavens."

"Do *all* of your poems address a later age?" asked Neferneferura.

"Yes, as does all of this art my artisans are producing, and all of the things I do, which have been ordained by agreements made in the Aton and enacted by me, and recorded by my scribes. *All* of it addresses a later age."

"Will we get to see that later age?" asked Meritaton, her eyes sparkling with enthusiasm.

"Yes," said Akhunaton, "if all goes well..."

Horemheb's departure from Akhetaton was sudden, spontaneous and secret. Not even Nefertiti suspected—all the queen knew was that she spent a nervous, tense evening with him and then he was gone. He departed when the full moon was at its zenith over the city. He was alone, unprotected, and taking a terrible risk, yet he let the impulse to depart from the king's city overtake him. He climbed a vertical crevice in the eastern cliffs, observed by Peser and Pewero.

Peser remained to spy on Akhetaton with his crude telescope while Pewero followed Horemheb over foot paths and animal trails, through bush, grassy hills and eventually desert. They ran over flat, sedimentary, dry washes, leaped up silted embankments, crouched low and scurried between bushes and thorn trees. The light of the moon made the land shimmer, turning rocks and sand to silver. The hills were black under the starry dome of the night sky.

Horemheb did not suspect he was being followed for Pewero was highly skilled. His childhood had been spent among the nomadic Bedouins and his initiation into manhood had included learning the assassin's art. It was this skill of which he was most proud.

Horemheb turned his back to north and spent the predawn hours walking parallel to the Nile. By dawn, Pewero had dropped back and was following Horemheb up and down hills, using his skills as a tracker. While Horemheb slept through the early part of the day under an outcrop of looming boulders, Pewero met with a courier and sent him to inform the local Amenist temple of the whereabouts of the General of Egypt.

Pewero returned to the wilderness and found Horemheb still sleeping. Pewero had watched over him for an hour when a priest of Amen approached, walking from the east.

"I am sent to relieve you," said the priest. "Return to your post over Akhetaton."

Pewero bowed to the priest, then returned an Egyptian military salute. He departed, running between the silent boulders, over the barren hills, walking, loping through grasslands, returning to the north

The king found Parannefer on the balcony of his apartment, smiling over the southern city with tears in his eyes.

"What is wrong, my Friend Like Whom There is No Other?" asked Akhunaton.

"Nothing is wrong, O King," said the tiny old man. "I had a dream of my wife last night, that is all. She…she said she missed me. She said she wanted me to come back home to her."

"I see. Well, my dear friend, perhaps she does." Akhunaton felt a twinge of sadness; in his empathic resonance with Parannefer he had lately felt a pain in the old man's heart. Now he knew that Parannefer was dying.

"I must make light my heart," said Parannefer, "like a feather. Like the Feather of Truth. Ankh em Ma'at."

"Ankh em Ma'at," Akhunaton repeated, touching Parannefer and feeling a surge of empathic resonance. He sensed sadness, but also hope.

"I *do* yearn to see her," said Parannefer, "but I think I may look back longingly at this world…"

"You already know what you need to enter the Tuat," said Parannefer's king and god.

The king's Best Friend looked up at the being who so awed him and smiled at the celestial man. "You have journeyed through the Tuat. Tell me, what is it like?"

"I have journeyed through the Realm of the Dead to get to this body," said Akhunaton. "I passed through the Presence of Living Light who is Osiris and communed with the love of the Embracer of Souls. This is the source of the Light that Lives. This is the presence of the Immortal Entity. You, Parannefer, keep in mind to look for the light and present your heart when you see it."

"What about the scales of Ma'at?"

"The scales themselves are light."

"What about Baba, the Soul Eater?"

"Nothing more than fear itself. Banish fear."

"How can I banish fear? Do I have a prayer?"

"Fear is a shadow. Light makes it flee. Seek light, seek light! Ankh em Ma'at."

Parannefer clutched the chest of the seated king, burying his face in the huge alien's shoulder. They embraced, the king and the king's Best Friend. Parannefer wept tears of gladness. They rejoiced while below them Akhetaton celebrated the endless festival.

For an instant Horemheb glimpsed a pit-black eye staring into his own. He sat upright, his heart pounding, shuddering, blinking. Gasping, shaking.

There was no one there. He was alone in his niche between boulders, this cool, dark pit of shade invaded by few slants of afternoon sunlight. It must have been a dream or a dream of a dream, suggested by something he heard, perhaps, here, under and between these boulders…

What, then? He looked around. He saw only a scorpion, fat and big, as long as his hand, scuttling over the loosely tumbled stones. He thought of Selket, the goddess of sorcery, and remembered that the scorpion was her creature.

No. He quickly extinguished the mental connection. The scorpion vanished through a wedge of sunlight.

Parannefer died during the night. He was assisted by the *nou* of his wife. She drew him into the Light of Osiris and his heart was received by the love of a god.

283

The news of Parannefer's death spread swiftly throughout Akhetaton. His funerary pageant was regal, in the grand tradition of Egyptian aristocracy, but without grief. It was a festive occasion, commemorating the reunion of two Earthly Lovers.

Nefertiti did not attend. Horemheb was also absent and after the festivities, Ai conferred with Akhunaton about the missing general.

"It is as I expected," Akhunaton said. "I intuited that he was planning a secret departure from Akhetaton to investigate the rumors of Nubian uprisings and the reformation of the priests of Amen. The violence of the Nubians has been exaggerated, but their discontent is real. I am aware that a number of outlawed priests survey us from the cliffs. And it seems certain that the priests of Amen will try to invade…"

"What will we do then? You have taught abstinence from fighting. You have

eulogized pacific themes. What if your noble city and the experiment it exempli-
fies is slain and erased from the records of time?"

"Oh, we will be waiting for them! When they arrive, I do not think we will wait
long to receive them. Perhaps we will go home."

"I think I understand," said Ai, chuckling.

Nefertiti awoke. The full moon gazed through a slot in the high ceiling. Her
bedchamber was empty but for herself for Horemheb had been gone for three
nights. He had not told her of his intended departure and she was worried. She
deduced that he had climbed the cliff after departing from her palace, gone through
the mountains to the east and journeyed into the desert.

She had expected him to be gone for weeks or months, but now she heard him
whisper her name.

"Horemheb?" Cautiously, she slipped from under her blankets. "Is that you?"

It was definitely Horemheb's voice, but thin and ghostlike. It issued from the
shadow behind a veil of beads hanging from a doorway.

She knew something was wrong. She went swiftly to the doorway just as Horemheb stepped through the curtain of beads and stood before her, catching her by the
arms. She embraced him, glad to feel him safely in her arms. Then she gazed into
his eyes…

A dark look clouded the face of the extraterrestrial king on being informed by
Ramose of his queen's departure—or abduction. He hung his head down

"'Do you feel infirm, O King?" Ramose tugged the Pharaoh's elbow.

"The worst has happened! Please summon Ai and Queen Tiy." Ani hurried from
the sunlit balcony and shortly returned with the queen and high priest.

"We have heard the news," Ai said.

Tiy scowled and shook her head.

"Do not scorn, my mother. Perhaps she did not abandon us. She might have been
captured."

"If true, her doubts and misgivings brought her abduction upon her!"

"Who would do this?" Ai begged, tears in his eyes.

"Kahotep," said Akhunaton.

"I thought his temple was sealed off and he was starving to death."

"He has tunnels all over Thebes."

"But his main tunnel between Karnak and Luxor was interrupted by the building of your first Temple of Aton."

"His tunnels lead into the serdabs of the wealthy. From the altars inside the
mastabas he takes the offerings to the dead for his sustenance."

Tiy stepped forward sternly. "Have we not gone too far in abiding by the principle of free choice and respect for life, Akhunaton?"

"Oh, we could have murdered Kahotep. If murder is acceptable, we can still indulge in it. Is murder suddenly acceptable now?"

Tiy was furious. "If one death can prevent many, then yes, murder must be committed!"

"Are you certain many murders will be averted by the one murder you propose?"

"Yes. Yes! What about your city? You said you would not have your citizens fight an invader with violence."

"I also promised my citizens that they would be safe here, free from the threat of murder."

"You fool! If Akhetaton is invaded, your followers will be slain!"

"No, Mother Tiy, no one will be slain in my city."

Ai spoke up. "Kahotep has been coming and going from his chambers under the Temple of Karnak."

"Yes, for several years he has been."

"And this has been *permitted*?" Tiy was incredulous.

"Of course. Unless involuntary imprisonment and starvation is suddenly acceptable…"

"Are you mad?" Tiy gestured toward the city. "How do you intend to protect your people?"

"By preparing them for translation, Lady Tiy."

The news of the disappearance of Queen Nefertiti caused ripples of dark uncertainty in Akhetaton. Throughout Egypt, it aroused feelings of dread.

Inside the palace, Akhunaton worked swiftly to respond to the threat he faced: a psychic attack. He carved out or painted over her name on every temple and palace wall, on statuary, everywhere he found it. He plucked or carved out the right eye, the Utchat, Eye of Horus, from every bust or statue of her.

Though he did not explain his actions, everyone in the inner court knew of the use of the right eye for telepathy. They knew of psychoholography, the creation of vivid mental images, and how to induce hypnosis with one glimpse, eye-to-eye. They knew of how one mind could dominate another and use its memories to project a psychic double to the places of those images. They knew of mind parasitism and the projection of strange attractors, pockets of chaos of psychic origin.

When the alien king finished removing Nefertiti's name and right eye, Kahotep's disruptive forces were effectively banished to the past, before the images had been altered. Psychic attack would be limited to times consistent with Nefertiti's memories.

They were truly a race of giants. When the daughters matured sexually, they were as tall as any Egyptian man and considerably taller than most. Smenkhara and Tutankhaton were diminutive for their family: about six feet tall when they stopped growing.

The youngest, was six years old when Nefertiti vanished. Beketaton was a precocious girl and understood well the grave implications of their father's genetic experiment on the planet—and the threat posed by Kahotep.

Their studies of mental physics became more concentrated after Nefertiti's disappearance. Though Smenkhara was not ordered to attend his father's sittings, he eagerly sought every opportunity to be with the strange man he had once hated.

The people of Akhetaton were hurriedly being prepared for an event their king called "translation." They had no idea and no expectations of a transformation for them..

Having no foreknowledge of the point of transformation will be their great advantage, thought Akhunaton as he looked over a terrace wall at the morning work crews. Since they had finished building the city., they assembled on the outskirts of the suburbs to tend to the fields. Every house was surrounded by ample courtyards and gardens. Fruit trees lined the city streets. There was ample food for all, everywhere.

The happy spirit of the people of Akhetaton soared. They found their hours at labor diminishing; many worked only half a day. Musicians played in every street and encampment. The steaming hot brew made from the roasted black beans from Asia Minor was becoming more popular than biscuit-beer, and imparted the opposite effect.

Dithyrambic drum circles propelled whirling dancers. The morning rhythms were at their peak when the children of Akhunaton joined their father on the terrace of the house.

"We will speak of mind and energy," said Akhunaton, "and of mind perception, internal energy and infolding-enfolding the *nou*, the psychic hologram inside all of us.

"You have been instructed to memorize the things you see, natural life forms, even room interiors and to be able to recreate such mental images perfectly. You have been practising these exercises for a reason.

"When reality becomes private for you, you are outside of the perceptual fields of any other life form whose sensory endowments are similar to your own. Then you have the opportunity for meditation, exempt from the theoretical bondage of sharing another's perceptual field. That is why I have given you creative visualizations of shared images—so you can combine your mental focus and common imagery to create holographic projections.

"I am impressed with your abilities. I have witnessed your levitations of objects, from a ceramic scarab to a polished stone ball, and two of you have experienced bodily levitation when you contemplated the meanings of *Ankh em Ma'at*. Meritaton believes she was teleported from one room of this house to another while sustaining a mental picture of that second room. If so, this is the secret which I have been teaching you: transferring information and ultimately mass through space and time without using kinetic or potential force.

"It takes a certain amount of mental force to establish and maintain complete mental images. But in every instant the human brain is utilizing *much more* energy! Tiny bursts of lightning, an energy very different from fire, spark from place to place in your brains whenever you think, solve arithmetic problems, recite a poem or dream.

"What is the difference in energy whether you are visualizing a stone or scarab *in the air* instead of where it is, on a shelf or in my hand? The answer is that there is *no* difference in energy! The brain is sparking with just as many tiny lightning bolts then as when you are dreaming at night. The difference is the *result*—a mental picture so perfect that it imposes itself on reality. A new reality is created. In effect, a new Universe splits off from the former, less perfect Universe—less perfect because more at the mercy of chance, chaos, entropy, the ever-present hidden random factors.

"Every time mind imposes itself on physical, material reality, the Universe becomes more perfect. The alignment of particles forming crystals when the planets first solidified is an example. The first life formed in the seas of the first mother-planet is another. The evolution of life, the cosmic disturbances that alter evolution and the transmission of spores into space for interplanetary fertilization and planetary breeding, all are this. Those spores are the multitudes of races, most of which are humanoid, who are represented by the word Amentii.

"In addition, purely terrestrial races who have incorporated such psychic skills into their cultures have sent wave-shifters to this timespace continuum of this planet. They attend our festivals. They hear our music and participate sexually in our fertility rites. Many pregnancies in Egypt and the world in general, are the result of visits by wave-shifters descended from this race, the three previously evolved human races, and the future evolutions of human races. By mastery of enfolding-infolding psychoholograms, humanoids may join the ranks of the timespace nomads."

"Is this what I did when I closed my eyes in one room," Meritaton asked, "and envisioned another room so completely that I was in that room when I opened my eyes?"

"Yes. You became a wave-shifter," said Akhunaton.

"Is this why you altered the statues and names of Nefertiti?" Ankhasenpaaton asked.

"Yes. She can only visualize what her memory sees, so her specter, which is probably controlled by Kahotep, can only be projected to times and places that can be visualized based on her memories. Akhetaton is inaccessible to Nefertiti's specter because her memories are no longer accurate to her icons."

Beketaton had been looking at her sisters and two brothers, then spoke up. "You said all wave-shifters had large heads. My brothers both have heads of normal size, and so does Ankhasenpaaton. Yet, Ankhasenpaaton and Meritaton combined their psychic imagery and levitated a ball of stone. Is Ankhasenpaaton capable of this on her own? Do our heads really have to be as large as mine?"

"Most wave-shifters have heads as only as great in size and volume of brain as any Egyptian. They are just humanoids.

"Your heads are at the limits for viable hybridization. Your offspring, one generation modified, will be capable of conception and birth without assistance. Your head, Ankhasenpaaton, is a normal size. This was done as proof to future generations that the depictions of your sisters are not exaggerations, since the relative sizes and shapes of all your skulls are consistently rendered.

"What we are doing here will have no meaning for nearly four thousand years. Then, all of the paintings and statues of you will have great meaning in a culture produced by five centuries of rapid change.

"You all face forty centuries of awesome danger. Then, perhaps some of you will see that period of immense change and you, too, will be translated. Ankh em Ma'at."

The moon hung in the zenith of the dome of night. The tcham-wrapped obelisks of the singing temples of Aton rang with the music of the distant spheres. Akhunaton closed his eyes. He sat cross-legged in the center of a circle drawn on the floor of his bare room.

When he opened his eyes, he was not alone. Around him stood multitudes of humanoid beings. Most looked entirely human: small, bearded men in hand-sewn clothing, many with slightly upturned, pointed ears. Others were descended from the ice-age races: tall, hairy humanoids.

Some were weird, otherworldly. They had huge, hairless heads without external ears: wave-shifters descended from the Age of Dragons, evolved from the smaller two-legged dinosaurs. Visitors from humanoid races which had yet to evolve, wave-shifting natives of a far future age, differed greatly from the humans. Some were hairless; a few possessed external ears and wrinkled faces, like skins of old human beings.

The walls faded beyond this sea of multiform humanoids.

Akhunaton spoke to them with his eyes and mind.

"Each one of you has evolved from a time that converges with this time on this world. You are all native to this planet, all liberated from the timespace continuum by your ability to project and sustain mental images. You infold-enfold the *nou* by lightness of heart in the spirit of the moment. Thus, you are all what beings who do not possess or practise such knowledge call 'magicians.'

"You know the events on this world that are pivotal to this time. You know of the parasite-priest who has stolen the crudest of all the secrets of longevity and seeks to enslave this world so he can perpetuate his addiction to living human pineal glands.

"Each of you has been summoned from more-perfect Universes that diverge from *this* Universe at *this* point in the timespace stream.

"I ask you to participate in the evolution of this world: to use telepathy and hypnosis to mask the visits of starships and to converge to project tangible hallucinations throughout the land during the visits of the translation ships. I ask you to impart insights into the minds of humans who are ready to give up the past and communicate new consciousness to their species.

290

"I ask you to harass with hallucinations and hypnosis the agents of Kahotep, who do their jobs believing they work for the common good of their people.

"You are all, either genetically or culturally, my children. You are related either to this body I now wear, or to my Horus-body from the beginning of this cycle. Possibly you descend from one of the bodies I helped design in previous cycles of evolution, or which I will create to assist in this world's future evolutionary cycles.

You are all my sons and daughters. I am asking for your help. Enlighten the brightest peasants with epiphanies. Harass the darkest men with hallucinations. Impregnate the women. And mask the activities of spacecraft with hallucinations that utilize the mythological imagery of future civilizations. Watch each culture emerge and stay sympathetic to the mythic images of these peoples.

"It is with love that I have summoned you here, and with gratitude that I receive you. Let us meditate together to reach clarity of mind and singularity of purpose. We join to avert catastrophe and to keep accessible the translation of any human mind that seeks it.

"Ankh em Ma'at."

When Akhunaton opened his eyes at the end of a lengthy meditation, he was once again alone in his private chamber.

Chapter Thirty

O ver the centuries the Beast had compiled a book, partly dream diary, partly a chronology of his most successful psychic experiments. His name for the book joined three Egyptian words meaning the specter embodied in the animal brain, the soul embodied in the human brain and the spirit of the sun, which imparts life to the mother planet. The book was called *Ka-Ba-Ra*.

He would not be satisfied until he had mastered physical immortality. He had mastered his sexual urge centuries ago, by self-castration, but he could not master psychoholography because his mind was constantly burdened, weighed down by doubts and fears. Greatest of these was his fear of death, a manifestation of his primitive animal mind. Thus, he could not enfold a psychohologram nor levitate mass, including his own, nor project himself to other points in the timespace continuum.

Some things he did well. He could create demons in his mind and then impart them eye-to-eye into other minds. He could hypnotize the unsuspecting. In states of astral projection, he could leave his body. Although his telepathy remained primitive, he was adept at imparting certain kinds of telepathic control to people who surrendered their will to his. He could arouse awe and fear, which granted his powers their illusion of superiority.

Akhunaton had secluded himself in Akhetaton and seemed not to care about the religion of Amen, though Kahotep was beginning to reclaim his empire. He had already established many contacts near Thebes via a system of tunnels he had built linking natural limestone caves. For over four years Kahotep had been leaving his secret chambers under the Temple of Karnak and using selected, controlled contacts to rebuild his shattered priesthood.

And now, he thought, looking up from the scroll he penned, he had two valuable assets, but for acquiring them he anticipated severe retaliation. To the north of Karnak, in a temple-cavern, The Beast had imprisoned General Horemheb and Queen Nefertiti.

To the eyes of Horemheb he had sent two demons via a haunted priest named Pawah. One was created to leap at first glance into Nefertiti's eyes. No direct contact with the eyes and mind of Kahotep was even necessary!

The demon imparted into the eye and mind of Horemheb was a dragon of fire endowed with all the attributes of fire, from a nasty temper to all-consuming passions. The dragon had flames for scales and it lived, as do all demons cast by black magicians, in the mammal brains, the limbic systems, of their hosts.

The demon created to live in Nefertiti's mammalian brain was a leviathan of water. It was the essence of tragedy, a drowning of her soul. It flooded her with tears, filled her nose and throat with colds. It was omnipresent in her mind, as if it had tentacles everywhere.

When Horemheb, commanded by demon-emissary Pawah, returned to Akhetaton, he had gone directly to Nefertiti. He awoke her, looked into her eyes and the water-dragon leaped from his eye to hers.

Nefertiti silently departed with her lover. He led her to the cleft between the mountains and into the custody of Peser and Pewero. Then they were delivered swiftly into the hands of Pawah, who lived in a limestone cavern south and east of Akhetaton. Pawah kept them in states of hypnotic stupor in separate sealed tunnels.

Paradise outside of the king's city was suddenly lost. Alive and strong, growing in numbers, recruiting only men, regaining control of brothels and beer-houses, the religion of the Hidden One flourished in every part of Egypt except Akhetaton.

The Beast allowed his Inner Circle to wander the tunnels, guarding the secret chambers in his absence. They knew how to pilfer the mastabas for their sustenance. While the twelve prowled endlessly, Kahotep experimented. In his dungeon he germinated spores of one mold after another in tiny airtight dishes of blown glass sealed with resin. The molds grew on crushed barley and oats, staples of the Egyptian diet. He also worked in his animal laboratory, connected to the Karnak tunnel system. It was in the open air, deep in a gap among ancient foundations in sacred, thus taboo, lands. Assured of privacy, Kahotep conducted experiments of breeding diseases in monkeys, available in any Egyptian marketplace, which he knew were closest in blood kinship to human beings.

"We stress the importance of the name of Amen meaning 'the Hidden One.' To be secretive is to be like Amen. To be stealthy is not cowardice; it is very close to being omnipotent, like Amen."

Pawah stood before first-degree initiates seated throughout the cave. Each man was alert, concentrating grim-faced on what the High Priest was saying.

"I have had Amen possess my body, and yet I still did not see Amen! He gave my body raptures and his voice echoed throughout the cave, but still I did not see Amen. Still he was hidden from me!

"I heard and understood his spoken message and the Hidden One gave me raptures for many hours — many ages of time in a single night! And I slept and dreamed of the stars for another Eternity. I felt all this and more — and yet I never once saw Amen! The Hidden One remained hidden from me, even while he was inside of me, where I could feel him.

"I came to Amen with a question, and I performed the rite, I recited the prayer that invoked Amen. Death came to me at once! And, after I died, I faced the One True Osiris with my question. The question was: how was it that the cult of Aton was allowed to flourish and displace the religion of Amen from the Pharaoic throne?"

His theatrics were masterful. He paused for emphasis. When he had gathered every bit of their attention, Pawah said, "I was told: 'It is a test of your faith.' Faith in Amen! Pampered by good years, our faith in Amen was taken for granted! So, a test was arranged, a challenge: a demon from *sheol*, the Evil World, occupies the throne of the Pharaoh.

"By law, no one can murder the Pharaoh. But if a sacred army sends a living demon back to the Evil World it came from, then they are not murdering the Pharaoh but exorcising an impostor! Such must always be accomplished in secret, for sake of our sacred, recorded history.

"Does any man fail to hear meaning in my words? Are your questions yet unanswered? Let all who do not understand step forth!"

All eyes remained fixed on Pawah. No one ventured forward.

"So be it. I tell you now to depart into the land, attend all secret services, and await orders from your priests. I will call upon you individually. Go in secrecy. In the name of Amen!"

Six weeks after the disappearances of Horemheb and Nefertiti, a messenger reached Akhunaton claiming to be from Horemheb. He reported the general had made it to the far south and wished to inform the king that the Nubians were casting off their chains.

"Have you seen Horemheb yourself?" the king asked the messenger, who had been telepathically scanned and was found to be neither a priest nor initiate of Amen, nor the innocent host of one of Kahotep's mind-parasites.

"Yes," said the boy. "He is in Thebes right now. He was with Nefertiti, whose face of perfect beauty I recognized. They will not return to Akhetaton until the Nubian uprisings are suppressed."

"In what districts are these rebellions?" asked the king.

"These are the districts." The youth held out a papyrus scroll. "Horemheb himself dictated this message."

Akhunaton unrolled the paper. He glanced over it. "Tell Horemheb that these districts are all former parts of Nubia that were created as possessions of Egypt to ward off invasion. But, until my reign, they were also a source of slaves. Therefore, the Egyptian Army will supervise the evacuation of all Egyptian citizens from the districts listed, all of which are far from Egyptian territories established on ancient Nubia."

The messenger was shocked. Queen Tiy, overhearing Akhunaton, was appalled and said so immediately. Nonetheless, the message from the king was dutifully recorded and stood as law.

Mother Tiy was furious. She argued with Akhunaton for hours. Even Ai found his sense of political caution strained to the limit. The debate came to naught and ended with Queen Tiy vowing never again to speak to her son.

The message gave Kahotep new information about the king. A pacifist. He had suspected all along that the abolition of the temples, the confiscation of the riches of Amen were only theatrics. The abolition of human sacrifice and death to prisoners, the evacuation of citizens and withdrawal of troops from lands held as Egyptian for centuries suggested that Akhunaton, as he called himself, was incapable of suppressing anyone, including the Priesthood of Amen.

Opportunities abounded for Kahotep, now that Akhunaton was isolated in his new city. Horemheb and Nefertiti were no longer held captive. They resided publicly in Thebes and sent out announcements of their dissatisfaction. Scribes recorded their dissident opinions, resulting in division among the people of Egypt.

Kahotep believed Akhunaton was ignorant of the world outside his sanctuary, that the king did not suspect that Amen's priesthood had reunified. He believed his departures from Karnak had escaped the king's attention. Kahotep felt a surge of self-confidence.

After several weeks, Akhunaton admitted another messenger Horemheb had sent a communique, this time from far south of Thebes, pleading for more support. The Nubians were casting off Egyptian rule everywhere. He needed more soldiers and weapons.

Akhunaton sent a reply: "Evacuate all citizens. Return all soldiers to Egypt."

Three weeks later another messenger arrived with word of outrage from Horemheb. Lady Tiy was sparked with anger and scolded Akhunaton, shaming him for disregarding her opinions after having preached the equality of kings and queens, men and women.

"Very well, Mother Tiy. We will continue this dispute after dinner, and after other business of the day. These summer days are long, and I have another visitor to receive."

"I shall retire after dinner until you are ready for me. If you are *ever* ready for me!"

"We will indeed discuss further the difficulty we are having in Nubia—but I would like you to be present to receive our late evening visitor. He is a judge from the suburbs of Memphis. He has a problem of his own on his hands."

"You will not need my help, I am certain."

"I will not require your assistance, Great Mother. Only your attendance."

"Very well."

The young messenger was asked to dine at the royal table. The dinner conversation was terse and sporadic. Queen Tiy said not one word and displayed a cold manner toward Akhunaton. Both were asked by Akhunaton to attend the meeting with the visiting judge. The emissary agreed to remain silent throughout the exchange.

The judge was a robust man named Hapu. He seemed a compassionate man to Akhunaton, who listened to the man's story intently.

"The essence of the case before me, O King, is that a young man may have been falsely accused of stealing precious jewels from his mother! Yes, his mother is the one who signed the accusation against him! The jewels were found in the young man's room. However, O King, there is much more to this story than these facts only. I have known this woman and her family for many years and I think the mother is being jealous and possessive of her son."

"Tell me," said Akhunaton, "why would this be so?"

"The boy's father died two years ago. Mother and son were alone. The woman fears that her son will abandon her, since he is of an age for courtship and the young ladies are beginning to catch his eye.

"When a young peasant girl captured his heart, it drew out his mother's wrath. She is from an aristocratic family and her son is in love with a peasant girl. She fears he will leave her palace, the city and the life of an aristocrat. Thus, she fears, she would die.

"He left home several times to visit his lover, each visit longer than the last. When he had stayed away for three months, she summoned the guard and swore that she had seen her son leave her bedroom and slip out a window. She also reported that some of her favorite jewels were missing. Well, her son showed up six days later and was arrested! She made us search his camel bags, bedroll, even his room in the palace. It was there that we, or rather she herself, found the jewels. She seemed to know right where they were.

"I am suspicious of her, and she is bringing to bear much pressure on family friendship and legal obligations. The whole matter has become objectionable to me in principle. Yet, I cannot let the young man go free! Thus, I appeal to you, O King, because my obligations to the law conflict with my personal involvement with the family."

"That is prudent of you, Hapu. You are unqualified because of your acquaintance with the people involved."

"I am so grateful that you were available when I sought your audience. Tell me, O King, what would you do if called upon to handle such a spurious dispute?"

Akhunaton turned abruptly to Queen Tiy. His eyes met hers. He said sternly, "Mother Tiy, would you imprison a man for a crime he obviously did not commit?"

Tiy was taken aback. She gasped, "Of course not!"

Akhunaton leaned back in his throne, no crown on his huge skull. He was naked, as usual. No one seemed to notice.

"Would you consider giving the man a life sentence?"

"Why , no! What are you implying, Akhunaton?"

"Does this man have a skill of any kind?" Akhunaton asked the judge.

"Well, yes, he is studying to be an artist and he is very full of ambition. He is also a skilled magician. He is just infatuated with this peasant girl, and has taken time off from his studies…"

"He is obviously very young. Periods of low ambition are no crime. Did you actually see his mother remove the jewels from some container in the young man's room?"

"No one saw her. We were all searching through clothes and travel pouches when suddenly his mother rattled a vase and announced she had found them. When I looked, she was holding them in her hands and the vase was back on the table."

"And your personal impression is that her accusation is a lie?"

"I feel that she is lying."

Again to Queen Tiy: "The people in our new prisons work in the fields, Mother Tiy. They are paid for their work, even though they are prisoners and have committed crimes. I am sorry that we have to treat rough, brutal, greedy people this way, but we have to remove them from gentler members of our society."

"Why are you telling me this, Akhunaton?"

"Because it is obvious that the young man is innocent. This good judge is merely coming to me because he has a personal involvement in the case and is unqualified to judge. I am glad that this is a man so honest! The young man would be the victim of a crime, far greater than the theft of mere jewels, if he were to be imprisoned."

"I would say so, yes," said Tiy cautiously.

"He would work on command, without choice. He would eat, drink, sleep on command. He would lose everything just by losing his personal sovereignty."

"What is your point?"

"I say there is no difference between being an Egyptian imprisoned in Egypt for a crime you did not commit, and being a Nubian in Nubia forced to live under Egyptian soldiers who have turned your homeland into an Egyptian jail."

Tiy was silent. The harshness in her eyes softened with a realization of the depth of his comparison.

Knowing he had proven his point, the king turned to the judge and said, "Let the young man be free because the evidence against him is not sufficient to justify the charges. Grant him a police escort to the township of his choice and protect him along the way. This is by order of the king, Akhunaton."

After the departure of the good judge, Akhunaton discussed the matter of Nubia with Queen Tiy.

"It is generally recognized that territory south of the Fourth Cataract of the Nile is within the former borders of Nubia. Yet Egypt has maintained colonies well south of the Fifth Cataract for over a century now, since Ahmes drove out the Hyksos Tribesmen and started this dynasty of our Kingdom. Since the Hyksos came from the east, what is the purpose of maintaining these southern military bases? You know what their reason was until you took the throne, Lady Tiy: Nubian slaves."

Tiy nodded silently, staring at her strange son.

"The Nubians are free to express resentment of Egyptian residents among them. Most of the Egyptians living in our southern cities are soldiers anyway, so a military withdrawal would constitute a fairly complete evacuation. Let it stand at that: all Egyptian soldiers are to assist in the evacuation of civilians. Then all soldiers will be withdrawn and what was once, will again be, Nubia. Any Egyptians who remain will do so at their own risk, without the benefit of the army."

Tiy shook her head. "What will prevent the Nubians who are uprising from invading Egypt? Killing our people north of the Third Cataract? The Second Cataract? Invading Thebes?"

"Any Nubians who penetrate north of the Fourth Cataract will be met by huge numbers of Egyptian soldiers with orders to kill invaders."

"So, you would fight a war!"

"I would protect Egypt from invaders. I only refuse to command an invasion or defend territories conquered by Egyptian invaders."

"You would not silence an uprising but you would fight invaders? Is this not contradictory?"

"No. Only oppressed, conquered people rebel. If no one invades, no one conquers and future generations need not rebel. By not oppressing the Nubians I seek permanent peace with Nubia."

Queen Tiy remained unimpressed. "I hope your plan works. That is all."

𓂀

Akhunaton's final refusal to support military outposts in Nubia delighted Kahotep immensely. The Beast realized that Akhunaton had no intention of leaving Akhetaton, nor of maintaining Nubian outposts and control over the Nubian-Egyptian border. He was an unmitigated pacifist!

If he will not suppress a Nubian uprising, he will not suppress an Amenist uprising either, reasoned Kahotep. *A perfect adversary: hopelessly idealistic and lacking understanding of human nature.*

Egyptians outside his dream-city have seen his wife and military commander turned against him. I can recruit many more from among the disillusioned men of Egypt. I can recruit an army.

I can imprison or kill this Pharaoh, but who will be his successor? What do I know about his sons, Smenkhara and Tutankhaton?

298

The Beast was finishing another stage of animal experiments in his rock-hewn laboratory. When his subjects died, Kahotep threw the corpses onto a flat rock in the sunlight. In this way he drew to him big, high-flying scavengers: vultures.

On this day, while they pulled apart a monkey's body, Kahotep screeched a few syllables of the native tongue of vultures. A big, jet-winged bird was alarmed. It watched as a man in black robes emerged from the shadows.

The bird cried out, "Ha! You speak! You must be intelligent!"

With little cawing sounds, the scientist-sorceror said, "I am intelligent! I speak your language. I feed you!"

"This is good! This is good, is good, is good!" The vultures all agreed.

"Good-good-good! I will be here tomorrow evening. Food then! Food then!"

He returned the next day and the next day, conversing with the birds regularly. He started teaching the biggest vulture to understand the language of humans. When the huge bird could finally understand rudimentary Egyptian, Kahotep sent her on errands to Thebes, listening to people in the marketplace, in the streets, in the courtyards, especially the courtyards, the private gardens of the Egyptian nobles.

When the Nubians discovered that the rebellion brought no resistance from the Egyptians, resulting instead in the evacuation of their soldiers, they responded with greater rebellion. Riots spread through the cities like fire through grasslands. The withdrawal of Egypt from Nubia was far from orderly as the Nubians, burning houses and throwing stones, behaved like stampeding wild animals or worse.

Many soldiers feared that these dark-skinned, unpredictable people would invade Egypt. Most longed for a time, almost twenty years before, when Amen, the Hidden One, had commanded the Egyptian Army. The soldiers who trudged north were broken in spirit. They returned to Egypt humiliated for they had lost land that had been dominated by Egypt for a century, and for centuries at a time before that. They did not know that, among the faces who would greet them at the end of their journey home, many would be friendly and charming secret priests of the war god himself.

Kahotep used Nefertiti's abandonment of Akhetaton as his greatest propaganda tool. While neither the queen nor the general endorsed the religion of Amen, both spoke out in a constant stream of public declarations against the pacifistic politics of Akhunaton.

Never before was the gulf between Akhunaton and outer Egypt so vast. Never had the division between Pharaoh and common Egyptian been so unbridgeable. Except in Akhetaton, sightings of spacecraft aroused fear and anger instead of faith and hope. Though the priests worshipped in secrecy and practised their craft in isolated caves and hidden indoor shrines, Amen, the Hidden One, had returned to the populace in spirit.

The High Priest Pawah was uniting the enclaves of priests and helping them recruit initiates. Many of these conveniently came from the ranks of returning soldiers, burdened with misgivings and apprehensions. Trudging footsoldiers returned to Egypt proper—and to belief in the Hidden One.

In his tomb-palace beneath Karnak, The Beast formulated plans to either prevent Smenkhara or Tutankhaton from inheriting the throne of Egypt, or else finding a way to control whichever of them replaced the interstellar king. His plans always began with an invasion of Akhetaton.

He used telepathy to prod the demons in the brains of Horemheb and Nefertiti into continuing their streams of letters of protest against pacifist Akhunaton. They issued public proclamations as well, which were copied by scribes and circulated throughout Egypt.

He could use long-distance telepathy with a demon of his own creation as a receiver. A demon-carrier could walk miles, trek for days, hunting the intended victim, and the demon imparted would still be a holographic part of the mind of its maker, Kahotep.

Creating demons was simple: daily, hourly mental projection of a visible, tangible, living and nonetheless imaginary entity. After the image is fully fleshed out, the personality of the entity becomes more defined. When it prowls the mind of its creator like a dragon in a cage, it is ready to be born as an autonomous creature, part of the mind of its creator but completely free of the will of the host-brain it will finally live in. Kahotep had perfected this act of magic better than any other.

He recorded the results of everything in his spellbook, *Ka-Ba-Ra*: his experiments with diseases of grains and simians, the cultivation of future plagues, his contacts, once or twice every week, in the limestone caverns with his priests, most notably Pawah.

To the elite of the priesthood, Amen had truly returned. The Beast was pleased with the progress of his disciples in recruiting initiates and organizing secret ranks. Drugging their ceremonial sacraments with ergotamine, he induced visions as he bellowed commands through tunnels and echo chambers, often "materializing" pieces of parchment to be discovered after awakening from the deep sleeps that followed the hallucinations.

His unseen, illegal army comprised several hundred thousand. Many more joined every day, trained soldiers home from the Nubian border. When he commanded a million, Kahotep planned to invade Akhetaton.

Nefertiti moaned. Her new palace was a prison, though she could come and go if she desired. Sometimes when she did long to escape, her will would abandon her as soon as she began making preparations. She did not know why. She only knew that she felt imprisoned.

She spent her days in tears. When her tears turned to rage, two or three scribes would appear. Nefertiti's rage would vent itself in emotional tirades against the horrible-looking king, her estranged husband. Every word was recorded and sent to Akhunaton or posted in Demotic script in public places.

Horemheb raged. He would awaken every morning next to Nefertiti, who seemed to sleep endlessly. He would sit upright and snarl, obsessed with the Nubian problem—which was the Akhunaton problem, as far as he was concerned. He would pace the room while Nefertiti gradually moaned herself awake. By breakfast he was bellowing about Nubian invaders, downtrodden soldiers and Akhunaton, Akhunaton, Akhunaton! At that point a contingent of scribes would appear and every angry word would be recorded. Copies would be made and circulated throughout Egypt.

"It is fairly obvious that Nefertiti has been possessed," said Akhunaton. "Her messages to me are disjointed, charged with emotion and full of hate. They are considerably less sophisticated, less articulate than I knew her to be capable of. Thus, I believe that only a small part of her mind is functioning, and it is under the control of Kahotep."

Ai and Queen Tiy listened in silence. Finally, Tiy said, "Why did you not prevent this?"

"Only Nefertiti could have prevented it."

Ai said, "That is true. We could have meddled...we just did not."

Tiy was furious. "That is asinine, Ai! Nefertiti is just a *girl!*"

"We offered her knowledge," Ai said. "We offered her the chance to become a *Seshat*, to receive the memory of Ptah through the eye. Now, because she refused, she received something *else* through her eye."

Queen Tiy shook her head. "This will not do."

"It will have to do," said Akhunaton. "We are limited in how we can deal with humans. Choice, even to make mistakes, must be preserved at all costs. She was warned that refusal to acquire knowledge would have consequences. But do you remember what she told you, Mother Tiy? She thought that your knowledge of things cosmic and human had made you— how did she put it?—you, Tiy, were 'strange and unnatural' to her."

Tiy summoned all of her self-control.

"So, we protected her freedom of choice," Akhunaton waved a hand demonstratively, "and she chose to preserve her ignorance. Not her *innocence*, though that is what the people in my city believe. She was not innocent. She was vain and proud and haughty and that was her downfall."

"Now she is rapidly becoming *your* downfall, Akhunaton. Now she no longer has freedom of choice."

"My children know of Kahotep. They are developing their psychic powers, choosing the path of least danger."

"And what of your city of followers?"

"Mass translation, Mother Tiy."

"And what about the rest of Egypt?"

"The rest of humanity will be bound to the bloody wheel of human history, Mother Tiy."

"And you have no intention of preventing mass mistakes?"

"No one learns anything when their mistakes are prevented by others."

"So you choose to do nothing. This has gone on for a year, Akhunaton! For a year, Nefertiti and Horemheb have been imprisoned in their own minds, enslaved by the Hidden One, who intends to destroy you and erase all record of your existence."

"That is true. I have very little time to prepare my people for translation and my children for their rightful throne."

Smenkhara would become the next king of Egypt. He knew it would be a dangerous task. He also knew he had, at the most, three years before he would inherit the throne of Egypt. His father arranged a coronation in the spring of the sixteenth year of his reign, when Smenkhara was fifteen years old. He reverently married his twin sister Meritaton and the next day solemnly accepted the Double Uraeus of an Egyptian king.

In the tunnels beneath the Temple of Karnak in Thebes Kahotep sat up and listened. The blind seer was having visions again. Amenhotep, Son of Hapu, wailed in a loud monotone and thrashed on the stone floor of his cell. Moaning, shrieking, gasping for breath, he uttered the words, "A new king! A new king cometh. Yes. A new king. A boy king. A new king…"

Kahotep entered the dark room with a candle. The blind visionary was caked in his own excrement. Kahotep asked coldly, "Who is this new king? Does he have a name?"

"…A new king…a boy king…boy-king of the star-king. The Aton Disc will be returning! Returning!"

The seer's few coherent words ended in a piercing scream.

"Still you do nothing!"

Tiy was angry again. Akhunaton and Smenkhara sat before her on their thrones. Her brother Ai stood silently beside her.

"For *two years* your wife and queen has been tormented by an evil magician and you allow it! It is obscene."

"What happened is obscene," Akhunaton acknowledged, "but it is not my fault."

"I do not blame you for Nefertiti's demise. I only blame you for prolonging it."

"What shall I do, Mother Tiy?"

"Has the Aton Disc lost its power?"

"Of course not. Aton has the power to control the human body, even the human mind, from afar. Aton can destroy an individual human body at a great distance, with forces similar to lightning or other forces similar to sunlight. And do you know what else the Aton can do? Incinerate an entire city in seconds. And an entire planet, like this world, in moments.

"Now, Mother Tiy, are those not wonderful powers the Aton Disc has? How much force shall we use to make Horemheb and Nefertiti stop writing nasty letters to me? Shall we take control of their minds and bodies and force them to walk back to Akhetaton and be silent forever? Or shall we murder them with powerful weapons? Perhaps we should locate Kahotep and murder *him*. Then we can start incinerating the bodies of his priests. Then we could use hypnotic controls to make the rest of the Egyptian people work very hard for us and believe in our religion. We could even force all Egyptians to learn our cosmology! We could take away their right to think because another Kahotep, another madman, might become leader of some future slave state. Perhaps we should do all of these things, Queen Tiy. There would be far less violence in the world if we did."

"Stop this."

"No, Mother Tiy, I will go on. People who are deprived of control over their own bodies resent it. A mind obsessed with resentment is enslaved by fear. Deprivation of choice results in hate, and people who are enslaved by fear, who then feel hate, cannot be enlightened until the pain and fear and hate are banished at the source.

"Such people would be broken in spirit. Such people have, through absence of choice, been bludgeoned into perpetual hostility. Their anger will end when freedom of choice has been restored to them. Ankh em Ma'at."

Tiy sat in silence.

"What do you think, my son?" Akhunaton turned to Smenkhara.

Smenkhara tilted his head and frowned. "I think that most Egyptians were not ready for this arrival of the Aton Disc."

"I think you are right, Smenkhara. That is the point of this arrival."

"I believe I understand, Father."

"What do you think we should do about your mother?"

"Can we perform an exorcism?"

"Only if Nefertiti gives her consent."

"She will not consent?"

"Not as long as she fears Aton, which, judging by her letters, she fears more now than ever."

"So, she must first choose not to fear Aton nor to hate you, and then decide to submit to an exorcism."

"Yes. She must make those decisions, in that order."

"Then it is up to her and to Horemheb to do combat with their mental parasites. We can only offer the means. We cannot decide for them."

"Can you perform a healing on an unwilling patient?"

"I doubt that such a healing would work. I think it would be meddling with the flow of life, if the recipient was unwilling."

"Very good, Smenkhara. What about an exorcism on an unwilling person?"

"Such an exorcism would not work. That seems certain to me."

"Why not?"

"You once told me that mind parasites feed on fear and exploit weaknesses in the host personality, its defects of character. I have observed that often people cling to their shortcomings and vulnerable conditions. A mind parasite might exploit any unwillingness that its host has to overcome vulnerability."

"That is valid, Smenkhara. Tell me of the two types of moral laws, and how they differ from each other."

"There are moral laws based on prescription, father, that merely consist of *do* and *do not*. These laws are not based on relationships between people and other sentient things, but on memorized dogmas. They constitute a low order of ethics.

"The second, higher order of moral laws are based on descriptions instead of prescriptions. These descriptions are of relationships between people, each other and all other life forms. These must be cause and effect descriptions in which results proceed from actions. They tell of the conditions of the process of life. With this order of law, moral abstention is replaced with freedom of choice. Better, more loving behavior is cultivated when people are aware that they are responsible for the results of their actions. This constitutes a high order of ethical principles."

Queen Tiy laughed. "Smenkhara, you talk more like your father every day."

Akhunaton said, "I am glad your mood has lightened, Mother Tiy."

Queen Tiy smiled. "Your point is well taken, Akhunaton. I think I must start preparing myself for translation, if the political situation in Egypt is as utterly hopeless as you say."

"Egypt has fallen as an empire twice before, Mother Tiy. Egypt will fall again and this time it will stay fallen. Forever."

"Is this inevitable?"

"Yes, but not soon. Egypt will thrive as a civilization for many more centuries. The collapse will be gradual until an invasion from across the sea renders her permanently crippled. Then a series of occupations will punctuate the flow for many centuries."

"That is terrible."

"But you will not live to see this unless you choose to become translated. Then, as a translated being, you will not be a participant in Earthly politics."

"What awaits me after translation?"

"You should know the answer to that, Mother Tiy. You should know that very well by now."

"Will translation be available to me also?" asked Smenkhara. "Yes, my son, but first you must take my place as king and use the power of your throne to protect the race I have created among the Egyptians."

"Suppose I am murdered? I fear that, Father."

"You might be, my son. Even so, you would survive aboard the Aton. You already live there, in flesh, blood and a detailed hologram of your body. You might leave the body you have now — in fact, you must. It will remain a mummified artifact of who and what you are. But do not fear death, my son. After your Egyptian body dies, will you be reunited with your alternate, more perfect body, that already exists in the Aton."

"Thank you, Father. I find that greatly reassuring."

"My son, my love for you has reversed the hate you once felt for me."

"I know, Father."

"That has reassured me more than anything else about the worthiness of this whole human experiment, Smenkhara."

"Bless you, Father."

"Bless you, Smenkhara." Akhunaton leaned forward and kissed his son.

Suddenly, Queen Tiy turned and fled from the room. The sound of her crying echoed through the hallway.

"Why do you weep, Mother Tiy?"

The evening blue beyond the vast windows of her private chambers was the only light. The Queen of Egypt turned slowly to face her strange son. She shook her head.

"Oh, Akhunaton…I have been wrong about much. That is all."

"We are compassionate races, Mother Tiy. We look upon this experiment as a dangerous process, but necessary to the elevation of Mind on this world. In a way, it is like every other childbirth: fraught with potential danger but necessary for the continuation of life."

"There is so much I have yet to understand! Even imparted knowledge causes confusion, arouses unanswered questions."

"That is true, Mother Tiy, and all of us must face the paradoxes and resolve them in our own ways."

"Akhunaton, is this some endless process?"

"As far as any beings know, yes."

"Then what is the point?"

"Ten million people must find ten million answers to that one question, Mother Tiy. That is the point. You are the point. I am the point. There is one question, and the Universe is different answers to it."

"That is an awesome thought, Akhunaton."

"It is the most awesome thought that I have ever contemplated."

"What is your solution, Akhunaton?"

"I have chosen to be an evolutionary midwife, Mother Tiy. That is what I am. A midwife."

She gasped and looked deeply into his face. She knew what he meant, and how dangerous his occupation was.

𓂀

Smenkhara ruled as Pharaoh and continued his training in the mental sciences. His father tutored him, sometimes with his siblings, often alone. He never developed the power to levitate either himself or objects. He failed to sustain long-distance telepathy. Yet, he looked back on his seventeen years of life and applied his consciousness to the development of ethical judgement. He understood the nature of love. He experienced much love daily. He gave his father much love.

Queen Tiy studied the arts of mental concentration. She applied her imagination to the creation of paintings, little renderings of nature in water-pigments on papyrus. She refrained from arguing with Akhunaton about his foreign politics. She seldom spoke with him, but attended the sittings and tutelage of his children often. She confided to her brother Ai that she regretted her sharp words and admitted that he was right that Nefertiti had turned her back on the knowledge that could have saved her.

𓂀

"Nefertiti, there is someone I would like you to meet," said Shep, her host in the mansion in Thebes. Nefertiti stood unsteadily in a shaft of sunlight falling through her bedroom window.

"This is Pawah," said the merchant aristocrat.

A huge man stepped into the light. He towered over Shep, and his body was bound with immense muscles. His eyes were covered by a black mask and he wore the leopardskin toga of a priest of Amen.

"No!" said Nefertiti, her lips curling back. "No! My king was right about your religion. No! No!" She burst into tears, her heart flooded with grief.

"I want to talk to you about salvation," said Pawah, stepping before her and kneeling. "Please listen to me."

"No! No...oh, speak if you must..."

"Nefertiti, you love Egypt."

"Go away…"

"You love all of Egypt and you wish to protect the land and the people. Only you can save Egypt."

"No…go away!" she shrieked at him, lunging with clawed hands, then burst into tears again.

"The Priests of Amen want to save Egypt, Nefertiti. It is not because of us that the Nubians riot at our borders. You know it is the fault of that horrible creature who calls himself the king."

"Be gone…!" Her tears incapacitated her. She feebly pushed at Pawah, moaning and convulsing with sobs as she attempted to struggle.

"Consider it," said Pawah, standing up.

"…You…you are…"

"You know he is right," Shep said, grinning and departing.

When Nefertiti was alone her anguished wails subsided, her sobs quieted, then silence emanated from her chamber. She broke a jeweled fish made of blue fiance and used the jagged edge to drain her blood through her wrists.

Chapter Thirty-One

Horemheb had always had an affinity for Ra. As a young man, before being swept into the religion of Aton, he had worshipped Ra and made journeys to Onn to offer his devotion in the ancient temple there. He had also been impressed by the priests of Ptah in Memphis. Unconsciously quite monotheistic, Horemheb liked the idea that Ptah was the all-God, the Universe and the Mind of the Universe, the supreme deity whose most important aspect was Ra, the solar Eye of God.

Pawah knew much about Horemheb. As he neared the general's chambers, he silently rehearsed his arguments. Shep burst in ahead of him and blurted out the necessary introductions. Then he stepped behind Pawah and retreated out the door.

The dragon inside Horemheb purred at the sight of a fellow warrior.

"You are a priest of Amen," said Horemheb, eyeing the mask and toga.

"Yes, Horemheb. Does that surprise you?"

"No, not at all."

"Like you, I fear for the future of Egypt, Horemheb." The silence that followed united them. "It is a pity that my religion has been abolished," continued Pawah. "Our war-priests would have a ready solution to the Nubian uprisings, my General."

After a long while Horemheb replied, "Yes, I appreciate that."

"I am sympathetic to your feelings, General. I have been reading your pronouncements avidly. I hope that the king takes your words to heart."

"But he will not! I know him. He is a lost idealist who thinks peace can be bought with privileges."

"Then, would you call him deluded?"

"Of course. His ideas are absurd."

"Do you know that certain…priests consider him to be a demon?"

Horemheb trembled at the word 'demon.' He did not answer.

"You know that my religion is still illegal to practise."

"Of course…I am aware of that."

"And under the rule of this disc-from-the-sky, we are forced to face defeat at the hand of Nubia."

"Do not tell me this," Horemheb snarled.

"As you wish, General."

The two men stood facing each other in silence for a moment, then Horemheb exploded into rage. "He is demented! I am certain of it. He is unnatural. Have you ever seen him?"

"No."

"He looks horrible. He is not a man, he does not understand men. He thinks we are all like animals."

"Is this so? Tell me more."

"It is that evil disc! I fear it, I always have. When it appeared in the sky…I felt afraid. I dislike fear, though I have felt it in battle, years ago, when I served under Amenhotep III. In war, it was not so bad because I was fighting, I could fight, I could kill to avert my own death…But this Aton Disc, it is unnatural, demonic…"

"You said that."

"Yes, so I said it! It is fearsome, strange. I can feel its power. It makes loud sounds, it looks like metal, yet it flies! It is strange, unnatural…demonic."

"How can we evict it from our skies?"

"Cast that filthy king out of Egypt! Kill his sons, that is the only way. But that would cause the world to end, because, demon or not, he *is* the Pharaoh."

Pawah nodded solemnly. "I ask you: can a demon be the true Pharaoh? I believe, others believe, that this is a trick, a trick of Seth, to take over our world by deception."

Horemheb raged, then snarled, "That might be true."

"Tell me about his sons. Tell me about Smenkhara."

Horemheb subdued his anger. His attention was caught by muffled voices in a far hallway.

"It is nothing, General. Please tell me about Smenkhara."

The voices subsided, the footsteps faded. Horemheb closed his eyes in concentration. "He used to hate Akhunaton."

"Oh?" Pawah gave his full attention. "How does he feel about his father now?"

"They have resolved their conflicts."

"I see. Is their truce a happy one?"

Horemheb strained the muscles in his face, then shook his head. "The last I remember, they were happy together."

"I understand. Tell me about Smenkhara."

"He is crippled. He now walks fairly well, but he cannot run nor dance. He is intelligent, a very serious boy. He studies mathematics and the law. I do not think he possesses the strange mental powers that Akhunaton's daughters do. *They* are unnatural."

"Tell me about them."

"They talk only of the king's mad ideas about nature and astronomy. They are very tall—Meritaton and Ankhasenpaaton are taller than their twin brothers. Some say they have levitated certain things. Sometimes they stare at each other for hours without talking, staring into each other's eyes, sitting with their legs folded, in silence, staring. Sometimes breathing strangely, fast and furiously or else slowly and deep. Their father teaches them these strange practices."

"It sounds like black magic," said Pawah.

"They are not natural. They are not human."

There was a scuffling of feet outside the corridor. Abruptly, Shep slid into the room. He whispered something to Pawah, who looked up gravely and said: "Nefertiti is dead."

"No!" Horemheb clutched at the air with groping hands. His teeth were clenched and his eyes widened with fury.

Pawah pushed Shep back out of the room, then stepped toward Horemheb.

"Leave me!" Horemheb bellowed.

"As you wish, General."

As Pawah left the room he heard the anguished wails and screams of rage.

Rumors of Nefertiti's death trickled out of Thebes because communiques from the queen and Horemheb stopped. It was as if the queen had suddenly ceased to exist.

Akhunaton said, "I sensed her death in my dreams last night."

"What did you dream?" Smenkhara asked.

"That I heard her call to me and I flew in a disc in the direction of her voice. She called to me from out in the sea and she drowned while I was searching for her."

"I am sorry, Father. I, too, believe she is dead."

"You loved Nefertiti, my son, did you not?"

"Yes, Father, I loved her."

"So did I, even if our life together was tainted with pathos and tragedy."

"Do you think…?" Smenkhara could not voice his fear.

"Do I think that someone murdered her?"

"That is what I meant to ask."

"I do not know. In my dream, she drowned."

"So death seduced her."

"Yes, Smenkhara, it would seem so."

"Perhaps she chose it, Father."

"Death is always chosen, Smenkhara. It can always be avoided."

"I do not understand this entirely, but I will remember it."

Akhunaton leaned forward, placing one hand on his son's shoulder. "Perhaps you should receive the imparted knowledge."

"Receive the memory of Ptah? Unite with Seshat?"

"Yes. Receive the beam of light through the eye from Aton, the illumination imparted by Yod himself."

"Yod is a being composed of light."

"A mind composed of energy, yes."

"A natural intelligence?"

"Yes, Yod is native to this Universe of stars and worlds."

"Then I would like to commune with Yod and receive his imparted knowledge."

"Remember, son, it cannot improve your character. It cannot make you a better person, not wiser, not smarter. It can only increase your memory to include a visionary history of the Universe and all things. I have received such imparted knowledge several times.

"I left the Horizon in Heaven for this, the Horizon of Earth. I created for myself this body, which I now inhabit."

"I understand that."

"I will not live among you much longer, Smenkhara. Another year at most."

"Then will you, too, like Osiris, depart back to Seti on the Aton Disc?"

"Oh, no! I have no doubt that I shall be delivered directly into the hands of Amen."

"Then you will be killed!"

"No, only imprisoned. I could live forever in this body, if I choose. I might not choose to if Kahotep decides to torture me while I live in it, or perform the Obscene Rite on my brain. He might do anything, anything at all to me."

"Do you think Kahotep will allow me to be Pharaoh?"

"That depends on the people of Egypt. Will they tolerate the murder of their Pharaoh?"

"I must surround myself at all times with people who are loyal to me."

"Yes, Smenkhara, and there are many such people. With their protection, no harm can come to you."

"I am grateful. Ankh em Ma'at."

"Ankh em Ma'at."

The sun was rising. The circle of priests hid among the rocks around the mouth of a cave.

"We must! We must see!"

"No!" a voice replied in a loud, throaty cry. "No! If he is still in communion with Amen, then he might die!"

"But it has been hours! The Hidden One gives rapture for only half the night! Pawah must be sleeping by now."

"Pawah has awakened!" boomed a voice from inside the cave.

The High Priest of Amen stepped from the cave. All eyes upon him, Pawah spoke.

"I have received an oracle! Amen has said the gods are displeased with Egypt! A demon was sent by Seti to test our faith in Ptah's supreme manifestation, which is Amen. As long as The Heretic rules, greater and greater plagues and pestilence shall be visited upon Egypt!"

Voices murmured. The jumbled boulders chattered with the shocked responses of the hidden priests.

"Amen says it is up to us to dethrone the Criminal King."

More voices were heard among the rocks. Finally, someone cried out:

"How shall we dethrone him?"

Pawah frowned. His eyes narrowed, peering through the slits in his mask. "Amen says—that is up to us."

"How shall we enter his city? We have sent assassins in and we do not hear from them again!"

"We must recruit more initiates! Every day soldiers return from Nubia. Go back among the people! Go back to your ordinary lives. Do not reveal your loyalty to the Hidden One. Just look for those whose sympathies can be cultivated and mention these prophecies discreetly and always in connection with Amen.

"Now go! All of you, go!"

Kahotep completed his experiments on grain molds and journeyed for several weeks by caravan, posing as a grain merchant. In his absence his Inner Circle prowled the tunnel complex and took care of the monkeys. They pilfered from the mastabas at night, stealing offerings and departing through hidden corridors that led back to Karnak.

When Kahotep returned, he called the vultures he had sent to spy on the human population.

"New king, new king!" said one of the huge black birds, screeching in his own tongue.

"Good, good," said Kahotep, cawing in the vulture's language.

"New king!" another bird chattered. "New king with old king. New king and old king. Father-son. Father-son."

"Yes yes yes. Queen dead." still another bird declared.

"Queen not dead! Queen not dead!" a fifth bird insisted.

"Queen dead, queen dead," argued the other bird.

"Queen alive! Queen alive!" The last bird was getting furious.

"Stop!" screeched Kahotep.

The birds were silent, regarding him with hostility. He fed them raw meat cut into strips. "Tell me calmly for more."

"New king like old king," one of the birds said. "New king like old king."

Kahotep learned little more than that there was a new king and there was a difference of opinion about the death of Nefertiti. He already knew the truth from his priests and from his travels.

Not long after his journey with the grain caravan a blight afflicted fields of oats on both sides of the Nile.

Akhunaton received confirmation of Nefertiti's death from Tefnut.

"Please tell me the cause of her death."

Tefnut sent him a wave of sympathy, then thought into his mind, "She ended her life by her own hand."

Akhunaton glimpsed briefly the image of his human wife, robed in her own blood. "I am deeply sorry, Shu."

While his wife-partner shared his human mind, Shu-in-Akhunaton wept on the bare floor of his chamber.

The death of Nefertiti plunged Egypt into a storm of doubt and anxiety. Soldiers returned home from Nubia with stories of riots and destruction in the south. Rumors of a blight laying to waste fields of oats and barley increased the worries of the people.

Yet, inside Akhetaton musicians still played and dancers still danced, citizens enjoyed much time to themselves. The city feasted nightly on the wealth of the gardens, rejoicing and reveling in the eternal procession of seasonal changes.

Akhunaton gave all his remaining possessions to his people. He distributed his jewels and works of art from terrace balconies and from the window of the bridge across the main avenue of the city. He gave his bedding to a poor family from the south and his clothes to a pilgrim he found naked in the rain. The king wore rags when he wore anything at all. He was unable to walk without a staff and would have appeared depraved and deteriorated to Nefertiti or Horemheb. But the smiles and the look of rapture that enveloped his face as he stared above the sun was a message of ecstasy written with his body to his family and courtiers. They were beginning to understand him. Smenkhara hugged his father often and told him that he loved him. Akhunaton returned affection to the boy he had always loved so much.

The king seemed to be a race apart from the human, and the people of Akhetaton seemed to be a world apart from Egypt. Rumors spread through the city that a time of great transformation awaited them. Music pulsated and rang over the fields and little hills surrounding Akhetaton.

The city had existed for only ten years. Three million people lived there and the brisk birth rate quickly swelled the number toward four million. Everyone was sheltered and well fed. With rare exceptions there was no death nor sickness. There had been tragedies, but the dance had not been interrupted. The happy citizens of Akhenaton were unaware that outside their city a storm of doubts and fears had spread a shadow over the rest of Egypt.

The king needed to know that there was famine to the south and west. The messenger from the Temple of Aton in Thebes had followed his unusual route to Akhetaton, running through the fields, crossing the Nile by ferryboat and heading north along the edge of the desert. When night came he would cut west through the mountains and enter the king's city to deliver his message about the grain blight.

But the messenger never reached the mountains. He was ambushed by a little man named Anpu, who cast the lad's body to the jackals and spirited all of the boy's possessions back to Thebes, to Pawah, High Priest of Amen.

Kahotep was quite pleased with his experiments. The grain spores had been very destructive: two new diseases were destroying oats and barley. Perhaps millet and wheat should be afflicted, too? No, that might be too severe…

Through certain brothels that specialized in young boys, Kahotep had purchased a number of human subjects. His experiments on simian diseases would next be performed on these wretched human beings whose bodies would receive his newly-developed bacterial strains.

"I said the gods are displeased, Horemheb," Pawah repeated, "so they take away the grain of the fields. How else can you explain it? You worship Ptah, my General; you worship Ra. Remember the highest form of Ra: it is Amen-Ra. Remember that!"

"Amen-Ra," Horemheb repeated over and over to himself. "Amen-Ra. Amen-Ra…"

"Amen-Ra is an excellent source of power to call upon, when your wrath at the punishment of Egypt becomes overpowering, Horemheb. Remember that. Amen-Ra."

All major buildings in inner Akhetaton had in the ceilings of their central rooms a round opening thirty to thirty-five feet in diameter. A circle of pillars supported these and open-air courtyards with potted plants stood at the base of the pillars. The only exception was the palace of Nefertiti, now abandoned and heavily guarded.

The people of Akhetaton saw the sky boats frequently during the afternoon and evening hours when they made dizzying shows in the sky that lasted for hours. The discs often descended directly into the wide circular opening in the rooftops of the king's house, the government offices, and the temples and palaces of Akhenaton, the city that was the Second Horizon of the Aton.

"Father," said Neferneferura one morning, meeting Akhunaton on his terrace. "I experienced a brief empathic contact with a vulture in the locust bush a few minutes ago."

"Tell me about it," invited the king.

"The bird was very inquisitive about me."

"Did it say anything? I have taught you the vulture's tongue."

"It said nothing. It looked me in the eye and I sensed it was intensely curious about me, Actually, about all of us here."

"Did you get any impression of why?"

"Yes. I felt it had been taught to understand the human tongue and was following me to eavesdrop on conversations I might have. To be truthful, I received a very specific mental impression from this bird, and it was one of intrusiveness."

Akhunaton placed his huge hand on his daughter's small one, which rested on his knee. He looked into her eyes and smiled. "The bird was a spy, Neferneferura. I have noticed black vultures watching and following people, spying. It is unnatural; birds are frequently employed by Kahotep to be his eyes and ears. He has tried to use human spies, too, but they are all easily found and easily seduced into Aton's festive spirit."

Neferneferura looked about, searching for a glimpse of a vulture.

"Never fear," said Akhunaton. "The mind of a bird is so limited by self-interest that it could never comprehend what Kahotep needs to know about this city of transformation."

In his rages and storms of anger during the months following Nefertiti's death, Horemheb summoned the power of Amen-Ra more and more frequently. He had been told little other than that Nefertiti had committed suicide and he wanted to know no more. He wholeheartedly blamed Akhunaton for the death of the woman he loved. After a year, his hatred culminated in his initiation into the religion of the Hidden One.

Queen Tiy's mother, Thuya, died in her sleep in the eleventh year of Akhetaton. She was buried in royal splendor in a rock tomb on the edge of the Valley of the Kings.

Tiy grieved, but briefly. Her parents were very old and Thuya had been happy. Tiy felt her sorrow give away quickly to the glad knowledge that such was an opportunity to rejoice.

Barely five months passed before her father, Yuia, joined his wife in an eternal embrace at the edge of the Valley of the Kings. Then Queen Tiy felt both joy and sorrow mixed in her stinging tears. Her heart was lightened by the loss of her father and mother and the freedom it gave her.

The *Atet* appeared in mid-sky an hour after sunset. It grew until it became an immense light. Then it dwindled, increased again and slowly became a ring of rotating lights encircling a cluster of white rays. It descended rapidly.

Smenkhara looked up at the stars from the center of the open-sky courtyard in his father's house. He was prepared to receive visionary knowledge imparted through his eye. As light filled the open chamber, he waited to be transported into the starship, as he had been many years before.

Instead, light filled his eyes until it burst into flashing pulsations. The light that filled his brain became a stream of mental images, overpowering his natural senses. He beheld an immense mental explosion and his brain rang with the name:

Ptah!

He saw the flash of light condense into stars. He saw the stars live for billions of years and some of them slowly brighten and die. Some burst into light and died, others shrank, darkened and vanished into the black night.

Out of these imploded stars came the timespace explorers: starships from an infinitude of Universes connected by the first black holes formed in this Universe. The explorers surveyed, withdrew, and were followed by the engineers. Working with Eternity, always at the edge of the timespace doorways that rotating singularities are, the timespace engineers used electromagnetic slingshots, magnetic nets and occasional detonations to propel many forms of matter, from asteroids to clouds of hydrogen, into stable orbits around the black holes.

Other stars were being born, living vast star-lives and dying. Some flared into novas, supernovas, or collapsed into black holes. Stars with planetary systems were born. Star-dust coalesced into planets wrapped in gaseous atmospheres, liquid oceans lapping the shores of islands and continents. Lively planets spun and circled through space as life took birth on their skins.

The spaces between worlds filled with starships. Frequently at first, then less often, wars were fought among planets. Conflict was abandoned as contacts between worlds increased.

Smenkhara watched the creation of the Ra system out of dust and gas. He saw the nativity of his planet. Then Smenkhara saw the Age of Volcanoes. He saw the Age of Oceans and the beginning of the pageant of evolution.

Smenkhara saw the great collision that pierced the second planet of the Ra system and gave his native world its moon.

Smenkhara saw the Age of Dragons. He followed the evolution of the first true humanoids from small, slender two-legged dinosaurs. He witnessed their first contact with extraterrestrial humanoids and he watched their ascent into the stars. Then he saw the great asteroid collision that ended the Age of Dragons.

Smenkhara observed the Age of Birds and Behemoths. He saw Gaia becoming cooler and the volcanoes subside. The birds and beasts grew huge until many birds could no longer fly but hunted on two legs like the carnivorous dinosaurs before them.

Smenkhara also witnessed the evolution of life on other worlds in the Ra system. He saw life emerge on the planet-sized moons of the fourth planet, a gas giant, star-like. Conflict between the humanoids of the two moons resulted in an interplanetary war. The resulting explosion of the gas giant scattered ice throughout the Ra system which condensed into a band of asteroids. It also burned all life off the third planet and from the vortex of the detonation a fiery body was ejected. It crossed the orbit of Gaia, the second planet and the near-collision hurled Gaia into a new orbit, third from the sun.

All planets in the Ra system were now lifeless save one: the jewel of the Ra system, Gaia, had been preserved by miracles of chance accentuated by intelligent, controlled intervention.

Smenkhara saw the evolutionary process of hominids on Gaia hastened by extra-terrestrial interventions. The three waves of evolution were punctuated by severe ice ages caused when debris from the violent death of the sister planets vaporized vast quantities of ocean water.

Then Smenkhara saw the fourth wave of human evolution begin in Egypt:

Thoth, whose body was engineered of human genes to be genetically compatible with a woman. The most highly-evolved human female was chosen and given the Living Information imparted through her eye. Her name was Seshat, because she had inherited the Memory of Ptah. They ruled for two thousand years. Thoth was succeeded by Osiris.

Osiris ruled for two thousand years, as the Egyptian people swiftly evolved. Osiris ascended into the heavens aboard the Aton Disc, leaving many descendants who were genetically compatible with evolving human females. This was represented mythically by his dismemberment, reconstitution and the belief that his penis stayed on Earth as a fertility principle among men.

Smenkhara then viewed the reign of Horus, his father's first humanoid form, and he saw the return of Horus to the sky.

The boy-king witnessed the first theft of life from the pineal gland of a murdered human victim by Kahotep, a hermit in the desert who had been trained as a scientist-priest. He saw then the terrible parade of human history that followed, the writing of murder upon murder upon ages of human lives by the Eater-of-Lifetimes, the vampire, Kahotep.

Smenkhara saw the return of his father to Egypt in the form of Akhunaton.

Smenkhara awoke from the visions as the *Atet* ascended into the night sky.

※※※

"You are right, Father," Smenkhara said soberly. "Imparted knowledge did not make me smarter, nor wiser. It has only made me more aware of my origins and of all of our possible destinies. I understand why Queen Tiy fears for our future. She believes violence is a last resort against Kahotep."

"Yes," nodded Akhunaton. "What do you think about that?"

"It is her moral paradox and she has to resolve it in her own way."

"What do *you* think of the use of violence against Kahotep?"

"I think it will stain future generations with even more unneccessary bloodshed. I think that Kahotep or even just the terrible spirit he has created in the minds of Egyptians will continue to play out the death-game of history."

"That is probably true, Smenkhara. And this principle confers upon us grave responsibility, for our smallest actions have cosmic repercussions."

𓂀

"We are completely sealed in," said Ai, pondering with detachment the realization that was upon him.

318

Queen Tiy spoke with extreme control in her voice, "Messengers leaving Akhetaton or attempting to reach us are killed. We are watched by two spies with an
ancient lens device, who hide in the eastern cliffs. We cannot get word even to
Thebes—and Nefertiti is dead by her own hand. Horemheb has vanished again and
soldiers returning home from Nubia report riots and rebellion in the colonies. We—
Egypt—have lost. The Hidden One has successfully reorganized his war-priests. The
ranks of his secret initiates have swollen into a huge army. Tell me, Akhunaton, how
do you intend to meet the threat of revolution?"

"Peacefully," Akhunaton replied.

The Priests of Amen had predicted famine: as blight spread through the grain
fields, famine was imminent. The Priests of Amen were now predicting plague.

Kahotep smiled over the body which lay on the stone floor of his cell. The bacteria had survived the transfer from the monkey to the dead boy's serum. The plague
was ready and the secret army had more than a million soldiers.

Each in turn, the daughters of Akhunaton received imparted information from
the Aton Disc. At the end of the sixth night, Beketaton awoke with the memory of
Ptah in her brain and hurried out to join her sisters. Her wish was not to discuss what
they had learned, but to meditate on it in the presence of others who also knew.

"It is nearly time, Smenkhara," spoke Akhunaton gently. "You know about the
rebel priest and human parasite. You know of all the danger you will face. And you
know about your double who awaits you aboard the Aton.

"I will be removed from the throne. According to the law, you will replace me.

" I have counseled you in ethics, but I have not made you ethical. I have merely
spoken to you at length of the problems and paradoxes of ethical thought. What can
make you a more ethical person?"

"Love," said Smenkhara.

Their spell had begun to captivate her.

Queen Tiy sat among her granddaughters, meditating, looking over the edge of
the terrace, far out over the city of Akhetaton, the Nile, and the blue hills under the
gleaming sky.

Suddenly Meritaton broke the silence. "Grandmother, you need not fear for the
future of Egypt. You need only make your heart feather-light and then leap."

"Leap?" Queen Tiy raised an eyebrow. "Is that the meaning of the vision I just
received?"

"Yes. The vision we shared was about the leap through the Horizon of Heaven."

Neferneferura added, "It is simple: whenever a heart has been prepared, whenever it is ready to leap, that soul shall be translated. Simply and instantly. There is no other way."

Meritaton continued. "Usually individuals are prepared for translation by shamans, the women and men they call 'wise.' But here are too many people. We must prepare them and—translate! They will make the leap together."

"And," said Neferneferuaton the Little, "they love you most, Grandmother Tiy. You shall be the one to lead them."

Chapter Thirty-Two

Horemheb and Pawah collaborated on the invasion. "We will strike first with barges. A hundred barges carrying one hundred men each. They are being built on the west bank of the Nile, just upstream from Akhetaton. The current will silently draw them to the king's city in about five hours. If we begin at sunset, the first barges will arrive at midnight. Of course, many citizens will still be awake. We have reports of their bonfires lasting until dawn! But they will probably be in stupors and unable to fight."

"Akhunaton is a king who does not believe in fighting," Horemheb remarked sullenly.

"That will make it all much easier," Pawah smiled.

The barges were finished and secreted along a remote bank of the great river, hidden by a veil of tall papyrus reeds.

One hundred thousand soldiers began taking their positions in the many outposts beyond the eastern cliffs. Another hundred thousand took their posts in the cities and townships west of Akhetaton. In addition, multitudes of secret soldier-priests had been surreptitiously alerted to be prepared for a journey to Akhetaton.

Indoctrinated that the alien king was a demon and an impostor and not the rightful king of Egypt at all, the rabid followers of Amen awaited orders to march, to bloody their swords and to obey a new king.

"I love you, Father."

"I love you, too, Smenkhara."

"It is almost time."

"Yes, the time for translation is almost upon us. You and Tutankhaton and your sisters should stay together, with Ai. Sitting in a circle, you are at your peak of power. Tutankhaton is betrothed to Ankhasenpaaton, so everything is ready in the clock of cosmic time."

"Where will you be?"

"I will meet the soldiers and allow them to take me captive. I will stay alive long enough to see that no harm comes to you."

"Father, I wonder if they will kill you and then kill us all."

"No. They will refrain from killing this family for one reason, something that every soldier understands better than anything else."

"What is that, Father?"

"Fear. They are afraid of us."

Amenhotep, son of Hapu was screaming again.

Kahotep pressed his ear against the wall to hear every word.

"I…I see fires! Dancers and…fires! Hundreds of dancers and they are *dancing into the fire!* They are *burning up!*" He screamed and was silent.

The Beast was content. He cetainly he understood *that* premonition! The followers of that creature-king were irresponsible children whose lives were spent in dance and merriment. Now, there was a fire on its way. *We will burn them,* thought Kahotep. *We will burn the dancers. Burn all of them. Burn them alive.*

Amenhotep, Son of Hapu screamed again.

Not even Pawah knew that the Hidden One was a man. But Pawah did know that Amen was a living thing, a god-in-man-form, much closer to human than Akhunaton was. Pawah inspected the lookout point that Amen himself was to occupy and arranged the secret caravan that would carry the Hidden One across the desert to the cliffs east of the city.

Kahotep emerged from the tunnels beneath Karnak the day before the invasion. He traveled in a canopied chariot drawn by eight horses with a priest at the reins. No human eye glimpsed the Hidden One. He was escorted by a caravan until he reached the mountains where he slipped away to his hidden post on the clifftops overlooking Akhetaton.

The battle would be over by then. But he did not need to witness the invasion— he needed to supervise the imprisonment and execution of Akhunaton and the choosing of the next Pharaoh.

He admitted to himself that this last problem did not have a really good solution: barring from choice both Smenkhara and Tutankhaton, who would Akhunaton's successor be? He *did* have a personal favorite:

Horemheb.

With his family, his mother and his children, before him, with Ai seated next to him and the setting sun touching the hills west of the Nile, Akhunaton felt the perfection of the moment settle like the instant of stillness between heartbeats. Drumbeats. All of the subtle intervals.

"Dear Mother," he said at last, "I have felt the love and trust in the future unfold in you like the Lotus of a Thousand Petals blossoming in your heart. You shall lead the dance, Mother Tiy.

"And you, my children, will return to my personal temple after the soldiers arrive. You will be safe there, but you must stay together. And remember: they fear you. You must treat your captors like they themselves were captured animals, frightened and ready to bite.

"So be gentle with your conquerors, my children. Be gentle."

His words ended and he was silent for many moments. They meditated until the sun was gone and the amber sky was darkening.

Finally, Queen Tiy stood and said, "It is time. I can feel it. Now."

She danced to the edge of the terrace, her lithe, ageless figure undulating, gyrating, spinning, leaping—dancing. The spirit of many drums, many musicians, flowed through her and all of the dancers became one dancer: Queen Tiy. She danced above the streets, above the city buildings, above the open-air Temple of Aton, which sprawled just a short distance away.

She danced out of the king's house. She danced through the streets. Like the first raindrop to fall leading the others out of a cloud, like the first molecule to come out of solution and crystallize, the dancing Queen Tiy drew all of the dancers and all the musicians together, drumming, skipping, twirling and flowing in the direction of the Great Temple of Aton.

Tiy danced around the temple in a clockwise path as multitudes joined her in gyroscopic pirouettes. From the terrace, the two sons and six daughters gazed down upon the spectacle and meditated, their minds open to the radiance of the moment, the life of the music.

The barges were cut adrift. One hundred barges carried ten thousand men inside their huge, flat hulls, all armed with spears, arrows and swords. All ten thousand made the long trip in complete silence.

The few out on the decks under the starry dome of the night could not tear their eyes from the sky. They watched the stars in silence and terror.

Pilot Tem guided the *Aton's* descent into the atmosphere. Slowly illuminating the disc, he caused the starship to become more and more visible to creatures on the Earth as it approached.

Peser and Pewero had been watching the strange festivities through their crude telescope. They did not know that the woman who led the dance was Queen Tiy. They only knew that every citizen seemed to follow her around and around the temple. They noticed the upright gold panels atop the rows of stone cubes were beginning to gleam with radiant light. The temple sang with a choir of celestial voices.

Pewero pointed urgently to the sky. A vast rotating ring of lights was descending from the zenith of the starry dome of Nuit.

"Holy Amen," said Peser in awe, "it is Aton."

"Let me see!" Pewero snatched the telescope from Peser.

"Give it back!"

Pewero peered through the lenses and gasped aloud, dropping the wooden tube. The glass lenses shattered and the wood splintered on the rock.

"You fool! You dropped it!"

Peser leaped forward and pushed Pewero. They struggled at the edge of the cliff as the starship drew near. Overcome suddenly by fear, they froze, staring up at the the vast disc, the rows of lights, the blinding rays.

"Look!" Pewero pointed.

The two spies could see that the dancing multitudes had followed the lead figure into the temple courtyard. A serpentine wave of human beings wove through the temple gates and past the awesome temple facade. They were dancing, leaping, spinning toward the central altar. The gold panels glowed with multicolored lights.

"Look there!" Peser pointed toward the starship.

It hovered only a few miles above the Great Temple. As the celebrants danced into the temple grounds, brilliant rays glared down from the belly of the starship and a beam of light was reflected up from the gold panels back to the starship until the entire temple ground blazed with white radiance.

"They are burning! They are burning up!" Pewero was nearly mad with fear.

Far below, the dancers continued to move past the temple facade of towering colossi, in a steady stream of moving limbs and heads and bellies, toward the central altar. The obelisk had been activated: the tip was blinding white and the panels were singing.

Queen Tiy led the populace into the color-shifting beam that obscured the altar stone—

Fearless, uplifted by the spirit of the moment, inspired by the dance of Queen Tiy, the people of Akhetaton weighed their hearts against the Feather of Truth and found the Universe to be loving—

They vanished from the face of the Earth.

𓂀

"It must be so," Peser mumbled over and over. "He was a demon. He led his followers into the fire of a dragon. They were burned up, right before our eyes. He *was* a demon. The Aton Disc was his dragon. It burned those people into nothing. It must be so. He *was* a demon. It *must* be so!"

"Silence!" Pewero struck the raving Peser on the back of his head. "Look!"

The starship had swiftly ascended and taken its place as a light among the stars. The Temple of Aton was silent. Below, the city was entirely empty. Akhetaton was abandoned.

Pewero pointed to the river. The first of the barges had arrived. A row of men with poles stood on the deck of each, pushing it to the shore.

The invaders had landed.

Their black figures bristling with speartips and arrowheads, cautiously, the soldiers crept through the utterly empty buildings. Many feared the Heretic King was not such a pacifist after all. Grim, unblinking eyes searched the dark facades and rows of pillars for an ambush.

The soldiers searched the streets, the temples, the government offices of the city, until they were satisfied that the citizens of Akhetaton had—somehow—vanished.

"What do you mean—burned up?" Pawah was impatient.

Horemheb, clutching his sword, was barely suppressing his rage.

Pewero groveled. "We saw it! It came out of the sky. The people— they danced! *Danced*, right up the steps of their damned temple to the altar. Then that dragon-disc shot down a pillar of fire and every man and woman was burned up in the flames!"

Pawah took Horemheb aside. "It makes no sense, General."

"I knew Akhunaton was evil! He abolished human sacrifice—then sacrificed all of his followers! I knew it! He is evil after all."

"Then you do not think these two are lying?"

Horemheb shrugged. "Torture one and then the other. See if they change their stories. I am going to join my troops and search the city myself."

"Horemheb! It is good to see you again!"

The General froze. Akhunaton was walking calmly down the steps of his house with open arms, smiling at the general and the troops he led.

"Do not fear me, Horemheb! It is over. I made light the hearts of all the people who would hear my message. I see you now command the rage and hatred of those whose hearts remained heavy. Do not fear me, Horemheb. I come not to threaten you."

"Take him into custody," commanded Horemheb.

Ten soldiers ran up the steps and brought down the huge and strange king. They bound Akhunaton's arms and feet.

"Be careful!" bellowed Horemheb. "Do not hurt him! We must keep them all alive."

Soldiers surrounded and entered the king's house. Horemheb led them through every room, every hallway and corridor until they found the central chamber. They entered the meditation room of Akhunaton's personal temple. They were met there by Ai and saw the faces of the strange-looking children, eight of them, staring calmly with eyes wide and faces blank with concentration. The general was speechless.

A young man wearing the double Uraeus crown stood and crossed his chest with the crook and the flail, speaking sternly, "Behold, you are in the presence of the King of Egypt, and you shall obey my commands as law."

Horemheb threw down his spear and roared with fury. The soldiers drew back, spears raised.

Smenkhara tilted his head back nonchalantly. "Lower spears in the presence of the King!"

Reluctantly, the soldiers obeyed.

"Seize him!" bellowed Horemheb, pointing to Smenkhara.

Two soldiers obeyed and Smenkhara was taken from the chamber.

"You, you, you—stand guard. Ten of you—guard these people!" Horemheb was close to helpless rage. He turned suddenly to Smenkhara. "What did your father do with the rest of his people?"

"That does not concern you. There is no one here except us, my father's little family. Everyone else is gone and shall never be seen in Egypt again."

"That is a lie! This is a trick! Where are they? What did you do with them? Where are they hiding?"

"Do not fear, Horemheb. No concealed multitudes will ambush a single soldier of yours."

"*You lie!* If harm comes to a single soldier, every one of you will die!"

"And if no harm comes?"

"Then…we will keep you as prisoners."

"Search the city, Horemheb. You have found everyone in it you will find."

By dawn only one possible conclusion stared Horemheb in the face: Akhetaton was deserted.

The people of Akhetaton teleported aboard the *Aton* had been directed by the energy folds of Yod to the many living quarters that comprised most of the hull of the starship. Still singing, the people of Akhetaton danced aboard the disc they had venerated as a god. Somehow they knew they were in another world and that was a great cause to rejoice.

Yod knew that one victim of horrible injustice had been denied rejoicing with the rest. Blind, he was imprisoned under the Temple of Karnak. Tem, Geb and Tefnut departed from the *Aton* as dawn fell upon Egypt. They flew south to Thebes to rescue Amenhotep, Son of Hapu, seer and prophet.

Amenhotep, Son of Hapu, awoke to the blackness that he had faced for the four decades since his captor had gouged out his eyes. His acute clairvoyance told him he was alone in these tunnels. Alone except for the blank minds of the Inner Circle, those living automatons controlled by Kahotep. They alone haunted the subterranean hallways and corridors beneath Karnak.

The blind seer sat in a corner, flexing his atrophied muscles and breathing slowly, laboriously, bewildered, confused. Something was different about the feel of this new day.

He sensed a presence somewhere above him. Excitement surged through him, thundering in his heart. His skin tingled in thrilling waves. Colored sparkles replaced the black absence of vision. He felt lifted, held by rapture. Light splattered over his brain. Colors blazed brightly in expanding patterns. The blind seer screamed but he had no voice. Crackling noises deafened him. His mind was turned inside out and, for an instant, became a canopy of stars.

𓏏 𓃥 𓃠

Amenhotep, Son of Hapu, stared at his hands. He could see them clearly. Over his head, the Egyptian sun was shining in the eastern sky. Fields surrounded him. Breezes caressed him. The fragrance of desert blossoms sweetened his nostrils and his seeing eyes blinked in astonishment. His heart leaped. A miracle had bestowed him with both sight and freedom!

He looked up and saw a silver disc descending rapidly toward him. When the disc returned to the sky, Amenhotep, Son of Hapu was also gone from the face of the Earth.

◠

"You have a visitor," Horemheb said.

"Thank you for announcing him," said Smenkhara.

The assassin-priest Anpu burst into the central chamber of the king's house. He moved in a crablike way, from side to side, eyeing the young king seated on his throne in the middle of the floor. The boy-king was surrounded by armed guards wearing black masks over their eyes.

Smenkhara had been forming a guardian in his brain. The visualization took intense concentration. He had created a living entity made of pain. He had suffered much as a child when his crippled legs had hurt him and he had hated himself, deformed, and hated his father, the unnatural giant from space. Now he had discharged it. It was an entity, his protector, waiting to strike in his defense.

Anpu was possessed by a new demon, created by Kahotep, implanted into his mind through the eye of a man behind a veil. But this demon was not intended to live in Anpu. It was a demon made of lightning, and it was intended for the young king Smenkhara's eye—and mind.

Anpu darted forward. Two guards grabbed Smenkhara and held him rigid. His crown fell to the stone floor and the gold disc that adorned it broke in half.

Anpu leaned into Smenkhara's face and when the demon of lightning flashed into Smenkhara's eye, the demon of pain flashed into the eye and mind of Anpu.

The lizardlike assassin screamed and fled from the room. He hurtled into the walls and pillars of the corridor until he found sunlight. From a terrace on the rooftop of the great house, Anpu leaped. He blessed himself with death upon the central avenue of Akhetaton.

Inside the chamber, Smenkhara said haughtily to Horemheb and Pawah, "Do not *ever* try to use black magick on the rightful King of Egypt. If you do, your worst fears will push all of you into the graves you have already dug."

Akhunaton was taken to a pit-tomb hewn into the foot of a cliff. He was placed inside gently—the soldiers both feared him and had been ordered to be careful.

Akhunaton sat cross-legged on the flat stone floor. Thirteen guards stood watch over him. They had been instructed to form a circle and to "Make certain no one takes their eyes off of him *for an instant.*"

Akhunaton smiled contentedly as he sat in their midst.

As he sat under his canopy, hidden behind a ledge in a niche in the cliff, surveying the city he had bloodlessly taken, Kahotep knew it was a stalemate. He pondered his prisoners, who they were, where they were and what to do with them.

He wished he could kill Smenkhara and Tutankhaton. He would rather not do it personally, but Pawah, in a trance, had told Amen that no soldier would make a move to murder Smenkhara. Smenkhara and Tutankhaton looked fully human in the shapes of their heads. The soldiers considered both boys to be not demonic. And one was the immediate heir to the throne, King of Egypt proper.

Kahotep's high priests were possessed by psychic parasites of his own creation. They associated with Amen the hallucinations of possession by the Hidden One. Still, not one among them, initiate or priest, would kill the Pharaoh. They knew Smenkhara was Pharaoh. They recognized his royal dignity as his authentic crown.

Pawah had rounded up a number of psychopaths, one of whom had gladly volunteered to assassinate the king. But miserable Anpu had failed the simplest and most direct method of attack—and thrown himself to a swift, welcome death. This had impressed the soldiers greatly.

Kahotep knew that the family was well aware of his existence and the means he used to prolong his life. He feared the strange children. The young man was probably clairvoyant and would refuse to eat poisoned food. He insisted on remaining with his brother and Ai.

Smenkhara had refused to join the cult of Amen, but he had also, casually and without intimidation, proclaimed that suppression of Amenism would hereby come to an end. He dictated this order to his scribes and prescribed modifications of some laws while erasing others entirely. Many of the war-priests found these revisions to be quite fair.

He agreed to the condition that he and his family be removed to Thebes. Their departure was almost immediate. The entourage crossed the Nile, boarded barges and pushed away from the western shore. Their vessels formed a caravan drifting south.

The soldiers again began massing in Akhetaton. When the sun rose the second morning after the invasion, the devastation began.

As if on some arcane cue, the war-priests of Amen arose and shattered the frescoes, statues, the three colossi rock-hewn outside of Akhetaton, and all the murals and statuary in the temples of Aton. The colossi at the entrance to the Great Temple of Aton were toppled by teams of horses pulling strong ropes. The vast facade was cracked and overturned, the singing temples overrun and the *tcham* wire stripped from the obelisk.

Countless paintings, busts and statues of Akhunaton and his family were smashed into rubble. Virtually all was destroyed, with a notable exception: a lovely piece of sculpture, a bust of Queen Nefertiti carved of limestone by the sculptor Tutmose. A war-priest, whose eye had long been ensnared by the beauty of the queen, entered its chamber alone and carefully placed it face down, cheek to the floor, facing the wall of the temple. When rioting Amenists invaded the room and scoured the walls, shelves and pedestals of every work of art, debris showered down upon the bust of the dead queen. After the soldiers had tired and moved on, three feet of shattered fragments covered the delicate face, whose right eye had been removed five years before, after Nefertiti's mysterious departure.

A few statues and rock paintings were pillaged from the temples by priests who lived at the temples outside the king's city. These were carried into the hills, through the deserts, and most were buried. All were hidden. Some of the war-priests themselves confiscated rather than destroyed the most beautiful of the works. Of these, a few were openly donated to the temples of Amen as contributions to their archives, but many were secretly taken by the priests for their own collection. Even artifacts which depicted long heads with lovely feminine faces were still taken, pocketed, palmed, preserved.

Amen required a secret, personally guarded record of the experiment. He needed to know more about genetics. From his distant past training he understood patterns of heredity and of genes and chromosomal transfer. But he lacked the technology to further his knowledge beyond simple animal and plant experiments, such as his very successful cultivation of new diseases. Microscopy, chemical engineering, selective breeding were all techniques he could only dabble in, severely limited by crude Egyptian technology.

Perhaps these statues and paintings will tell me much, he thought, pondering some of the treasures which had been brought to him. The stunning beauty of the faces of the daughters and their fantastically long heads fascinated him. He remembered the weird experimental beings he had seen born in Egypt during the reigns of Thoth, Osiris, and Horus. They had repeated it, he realized. And this time they had left a record in art, stone, and cuneiform, of the creation of their stellar race. If left to survive, this record would inform future generations of human origins. It would be evidence of a larger world, a greater-than-human family, one that is not always visible but is always nearby...

These things cannot be known. The world is flat. The stars are not as big as Ra, the sun, but are tiny, ins

*ignificant, painted on the belly of a giant cow....*Kahotep glared into the darkness, his brain concentrating. *It is most important that all strange looking things in the sky be regarded as evil, demonic apparitions—invaders.*

Kahotep thought: *War shall be my emissary. There is no war except war against knowledge...*

𓂀𓅃

Akhetaton was destroyed, its buildings had been toppled and their foundations buried under heaps of rubble. Kahotep hoped, the destruction of the vast body of art was complete. The heads, the faces, that realistic style of rendering, that heretical departure from the millennia-old rigidity—all of it had to be eliminated. All record of this king and his aberrant, unnatural family, all stamped, carved, painted artifacts had to be shattered into dust, along with all memory of them. Propaganda would replace art, and a lie would grow in place of the record.

So be it, Kahotep said to himself, *so be it. I will be king again.*

𓂀

After Horemheb's departure and return to Thebes, Kahotep slipped out of his hiding place and, escorted by a little caravan, journeyed by night through the desert to Thebes and, from there, underground to Karnak. Upon arriving at his subterranean sanctuary, Kahotep flew into a rage when he discovered that his seer, Amenhotep, Son of Hapu, had inexplicably disappeared. He vented his wrath by flogging to death several young boys who had been smuggled to him by his trusted priests.

His rage was compounded when he discovered that his spellbook, his only written record of extraterrestrial knowledge, the *Ka-Ba-Ra*, was also gone.

Chapter Thirty-Three

The soldiers never felt their fear of Akhunaton lessen. Thirteen guards were ever on duty around Akhunaton, in six hour shifts. They alternated watching the naked alien man and watching the tomb door. Never were fewer than nine pairs of eyes staring at the former king. Some were braver than others, but all found standing watch over a being who might vanish during the slightest lapse of eye contact to be severely disconcerting.

Akhunaton could not help feeling empathic echoes of the pain of their fear. He knew they feared him so much that his mere spoken words might panic them. He focused his mind on the projection of tranquility. It was this influence that kept them from succumbing to panic and violence.

When he sensed that Kahotep had departed, he realized he would not be fed. He was to be starved.

Smenkhara returned to the palace he had lived in as a boy. The memories evoked were curiously dim and not at all painful. He strolled the hallways and gazed out from the terraces. The young pharaoh surrounded himself with the Theban priests of Aton, the few who had remained, who had not journeyed to Akhetaton. They protected the young king because they knew huge fortunes had been promised for the murder of Akhunaton's eldest son.

Every day priests from the religions of Amen and Thoth petitioned the young king to legalize human sacrifices and sanctify the death penalty. To these demands Smenkhara hurled unbending denials and the emissaries were instantly dismissed.

High Priest Ai was strangely feared by the soldier-priests who kept Smenkhara under their own surveillance. They were always searched for weapons and poisons and psychically scanned before being allowed into the royal presence. They were generally sincere, mostly wanting to participate symbolically in the protection of their king, while also assisting the Priests of Aton that their religion might not be abolished again.

Thus Smenkhara ruled well. He watched the passing of the plague that had been predicted by the priests of Amen. He grieved while a million people died; he rejoiced when no more deaths were reported.

A year passed, a year of contending with Smenkhara. His father had taught the boy well, Kahotep lamented.

Smenkhara successfully commanded Egyptian troops and settled border skirmishes in the south. The Nubians, skillfully defeated, no longer contemplated an invasion. Losses to the Egyptian Army had been minimal; fewer than a hundred men on either side had been slain. The battle had been purely defensive on Egypt's part. Smenkhara's promise was made true: he would defend and protect Egypt while upholding his father's reforms. Because Amenism was no longer suppressed, and because Egypt had been defended and thus protected by Smenkhara, the Egyptians gave Smenkhara their devotion.

They are like children, Smenkhara often thought while looking over his balcony upon the masses who had come to adore him, as they had his father. *They are fickle, unstable like children. One minute happy, the next minute, crying. I was like that, long ago…It seems like somebody else now, not…not me….*

Kahotep lived infuriated by the disappearance of his spellbook and his seer. This last was a matter of pride only, but to Kahotep it represented an intimate invasion of his privacy. Only after three years did his rages begin subsiding.

Horemheb had vanished from public life. He was in the limestone caves to the south and east of Thebes receiving training as a High Priest of Amen.

Kahotep had desperately hoped that the inexperienced Smenkhara would fail the defense of Egypt when the Nubians crossed the border to invade, but Smenkhara had not failed. Smenkhara had emerged victorious.

Kahotep plotted incessantly to dethrone the young king, but he dared not act: Akhunaton was still alive.

The starvation of Akhunaton was taking much longer than Kahotep had anticipated. The king sat in his tomb smiling vastly as his guards became more disconcerted. Kahotep visited the ruins of Akhetaton seven times hoping fervently for a sign of death, but after several years of waiting, Kahotep formulated a desperate plan. He summoned his Inner Circle for protection. Without giving up his secrecy, he would visit Akhunaton.

The journey took several days and nights. Kahotep and four of his High Priests took up residence in the outpost overlooking the devastated city. He relayed his instructions to Akhunaton's guards: they were to leave Akhunaton alone for one hour upon the appearance of four masked figures. When the rock tomb was completely empty except for the dethroned king, the Hidden One would slip inside in the company of his escorts. They would keep their eyes upon the king, for it was essential that a perceptual field be maintained over Akhunaton. If the king was as expert at wave-shifting as Kahotep feared he was, glancing away for an instant would be the chance he would need to enfold a psychohologram and vanish forever.

Viewing the motionless, smiling king terrified Kahotep. *Yes,* he thought, *he is one of the star-kings, a true Horus. His skull must contain a brain five times the average human brain. But how has he managed to stay alive all this time without food or drink?*

Taking a small piece of polished silver from the pocket of his robe, Kahotep placed the cool metal under Akhunaton's nose. He held it close to the king's nostrils and peered at it intently. No vapor condensed. Nor did the king's chest stir.

Kahotep realized there was something drastically unnatural about his stillness. Extending a trembling hand, Kahotep touched the king's bare shoulder. Akhunaton's body was stone-hard. His grey-brown skin felt like contoured marble, solid and cold.

Kahotep stared with wide eyes at the man sitting cross-legged, smiling. *This powerful adept, with his giant brain, perhaps assisted by some machine aboard the spaceship, has somehow slowed the passage of time…He has tricked me,* Kahotep thought feverishly. *He has tricked me! He can stay in this state indefinitely—forever, if he chooses.*

In a million years he could still vanish in an instant, even return through time to his starship…

He ordered his four priests to lift Akhunaton, but the alien's body was endowed with immovable mass.

I will make certain that this ploy will fail. He will become a living, unchanging artifact. So be it! He will be guarded forever, that is all.

Kahotep returned to Thebes and the tunnels under Karnak. His grain blight and plague of fevers had passed, causing the devastation that had been predicted. The bacteria afflicting the grain and the virus causing the fevers both mutated into strains that were either compatible with their hosts or were destroyed by their immune systems.

When after several years the plague and blight had subsided, Smenkhara was still king.

Kahotep awoke with a jolt. Adrenalin tingled in his body and exploded in his chest. He gripped the sides of his throne and peered into total blackness: every tiny electrical lamp, oil lamp, and candle was unlit.

Sweat burst from his forehead and palms. Adrenalin evoked colored phosphenes splattering across his vision. He blinked. Tears streaked down his cheeks. He gritted his teeth.

He knew he was not alone. He could not see who or what stood in perfect silence across the room from him. He could only sense the towering entity: the immense figure of a man, familiar and overpowering in presence…

Chapter Thirty-Four

"Greetings, Kahotep," said Akhunaton. "It is time we talked, you and I."

Kahotep cringed and drew back against his throne.

"You need not fear me. You radiate terror, Kahotep, and that is an inertia you cannot overcome."

"Go!" Kahotep hissed. "Do not torment me! Leave me alone!"

"Your visit was appreciated. By seeing me and touching my skin, you imparted your vibratory field to my own. Your guards suddenly fell asleep, simultaneously. I used our connection to wave-shift to this timespace locality.

"You, Kahotep, will forever be unable to lighten your heart from the grief you both cause and contain."

"I curse you, Akhunaton," croaked Kahotep.

"Fear is the anchor that binds your body to this fragment of time and space. You fear me right now. Your throat constricts with fear. You can barely speak."

Almost inaudibly: "You torment me."

"Do I? I have not touched you. I have not inflicted any pain upon you. And you know in your heart that I will not, ever."

"Be damned…you…monster!"

"You know the meaning and importance of my physical proportions. Future generations will compare my brain and body and gaze upon me with wonder. They will realize that I came from the stars and took a human wife in Egypt. They will ponder their own stellar origins."

"Show yourself, Akhunaton! If you intend me no harm, come out of the darkness."

"I am greeting you in darkness because you have chosen to live in darkness. If you wish to come into the light, you must create light yourself."

"You are…tormenting me."

"You are a coward."

"Damn you. Forever. Damn you."

"All you can do is hurl curses, Kahotep. Your path has ended. Another has begun in its place."

"You will be forgotten, Akhunaton. I will make certain of that."

"You have destroyed multitudes of artifacts, but not every one. Some works survive that depict me as I am. You yourself have here the most accurate of the smaller depictions of me and my children, in your hope to decipher the genetic code.

"Watch those artifacts very carefully. You must keep close attention to everything you have taken, for those things can be taken back as well."

Kahotep snarled with rage. "You stole my book! My book of secrets—you stole it, you tyrant. You stole it!"

"It is still on Earth. It is in the possession of a priestess of Isis, somewhere, on its way to new owners. I admit, I stole the *Ka-Ba-Ra*. You shall never have those scrolls again."

"You! That is immoral!"

"Yes, in principle an act of theft is not justified in and of itself."

"Then you are no better than I, Akhunaton."

"The theft of a book containing knowledge that can be used to inflict pain and death upon multitudes is different in principle from the theft of a living human pineal gland from a still-conscious brain."

"Lord God Ptah condemn you!"

"The theft of the *Ka-Ba-Ra* is more than symbolic. It is a final statement: you are on your own. We could kill you, but we will not. We could have you transported to a time before humans, so you could inflict your unholy rite upon nothing. We could do these things, but we will not. We will simply leave you alone.

"Smenkhara, my son, is king now. He will rule for the rest of his life. If he has a son, he, too, shall be Pharaoh. If Smenkhara does not live long, he will be succeeded by Tutankhaton. The lineage I have established will be preserved. This lineage shall be preserved."

Kahotep grumbled inarticulately.

"We knew who you were when we selected you in Siberia, Kahotep. Your name was Nagarjaruk and you were a shaman. You have not changed. Your mind is the same as it was more than eight thousand years ago.

"We gave you the name you still wear: Kahotep. You know what it means: 'Fulfillment of the *Ka*.' And yet, you do not know why we gave you this name, nor what the *Ka* truly is.

"*Ka* is a mind that inhabits a brain within your brain. The large brain, the cortex, occupies most of the volume of the human skull, but it is a trait that was imparted by genetic manipulation, not by gradual evolution. The older, smaller parts of the brain are still as they were when humans were like small apes.

"In the skulls of these apes resided a small, efficient brain, interested in the preservation of the individual ape alone. For the convenience of mating and mutual grooming, of females watching over their babies, did a concern for the species manifest.

"In this brain was the small, selfish mind we call the *Ka*.

"The *Ka* still lives in the brain. It still thinks its own thoughts, suffers its own anxieties, and fights for its own selfish survival. There is nothing wrong with this.

If an animal gives up its *Ka*, it dies. If a species loses its *Ka*, it becomes extinct. If life in this world loses its *Ka*, all life will end. So be it. We who are from the stars did not make this so. It is a condition innate to life.

"You, Kahotep, have taken upon yourself the destiny of the *Ka* of humankind. You represent the monkey in the snake-filled jungle, the mammoth-eater of the glacial tundra, the human predators who lost their fruit forests to sheets of ice and learned to hunt mammoths.

"Your human *Ka* discovered that mammoths charge and stomp, and that a broken leg on the ice means lingering death. Your human *Ka* also came to learn the grim truth about members of your own sex: when hunting conditions become extreme, individual males become expendable. The bounteous male fertility insures the survival of the species. The children are the future of the tribe, but the men—if they fail to kill so the tribe can eat, then they might be dragged back to the tribe—and eaten.

"So it was when we found you, Kahotep. You had imbibed many potions from the sacred mushrooms. You were able to conjure spirit-visions without imbibing the alkaloids, and your clairvoyance was expansive. But you were also a hurt, frightened boy.

"Then in our absence, you stole life from the skulls of your fellow humans in order to prolong your own life. This is evil. To procure the increasing number of pineal glands you needed to perpetuate this addiction, you institutionalized murder."

There was silence. Akhunaton resumed slowly:

"You no longer have a connection with the *Ba*.

"*Ba* is the mind of the great brain that surrounds the animal brain and composes the greatest mass inside the skull. *Ba* is the mind of the brain *we gave your people*, Kahotep. The minds and hearts of Egyptians have grown heavy from forced labor, death, grief and sorrow which make impossible the ideal of walking with a heart light as a feather, as if to meet Osiris at any moment. Which even you must prepare yourself for, Kahotep.

"At this moment, your *Ba* is not even in your body. It has gone mad with empathic horror at what you do, Kahotep, to prolong your life. It has abandoned control over your body to the angry mammal-mind of your *Ka*.

"This is something we who watch this world cannot undo by anything short of forceful intervention. But that would be an example of the violent politics we have chosen to refute. So we will watch you. We will remain close at hand, invisible to most, and we will awaken these evolving humans to our presence slowly and in ways that will harm none.

"The spheres in space will prevail over false cosmologies that flatten the Earth and shrink to lifeless the starry Heavens. Whenever a human child, man or woman, reaches that bliss of lightness when the *Ba* puts the *Ka* to sleep, then shall come contact and translation.

"You will try to prevent this. You will oppose the unfolding of the new cosmology, the rediscovery of the old cosmology, and you will try to stigmatize the process of contact and translation. Only the most subtle minds will be able to discover a path out of the maze. In truth, a leap over the wall is required, for all the tunnels of the maze lead to the same place: doubt. With lightness of heart, the leap is made. The *Ba* is a subtle spirit, radiant with invisible energy.

"The *Ka* must go to sleep, which it fears because it knows it will never wake up. Must humans do this by dying. Before death, if the organism faces translation, the *Ka* must voluntarily go to sleep. It can do so only if it knows that there is nothing more to fear, that the jungle is no longer crawling with poisonous snakes, that the mammoth hunt will cost the lives of no more mammoth hunters. Because you have perpetuated violence, such reassurance is not possible among the humans whose *Ka* has heard your message. But you shall not stop the realization of *Ba*.

"You have become a god of your own realm, but Egypt is only a tribe of screaming children in a desert on a very large and wild planet. In causing and absorbing so much pain, you have sealed yourself off from mobility in the timespace stream, for a heart as heavy as yours would not survive the potential danger of a black hole translation.

"Your body is therefore imprisoned in linear time, apart from cosmic time, and local space, apart from cosmic space. You innately doubt that Ptah, God of this Universe, is benevolent. All this has severed you from that greater cosmos, accessible only to a heart that is feather-light.

"Forever banished to an infinitesimal space and fragment of time, you shall continue to use your parasitic means to lengthen your lifetime. You shall seek to conquer all of this planet with wars. You shall not be prevented from this by anyone—except the people to whom you deliver orders. When those commands fall on deaf ears, you shall then face what you fear most: you shall die.

"This is the ultimate punishment you have visited upon yourself: you shall spend a lifetime living the memories of every one of your murdered victims. If you live ten thousand years, you shall relive the millions of lifetimes you have literally eaten to sustain your longevity. In this way will the souls you have eaten be released.

"You call yourself such names as The Beast and Kahotep and Amen. In spirit you are Baba, the Soul-Eater.

"So be it. I can no longer remain in proximity to your pain or fear. Bless you and may you choose to die before another dies for you.

"Ankh em Ma'at."

Silence filled the room. Kahotep was again alone.

Chapter Thirty-Five

"Father, why are you here?"

"I came to say goodbye to you, my son."

"Oh! Let us look at the moon and stars." A long silence passed. "Tell me which star you came from again."

"This bright star in the southern sky. Just above the horizon."

"I see." Another immense silence passed.

Akhunaton put his arm around Smenkhara's shoulder as they leaned forward, peering into the sky from the window.

"It is lovely," Akhunaton said. "Smell the sweet fragrance of the lilies of the Nile and the desert blossoms."

"Yes, Father. The moon is almost full."

"Yes, Smenkhara."

"A great ball like the Earth! How good to know."

"Yes, it is good to know."

"Tell me about the Sirius system."

"You will go there very soon."

Smenkhara beamed at his father with the eyes of a child. "Really?"

"Yes," Akhunaton said. "Soon."

Tutankhaton had been unable to sleep. He received his father wide awake, with arms extended, palms out, in greeting.

"I love you, Tutankhaton."

"I love you, too, Father."

"You will be the next king, Tutankhaton."

"Really, father?"

"Remember that star."

"The star of Anubis?"

"Yes. With the Horizon of Heaven in it."

"Yes, Father, and I will remember the times I saw the Aton Disc."

"I am glad. You live aboard that disc already."

"That is what you and my sisters have told me! I rejoice to know it."

"I rejoice to know that, too, Tutankhaton."

"How will it be for me as king?"

"I will not lie to you, my son. It will be horrible."

"Oh please, will it?"

"Do not fear. Those few years will be nothing compared to cosmic time, which is what you will be translated into."

"Is this certain, my father?"

"Tutankhaton, remember that time you and your sister Ankhasenpaaton were playing together in the fields and you saw a big light shining down from the blue sky?"

"Yes! And it enveloped me and my sister in light…"

"Do you remember the dreams you had then, after the light surrounded you?"

"Yes! They were dreams of Ankhasenpaaton, only she was a woman, not a girl…"

"Bless you, Tutankhaton. Do you remember anything else? What came after?"

"No…" The innocent boy knitted his smooth brow and gazed into some potted irises below the window ledge.

"Think. Think deeply, Tutankhaton."

"…Oh, yes! I found myself in that same field, lying down, breathing hard…and there was a cut on my knee. It hardly left a scar." Akhunaton smiled. "What does that mean, Father?"

"It means that a part of you lives aboard the *Aton*, ready to be reunited with the hologram, the *nou*, that is your spirit, Tutankhaton."

"Tell me, Father, is this why all Pharaohs up to you have been mummified?"

Akhunaton said, "Yes."

🜏⌒

"I have loved you deeply, Meritaton. And all of you, my daughters."

Meritaton and her sisters looked up at their father, glowing in the rays cast down by the Aton Disc. The six girls sat in a circle around the cosmic king. Queen Meritaton stood and faced him.

"We love you, Father," said Neferneferura, standing and smiling gladly. Akhunaton kissed her on the forehead.

"My daughters, it is beautiful to come together. We are singing our final harmonies with our hearts. We will be together again, a long time from now. And for a long time we will have only our love between us. I love you all, my daughters, and I bless you endlessly in the name of Ptah."

"We bless you, Father."

"My father," Meritaton said. "My heart unfolds like an infinite lotus before you."

"You shall be known as the Seven Sisters," said Akhunaton. "Maketaton shall be among you in spirit. Her *nou* lives aboard *Aton*, and her intelligence is present here."

"I feel it," Neferneferuaton the Little said.

Ankhasenpaaton said, "I feel her, too."

"I feel her."

Akhunaton gazed fondly at the young women, his daughters, who constituted his tall and large-brained seed-race. Their children would be assimilated by the emerging races throughout the land. Their many descendants would lose their differences and blend perfectly among humans who were not their kin.

So much of the record of Akhetaton had been lost that the time capsule that Akhunaton had intended it to be might no longer exist. He knew that this demonstration might have been in vain.

"We do not know how much of the art or the record has been preserved." Akhunaton lowered his eyes. "We know that much has been spirited away by my priests, at great risk to their own lives. All of my temples were forewarned and my priests are loyal and efficient, so there is hope. I know also that many of the invading priests of Amen stole many small pieces by Bek and Tutmose in advance of the destruction. Preserving the rest of the story depends on what each of you do in my absence.

"Meritaton, you have your brother's seed in you and shall bear him three sons. They shall be, in every respect, normal boys.

"Beketaton, Setepenra, Neferneferuaton the Little and Neferneferura, you depart tonight for distant lands. Beketaton and Setepenra, you are pregnant with twins. Both your brothers are the fathers. Neferneferura is also pregnant; Smenkhara contributed the genes. Neferneferuaton the Little, you are pregnant with a boy conceived from genes selected from Tutankhaton's seed. You four shall disperse into the east tonight, to be taken in by powerful nomadic empires who show great promise of surviving into the future.

"Ankhasenpaaton, and you, Meritaton, shall stay with your husbands who are your brothers, and oversee this dynasty as guardians and protectors of your brothers, which is something they cannot be.

"You are all adepts at wave-shifting; your two brothers are not. Smenkhara is bound by the circumference of his intellect; Tutankhaton lacks the will power and concentration, though this is irrelevant since protoplasm has been taken from their bodies for restoration, and their personalities have been prepared for transfer. Their bodies shall remain here, mummified and preserved. They shall be protected in their tombs. I shall protect them myself.

"This is the best protection from harm: to gather only love around you. You will each be contacted shortly before your assassinations are to take place. The contact will be made by humans, not extraterrestrials.

"Let us meditate together before I depart. Ankh em Ma'at."

The circle of seven figures sat in the desert holding hands. They gazed at each other in silence for a long time.

Then, one star descended from high among the rest. The desert was filled with the light of day. When the star returned to the center of the sky and disappeared, only two remained.

Kahotep received confirmation of Akhunaton's departure with elation. The news that four of the daughters had vanished and that the remaining priests of Aton in the temples throughout Egypt were also missing, along with Aper-El, Akhunaton's minister in Memphis, aroused mixed feelings in Kahotep. He hoped it meant that he now had fewer rivals to contend with, as he still did not control the throne.

Queen Meritaton was pregnant. The Aton Disc was seen over Thebes and Tutankhaton married Ankhasenpaaton the day after the visitation .

Smenkhara knew he faced his final grim years. The times were tempestuous and combative for the young king as a defender of his religion, worship of the circumferential metal disc. Kahotep daily sent his priests to argue, petition, debate with Smenkhara over the issue of human sacrifice. The Pharaoh was intransigent: no human sacrifice, no death and, whenever possible, no war.

Kahotep was desperate to seize Egypt away from the Atonists. After another unsuccessful attempt to poison the young king, The Beast conceived a more far-reaching and viable strategy.

Kahotep wandered across the desert at night, looking for a gravid cobra. When he found one under a boulder he returned every night and on the fourth night, he found her writhing in the pangs of birth. He watched the babies spill out of her and twist away into the crevices between tumbled boulders.

He caught one of the little snakes and placed it inside a leather pouch and cinched it up. At dawn, in his inner chambers, he released the tiny one inside a wooden box with a layer of sand in the bottom. He offered the newborn serpent a baby bird. The snake struck at the bird and it died instantly.

Kahotep had chosen a cobra because of the temperament of its race: patient, tolerant of humans. They were intelligent and followed instructions readily and Kahotep knew the language of cobras.

Smenkhara's last year as king was marked with constant harassment from the priests of Amen. They plagued him with arguments in favor of human sacrifice, interrogated him about the whereabouts of his father, his sisters and what had happened to the population of his father's city. Had Akhunaton's followers not been sacrificed to the Aton Disc?

No, Smenkhara would say, all of those people are alive except for Nefertiti, who chose to die.

He longed for the sheltered, peaceful days of his childhood in Akhetaton. He spoke little to anyone except Meritaton and Ai, who advised him on matters political. He looked forward to the pageants, which gave him welcome diversion.

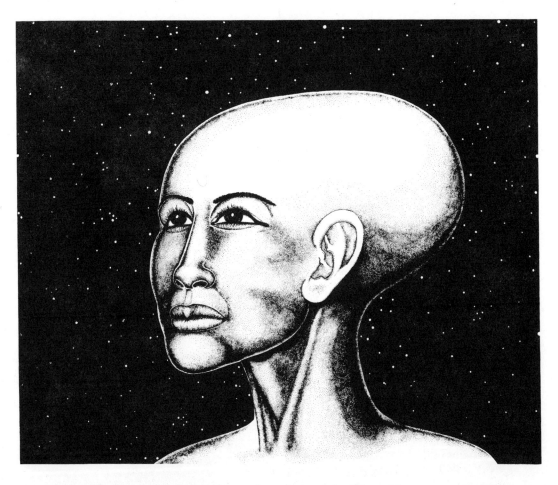

It was during preparations for such a pageant that Tutankhaton vanished. The palace was searched and Ai discovered that two guards were also missing. Ankha-senpaaton, the young prince's bride, knew instantly that the guards had abducted him. No announcement was made while the Egyptian Guard quietly searched all of Thebes.

After several hours, Tutankhaton was found. He was indeed with the two guards, hidden in a room behind the altar in the inner temple of the palace. Tutankhaton was unhurt and, like both the guards, he was quite drunk.

Smenkhara was furious. He shouted at his younger brother, reminding him of the next day's pageant and how he had held up the elaborate preparations, which now would not include him. He stormed out of the room. Tutankhaton blubbered after him, stumbling.

The pageant had not gone well and neither had the ceremony, but the feast more than made up for it. The first good harvest in years contributed to an endless banquet. The people were grateful. Tutankhaton, as expected, did not attend, vanquished by the wine.

Later, in their private chambers, Smenkhara and Meritaton joined Ankhasenpaaton in agreeing that Tutankhaton's behavior had not been natural for him at all.

"They just wanted a private place to drink," Tutankhaton had protested. "They said they were off duty and just not out of uniform yet."

"And you believed them?" Smenkhara was astonished.

"It seemed unlikely that they would lie," Tutankhaton admitted.

"And you let them into the temple! To drink! And you drank with them!"

"I did not intend to! Just one glass, but the wine was so good…"

"Do you know how much you drank?"

Tutankhaton shrugged. "Suddenly there were all these empty bottles!"

Smenkhara departed up the stairs to his chamber to retire at the end of a long, exhausting day.

Tutankhaton called up to him, "I am sorry, my brother!"

"I have grave doubts about my brother," Smenkhara told Meritaton as they lay side by side in their beds.

"We share doubts," said Meritaton.

"You said Ankhasenpaaton feels this way as well?"

"Yes, she told me so after dinner."

"What did she say was different about him?"

"Well, he has always had a difficult time asserting himself. Now, part of him is somehow *gone*. Or so it seems…"

"We must watch over him."

"Yes."

"Bless you," he said to his sister-wife.

They embraced and made love in the moonlight.

Kahotep spent two years learning to communicate with the cobra. He fed it and gave it a warm lair in the rocks near his animal laboratory and attempted to communicate with it while it slept. With barely enough candlelight for eye contact, Kahotep meditated until his mind shared the legless slithering dreams of the serpent.

Finally, Kahotep imparted dreams of his own into the reptile's primitive mind:

the floor plan of Smenkhara's temple-palace, designed by himself, centuries ago. The snake departed in the morning with memories of a place it had never seen.

Ai, in his bedroom chamber, could not sleep. Something ached in his heart, something was wrong. An hour before dawn, he heard Meritaton scream. Ai leapt from his bed as footsteps clamored through the palace halls. Lamps were hastily lit as a woman's voice wailed in anguish.

Ai found Meritaton in a corner of their room, clutching Smenkhara's lifeless body.

"A serpent…" Meritaton sobbed, pointing an unsteady arm toward the window. "A cobra. It went out that window…"

Smenkhara's funeral was brief and led immediately to the coronation of Tutankhaton.

Meritaton grieved. On the third night following his death, Smenkhara came to her.

She awoke with a jolt. "Yes, my love?" Her senses were clear, her heart was light.

"My dear sister." He stood in a shaft of moonlight. She flew into his arms. Their bodies came together in this world. When the light subsided, they continued their embrace in another.

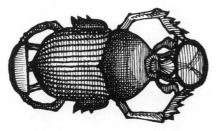

Chapter Thirty-Six

The body of Smenkhara disappeared from its formal tomb shortly after the funeral, but not, as was purported, into the powerful rays of the Aton Disc. The young king had been hastily preserved without the year-long mummification process which had been abolished by his father. It was secretly disinterred and taken to a rock-pit tomb on the edge of the Valley of the Kings. The mummy of Smenkhara was placed in it without funerary objects. His own *ushabti* and other spiritual devices were left behind in his first tomb and Smenkhara's second tomb was decorated with the funerary paraphernalia of his grandmother, Queen Tiy.

The High Priest Pawah had ordered the mummy to be destroyed at all cost but the Priests of Amen found the tomb of Smenkhara empty.

The disappearance of Smenkhara's mummy and of his sister-wife Meritaton infuriated Kahotep, but he consoled himself that at least he had partial control of the throne, even if it was through a reluctant king.

Every afternoon Pawah visited Tutankhaton to convince him to reject his father's reforms. Pawah never once touched the young king with his hands; still, young Tutankhaton was afraid of the priest and always greeted him with a shudder of horror. He spent the visits locked inside himself in dread, for Tutankhaton had been invaded by an evil entity of Kahotep's creation, a demon made of fear. To the king it was black, yet invisible; formless, yet seemed tangible; nowhere and everywhere.

By Pawah's fifth visit, Tutankhaton was ready to utterly reject the religion of his father. He made a brief display of bravado when he announced to his family that he had decided to change his name to honor the god of his new religion: Amen. And that this change of names applied to the other members of the royal family as well: Tutankhaton would change his name to Tutankhamen; his queen would become Ankhasenamen. The old religion had returned, he declared. The historical fluke called Atonism was no longer recognized as a religion.

After the coronation pageant for the new king-names, Ankhasenamen cried. She walked with him once in their garden courtyards. She gazed upon her brother's beauty and tried not to see the vacant look in his eyes, but thereafter she refused to see the king.

The Beast was not satisfied. To have complete control over Egypt, Kahotep needed a king whose mind received his direct telepathic commands. He had instead a king who was volatile and responded only to proddings by imaginary fears.

Such a king will not do the thing I want, Kahotep worried. *He will not go to war against Mitanni or Nubia.*

After five years of the reign of the pitiful, tormented Tutankhamen, Kahotep decided to murder him. The assassin had been in training for ten years, recruited for the task before the invasion of Akhetaton. This killer was a true warrior and received his instructions directly from the mind of Amen, his god. He was completely submissive to the will of Amen. He would make a good king.

Tutankhamen had ruled for exactly five years on the day of Horemheb's return. The general was taken immediately to the courtyard where Tutankhamen and Ankhasenamen sat silently facing each other on a stone bench. Tutankhamen stood and greeted Horemheb with the blank smile that had haunted his face since before his coronation. He walked to Horemheb and embraced him.

Horemheb gripped a leather strap that ended in a lead ball. He struck the back of Tutankhamen's head. The king crumpled in his arms. Ankhasenamen gasped and cried out. Throwing the king's corpse aside, Horemheb seized Ankhasenamen. The Queen of Egypt let out a fragment of a scream as the huge hand closed over her mouth.

Pawah had been saddled with a particularly nasty dragon intended to occupy Ankhasenamen's brain, but the psychic entity would not make the leap from Pawah's eye to hers. Her mind simply would not take an evil spirit. She emerged from the Temple of Amen inside the palace after several hours of resistance and was assured that Horemheb was safely under house arrest for the murder of King Tutankhamen.

She also learned that High Priest Ai had offered to marry her, being brother of the queen who was the mother of the stellar king. Ankhasenamen immediately accepted Ai's offer. He was an old man, but with a measure of youthful vigor and Ankhasenamen was carrying a son by Tutankhamen, a boy scheduled to vanish at birth.

Though the Priests of Amen railed against this union, Ai's kinship could not be denied. He was handed the crown of Pharaoh.

Horemheb attempted to escape and was killed in the struggle when he fell and struck his head against the stone floor. The body was examined and pronounced dead. Horemheb was interred without mummification, placed in a common grave.

Horemheb's grave was secretly disinterred the second night after burial. The body was all that was taken. Not even his golden *ushabti* was touched.

King Tutankhamen was mummified in the complex year-long ritual that had been practised upon the bodies of kings for thousands of years. He was buried with full funerary regalia, complete with ceremonial objects and his own father's throne. The emblem of the Aton Disc, with a fan of rays spreading from the disc, turning into human hands holding ankhs, was preserved on the back of the throne.

Also entombed with him, in a canopic vessel surreptitiously left by a covert priest of Aton, was the mummified remains of Nefertiti's first intended offspring, the sexless, mutated cluster of protoplasm that had been the first and only attempt to fuse her genes with Akhunaton's.

In the two years Ai and Ankhasenamen ruled Egypt, they tried valiantly to restore reforms imposed by Akhunaton. Tutankhamen had legalized human sacrifice; Ai banned it again, but his decree only caused the grisly ritual to be practiced in secret.

The priests of Amen condemned him for being too old, but Ai heroically defended his throne. Among his problems were the Nubians raiding the Egyptian border and the kings of Mitanni, who were threatening to sever diplomatic relations with Egypt because no king since Amenhotep III had given them gifts or marriageable daughters for their princes.

When, after two years as Pharaoh, Ai died of a heart attack, Ankhasenamen was alone.

The Hittites circled the city of Amki at night and attacked it at dawn. They rode in on an avalanche of horses' hooves and their swords and scimitars slaughtered thousands of citizens. The undefended city was destroyed and virtually no Hittites were harmed. King Suppiluliumas watched the carnage from a high desert hill. When the one-sided battle was over, he rode his chariot through streets lined with rubble to ascertain that every Egyptian was dead.

When he returned to his palace, the Hittite king discovered a message inscribed in cuneiform in a clay tablet, a letter. An accompanying stone bore a seal—Egyptian.

King Suppiluliumas read the letter:

"My husband is dead and I have no son. The people say that your sons have grown. If you will send me one of your sons, he will become my husband, for I have none among my subjects suitable to become my husband.

"Dahamunzu"

She had signed the letter with the word "queen", nothing more. Suppiluliumas knew this was Ankhasenamen, the Egyptian queen.

He was puzzled. His raiders had slaughtered all who had tried to escape Amki; news of the invasion could not have yet reached Ankhasenamen. Thus the letter had been sent in innocence—or had it? *Egyptians are treacherous people...*

From his throne in Khatti, Suppiluliumas looked west, toward Egypt, with suspicion and misgivings. He had wanted to wage war, but the queen had chosen to wage peace.

⊰⊙-

King Suppiluliumas called his council. He addressed his comments to all, but especially for the benefit of his generals, Tarhuntazalmas and Lupakkis.

"This has never happened before," he repeated endlessly. "Such a thing is unknown. I have never in my life faced such a dilemma..."

"Do you suspect it is a trick?" his vizier inquired from across the table.

"Of course! But if it is not, would it not be an opportunity? We were lucky when we took Amki, they were unprepared. Our next battle might cost us much blood."

"I understand," said Tarhuntazalmas.

"If it *is* an opportunity," King Suppiluliumas continued, "and if the Egyptians are slow to notice the devastation of one of their cities, then we, by marriage, might conquer all of Egypt in a coup that will also cost us no blood."

The council pondered these words, then formulated their plan.

👁

King Suppiluliumas feared that any of his sons sent to the city on the Nile would die there, so he sent his chamberlain, Khattusaziti, on a secret mission to Akhetaton and Thebes, in search of the sender of the mysterious letter. Knowing he would die in Egypt, and yet unwilling to disobey his king, Khattusaziti travelled a long, complicated path west. He arrived alive at the court of Ankhasenamen.

He confided to the Queen of Egypt that his king was deeply suspicious of the offer to grant the throne of Egypt to a Hittite prince. Ankhasenamen was frantic. By law she had only one season, ninety days, in which to find Ai's successor. In the reestablished royal funerary rite, the true successor had to be chosen in time to perform the opening of the mouth ritual.

She send Khattusaziti back to Babylon with a second message. She pleaded:

"Why did you say 'they may deceive me?' If I had a son, would I write abroad to publish the distress of my country? And because you did not believe me, you have spoken thus. My husband is dead and I have no son. I have written to no other king but you. I have been told you have many sons. Select one you wish to rule Egypt.

   "Dahamunzu"

Khattusaziti was accompanied by a messenger of the queen, a young man named Hani. Both had returned from Egypt to find that Suppiluliumas was gone from his palace, conquering cities to the south and east, away from the Egyptian border. Word came that he had conquered Karkhemish, a vast city on the right bank of the Euphrates. They departed immediately.

After a bloody battle of eight days, King Suppiluliumas was rampant with emotion in the aftermath of a successful battle. This weakling Egyptian who dared call himself an ambassador was too much for the Hittite king to bear. He raged at Hani.

"I was friendly!" Suppiluliumas leaned into Hani's face. "I was a gentleman. But Egypt did me evil. You attacked the Prince of Kadesh, whom I had rescued from the king of the Hurri land. When I heard this, I became furious. Even the gods were angered! I sent chariots and troops. They attacked attacked Amki, in Egypt. You Egyptians were afraid. You keep asking for one of my sons, as if I owe you one! You will only make him hostage, do you hear me?"

Hani was not deterred. "Lord and king, it is my country's shame. If we had a king at all, would we come to a faraway land to beg a hostile king for a lord for ourselves? Nubhururiya, that is, the queen's husband, is dead and has left no son to be his heir…"

After hours of negotiating, King Suppiluliumas made a startling proposition: that an old treaty, known as the Charter of Kurustama, be renewed. The Charter, which had been drawn up after many bloody wars, clearly stated that both sides should leave each other alone.

King Suppiluliumas read the codicil aloud:

"Of old, Khatti and Egypt were friendly with each other, and now this, too, has taken place between them. Thus, Khatti and Egypt will be friendly with each other continuously."

Hani and the king signed the codicil.

Prince Zannanza was chosen by his father to be the next Egyptian Pharaoh. He departed with Hani and a small armed military escort. But they never made it to Egypt. Far into the desert they were met by warriors who had waited in ambush. Their leader was a huge man who wore the leopardskin robe of a priest of Amen.

The realization that his son had vanished in the desert came as a great shock to King Suppiluliumas. He flew into a rage that was only temporarily dampened when he received another urgent plea from Queen Ankhasenamen, begging again for a prince who had not arrived. The king roared again in grief and fury and swore to invade Egypt.

Ankhasenamen was gone, vanished without a trace while alone in her chamber. Her handmaidens reported they heard the voice of Tutankhamen speak the words "I am healed, my sister."

But Horemheb had not died. His return to Thebes was greeted by much fanfare. The older priests of Amen recognized him and attributed his miraculous return to life to the divine powers of Amen—reanimation, a favor bestowed only upon mortals deemed extremely worthy.

The news of Horemheb's revivification overshadowed everything else. Apparently forgiven for the murder of Tutankhamen, the regicide was officially forgotten as well.

He performed the rite of the Opening of the Mouth immediately upon his return and was proclaimed Pharaoh by the unanimous acclaim of the priesthood of Amen and the people of Thebes, who were again overwhelmingly Amenist. Horemheb went from prisoner to corpse to Pharaoh.

As his first task as king, he organized the army and sent it east to fend off the invading Hittites. His defense of Egypt was successful; King Suppiluliumas returned home defeated.

Then the Amenist king engaged in the first of many campaigns to remove the name of Akhunaton from every tomb and temple record throughout the land. Wherever the names Akhunaton, Nefertiti, Tutankhamen or Ai were found, they were erased. The walls of buildings, the inner corridors of crypts and tombs, all were entered and the inscriptions bearing the record of the reign of the Heretic King were stricken. Whenever hidden statuary was discovered, it was destroyed.

After twenty years of Horemheb's reign, the obliteration of the names of Akhunaton and his family was nearly complete. When Horemheb, the last Pharaoh of the Eighteenth Dynasty, died, the campaign to strike the Heretic King's name from recorded history ceased. For a time.

Chapter Thirty-Seven

An unknown tomb had been discovered. Three Beduin tribesmen and two priests of Amen entered the tunnel and followed the stairway down, their torches lighting the way.

Two huge men pulled the final block from the wall of the sealed chamber. Two young boys crawled into the tiny opening. The sound of objects toppling echoed through the yellow glare and the darkness. Voices exchanged whispers, and the two smallest figures disappeared into the darkness.

After more excavation, the burly priests of Amen squeezed through as well. They stood among a treasure trove of gold, illuminated by their torches. They knew they had entered the tomb of Smenkhara. They drew mallets from their belts and leaped into the stacks of precious artifacts. They smashed the canopic jars, the *ushabti*, the panels of wood covered with gold foil—the only panels remaining from the Temple of Aton.

Then the torches, held by the awestruck boys, flickered and dimmed. The flames nearly died although the ancient air had not stirred.

Akhunaton stepped out of the shadows. He towered over the smaller desert humans, tilted his huge head forward and smiled, leaning over the mummified body of his son. The priests of Amen dropped their mallets. They froze, then backed against the far wall. The trembling boys scrambled through the hole in the wall.

The priests of Amen collided and fought over the right to crawl out first. A voice on the other side demanded to know what was wrong. One priest knocked the other down and struggled through. The second dove through as Akhunaton approached from the darkness. He picked up the torches and tossed them through the hole.

The priesthood of Amen converged in force to reseal the opening of the tomb and bury it under tons of rock and sand. The Beduins restored the ground to a natural appearance, so that the region would appear as though it had never been touched.

Centuries passed before anyone, including the Beduins, dared utter the name Akhunaton.

The tomb of Tutankhamen, discovered by Beduins, was excavated by night. It was entered before dawn by two small boys trained in the art of tomb-robbing. They had just passed a gilded *ushabti* out of the tomb when one of the boys opened a jeweled box near the empty altar. He quickly snatched up the eight gold rings within and tied them in the scarf he wore as a headband. He prepared to pass the little treasure box out through the square hole when he heard footsteps tapping in the darkness, coming toward him.

A huge man with a massive, elongated head stepped into the torchlight and looked down upon the Beduin children. He smiled. The boy dropped the scarf containing the rings and scrambled through the hole, followed by the other boy, who wailed in terror.

Akhunaton passed the torch out through the hole, then laughed loudly in the darkness.

Chapter Thirty-Eight

Kahotep again reigned long in Egypt. The invasion of Asia Minor and Egypt by Alexander was Kahotep's first world conquest. The burning of the Great Library at Alexandria was his attempt to eradicate the ancient cosmological knowledge.

The Mycenians ruled Egypt through astronomer-priests, the Ptolemies. Lepsuis Ptolemy replaced the ancient cosmology with a system describing the Earth as flat and encased by moving transparent domes, lighted by the sun, moon and planets. Half the outer dome was blue and half was black with tiny white lights.

Wars of conquest were fought throughout Europe, Asia Minor, and Africa spread the cosmology of the flat Earth and smallness of space. Luminous objects were still seen moving in the sky, but only the followers of Plato and Proclus knew that these were starships and not demons.

Though Kahotep conquered the world many times, still the light of knowledge imparted from the Sirius system was not altogether lost. After the death of Jesus Christ, the followers of Plato merged with an eastern school of thinkers and became known collectively as the Gnostics. Preserving old records and artifacts, in secret they educated men and women of intelligence. The Invisible College preserved the heliocentric cosmology by educating such scholars as Copernicus, Da Vinci, Galileo and Sir Isaac Newton. Carefully controlled experimentation and mathematical models gradually replaced interpretations of Biblical scriptures as the most reliable method of factual discovery.

Paul of Tarsus did Kahotep's bidding and established the great Christian Church. Centuries later, by command of the Holy Inquisition, torturers and executioners were sent after the keepers of old secrets. In the name of Jesus Christ, thousands of women and men were burned as witches and heretics. For hundreds of years anyone teaching that the Earth was round was tortured to death for heresy.

When science replaced superstition, Kahotep financed the Industrial Revolution. His puppet, John Pierpont Morgan, exploited the visionary genius Nikola Tesla, himself a human artifact created to receive visionary knowledge of extraterrestrial origin. With a limitless treasure of technology at last at his disposal, Kahotep decided to do more than rule the world. He determined to build up to its destruction on that inevitable day when the Star People and the God-Kings returned.

PART V

THE RETURN

Chapter Thirty-Nine

I n the aftermath of Napoleon's invasion of Egypt, a slab inscribed with hieroglyphics, hieratic Egyptian and classical Greek fell into the hands of scholars. The Rosetta Stone provided the world with a standard translation for Egyptian heiroglyphics.

Richard Lepsius was thirty-two, brilliant, and as fascinated by truth as by treasure. In 1882 he realized that vast amounts of information pertaining to the era between the reigns of Amenhotep III and Horemheb had been deliberately erased from all Egyptian temples and tombs. No chapter in history had ever been so completely obliterated.

He was excavating a tell near the city of Amarna when he discovered the name *Nefertiti* inscribed on the back of a piece of ceramic jewelry. He had heard of the legendary queen whose beauty was unfathomable, but now he had the first real proof that she once existed. Before a week had passed, Lepsius uncovered a scarab with the name *Tutankhamen* engraved on the back. The hieroglyphics were circled, indicating that this was the name of a king. Lepsius knew he was uncovering the forgotten era.

Before the end of the year, Lepsius was diligently uncovering the story of the successor to Amenhotep III, a man called "the Heretic" and "the Criminal King," a man who changed his name from Amenhotep IV to Akhenaton, or Akhunaton.

In the years that followed, Richard Lepsius uncovered a secret chapter of history when four Pharaohs ruled during a scant thirty years, ending when a general named Horemheb erased all records of their reigns.

⟨glyph⟩

The starship *Aton* returned to the Ra system because of powerful stirrings of emotion and upheaval which had been sensed emanating from the planet Gaia.

"I believe it is the upheaval of awakening," said Shu to pilot Tem as they neared the blue-green planet swirling with white masses of clouds.

"I hope you are correct," Tem replied cautiously.

Isis watched the viewscreen, her eyes wide with anticipation. Smenkhara and Tutankhaton stood behind her with their father. Beside them, Tiy and Meritaton held their breath.

"'When the fledgling in the egg chirpeth in the egg, thou givest him breath to preserve him alive'," Shu quoted. "Fledgling humanity is, indeed, chirping in the egg. The fledgling can stand on two legs. The fledgling can sing. Soon the fledgling will break the egg and fly."

"If young humanity does not perish," said Tiy. "They are industrializing their planet now, with disastrous effects. Kahotep effectively controls this world now, through banks and money and political power to keep the nations divided. While nations war, Kahotep sells weapons to every tyrant."

Shu merely shrugged and smiled. "Nearly every civilization knows their world to be a planet, round and with neighbors in space. Kahotep could not suppress this knowledge. He tried, but failed."

Tutankhaton grinned. "Kahotep knows that we promised to return."

"Kahotep knows that we never departed. There have always been lights moving in the sky, discs of metal among the clouds."

Tem nodded. "And now we return with great subtlety and discretion, to reveal ourselves without inflicting culture shock on frail human minds."

"I have communed with Yod and formulated a series of demonstrations we will arrange for the benefit of humanity on Gaia," said Shu.

"These demonstrations," interjected Tem. "They will be dangerous. We are returning to a hostile planet whose secret ruler knows our intent and will do anything to repel us."

"He fears us because we represent a superior power."

"He rules through propaganda and deception."

"His lies are breaking down," Shu chuckled ruefully. "We kept the knowledge of Aton alive through Egyptian priests. The priest Solon spoke the truth to the Greek Socrates. The Greeks were so infatuated with philosophy then, they were the perfect people to receive this knowledge. Plato recorded it in cryptic dialogues which Proclus brilliantly interpreted and derived the spherical cosmology. Other Greeks, Aristarchus and Eratosthenes, correctly measured the diameter and circumference of their round Earth.

"Visionary knowledge has always been available to the common people. The Gnostics kept it alive through times of severe suppression. They educated such humans as Kepler, Copernicus, Da Vinci, Galileo, and Newton. Look at the sciences they gave the world, in the face of imprisonment, torture and death!"

"Bruno was killed," said Tiy. "And thirty-five years later, Galileo was forced to disclaim his cosmology."

"Yes, but in that same century Newton reinvented calculus and Olaf Roemer measured the speed of light. Two brilliant successes, overseen by us."

"We have been watching over this world too closely to lose it now," whispered Father Tem.

❧

Albert A. Michaelson, the world's greatest expert on the velocity of light, teamed up with Dr. Morley, a chemist whose specialty was the illumination of gases. Together they built the most sophisticated device ever conceived for the purpose of measuring the speed of light: the interferometer. In the year 1882 they collaborated on the first controlled scientific experiment to accurately measure the velocity of the Earth through space, utilizing minute variations in the speed of light that they expected to find.

The interferometer tuned to bands of light at parallel or traverse trajectories to the rotation of the Earth. A shift of $1/25$ of a wavelength toward the yellow end of the spectrum should have appeared when the beams interfered with respect to the motion of the Earth. The experiment was performed, then repeated. It was repeated many times.

"Stop!" cried Dr. Morley, looking up from the lens. He frowned. "There is still no difference."

"That's impossible," Michaelson called down to him.

"Yes, it seems impossible." Morley gritted his teeth and wiped the sweat from his forehead. "Either this planet is perfectly motionless in space, or the speed of light never varies, no matter what direction we intercept it from."

In 1886 a peasant woman was digging for fertilizer in the vast alluvial deposits near the town of Amarna in Egypt. Her spade struck something solid. She cursed. Stones! Here, just a foot below the ground, preventing her from digging any deeper.

Turning up the soil to recover as much as she could, she was surprised to find clay tablets instead of river stones. They were inscribed. She knew that these tablets, like everything else excavated in Egypt, must be valuable. Local officials were notified and scholars were summoned to the site.

The tablets comprised a series of cuneiform letters written by a king named Ikhnaton, or Akhenaton, to his Minister to the North, Aper-El. Collectively, they became known as the Amarna Letters.

One thousand nine hundred years after the crucifixion and revivification of a humanoid artifact named Jehoshwa ben Miriam inspired the mythos of Jesus Christ, the Aton Disc watched over another humanoid artifact. Nikola was the second and of two brothers genetically designed to be telepathic receivers of psychoholographic signals detailing extraterrestrial technology. The older brother was Daniel. He was monitored throughout his youth and his brain was found to be critically defective. He was taken back aboard the *Aton* and translated into a new body and a new world. His younger brother was left to fulfill a great destiny.

After transforming the industrial world with polyphase motors and generators producing alternating current, Nikola Tesla experimented with transmission and reception of electromagnetic waves. In June of 1900, Tesla and his assistant George

Scherff had assembled the greatest scientific minds in Europe and the United States for a demonstration of his radio wave receiver. With his directional antenna aimed at the planet Mars, Tesla was amazed and delighted to hear loud, clear blips of intelligently coded signals beeping from his loudspeakers.

Tesla had experimented with wireless transmission on two occasions before, in 1895 and 1897 but had never received anything like these loud, clear signals from an unknown source. Since the antenna had been pointed at Mars, he logically postulated that he had received radio signals from an intelligent civilization on that planet.

The source of signals was the starship *Aton*, in a geosynchronous orbit high above Tesla's New York laboratory.

Tesla's announcement that he had established contact with extraterrestrials caused the great inventor to lose his credibility among scientists. Acclaim turned to derision, although witnesses to the initial contact swore that Tesla's claims were true.

☥ 𓅦 𓅨

"We must arrange a demonstration that will be unmistakable," said Pilot Tem.

Shu spoke. "Their cultural development is accelerating. Already they have instituted many reforms. Notice: in the last four hundred years they have abolished human sacrifice and the dogma of the Divine Rights of Kings, and replaced monarchies with primitive but effective republics of elected officials. Slavery has been abolished by nearly every government except the most oppressive. Women of some democratic states are on the verge of acquiring rights to participate equally with men in politics. I predict the species will abolish war in less than a hundred years, despite the influence of Kahotep."

"I hope you are right," said Tiy.

Smenkhara nodded. "I feel different empathic emanations from the people of Gaia now. They are waking up, both scientifically and ethically."

Tem stated, "We must stage a series of demonstrations of our presence here."

"The first will have a clear, decipherable physical signature. The next will have a social and religious impact which will also be unmistakable. Neither will cause culture shock at the time," said Shu. "I hope culture shock will be a delayed reaction."

⊗

At 6:45 on the morning of June 9, 1908, a ship off the coast of India reported the passage of an immense fireball moving from south by southeast to north by northwest. It passed silently overhead. As it slowly descended to the north, a piercing whistle began and grew louder and louder until it snapped into a mighty roar.

The people of India and China were jolted by the shock wave of a powerful sonic boom. The fiery object had changed direction slightly and shot toward the north-

360

east. Tents and animals on caravans in Mongolia were toppled by the roar the cylinder made.

The time was seven a.m. The nomads of southern Russia had for generations been victims of cruel Czars. They were praying for a sign from God. A mighty cylindrical object spouting a V-shaped crimson flame ripped the sky, leaving a path of white vapor.

At 7:07 a.m. the object roared over the town of Keshma. The startled inhabitants witnessed the abrupt maneuver as it veered east.

At 7:11 the object passed over the town of Preobazhenka. There, it veered again in full view of the startled Siberians. The vapor trail it left was proof as the fiery cylinder moved west, toward the town of Vanavara.

At 7:17 a.m., to the north of the town of Vanavara, over a desolate forest of semifrozen swampland called the Stony Tongus, the object ascended into the sky and exploded on the upper edge of the atmosphere.

Without harming human life, an eighty-megaton hydrogen fusion bomb had been detonated over the isolated wilderness.

Ilya Popovitch had crawled into a well to rescue a lamb. Above him the sky turned white. Ilya buried his face in his hands and the bones of his hands flashed against his closed eyelids. When he looked up moments later, he saw a vast white cloud billowing upward like a glowing mushroom, towering against the sky.

There were others who witnessed the explosion, many others. One man who had kneeled behind a stone wall to tie his bootlaces and another who had simply looked away for an instant were spared the radiation and shock waves.

Regrettably, the reindeer were not so protected. Many died within two days of the explosion, victims of a strange disease. Then many calves were born deformed and abandoned at birth by the herds.

The peasants of the Stony Tongus region would never forget that mysterious explosion.

❧⦿☙

"Mistah Ludwig! Mistah Ludwig!" Ludwig Borchardt looked up and shielded his eyes from the glare. A brown-skinned Arab boy was running toward him caling, "Come see!"

He followed the boy to a square cut deep into the desert floor. The debris consisted mainly of shattered statuary. Several laborers stood around a tiny pit in the wall of the excavation. Facing into the rubble of the wall was the bust of a woman with a high, conical crown. The limestone bust of Queen Nefertiti, carved by Tutmose, was unearthed intact after more than three thousand years.

"As if someone put it there on purpose," mused Borchardt.

Five years later, the statue vanished from Egypt.

The starship *Aton* returned to Europe to continue to demonstrate its existence.

In Portugal a little peasant girl was singled out for contact. The *Atet* approached, wrapped in invisibility. Isis descended to the ground, illuminated by ionized air which obscured her face. She spoke in Portuguese to the child, who immediately made the sign of the cross over her chest.

Weeks later the girl was playing with her sister and brother near the mouth of a cave. The *Atet* returned, again cloaked in a mirage field. A hologram of Isis was projected into the shadows inside the cave, where the image appeared luminous and transparent.

The voice of Isis whispered gently, "Do not be afraid of me. I am an angel of peace. Come, let us pray for peace."

Carefully phrased to fit the children's Christian belief system, they had been chosen to deliver news of an impending manifestation, a "miracle," to a community of faithful and spiritually simple people.

Kneeling beside the humanoid apparition, the children demonstrated their capacity for deep faith and acceptance of the seemingly impossible to the voice and glowing figure of "the Great Mother," whom they believed to be the Virgin Mary. She dissolved into clouds of glowing light as the children prayed for an end to war.

The year was 1916. War was again blasting death upon the face of Europe. There seemed to be no way the children's prayers could come true.

"What do you mean, an angel of God?" The girls' mother was skeptical, but she knew her daughters did not lie.

"It is true, Mama! We prayed together for peace!"

On April 6, 1917, Lucia Abobora was playing with her friends, Francisco and Jacinto Marto, in a meadow in Cova da Iria, just outside the Portugese town of Fatima. Lucia was first to see the sphere of light descending from the sky. In it was a holographic image of Isis, clothed in long robes.

"Do not be afraid," Isis said, "I will not hurt you."

"Who are you? Where do you come from?" Lucia eagerly asked.

"I come from Heaven, Lucia. Listen carefully to me. You and your friends must return to this spot every month on the thirteenth day at this very hour. I will return six times. The seventh time, seven months from now, you will see a miracle."

Every month the three children returned and brought their friends. Skeptical parents followed and each meeting was marked by and more impressive manifestations.

On the twelfth of August, the Administrator of Ourem imprisoned all three children. The following day, pilgrims to the site stared in awe at a green glowing cloud: the mirage field around the *Atet* was carefully weakened to allow faint glow of visible light, giving the crowd the sign they craved. The children were released on the seventeenth of the month and the authorities hoped the "hoax" would not go on.

On September 13, dozens of pilgrims from throughout Europe gathered at the Cova da Iria seeking deliverance from their sufferings. The sick and the crippled begged the three children a miracle. Then the sun dimmed and a globe of light appeared in the sky. Incurable sicknesses gave way to instant recoveries. Crippled limbs and sightless eyes were healed.

On the thirteenth of October the sky was heavy with clouds. Rain drizzled, then poured as seventy thousand people waited in the Portugese town of Fatima, desperate for a miracle. Many were the mutilated victims of Kahotep's latest war. All were suffering—or they were skeptics.

Professor Almeida Garret was a scientist from Coimbra University. He was among those who had made the trek to scoff at the masses and their gullibility. The rain pelted him and he had decided to leave when the sun burst through the clouds, but in the wrong part of the sky. He turned and gasped. It was not the sun—it was an immense disc, turning slowly on its axis as it descended through the clouds.

"It was raining hard," the scientist later wrote. "Suddenly the sun shone through the dense cloud that covered it. Everyone looked in its direction. It looked like a disc, of very definite contour. It was not dazzling. I don't think it could be compared to a dull, silver disc, as someone later said at Fatima. No. It rather possessed a clear, changing brightness, which one could compare to a pearl. It looked like a polished wheel."

Seventy thousand Europeans witnessed the descent of the *Aton* starship in Fatima, Portugal.

In 1920 the bust of Nefertiti discovered by Borchardt's team appeared as mysteriously as it had vanished, in the British Museum. Two years later, on the fourth of November, Howard Carter discovered the tomb of Tutankhamen. After twenty days of painstaking excavation, the stairway to the chamber was cleared and the tomb was opened. The Beduin scarf containing eight gold rings was the first thing found.

Carter's benefactor, Lord Carnarvon, was bitten on the face by a mosquito shortly after entering the tomb. He died three weeks later of fever induced by blood poisoning. At the exact instant of his death, on April 6, 1923, the lights throughout Cairo fell dark in an unexplained power failure.

As the years passed, Howard Carter himself suffered strange ill effects of what he himself considered was the result of having opened so many tombs, including Tutankhamen's: fevers that defied diagnosis, screaming nightmares, auditory and visual hallucinations by day. He died in 1939, at the age of 56.

In 1927, Leonid Kulik led an expedition into Siberia to find the crater left by the Tongus "meteorite." He found a vast ring of fallen trees. Their trunks all pointed toward the center of the ring like a great fan. In the center Kulik found a cluster of limbless conifers, pointing skyward. There was no impact hole, no crater, no meteoric fragments at all. Just strange stories and a circle of fallen trees many miles wide.

The mummies of Smenkhara and Tutankhamen were studied by many Egyptologists for many years and were debated hotly. Smenkhara's mummy had an enlarged female pelvis, so at first experts identified his mummy as that of Queen Tiy, then of Akhenaton himself. But this king had died young, too young to have been the radical king of legend.

Examination of the skulls showed that both had elongated occipital lobes, far in excess of the volume contained in a normal human skull. Hydrocephalus was considered as an explanation for this anomaly, but the occipital lobes of the brain are unaffected by that disease. No evidence was found of a similar genetic or glandular precedent among the billions of humans alive during that century. After years of controversy, these mummies were determined to have been sons of Akhenaton.

Chapter Forty

Kahotep was dying and knew it. In theory, he should have been able to extend his life forever but there were apparently hidden variables; he had postponed death, delayed it, nothing more. After twelve thousand years of living, Kahotep stared in his scrying mirror at the deep creases in his face. He gazed long at the wrinkles on the backs of his hands. He was no longer able to fight off the ravages of old age, not even with his ever-increasing appetite for living human serotonin.

He had mapped the brain, charted the ductless glands and isolated their hormones. He could speed the aging process with dopamine, induce trances with endorphins, and synthesize serotonin, which helped his battle against aging. It was not enough. He determined to attempt one last experiment to find an alternative to the Obscene Rite. He required five million human guinea pigs for the greatest lab experiment of all time.

And if his desperate effort failed, he would still have his revenge against the star-gods and all of cruel Nature. If he, Kahotep, had to die, he would take all of humanity and much life everywhere, with him.

Czar Nicolas Romanov II fell under the shadow of the black magician, Grigori Rasputin. From the instant he planted a demon made of blood into the eye of young Alexi Romanov, to the terrifying assassination conducted by Felix Yussupov, Rasputin engineered the fall of the Soviet Parliament and delivery of the Russian people into the hands of the Bolsheviks. Russia was Kahotep's domain.

Through puppets like Aleister Crowley and Dr. Joseph Mengele, Kahotep established occult orders. The infamous Thule Society initiated a young, aspiring magician named Shickelgruber, who yearned to live forever. Long after Schickelgruber had changed his name to Hitler he was allowed to glimpse Kahotep in a secret underground temple. Later, Hitler spoke of the event:

"I have seen the superman…and I found him to be terrible."

Longevity experiments proceeded under Stalin and Hitler. Kahotep used international business interests to conquer the last great nation beyond his control. He used the promise of immortality to persuade industrialists John David Rockefeller and Henry Ford to endorse the German experiments and support Hitler.

The resulting legislation was his greatest achievement. With it he owned, just like a bank or a company, the United States of America. The law read:

By virtue of and pursuant to the authority vested in me by sections 3 and 5 of the Trading with the Enemy Act as amended, and by virtue of all other authority invested in me, I, Franklin D. Roosevelt, President of the United States of America, do prescribe the following:

A general license is hereby granted, licensing any transaction or act proscribed by section 3(a) of The Trading with the Enemy Act as amended, provided, however, that such transaction or act is authorized by the Secretary of the Treasury by means of regulations, rulings, instructions, licenses or otherwise, pursuant to the Executive Order 8389, as amended.

> Franklin D. Roosevelt,
> The White House,
> December 13, 1941

The man stepped out of a black car and strode briefly through the snow flurries into the concrete building. His black cape billowed and his face was veiled. Terror spread like a powerful wake behind him. Even jaded sadists, torturers of countless Jews, shuddered in the presence of Dr. Joseph Mengele's friend, "an ascended master of the Master Race." No one knew who he was, only that he was revered by the Nazi elite, perhaps "the superman" of whom their leader spoke.

He went directly to the chamber prepared for him. Two guards, faces blank, hoisted their rifles and departed from the room after the veiled man entered and the door boomed shut. Twelve young Jewish men lay alive on operating tables, their spinal columns severed, their skulls opened like blossoms, their brains exposed and spread apart like gelatinous petals. Conscious, paralyzed.

He pulled down his veil and drew a small wire loop out of a pocket inside his cape. Swiftly as fleeting shadow, he swept from one table to the next, pausing long enough to flick away the living pineal bodies from the centers of the exposed brains.

The last thought, which all victims shared,was, *God in Heaven, he's eating our brains!*

But the longevity experiment had not succeeded. Hitler's forces invaded Egypt and Rommel searched the ancient land for a book of scrolls, a lost relic that his führer called "The Pagan Grail." Kahotep knew that fragments were crudely preserved in the Kabalas of the Old World, but nothing really substantial remained.

Many before had searched for the Pagan Grail, from Alexander the Great to

European kings who fought a thousand years of Holy Wars, never knowing that what the popes who commanded them were seeking was not a cup at all. Napoleon was sent by The Dark Lodge to search Egypt for the ancient spellbook. The Dark Lodge was again trying to locate the object of Kahotep's obsession.

But the *Ka-Ba-Ra* was never found.

Rage stormed into hate and sickening self-loathing as Kahotep put into effect his final plan. He would not die alone. If he had to die, then he would take all human life and much life everywhere on Earth.

The empire of Hitler collapsed and Germany fell. Japan surrendered after being bombed with "a new kind of weapon." His war had given him much, though. He controlled every nation through banks and vast companies. He bought and sold virtually every weapon of war anywhere on the planet, and war ruled all industrial economies. He was still the god of war, nameless and unseen.

Kahotep found a new home from which to rule. The victorious United States gave him what he required: Einstein announced to the world a formula by which matter could be converted into energy, and a man named Teller used this formula to build an atomic bomb.

His two greatest empires, the United States and Russia, leaped at the chance to arm themselves with nuclear weapons. Uranium was mined in vast quantities, processed and concentrated into bomb-quality uranium, and assembled into mass-produced nuclear warheads. Kahotep ordered production of ten times the nuclear explosive power necessary to render extinct human life.

Chapter Forty-One

"They are a different people now than they were in Pharaoic Egypt," Akhunaton said. "Very different. They are maturing as a race."

"Do you really think so?" Tiy asked.

"Yes. I have seen changes. Do you not think they have changed, Smenkhara?"

"Yes, they have, Father."

"Look at them," Akhunaton said. "Look at them!"

They peered into a hologram, projected through time, of the events on Earth: humanoid evolution, the procession called "history."

The image was of an atomic cloud billowing through the upper atmosphere.

"Look now."

The image changed to a train station in a Siberian forest. Men standing in line to board the train were pointing excitedly the picture on the cover of a magazine of that same atomic cloud. They were remembering an event witnessed by many of them: the bizarre explosion over the Stony Tongus swamp forty years before.

"This news will sweep Russia," Akhunaton said. "The people of the world will have to answer for themselves the question of whether an extraterrestrial craft detonated an atomic explosion over forty years before Earth scientists discovered the process and used it to win a war."

"So now they know more science," said Tiy. "That does not mean their race has integrity."

"The people have turned away from many evils," said Akhunaton. "Where do you see human sacrifice? Slavery?"

"It is true that much has been discarded," Tiy admitted reluctantly. "Desperate leaders making concessions to avoid revolution."

"Exactly," said Akhunaton, smiling. "Terrified leaders have made frightened concessions to multitudes who no longer tolerate evil inflicted upon them. In some places women are attaining equality with men. Everywhere the people participate in the process of government. Parliaments and congresses are elected. Representatives compete for public approval."

Tiy nodded. "Let us see what future these warlike people make for themselves."

Smenkhara looked at his brother and the two smiled.

"I think that my two sons see improvements in the society of their fellow male Earthlings," Akhunaton said happily.

"Yes," said Smenkhara. "I feel much in common with this angry, childish race. Like me, they spent their childhood hating their true fathers. Now we all want love and *we* are fathers!"

Tutankhaton smiled.

"A father's love can cross a Universe to all of his children."

"Bless and thank God Ptah for that," said Smenkhara.

"Now," Akhunaton said slowly, "we have announced our return. Let us begin."

A starship off the western coast of North America dispatched a formation of shuttlediscs which flew toward the volcanic mountains of the coastal range. The pilots enjoyed the thrill of landskimming, skipping, circling around glaciers and peaks, diving into canyons and valleys, Shrouded in force-fields that obscured radar and direct sighting, the nine discs found a lone passenger plane. They lifted their mirage screens.

Kenneth Arnold, pilot of the plane, looked up and gasped in astonishment. Nine spinning, silver discs danced in perfect formation through blue air toward snow-crested Mount Rainier.

Arnold reported the sighting. He described the discs to reporters, saying they moved "like a saucer would if you skipped it across the water."

Thus the phrase "flying saucer" was born.

On the sunny afternoon of April 24, 1964, at 5:45, highway patrolman Lonnie Zamora was pursuing a speeding car north toward the town of Socorro, New Mexico, when a blue flame descended from the sky with an ear-splitting, screaming roar.

He watched with horror as the blue fire landed on a storage shed that Zamora knew housed explosives for a mining company. He radioed his superiors and drove off the freeway and over winding dirt roads that wove between the desert hills.

In a ravine two visitors from the star system of Procyon IV eyed Zamora as his patrol car approached. Their particle-beam exhaust had burned a wide circle of vegetation. Their craft weighed six tons, selected especially for this demonstration because its landing pods would leave unmistakable prints in the desert rock.

Zamora thought the two small figures in silver suits were young teenagers who had rolled their car. He followed the road up the slope of a mesa overlooking the ravine. At the edge of the mesa, he looked down upon a profoundly strange vehicle, but the two figures were gone. He heard the slam of a heavy metal hatch. Then, as the lawman walked down the side of the slope toward the elongated white egg, it exploded with blue flame and ascended. Zamora was flung to the ground by a blast of hot air. The object sailed up twenty feet, then the flame disappeared. It accelerated horizontally at fantastic rate and was instantly out of sight.

Lonnie Zamora reported his encounter over police radio. He waited for backup by his patrol car, looking at the prints of the landing gear in a circle of smoldering bushes and charred earth. He had observed an insignia on the craft, though he did not know what it meant. In fact, the UFO bore the alchemical symbol for the planet Venus.

In 1967 a meeting took place. One of the principals was Dr. James D. Mac-Donald, an atmospheric physicist who would one day warn of industrial damage to the ozone layer, patent computer hardware, liquid crystals and digital gauges. However, he was not there for reasons of science. He was there to vent his rage.

Astronomy professor J. Allen Hynek was the target of MacDonald's anger. For years Hynek had been the scientific consultant to the United States Air Force on their special Project Blue Book, a team assembled to investigate UFOs. Hynek was a quiet and introspective man, not given to brash claims nor hasty conclusions.

The place was an apartment on Bryn Mawr Avenue in Chicago, near the campus of Northwestern University where Hynek taught. The young French couple who had arranged the meeting were struggling to keep peace between the two men. Jacques was pouring coffee while his wife, Janine, served chocolate cake. They called their small discussion group the Invisible College, in honor of the secret society of intellectuals who had braved the Inquisition to launch the Renaissance.

"How could you?" MacDonald cried, "How *could* you have sat on all that data for so many years and never alerted the scientific community?"

Hynek shrugged. "For years I just felt lucky to have *access* to it. If I had tried to go too far, the Air Force would have fired me. In fact, when I tried to call attention to it, I was ignored! How do you think I felt, caught in the middle like that?

"Listen, Jim, I published an article in 1953 saying that this was an important phenomenon. I sent word of unsolved cases to some of the big guns — Carl Sagan, Robertson, Lou Alvarez — who were all saying that there was no such thing as a flying saucer! As I recall, I tried to contact you, too, but you paid no attention. Where were *you* all this time? Why were you not interested then?"

※

On several continents and in many nations, college students marched with signs and sang songs of peace. Some demonstrated against a war in Viet Nam, others against a war in Czechoslovakia. Some were gunned down by soldiers in obscure Third World countries. Everywhere people were refusing to fight wars.

From his chambers below the Pentagon, Kahotep watched television footage of peace marchers. He snarled in contempt and fear. These humans were rebelling, refusing to fight and kill. Soldiers even turned their weapons on their own commanding officers. Kahotep had never seen such disloyalty. He had never seen anything like it in all his thousands of years.

"Major, I have something to show you."

"Yes, General?"

"Follow me."

The intelligence officer led the security officer downstairs to a department in Military Intelligence Headquarters. This young officer had been chosen for a glimpse of a closely-guarded secret because he would be handling documents of a very sensitive nature, and because his personality profile showed that he was clearly capable of keeping the awesome secret.

The general pushed open a door. "Come in." The door closed behind them and the general turned on the lights.

"My God! What are these things?"

"Relics from ancient Egypt."

"Oh, Jesus, how strange! How utterly…insane."

"Take a good look at all of them, especially that one. That statue, there. Look at him. See how horrible and unearthly he must have looked."

"I suppose he didn't actually look like that. Those artists, I mean, they had a strange style, didn't they, sir?"

"Not during this era. We're very sure that's how this king and his family really looked."

"Why? Why those horrible long heads?"

"They are from outer space. They eradicated more than a million people."

"Killed them?"

"Somehow an entire city was murdered. The city was called Akhetaton. Follow me."

The general led the major down another corridor to a room with a flickering videoscreen set in a dark wall. On the screen was a man wearing a toga with a leopardskin cloak over his shoulders. He sat on a throne, staring into space. His face was gaunt, his skin deeply riven.

"Look at him. He is all that stands between us and a new invasion from outer space."

"Him, sir? That man? Why him?"

"Because he was there when it first happened."

This man was alive when that extraterrestrial king was in Egypt?

"Yes. He was one of their guinea pigs. They experimented on him and then let him go. He says he escaped their infernal city and tried to prevent them from murdering those people. Whatever they did to him, he hasn't aged in more than three thousand years."

"This is incredible. sir! I can't believe it."

"Believe it, Major. It's fantastic, but it's true. But also think of the fear and panic if the public ever found out."

"Oh, yes, sir! Of course!"

"Major, have you heard of the Orson Welles radio broadcast of *War of the Worlds?*"

"Yes, sir. A lot of people panicked when they heard it."

"They sure as hell did. And that was a radio show, not a public announcement!"

"Yes, sir."

"This man's name is Kahotep. He was a high priest, but he was persecuted and forced to live in secret because of his long life. People became suspicious when he didn't age, so he was forced to live most of his life in darkness, knowing that his world could be invaded again at any time and he would be powerless to stop it."

"That's terrible, sir."

"Yes, it's terrible! He gave us humans a little knowledge at a time. On that screen is the man responsible for the Renaissance, all the sciences, everything."

"Amazing. I've got to sit down."

"Have a seat. Look at him. We still don't know how he stays alive. But he's given our military a lot of information about UFOs."

"Flying saucers?"

"That's right, exactly."

"So, if I understand you, sir, they're back and trying to invade again!"

"Just so. We are developing many new nuclear weapons and missiles to avert this catastrophe. Major, are you religious?"

"No sir."

The general handed the security officer a copy of the Bible. "Read this book. There's real history in it. And pray."

"Pray, sir?"

"Kahotep is our most vital intelligence resource. He was around when Christ was alive. He even met Jesus, in fact. He is a Christian."

"I'm confused, sir."

The general laughed. "You'll adjust. Come — let us bow our heads in prayer."

Awkwardly, the intelligence officer obeyed. He spoke a simple prayer about world peace and protection from God. He ended it with, "In the name of Jesus Christ, Amen!"

As the two men uttered the final word of the prayer, the face of the Egyptian on the videoscreen smiled.

"I am proud of these people," said Smenkhara. "I am amazed. Their consciousness as a race has progressed more in two centuries than in the preceding twenty."

Akhunaton laughed. "It will be exciting to return to that world. Wonderful to go back without having to rule anybody."

"That will be wonderful," Smenkhara agreed.

"We will return just to dance and rejoice among our fellow humans again," added his brother.

Pilot Tem smiled. Also smiling were the seven daughters of Akhunaton.

Chapter Forty-Two

The Ra system is located in a spiral arm of the Milky Way Galaxy. There are over two hundred billion stars in this galaxy. More than eighty billion are single, solitary suns. Twenty billion of these are either red giants or white dwarfs, without natural planets. The remaining sixty billion stars are small, hot and yellow, and many are circled by planets.

The Ra system originally had four living bodies. War annihilated two life-supporting moons and detonated the gas giant they orbited. Only asteroids remain to tell the story. Mars was irradiated and pelted with meteoric hail. Gaia, also called Earth, was on the far side of the sun, shielded from the blast. She survived as the only living mother-planet in the system. Travelers from eighty billion stars systems had mourned the devastation in the Ra system.

Humanoid races were the natural result of evolution on Earthlike planets. The forces of parallel evolution and a mother-planet's need to reproduce herself in kind, like any other fully living organism, gave rise to similar offspring. The great galactic civilization was a father-force to the mother-worlds forming in the life-zones of the many yellow type-G stars of the galaxy.

The process of seeding planets on which had evolved hominid species with genetically idealized humanoid seed-races was billions of years older than the existence of the Ra system. The process of galactic civilization assisting a difficult and traumatic evolutionary birth had been done many, many times. It involved manipulation of the cultural consciousness of the emerging humans by means of their popular arts and scientific notions. A thousand genetic samplings were made by survey teams, but many more abductions were staged to awaken the people of Earth.

Many of the billions of humanoid races throughout the galaxy were genetically similar to the people of Earth, having evolved from related seed-races cultivated by the evolutionary overseers. Some of them traveled to Earth to refuel with the heavy water from deep in her oceans and to view her forests and mountains. A few of the more human-appearing of these galactic races infiltrated to influence the human species, which was conducting mass exterminations of life with industrial logging and pollution and strip mining. In spite of derision from scientists, many people believed that aliens lived among them in great numbers and that UFOs were of extraterrestrial origin.

Starships from a million worlds converged on timespace terminals and rocketed in hyperbolic arcs through the event horizons and around the singularities that led to the first Black Hole. They materialized out of the event horizon of Sothis III, the black hole near the Sirius system. From there they journeyed a distance of 8.714 light years to Gaia in the Ra system. This vast fleet converged beyond radar range over Earth's armed cities and nations. The star craft shielded and entered the atmosphere. Sudden, simultaneous interaction with human beings on a vast scale was the goal.

Contacts were made on the visitors' terms. Many humans were abducted and examined in laboratories. A few women returned impregnated. Motorists were intercepted at night on remote highways and put through experiences they did not remember. Families who lived on the edge of wildernesses were visited by translated beings, though few remembered these encounters. People vanished without a trace. The ships irradiated grass and trees with powerful microwaves.

People in cities received a different kind of unremembered encounter. They were struck in the eye by blinding beams of light that imparted strange, almost religious concepts and memories of ancient Egypt directly into their brains. Then their memory of the experience was wiped clean.

Governments denied everything, saying mass psychosis and delusions explained sightings over population centers. Individual contacts were decried as hoaxes.

Kahotep had successfully detonated fission and fusion bombs and was applying particle physics to advance technological weaponry. He intended to detonate all nuclear stockpiles when contact with extraterrestrials was made.

Knowing this, Akhunaton stood before the viewscreen of the starship *Aton* as it returned from a roadside encounter in the Australian desert. Over the image of planet Earth he spoke, "This process has been repeated so many times that all that is needed now is a triggering event that will discharge the hidden memories of the hundred million people processed by the star craft. It is time to show ourselves."

Geb and Nuit stood beside him as he piloted the shuttledisc. Geb asked, "How can this be accomplished without culture shock?"

"Many people on Earth believe that discs like the one we are flying are from other worlds. They are subconsciously adjusting their minds to the idea that peaceful extraterrestrials visit their world. Now we shall use culture shock as a weapon disarm the nations and avert nuclear war."

Nuit was skeptical. "Deliberate escalation of culture shock sounds dangerous."

"It is dangerous. The situation on this planet is dangerous. Mass extinctions will result if events are allowed to proceed without interruption."

"Interruption means intervention," Nuit observed.

"That is why we are here. We shall announce ourselves slowly and unmistakably."

On the screen now was the image of a small house.

The oldest of the three children who lived in the house had just acquired what his therapist described as an "imaginary playmate," invisible to all except the boy. Even though he talked to it, he would not tell anyone what it said to him.

In fact, the playmate was a telepathic link to a psychic instructor. The boy was learning on the subliminal level to control out-of-body experiences and utilize the great creative forces of his *ba,* the mind contained in the outer cortex of his brain. When the child was seven years old, the entity departed.

The boy remembered the visions he had shared, despite the skepticism of his parents and schoolteacher, so he added another lesson to the many his invisible mentor had taught him: never trust adults because they have forgotten too much since they were children.

"There are many more children prepared to annouce our return," said Akhunaton, "but this one shows great promise. He is intelligent and psychic. His father is a scientist and he will learn much, though he will not make science his profession. It is more expedient to us for him to choose the arts, for we must make our announcement through the language of metaphor."

Tiy chuckled. "In Egypt you used the arts to build Akhetaton. You used music and dance to translate millions of people. With the worldwide electronic communications media on this planet, affecting global change through art and music and literature is imminent."

"Yes," Akhunaton agreed, "and popular arts worldwide is so vast that monitoring it is entirely beyond the power of Kahotep."

Ai burst into laughter. "Perhaps this little boy will create a great work in your honor when he grows up."

"That is the plan," said Akhunaton.

The young man remembered many visionary experiences from his childhood. He learned to read and write and spent his time illustrating his own imaginative stories with drawings and paintings. When he read a book entitled *The Flying Saucers are Real* by an Air Force major named Donald Keyhoe, the boy acquired a fear of being under a starry sky. The phobia lasted several years.

He learned to play the guitar and during his youth played in neighborhood rock-and-roll bands. Science fiction intrigued him more than any other form of literature. He wanted to become a science fiction writer.

The turbulent decade of the nineteen sixties awakened the boy to social and political realities: nuclear weapons and the possible devastation of nuclear war; chest-strangling smog over the southern California sky and the possibility of human extinction due to a global environmental crisis. He learned that his father, the scientist, could be as dogmatic about life and death political issues as the clergy of his

mother's church were about moral and spiritual issues. Young people around him whispered: "Don't trust *anyone* over thirty!" He cynically faced a grim future.

He retained his interest in extrasensory perception and out-of-body experiences and continued to write science fiction stories, although he found them hard to publish. His elders encouraged him to forget being a writer. They said he should go to college and get a job.

So he went to college and soon dropped out. His heart ached to find an alternative to the reward system of money and status that his parents' civilization offered him. Huge numbers of young people felt the same way, but the only thing any of them knew with certainty was that they were not alone.

The young man became obsessed with the idea that some great clue to human destiny was buried in the lost history of ancient civilizations. At the age of twenty-six, he found himself with three friends sitting around a campfire in Blythe, California. They had spent the day photographing and measuring, with a surveyor's transom, a compass and a sextant, the giant figures of human beings and animals etched into the black desert pavement atop mesas in the desert west of the Colorado River.

The night was a Saturday, the 28th of May, 1977. He was arguing with one of his friends, defending the reality of UFOs, when an immense disc streaked into the atmosphere directly overhead. The young men watched it for twenty minutes as it zigzagged and skipped across the sky, leaving behind a blue-white ionized trail and a stream of golden sparks. Though the men who beheld it agreed it was too spectacular to fit any conventional explanation, the sighting went unreported.

The next day he saw and photographed an opaque orange object close to the ground. His friend beside him in the front seat of the car did not see it. Neither remembered the brief experience when they met the other two at a cafe in Blythe for breakfast. He remembered the second incident only when the film was developed and he saw a photograph of an orange *something* among the other snapshots.

His research into paranormal events and ancient clues to undiscovered secrets lured him into extensive travel. Eventually he lived in a tiny mountain cabin in the county of Mendocino and made a meager living selling his paintings of nature.

One Monday night, a June 6, he was driving along Interstate Highway 5 when he saw the planet Venus in the wrong part of the sky and shining too late at night to be Venus. The silhouette of a mountain passed *behind* Venus, then a tall tree also passed behind the light. The young man experienced a surge of terror as he realized the silent object with a single light was approaching his car rapidly.

He made it to the top of the Grapevine at 11:30 and passed the Gorman Lancaster-Palmdale exit. The brilliant blue-white object was still there.

The nest instant he was driving down a freeway on-ramp, laughing and giggling to himself and repeating, "I've just had a Close Encounter of the Third Kind! A UFO encounter—of the Third Kind!" He saw the sign for the Lancaster-Palmdale exit looming up ahead.

But—he had passed that exit just minutes ago. Or had he? His laughter ended with a surge of horror.

He entered the Gorman Cafe a few minutes later at 2:30AM. He ordered coffee and pondered silently the implications of three missing hours.

He never reported the incident. Something inside him refused to seek out the memory of those missing hours.

"There he is," said Akhunaton.

Below the *Aton*, shielded from radar and visibility, was a lone blue station wagon speeding on a highway north of Los Angeles. Below also was the *Atet*, guided by the electromagnetic mind of Yod.

Yod first took control of the vehicle, then of the autonomic nervous system of the driver. The car drifted down an off ramp and cruised along a dirt road that led into the desert mountains, away from the highway.

"It is pathetic how these experiences terrify these young humans," Akhunaton said sadly as he shared empathically the anxiety the young man far below was experiencing. "However, the world must know who and what we are and why we are here."

"Agreed," said the man in silver robes.

"Of course," said the stout man in the burgundy-colored suit standing beside the living chair in which Akhunaton sat. They were awaiting the young man's arrival in the teleportation chamber of the *Aton*.

Far below, the *Atet* bore the energy body of Yod toward the car parked on the mountain road. The superintelligent field-mind sensed the terror of the young man inside. It caressed his nervous system with empathic tranquility, saving the fragile human being from overwhelming trauma. Then Yod projected the gnosis into the young man's unblinking eye. The flashing lights blinded him as they imparted images into his brain: memories of ancient Egypt.

Hours passed during which the essence of thousands of years of Egyptian history was conveyed along with the impression of direct interaction between human beings, extraterrestrial beings, and huge discoidal metal ships.

When Yod's transmission ended, the *Atet* departed and a translation beam teleported the young man directly aboard the *Aton*, several hundred miles above.

The blinding colors and tingling sensations subsided. Dazed, breathless, overawed, the young man saw around him a vast room crisscrossed by shafts of multi-colored lights. He sensed figures on his left and right. His knees buckled but strong hands kept him from falling.

He was supported on his right by a man with long white hair wearing silver robes, and on his left by a man in a burgundy-colored double-breasted suit who wore a thick moustache. Both were apparently human beings.

They led him toward a huge, jeweled chair in which sat a silhouetted figure. The dark form was that of a giant man with a vast dome-shaped head, five times the size of an ordinary human skull. His face and unclothed body were grotesquely elongated, his external ears unnaturally long, and his eyes several inches wide. His thick lips looked Negroid and his skin was greyish brown.

Through waves of nausea and fear, the young man thought: *I am being taken before a Negro man more than a million years ahead of me in evolution!*

Supported only by two smiling, friendly souls, the faint young man studied the fantastic being before him. He noticed that the naked giant had normal looking human sexual organs. *He is a human being, just like me!*

The giant leaned forward, looked the young man in the eyes and smiled. Their minds met and shared the thought: *You will do very well. There is much to go through, but you will serve your people and mine very well. Thank you.*

The young man was silent, internally pleading to know more, to know more. . . .

You will sleep now, young human. You will awaken fully and remember all you have learned tonight only when you encounter me again.

The young man's vision dissolved again into brilliant phosphenes. His skin tingled as though caressed with electric current. He heard a crackling roar and regained his senses as his car drove, as if under its own guidance, back onto the highway.

✸

"He remembers nothing," Akhunaton announced as the image of the young man sitting in the cafe drinking coffee filled the viewscreen. "His talents will suit us. He will soon marry. He will father a son and understand firsthand the miracle of birth. Then we will trigger his memory. He will do for his time what we have done for ours, in the same way."

"There is not much time left," said the man in the double-breasted suit.

"Will he be able to fulfill his task in the few years his race has left?" asked the man in silver robes.

"He will suffer adversity like you did, William. He has much to do and little time. We selected him because he lives his life with a sense of urgency. His talents are considerable. He is a perfect candidate for translation, but he must learn the lessons of a lifetime in less than two decades."

Charles Fort tugged at his moustache and frowned. "This will be a difficult transition."

William Blake nodded. "There is just so little time…"

𓂀

The young man's love for his son was overpowering. He vowed never to give the boy a false or dogmatic answer to any question asked. He swore never to dismiss any of the child's experiences, no matter how strange they might sound.

He never attempted to recover memory of the lost three hours of his journey on Monday, June 6, 1977. Then, in January of 1986, he and his small family missed a flight out of the San Jose International Airport bound for Los Angeles. Impulsively, his wife suggested they pass the time until the next flight at the Rosicrucian Museum of Egyptology in San Jose. Neither had visited the museum before, and he enthusiastically agreed.

Upon entering the building, he felt an urge to climb the nearest flight of stairs. He walked ahead of his wife and son toward an exhibit under a big sign that bore the word: AMARNA.

He halted in front of a huge statue. He stared up at it in astonishment and awe. Tears flooded his eyes. His hands trembled.

He stood before a colossus of King Akhenaton.

Another image imposed itself over the the strange-looking face on the statue: a living face, one he had seen eight years before.

His wife tugged at his arm and asked if he was all right. His son demanded his father's attention.

The young man was remembering: the unearthly face of the extraterrestrial king, the night of terror, the images of thousands of years of human history beamed into his eye from a flying saucer.

You will go to sleep now, and awaken fully when you encounter me again!

Akhunaton witnessed the awakening on the viewscreen of the *Aton* with William Blake and Charles Fort, Ai, Tiy, and his children gathered beside him. They watched with satisfaction the intensity of their student's awe and rapture.

"He is already considering composing and illustrating a book containing his holographic memory of Egypt," Akhunaton explained. "His imagination has been filled wih inspiration, and he will accept his duty. He will perform his service for us and his own humanity, even though it will cost him dearly. But if he and his race are to become translated into the galactic community, they must be tested for strength and integrity."

"Can a being so primitive comprehend the implications of these visions or the urgency of the task at hand?" Tiy asked.

"He lives his life in a state of urgency," Akhunaton said. "The book he will write has been started by several others before and never finished. Death has ended the other writers and artists who have attempted it. Earth is still Kahotep's world, Mother Tiy."

"It is an impossible gamble." Tiy shrugged.

"So is the leap in organization from atom to molecule. So is the alignment of molecules in a crystal. So is the desperate struggle to become a single cell. In each case, entropy is reversed and life continues to evolve."

"He will succeed," said Smenkhara. "He has a son and he loves him."

"That is the counter-force to entropy, Smenkhara," Akhunaton smiled. "It is Love."

"I love you, Father. And I love that poor young artist down there."

"Pity him not," said Akhunaton, "for he has much to learn, but he already knows Love."

The young man and his wife struggled for two years while he studied ancient Egypt and drew strange and fantastic drawings. Obsessed with the ancient king Ikhnaton, he expounded weird theories about time, space, and faster-than-light travel.

381

His wife finally left him. Their small family had broken up. He struggled to remain on good terms with her. She assured him his fears were unfounded.

He continued composing and illustrating his strange epic novel. He lived in the forest of northern California in an old van. His friends listened to the theories with amusement and wished him well. He did not know how to tell them what it meant, how to explain that momentous night ten years before, which he now remembered in minute detail.

Skimming just above the singularity in a black hole of contrition, the young man kept the image of the huge, elongated living face in his mind when the acute pain of divorce and the dull agony of poverty threatened to pull him into the pit of despair.

You will awaken completely…when you encounter me again.

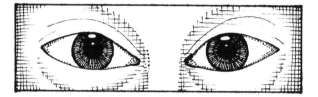

About The Author

Daniel Blair Stewart is a novelist and graphic artist born in Utah. His specialities include mystery phenomena—paranormal energies, crop circles, the Loch Ness monster. He has just completed his second illustrated novel called *Edison, Morgan and Tesla*. He lives in Ukiah, California.